SANCTUARY

THE AFTERMATH SERIES

Shelter, Dave Hutchinson
Haven, Adam Roberts
Sanctuary, Dave Hutchinson

ALSO BY DAVE HUTCHINSON

Europe in Autumn
Europe at Midnight
Europe in Winter
Europe at Dawn
The Return of the Incredible Exploding Man
Cold Water

DAVE HUTCHINSON

SANCTUARY

BOOK THREE OF THE AFTERMATH SERIES

SOLARIS

First published 2023 by Solaris
an imprint of Rebellion Publishing Ltd,
Riverside House, Osney Mead,
Oxford, OX2 0ES, UK

www.solarisbooks.com

ISBN: 978-1-83786-030-2

Designed & typeset by Rebellion Publishing

A CENTURY OR so ago – nobody's quite sure how long because for some considerable time afterward the survivors were too busy trying to survive to worry about the date – Earth was struck by the fragments of a shattered comet, some small, some ruinously large. Nicknamed 'The Sisters', the fragments rained down for several days. Hundreds of millions were killed by the initial impacts; billions more died of disease and starvation in the following years.

Had the comet struck intact, it would have destroyed all life on Earth. As it was, the fragments caused the Long Autumn, a climatic event lasting decades, a howling nightmare of rain and hail and sleet, bookended year after year by harsh winters.

In England, the population – and if they had ever known just how small it was now, the despair alone would have killed them – banded together in small communities, farms, villages, and survived on what little agriculture they could manage, and by stripping the old society's shops and supermarkets for supplies.

In some places, larger population centres grew. In Plymouth, the Royal Navy took over the city and began organising the community, and like everyone else they huddled together, mostly cut off from the world by the weather, for decades.

Almost a century later, as the weather gradually began to ease, Plymouth – now calling itself by an old nickname, Guz – directed its intelligence organisation, the Bureau, to begin to send operatives out to make contact with other communities and assess the state of the country.

One of these, Adam Hardy, newly returned from a rough assignment in Wales, was sent out again almost immediately to investigate the disappearance of another operative in Kent. In Margate, Adam found the town being run as a huge work camp by Frank Pendennis and his gang of enforcers.

In response to Frank beating a woman, Adam stole Gussie, Frank's prized antique sniper rifle, and barely escaped from Kent with his life.

Directed to the Chilterns, where a group from Guz would meet him to debrief him about Margate, Adam found himself staying at Blandings, a fortified country house where Betty Coghlan and her son were running a weapons manufactory and trying to build some kind of society.

While waiting for the force from Guz to arrive, Adam was asked by Betty to take some antibiotics to the Parish, a community of farmers further along the Chilterns. Unbeknown to Adam, though, the people of the Parish were in the middle of a war, and almost as soon as he arrived, he was robbed, savagely beaten, and left for dead.

Rescued by a local family, he was nursed back to health, only for the family's compound to be attacked by other farmers. Only Adam managed to escape, and he set out to take a gruesome, bloody revenge on the people of the Parish, carrying out a number of atrocities under the guise of Wayland, *a legendary local figure.*

His campaign of terror, and the war, was finally brought to an end by the arrival of a force of Marines from Guz, accompanied by Chrissie, his superior.

But Adam's trials still weren't over. There were rumours of something happening to the north, in Oxford and the Cotswolds, and Guz needed someone to take a look.

Now...

A STRANGER COMES TO TOWN

ONE

MELLOW WAS IN her office trying to get the week's rotas to make sense when there was a knock on the door and Sergeant Fleet looked in.

"Boss?" he said. "The super says the chief super wants a word."

She looked up from the worksheets strewn across her desktop. "And is there some reason why Superintendent Todd couldn't have told me that himself?" Fleet started to reply, but Mellow held up a hand. "Don't bother. I can guess." Her immediate superior was an enthusiastic exponent of delegation, and his first instinct, on being told to deliver a message, would have been to get someone else to deliver it for him. "Did he say when?"

"Right away." Fleet looked apologetic, even though none of it was his fault.

She sighed and looked at her paperwork again. "All right, Peter," she said. "Message received." She gathered the sheets together untidily and locked them in a drawer of her desk. "Let's see what the chief super wants, then."

The original headquarters of the Thames Valley Police Force, out in Kidlington, had been abandoned in the earliest days of the Long Autumn and everything of use brought into Oxford. At almost the same time, the old central police station on St Aldate's had been rendered uninhabitable by a gas explosion and fire, so the remains of the force had commandeered a recently abandoned office building and made their headquarters there. There was no one alive now who remembered what it had been, in the final days before the coming of The Sisters. Mellow suspected that its purpose had ceased to exist the moment the comet fragments rained down all over the world, that no one now would understand what had once been done here.

Still, it was warm and dry, because a big woodburning boiler had been installed in the basement to power the radiators, and it had electricity because of the little grove of wind generators mounted on the roof, and the canteen was just down the corridor from her office, so things could have been worse. Some of the city's outlying police stations had still not been properly renovated, and were miserable, cold, mouldy places.

The lower floors of headquarters were bustling with support staff and plain-clothed detectives and the occasional constable and sergeant in their black uniforms, but as Mellow climbed the stairs towards the fifth floor she saw fewer and fewer people, until she emerged in Executive Country and found it deserted.

Almost deserted, anyway. She stopped at a door bearing a plaque with CHIEF SUPERINTENDENT MAXWELL painted on it, paused a moment to make sure she'd got her breath back after the stairs, knocked, and went in.

In the outer office, Lucy, Maxwell's secretary, was sitting at her desk. Mellow had no idea quite what Lucy actually did; on the very rare occasions that she'd been called up here, the secretary's desk had always been completely bare, as indeed it was this morning.

"Go on through, inspector," Lucy told her with a bright smile.

"He's expecting you."

"Yes," Mellow said. "I know." She walked across the office to another door, with another plaque bearing Maxwell's name and rank, knocked, and waited until a voice from inside called her to enter.

Andrew Maxwell's predecessor, Chief Superintendent Scott, had been content with a pokey little office on the third floor, next door to the squadrooms. He was a fifteen-year veteran of the force, had worked his way up quietly and competently from the rank of constable and had never forgotten that he was one of the team. Maxwell was cut from different cloth; on his arrival he'd decided a big corner office, insulated from the other ranks, was more suited to his status. He was rarely seen in other parts of the building, and some constables wouldn't have recognised him at all if it wasn't for the gold braid on the shoulders and over the breast pocket of his uniform.

Scott's office had been comfortingly untidy, paperwork permanently scattered across his desk, and files and folders stacked against the walls; Maxwell's was almost bare. There was a row of filing cabinets, and a couple of landscapes on the walls, and there was a huge desk innocent of any evidence of work, with a single uncomfortable visitor's chair in front of it, and that was all. Maxwell was standing at the window behind the desk, looking out at the rain and sleet lashing down on the city.

"You asked to see me, sir?" Mellow said, standing beside the visitor's chair.

Maxwell didn't answer immediately, and Mellow knew he was counting to ten, keeping her waiting to assert his authority. She'd put up with more than enough of this sort of thing during her career, and these days it just bounced right off her.

Finally, he turned from the window. "Inspector Mellow," he said ponderously, sitting down behind his desk and clasping his hands in front of him as he looked at her. "I have a little job for you."

Mellow felt her heart sink. "Yes, sir," she said.

Maxwell opened a desk drawer and took out a sheet of paper. "This comes directly from Chancellery," he said, holding the paper up. Mellow took a step forward to look. The handwriting was nearly illegible, the signature a wavy line with a dot at the end, but it was on official notepaper and the Chancellor's seal was at the bottom.

"Yes, sir," she said.

"At some point in the next few days, someone will try to enter the city," Maxwell said, putting the memo back in his drawer. "That person will be detained and brought here, and you will interview them."

Mellow waited for more information, but it seemed none was coming. She said, "I don't understand, sir."

Maxwell sat back in his chair, a big man with short-cropped grey hair, a broken nose, and old scars on his knuckles. "I made it as simple as I could, inspector. What don't you understand?"

Mellow was at a loss where to begin. Who was this person? Had the closed-border policy been relaxed without anyone bothering to tell her? "Do we have any idea *when* this person is coming?" she asked.

Maxwell shook his head. "We do not, or where they'll be coming from. An advisory has been issued to the militia units manning the checkpoints. They're to report any and all people approaching the city."

"And when this... person does arrive, what am I to interview them about, sir?"

Maxwell gave her a hard stare.

"It's often helpful to have some background, sir," Mellow went on. "It gives us some idea what questions to ask."

Maxwell cocked a bushy eyebrow. "Get their details," he said. "Name. Where they're from. What they want."

"Yes, sir."

"Use your initiative, inspector."

"Yes, sir."

"You'll report directly back to me," he went on. "Not to Chancellery. Understood?"

"Yes, sir."

Maxwell sat looking at her until she realised she'd been dismissed. She left the office, nodded to Lucy, who was still just sitting at her desk doing nothing at all, and went out into the corridor. She closed the door to the outer office behind her, then just stood there for a few moments. It was not her custom to get angry in public, although it wasn't unknown. She knew it wasn't healthy to bottle things up, but there was no other way to survive in the force these days, particularly if you were of a certain seniority. You did your job and you nodded nicely, and you kept your mouth shut. Detective Chief Superintendent Scott had learned that the hard way, and he had been far from an angry man.

She went back downstairs and poked her head into the squadrooms, but they were all empty. A dozen detectives were out in Blackbird Leys, looking for an illicit still which was producing a form of vodka that had already killed three people, and the rest of her team were investigating a spate of robberies in one of the Colleges.

She found Fleet in the canteen, tucking into a bacon sandwich, a mug of tea on the table in front of him. She sat down across from him and said, "We've been given a job."

Fleet washed down a mouthful of sandwich with a swig of tea. "Is that what the chief super wanted?"

Mellow nodded. "Someone's going to be arrested at one of the checkpoints in the next couple of days. We're to bring them back here and… interview them."

Fleet frowned. As well he might; put like that, it sounded particularly absurd. "Do we know where and when?" he asked.

She shook her head. "I'll do the interviewing, but I'd like you to go out and collect them, so stick around the office for a few days.

Catch up on your reports or something."

He shrugged. "Okay."

"And don't tell anyone else. Not even the super."

Fleet blinked at her. "What's going on, boss?"

"I don't know, Peter, but the chief super seems to want it all kept hush-hush, so let's do that." She got up. "You don't have anything else on at the moment, do you?"

Fleet shook his head. "Nothing that can't wait." He paused. "Is this something dodgy?"

Once upon a time, there would have been no need to ask, but petty politics had begun to engulf the upper reaches of the force in the past few years, and these days it could sometimes be hard to tell what was legitimate police business and what was various senior officers jockeying for position. It was wiser, if one wasn't sure, to stay well away. If that was possible.

"I don't know," Mellow told him. "But if it is, I'll make sure there's no comeback on you."

They both knew this was a bold claim. Fleet said, "Watch yourself, boss. I like working for you."

Mellow smiled. "It'll all be fine, I'm sure."

Fleet shook his head and looked around the deserted canteen. "Hell of a way to run a police force," he said.

"It's all we've got. I'll talk to you later. And don't worry."

Fleet nodded glumly and went back to his lunch. Mellow returned to her office, took the worksheets out of her desk, and sat leafing through them, but trying to get the rotas to work smoothly was like doing a particularly fiendish puzzle, one where the pieces whined that they weren't being treated fairly, and her mind wouldn't settle anyway.

She got up and went down to the ground floor, where, in a little room at the back of the building, a sergeant named Sharpe was sitting surrounded by radio equipment painstakingly built by engineers from Trinity College. One console was permanently tuned to the force emergency frequency, and Sharpe was using the others to constantly scan through the wavelengths, keeping an eye on police communications.

"Haven't seen you down here for a while," she said when Mellow entered the room. "Bored?"

"Sick of doing admin," Mellow said, pulling up a chair and sitting down at the comms desk beside her. "Anything going on?"

Sharpe reached out and flicked a switch and a burst of static emerged from a speaker mounted on the wall above the desk. She adjusted a dial minutely and Mellow heard a man's voice. "That's Dominic Baker," Sharpe told her. "Out in the Leys. They haven't found your still yet."

Mellow suspected the still had been dismantled and moved to another location, but that was no reason to stop looking. "Anything out of the ordinary?"

Sharpe looked at her. "Like what?"

Mellow shrugged. "Don't know. Something interesting." She and Sharpe had gone through training together and had spent some time paired up on the beat, but Sharpe's career had stalled and Mellow's hadn't. "Anything interesting."

Sharpe turned the dial quite a distance, and the speaker started making a garbled noise. "There was a *lot* of chatter here a month or so ago, but it's all scrambled, which means they're pretty skilled-up, not just using bits and pieces of gear they've managed to repair."

"Where is it?"

Sharpe shrugged. "It was very faint, like it was a lot of people using hand-held radios. It's settled down a bit now, but you can still hear them sometimes." She nodded at the speaker.

Radio equipment didn't grow on trees; a community that was using it must, by definition, be technologically advanced. The force had triangulated two sources in the years since electronics manufacture had begun again in Oxford. The first, dubbed Red One, was somewhere in the Chilterns, not far from Goring.

The other, Red Two, seemed to be quite some distance away to the southwest. Both of them were scrambled. There were sometimes others, when the atmospherics were right, unknown voices somewhere out there in the rain and the night, but not very many. Even allowing for the massive loss of life caused by The Sisters and the subsequent Long Autumn, England was a lonely place.

"Have you tried RDF?" Mellow asked.

Sharpe snorted. "Not worth asking for the manpower." Radio direction finding was a painstaking process involving taking a radio set out, finding in which direction a transmission was the strongest, then moving some distance and repeating the process. It could take a while, and the equipment the police had wasn't easily portable.

"Did you report it?"

Sharpe nodded. "Reported it and never heard anything else about it. Chancellery probably already knew about it; they've got their own receivers."

Chancellery, in this context, meant the Transport Unit, people best left alone. Mellow didn't doubt that they knew exactly where and what Red One was; it was a powerful transmitter and close enough for them to have sent someone to the Hills to check it out. If they had, the information wasn't being shared with the Thames Valley Police.

"Politics," Mellow said.

Sharpe adjusted the dial again and the mysterious garbled message was replaced by the voice of an officer reporting in to a police station in Cowley. "Sometimes I think they're talking to each other," she said. "Red One and Red Two."

Mellow looked at her. "Really?"

Sharpe shrugged. "It's just a feeling. I listen to them, sometimes. Can't understand a thing they're saying, of course. Just a sec." She took a pair of headphones from the desk and held one of them to her ear while she twirled one of the dials forward and back in progressively smaller increments, until she was barely moving it with her fingertips. Her eyes took on a faraway look, then she lowered her hand and listened for a moment. "There." She handed the headphones to Mellow. "Have a listen to that."

Mellow put the headphones on. At first, all she could hear was static. Then she began to make out, so faint that it was on the far edge of audibility, an irregular beeping sound almost buried in the background noise.

"What is it?" she asked.

"That's Red Three," Sharpe said with a big smile.

Mellow listened again. "No," she said.

Still grinning, Sharpe nodded. "It's another transmitter, and they're talking in Morse."

"What are they saying?"

"It's code. Just lots of numbers. My guess is it's a powerful transmitter and it's a long way away. A lot further than Red Two. Maybe it's France."

Mellow didn't see how that would help. She didn't think there was anyone in the country who still spoke French. She said, "Do Chancellery know about this?"

"Not from me, they don't."

This was dangerous territory. Mellow glanced at the door. "You should tell them, Ruth."

Sharpe shook her head. "I told you, it's a really, really weak signal, and it doesn't have a schedule. I only found it by accident. Chancellery's comms room makes this one look like a scrapheap; if they *have* heard it, they won't expect anyone else to." She beamed at the consoles, the dials and switches. "No," she said. "This is my secret."

"*Our* secret, now," Mellow said, wishing she'd stayed in her office and forced herself to work on the rotas.

"Yeah, but I know you can keep a secret, Leonie."

Do you? Do you really know that? "You can't trust anybody

17

these days." Mellow stood up. "Maybe you should try to think of some way to tell Chancellery. Maybe pretend you've only just found it."

Sharpe shook her head again.

"Then don't tell anybody else."

Sharpe looked unhappy. "I thought you'd be interested."

Mellow sighed. Sharpe was bright and she was a good copper, but she was almost entirely guileless, which was a bad thing to be these days. "And I am," she said. "I really am." She squeezed her friend's shoulder. "But if you're not going to report this, keep it to yourself, eh?"

SHE STAYED ON for an hour or so after her shift finished, just in case Maxwell's mysterious intruder turned up, but when nothing happened she stuffed the rota sheets into her desk, locked the door of her office, collected her bicycle from the yard behind the building, and went home.

The centre of Oxford was an island, pretty much. The Thames and the Cherwell, swollen by decades of rain, had long ago washed their banks away, along with the bridges that used to stand there, and now the only way to cross them was by a series of steam-powered chain ferries. Most of the population lived in the suburbs, on higher ground or beyond the reach of the floodwater, but all the shops were in the centre of town. On her way to the ferry across the Cherwell, Mellow stopped at a butcher's and bought a chicken. The earlier heavy rain had given way to the usual miserable drizzle, and there were quite a few people out and about. Horses and carts choked the streets, work crews busied themselves with the unending task of reclaiming derelict buildings. She nodded hello to the occasional patrolling bobby she saw, but she was conscious that she recognised fewer and fewer of them these days. There had been a time when even in the outlying police stations she could have counted on seeing at least a few familiar faces, but now they were staffed by strangers, no way to know where their loyalties lay.

At the ferry crossing, the big flatboat was on the other side of the river, and after buying a ticket she had to wait for twenty minutes in the shelter beside the engine house while it loaded up with wagons and carts and foot passengers. When she'd been little, the Cherwell ferry had been the most exciting thing in the world, with the chimneys of its steam engines pumping smoke into the air and the sound of the machinery, the sense of being out in the middle of the river with the water running strongly beneath your feet. When she was seven, though, a cable had snapped and twenty-six people had drowned, and for ever such a long time after that she had refused to go on the ferry because she couldn't stop thinking about the horses, still hitched to their wagons, being dragged down into the swirling brown water.

It was a long time since there had been a major accident on any of the local ferries, although the engines still broke down periodically, stranding the boats on either bank, or sometimes in the middle of the river. Now, it was just one more part of her journey to and from work, and she hardly thought about it.

Movement on the other side of the river caught her eye. When she looked, she saw that the green flag had been raised on the opposite engine house to signal that they were ready to pay out cable. She stepped out of the shelter and watched a similar flag rising up the flagpole over the engine house on this side, and a moment later there was the sound of escaping steam and the winch starting up, and the ferry began to make its slow journey.

It was actually an operation of no small precision. The two winches had to operate in perfect unison, one reeling in and the other unreeling, otherwise the cable could snap or sag uselessly towards the bed of the river and let the current take the boat. When her father had realised why she was suddenly unwilling to go near the ferry, he had taken her down to the crossing one day and one of the ferrymasters had shown her the steam engine and the huge drum of the winch with its quarter of a mile of cable wrapped round it, still dripping from a recent immersion in the river. She still remembered vividly the smell of the tobacco he was smoking in his pipe. "The trick, little miss," he had told her solemnly, "is to keep just enough tension, but not too much."

She looked at the ticket in her hand, the poorly printed little slip of card that proved she had paid ten pence to use the ferry. And right there, really, was proof of how much things had changed since she was a girl. The tobacco that long-ago ferryman had been smoking had probably been given to him by a passenger in return for being carried across the river, because that was how it had been done for decades. Now, he'd have to go to a shop in town and buy it, and it would be very expensive because supplies were running low. Somewhere, the person who controlled those supplies had become rich. They could only spend that wealth in Oxford, it was true, but these days in Oxford wealth bought you influence, and influence bought you power, and that, she thought, was the whole problem.

The river crossing took about ten minutes. Then there was another five minutes to wait while the incoming passengers disembarked from the boat. Then there was ten minutes or so while the outgoing passengers boarded and the ferrymasters arranged them so that the weight of people and carts and wagons was evenly distributed. There was always one arsehole who insisted on parking his cart where he wanted, in spite of what anyone told them, and there was a period of shouting before everyone was settled and the flags went up again on the enginehouses and the ferry began to inch its way out across the river.

Mellow lived where she had always lived, the neat detached house on the corner of a street in Headington where she was born, where her father had been born, where her grandparents had somehow survived the fall of The Sisters and the first terrible years of the Long Autumn, the house her great-grandparents had moved into just after their marriage, back in the days when there had been cars and aeroplanes and television and all the other things she'd read about when she was growing up. A lot of people had fled the city in the early days of the disaster, but many had remained, either because they were too fearful or because they simply had nowhere else to go. They were the ones who had finally organised themselves and begun to reclaim the city, old families who had gained a certain status in Oxford and then seen that status quietly and almost imperceptibly undermined.

It was dark by the time Mellow finally cycled along her street, but this had been a safe, quiet area for a long time now. Headington police station was just a couple of streets away, and the Neighbourhood Watch had always been strongly active. Most of the houses on the street were occupied and well looked-after. Each one had a windmill in the back garden and there were lights in almost all the windows.

The lights were on in the front room and the hallway of her house, to illuminate her way up the front path. She wheeled her bicycle around to the back of the house, took the bag containing the chicken from the pannier, then went back to the front, let herself in, locked the door behind her.

"Is that you?" a voice called from one of the rooms off the hallway.

"Transport Unit," Mellow said, putting her bag and knapsack on the floor while she took off her coat and hung it up. "You're under arrest."

"Funny as ever," her father said, wheeling himself out of his room and into the hallway.

"That's life in the force," she said, bending down to give him a hug and kiss the top of his head. "Nothing but comedy. How was your day?"

He shrugged, a big man in his late fifties with wild grey hair and legs that ended at the knees. "Same as yesterday. And the day before that. And the day before that…"

"Yes, I get it, Dad." She picked up her bag. "I got a chicken," she said. "I thought we could have a roast tomorrow."

"Sounds good to me." He turned his wheelchair expertly in the narrow hallway and propelled himself towards the kitchen. "We've got the last of that stew for tonight."

Mellow followed him into the kitchen, where saucepans of stew and peeled potatoes were waiting on the edge of the range. Her father reached over and set them on the hotplates while Mellow put her ID badge, radio, and sidearm on one of the worktops and her shopping on the kitchen table. He wheeled over and looked in the bag.

"Are you sure this is a chicken?" he asked. "Looks more like a pigeon."

She sighed and opened one of the cupboards. She took out a plate and a big mixing bowl.

"Can we afford this?" her father said.

Three years ago, he wouldn't have asked. Back then, Sergeant Jack Mellow had a pension from the Thames Valley Police, which in practice meant his old pals from Headington nick coming round every week with food and doing odd-jobs – one of them had built a series of low ramps around the edge of the kitchen so he could reach the range and the sink from his chair. Nowadays, his pension consisted of a constable coming round every two weeks and popping an envelope containing twenty quid through the letterbox. Added to Mellow's inspector's salary, they were barely getting by. They made their own electricity and grew their own veg, but they had to pay a monthly fee to the Municipal Utilities Department, which kept the water running and the drains clear, there were always repairs that needed doing, and food kept getting more expensive.

On the other hand, they were wealthy. The previous year, a

couple of neat young bureaucrats had come down the street with an authorisation from Chancellery – a lot like the one Mellow had seen earlier today but this one had been printed – to assess the value of all the properties in the city. She'd been at work, but Jack said he'd expressed an opinion that there were a lot of houses in Oxford and the bureaucrats would probably be old men by the time they finished the job. Still, they had the official paper, so he let them in, and they poked about for ten minutes and left, and a few days later someone delivered a letter – again on headed paper – bearing the news that the house was worth fifteen thousand pounds. Which was grand, obviously, but Jack pointed out that it was still effectively worthless unless there was someone willing to buy it, and neither of them knew anyone with that much spare cash.

It occurred to Mellow, though, that an exercise like this would be an ideal way of checking who was living where, a sort of unofficial census. There was a convention, going back to the early days of the Long Autumn when everything was chaos and resources were tight, that only registered residents of the city could live and work there. It was still quite a tightly enforced convention, although people did slip through the checkpoints from outside, and in a little corner of her mind, Mellow wondered whether someone was looking for unregistered residents. If they were, nobody had bothered to tell the police.

She put the chicken – and in truth it must have looked particularly pathetic in life – on the plate, popped the bowl over it. "It'll do for us," she told him. "And you can use the leftovers to make soup." She carried the plate over to the larder and put it on a shelf. She'd heard rumours of a move to bring people's wind turbines under the Utilities Department. She wasn't sure how that would work, and it would cause a lot of resentment; the turbines belonged to the residents – Jack's father had built theirs. But Chancellery had ways of dealing with resentment.

Mellow washed her hands at the sink, dried them on a

threadbare towel. "I'm going to have five minutes," she said. "I'll be down in time to sort out dinner."

"No rush," Jack said, wheeling back towards the range. "I can cope."

Upstairs in her room – the same room she'd been in since she was little – Mellow changed her clothes and then stretched out on the bed and lay staring up at the stain in the corner of the ceiling. It seemed a little larger today, which suggested the roof still hadn't repaired itself. Once upon a time, one of her father's old mates from Headington police station would have popped round one lunch break and fixed it, and she'd have given them a bag of potatoes or some carrots from the garden in return, but the last time she'd visited Headington nick she hadn't seen a single familiar face – she'd actually felt rather unwelcome, if she was going to be honest – and people who did repairs and various odd-jobs professionally wanted cash and quite a lot of it.

It occurred to her that coping was something they did, and compared to a lot of people in England it was something they did quite well. From what she'd heard, the rest of the country was a sodden, half-drowned catastrophe populated by farmers who were barely keeping starvation at bay. She didn't know how true that was; she was thirty-five, and although she'd learned about the country's geography at school, she'd never left Oxford. The presence of Red One and Red Two, and the apparently more recent discovery of Red Three, suggested the picture was more complicated than that, but that was the impression one got from outsiders who visited the city. At least, when outsiders were still allowed to visit.

Mellow closed her eyes and put a hand over her face, feeling the day suddenly weighing down on her. For the past eighteen months or so, Oxford had been turning outsiders away. The reasons given for this were many and vague, but seemed to centre around an assertion that the city was full, which it was not. Roads had been blocked and checkpoints set up, and a unit of the militia carved off under the auspices of the police to form a new Border Guard to man them, and anyone approaching Oxford was told, politely or otherwise, to go away.

In truth, it wasn't that hard to slip into the city unseen, so long as you avoided the roads, and some people still did that, although they tended to stand out because they had no money and very little idea of how it worked and most of them were easily picked up, baffled at what was going on in Oxford, and handed over to the Transport Unit.

Maxwell's mysterious visitor sounded different, though, and Mellow sensed hazard here, Politics, which was something she was careful to try and avoid. Whoever they were, Chancellery wanted them allowed into the city, and Maxwell wanted to take a look at them first, and now she was mixed up in the whole stupid business. As if being a copper wasn't complicated enough already.

She must have dozed off, because the next thing she knew her father was calling her from downstairs to let her know dinner was ready. She got up stiffly and went down to eat, unable to shake a sense of foreboding.

TWO

MILES TO THE south of Oxford, across the drowned and forbidding landscape of the Vale of the White Horse, peace was returning to the many little communities and holdings and fortified farmsteads of the Chiltern Hills.

It was not returning willingly. For weeks, in the part of the Hills where Berkshire met Oxfordshire, former friends and neighbours had fought each other, for reasons they couldn't later articulate and with a ferocity that they couldn't properly explain. The savage little war which had overtaken the Parish had only been ended by the arrival of several hundred quiet, serious men and women wearing military camouflage and armed with the kind of weapons few in the area had ever heard of, who had ended the violence by the simple expedient of being massively more violent than anyone else.

They were not soldiers, the people of the Parish learned in the shellshocked days following the end of the conflict. They were *Marines*, and they came from Plymouth – *Guz*, as it called itself now – a city which had survived the Long Autumn under the control of the Navy. It was a place, so gossip had it, where there was plenty of food and housing and hot running water and even flush toilets, and quite a lot of the people of the Parish, perhaps in an effort to put their recent shame behind them, wanted to go there.

This was not part of Guz's plan. The Marines hadn't been sent to end the conflict out of the goodness of their hearts, but to create a stronghold situation in the Chilterns, and they needed as much as possible of the population to stay in place. So they helped the people of the Parish repair the damage they had done to each other's homes. They set up health centres and community centres. They erected wind turbines and brought electricity and electric light to the area for the first time in a century. They rode east and west along the Hills, bringing more communities under their control. They rode up to Streatley, where the Thames, swollen by almost a century of rain, passed through the gap in the hills on its way towards the ruins of London. There weren't enough of them to take the town, or Goring on the other side of the river, but they came to an accommodation with the local population and set up a permanent garrison there.

Adam watched all this with something of a sinking heart. He didn't know what the Parish had been like before the war – he'd ridden right into the middle of it, had in fact been robbed and beaten up and left for dead within an hour of arriving – but he'd seen Guz behave like this before. It was standard policy. They arrived in a spirit of partnership, and woe betide anyone who might be foolish enough to disagree. The origins of this particular intervention lay in a stew of rumours and garbled intelligence about what was happening in Oxford and further afield in the Cotswolds, a sense of unspecified threat that Guz had felt impelled to respond to.

In the days after peace was imposed on the area, Adam had been talking to some of the locals. In the past it had been, he gathered, something of a rite of passage for some of the young men of the Parish to go off adventuring to Oxford, but when you asked them about it, it turned out that none of them had ever actually entered the city. Most of them came back after a few months, and, talking to a few of the old gaffers who had done it in their youth, Adam gathered that their great adventure had amounted to not much more than a season working as hands on one or other of the farmsteads in the area, which they could have done without leaving home and spared themselves a slog across country.

The nature of the farmsteads down in the Vale of the White Horse seemed to have changed lately, though. More recent visitors reported the locals becoming more and more standoffish. "They just told me to fuck off," said one young man.

"How?" asked Adam.

The young man, whose name was Roger, narrowed his eyes. "How do you mean?"

"How did they tell you to fuck off?" Adam asked. "Were they angry? Did they threaten you?"

They were sitting in one of the big command tents the Marines had set up in a burned-out farm compound, and it was obvious the boy was a bit overwhelmed by it all. He'd left the Parish a few days before the beginning of the war, and had returned to find his entire family dead, his home a pile of wet ashes, and an army of strangers in control. He was also perplexed to find himself being questioned, not by one of the Marines with their uniforms and interesting military equipment, but by a dishevelled and exhausted-looking man in dirty clothes slumped in a camp chair across the table from him.

"What are we doing talking about Oxford?" he asked. "What's that got to do with anything?"

Adam rubbed his eyes and wondered if he'd ever get a decent night's sleep again. "It's not got anything to do with anything," he said. "I'm just tying up loose ends. Sooner I finish this, sooner I can go home."

"What about me?" Roger demanded. "I can't go home. Somebody's burned my fucking home down."

Adam looked at the pen and the little stack of notepaper on the desk in front of him. He hadn't made any notes; like the majority of the country's population, most of the people of the Parish were illiterate, and he'd found that it upset them when somebody wrote down what they were saying. "You went up the Wantage road, right?" he said.

Roger nodded, not seeing where the question was going.

"That's a pretty good road," Adam went on. "It's, what, a three-day trip to Oxford on foot? Four at most? Four days there, four days back. You said you were gone about six weeks."

Roger stared at him. "What have *I* done?"

"You haven't done anything. I just want to know where you were all that time, that's all."

"There's a girl I'm sweet on in Abingdon," Roger said defensively. "Her dad's got a forge and I worked for him for a while, till I heard what was going on up here."

"Will you go back there, now?" Adam asked.

Roger's mouth dropped open.

"There's nothing left here for you, right?" Adam said.

Roger blinked at him. "I don't have to talk to you."

"Yes, you do," Adam told him, looking past him at the two Marines standing either side of the tent's entrance.

Roger turned in his chair and looked at the Marines, then turned back to look at Adam.

Adam said, "They told you to fuck off."

For a second, he thought Roger was going to come across the table at him, which would probably have resulted in one or both of the Marines shooting him. There had been attacks – not much more than fistfights, really – on Bureau personnel, and a Marine had gone missing, presumed killed. The Bureau had expected these things, and planned accordingly; it was currently employing a zero-tolerance policy with regard to attacks on its people. Eventually the inhabitants of the Parish would learn who was giving orders.

But Roger didn't do that. He sat glaring at Adam and said flatly, "I tried a farm a couple of miles outside Abingdon, but they didn't let me in. They didn't even open the gate, just shouted at me from the wall."

"What did they say?"

"I told you. They told me to fuck off. Said they didn't need any hands." He shrugged. "So I fucked off to Abingdon instead."

"Did you believe them? About not needing hands?"

"You're not a farmer, are you?" Roger said with a sneer. "Farms always need hands. There's never enough help."

"So why tell you to go away?"

"You tell me, you're the clever one here. I don't think they were even the same people."

Adam raised an eyebrow.

"We know the family," Roger said. "Old man Meaden and his wife and their kids. My dad went to work for them when he was younger, that's why I went there rather than somewhere else."

"And if they knew you, they'd have let you in," Adam finished for him.

"You'd think so."

"Did you have a row with them? Something that would have made them turn you away?"

Roger shook his head. "My dad wouldn't have told me to ask them for work if we had. He hadn't even seen them for two years."

Adam thought about that. "What *will* you do now?" he asked finally. "Out of interest."

"I don't know." Roger stared at him. "Any ideas?"

When Roger had left, Chrissie, who had been sitting quietly on the other side of the tent taking care of some paperwork, came over and sat in his chair. "You didn't have to be so horrid to him, you know," she said.

Adam stretched as much as he could in his chair and looked up at the roof of the tent and listened to the rain falling on the fabric. "Don't tell me you're starting to get soft in your old age," he said.

She was a stout red-haired woman in her mid-thirties, wearing black combat coveralls and an automatic pistol in an underarm holster. "He's a bright lad," she said. "I've had my eye on him, thought about maybe taking him back to Guz when the command staff pull out."

"Train him up for the Bureau?" he asked, closing his eyes.

"We're like farmers. There's never enough hands."

Adam rubbed his face. He'd had a haircut and a beard trim, and he'd made use of the field showers the Marines had installed, but he still felt dirty.

"What do you think of his story?" she asked.

Three other people who had gone out into the Vale over the past few months had reported that smallholdings seemed to have changed hands. He said, "It sounds as if Mr and Mrs Meaden have been quietly replaced." He sat up and looked at her. "And all the little Meadens."

Chrissie gave him a long, level look. "Why?" she said finally. "And by whom?"

"That is the question, isn't it?" he said. "Questions."

She turned and waved the Marines – who were actually there to guard her and not the tent – out, and when they were safely outside, she said, "Roger doesn't know how lucky he was. He walked right through whatever it is Father John's people are doing down there and he knocked on their front door and they let him go. They could have just shot him, and nobody would have been any the wiser. Considering what happened here it would have been a miracle if anyone ever missed him."

"It's not likely to be Father John though, is it?" he said. "Not after all this time."

"The people we ran into were more than happy to drop his

name." She shook her head. "It doesn't matter *who's* in charge. Something's going on. Those people were well-armed and well-organised, and they weren't a walkover."

Personally, Adam thought the Bureau was jumping at shadows. He and Chrissie and the little expeditionary force she had led from Guz were here chiefly because of rumours of *something* happening in the Cotswolds and around Oxford, and really rumours were all they were. Signs and portents, gossip and supposition. On their way to the Parish, Chrissie and the Marines had encountered a small armed force in Wiltshire. A firefight had ensued, and interrogation of the few survivors had only turned up more rumours and gossip. The one concrete piece of intelligence they had obtained was the name 'Father John', which had a terrible resonance for Guz. But it was, when all was said and done, only a name.

"What were they doing in Wiltshire?" he said.

"You know what they were doing there. They were *showing us up*, is what they were doing. Stomping about as if they owned the place."

"I didn't realise we had a claim on Wiltshire now."

"Don't be an arse, Adam. They were challenging us."

In Adam's opinion, Guz was far too prepared to believe that everything was a challenge. It had also had things its own way in the West for far too long. Wiltshire was rough country, but a large enough armed force based there could control the few existing routes in and out of the West. Guz had never had to consider that before, and Adam sensed an uncharacteristic policy failure, somewhere high up in the Committee; they were moving quickly to add Warminster and Salisbury to the string of garrisons they had already established across Devon and Somerset. If you had any doubt at all that war with *somebody* was coming, you only had to look at those deployments.

Chrissie said, "I wouldn't be sending you if there was anyone else."

"Yes," he said. "You said that last time you sent me out."

She sighed.

"You signed something to say I could have some leave when I was done in Margate," he said. He made a weary show of searching his pockets. "I seem to have lost it, though."

"We know next to nothing about Oxford, and that's an intelligence failure," she told him seriously. "We've been busy with other stuff, but that's no excuse for taking our eye off the ball. We know it's a big population centre, but we don't know how big. We assume there's some kind of organisation there, but we don't know what it is. Just go and *look*. Find out who's running the place; make contact with them, if you think it's safe. Find out if they're a threat. Don't kill anybody or start any wars. Just look and come back. Then we can go home."

He nodded. She made it sound as if there was a choice, but really there wasn't.

IT FELT ODD to be moving openly around the Parish. For most of his time there he had moved from cover to cover, mostly coming out at night. Everyone who had known he was there was dead. Not that the people of the Parish had been paying attention; at the time they'd been too busy trying to kill each other to bother very much with a lone stranger.

On Chrissie's orders, when he did leave the encampment, he took a Marine with him. Not for protection – there had been some initial resistance to the occupation, but that had been put down with a series of brisk hangings and most of the local population seemed too shellshocked to be much of a threat – more as a mark of status. It made Adam feel uncomfortable, but for his designated bodyguard, a massively muscled monosyllabic sergeant named Boult, it was just another duty, so he kept his opinions to himself.

Everywhere he went, there were marks of the war. Abandoned

farms, their gates broken down and their buildings burned out, graves seemingly placed at random in ones and twos, livestock wandering about. At the moment, the people seemed docile, as if the war had burned something out of them and they were afraid to remember it. Guz knew that it was going through something of a honeymoon period at the moment, and once that was over the locals would begin to resent its presence, so it was using the time to make itself indispensable. There were field kitchens dispensing free food, a ready supply of Marines to help with rebuilding, even a school in one of the big tents. Guz was, of course, recruiting an army, but hopefully by the time the people of the Parish realised that it would be too late.

There was a big farm not far from the northern edge of the Parish, one of the biggest farms in the area, and it was a wreck. The clearing it sat in was churned up by horses and people, and to one side there was a hurriedly dug mass grave containing the bodies of more than a hundred people who had died during the final, spasmodic battle of the war. The wall around the farm compound itself was broken down in several places, and in other places it bore the marks of explosions. The gate had been blown apart by a rocket propelled grenade, and another RPG round had all but removed the upper floor of the main house. The compound was full of people trying to clear up the mess, but they all looked exhausted, and when Adam and Boult stepped through the gate only a few paid any attention. And even then, Adam thought they were looking at the sergeant rather than him.

"Try not to shoot anybody," he murmured to Boult.

"Sir," Boult replied, in the tone of a man who had long ago come to the conclusion that his superiors were never going to stop stating the fucking obvious.

Adam walked up to a man who was stacking the broken boards of a demolished shed and said, "Hello. I'm looking for Harry Lyall."

The man looked at him, then at Boult, then back at Adam. He waved at the house, then went back to piling up boards.

The door of the main house was open, but it was impossible to see much further inside than the front hall. "Harry Lyall?" Adam called, and after a moment a tall middle-aged man emerged from one of the doorways off the hall. He came to the door, looked first at Boult, then at Adam. "Are you Harry Lyall?" Adam asked.

The man nodded. He appeared gaunt-faced and hollowed-out. His clothes seemed to be for someone a lot stockier and he didn't look to have slept for a very long time.

Adam put out a hand, but Lyall didn't shake it. "I'd like a quiet word, if that's all right with you."

Lyall looked at Boult again, back to Adam. "About what?"

"This and that. Won't take long. Is there somewhere we can talk?"

Lyall heaved a sigh. "I'll get my coat."

THEY HAD BEEN walking for a while when Adam became aware of an angry-looking woman with a pump-action shotgun following at a respectful distance.

"That's Wendy, my foreman," Lyall said. "She probably thinks that if you've got a bodyguard, I should have one, too."

Adam glanced over his shoulder at Boult, who was following at a similarly respectful distance. "I don't want a bodyguard," he said. "My boss just ordered him to follow me everywhere and I can't stop him."

"Red-haired woman? A bit fierce?"

"That's her."

Lyall nodded. "I talked to her. Is she like that all the time?"

"We don't normally see that much of each other. I'm away a lot."

Lyall looked at him. "Doing what?"

Adam shrugged. "This and that."

They walked for about half an hour. Occasionally they passed locals, but when Lyall nodded hello, they ignored him and walked on by, and eventually Lyall gave up. Adam wondered how long it would take the Parish to recover from the war. It would never be the same again, even if Guz hadn't invaded the place. Maybe, he thought, it was best they had. At least it gave the locals something to hate other than each other.

Eventually, they came to the edge of the hills and stood looking out across the Vale of the White Horse, an overgrown landscape of marshes and lakes that extended into the far distance until the drizzle made it impossible to make out details.

Lyall pointed at dark smudges in the distance. "That's Didcot there," he said. "And over there's Abingdon." He gestured to the north. "Oxford's that way. Some say you used to be able to see it from here, once upon a time, but I never have. It's always too rainy."

"Do you know anyone down there?" Adam asked. He could just make out buildings in the near distance, almost lost in the general overgrowth.

"We bump into each other in Goring on market day, but otherwise we don't mix much."

"How about Oxford? Have you ever been there?"

Lyall shook his head. "It's a long walk over rough country," he said. "There's only one road that's even halfway usable, and that's mostly overgrown or washed away; you can't get a cart along it."

Adam wasn't sure that was entirely true anymore. He said, "Have any of them ever come here?"

"From Oxford?" Lyall shook his head. "Not that I know of. Why would they come *here*?"

"Trade? Curiosity?"

Lyall chuckled, but it was a forced, bitter sound. "Nah. Streatley or Goring, maybe. But not here."

Adam nodded into the distance. "We've been hearing rumours about something going on out there."

Lyall grunted. "Your boss was going on about that, too. I don't know; I haven't heard anything. I've been a bit busy."

"Some people say you tried to stop the fighting."

Lyall snorted. "And a bang-up job I made of *that*."

They stood looking into the rain for a while, then Adam said, "What *happened* here?"

Lyall shook his head. "You can read the report, if you can read. Your boss interrogated me for hours."

Adam turned to him and said, "She debriefed you, Mr Lyall. If you'd been *interrogated*, you wouldn't be able to stand here talking to me."

Lyall looked at him for a few moments, then turned back to the view. "My son and a couple of his mates tried to rob one of our neighbours, and he killed them," he said. "Then all of a sudden everybody was shooting." He put his hands in his coat pockets, rummaged around absently, took one hand out holding a piece of string and the stub of a pencil. Adam watched him. He had read the report, and a lot of other reports as well.

He looked over his shoulder to where Boult and Wendy had stationed themselves out of earshot and were filling in the time by giving each other the stink-eye. He said, "I'm sorry this happened to you and your people, Mr Lyall," he said.

"We did it to ourselves," Lyall told him.

"I'm still sorry." And he turned and started to walk away. He heard Boult fall into step behind him.

"You didn't tell me your name," Lyall said.

"It doesn't matter," he called without looking back. "I was never here."

THREE

FOR MORTY ROBERTS, the sudden and explosive end of the war in the Parish came as an unwelcome surprise. While the locals had been rampaging around slaughtering each other, he had been able to move unseen through the forgotten, overgrown spaces of the area and carry out his own killings, his victims lost among the general body count. Now, though, that was over. Nobody was killing anyone anymore. And worse, there were new people in the Parish, and while he admired their work and coveted their weapons, he knew instinctively that if he came to their notice he wouldn't survive for long.

This was something of a problem for Morty, because he wasn't remotely ready to stop killing yet. The people of the Parish hadn't even begun to suffer for the years of humiliation they'd put him through. And besides, he'd discovered that killing was the only thing he was good at.

He retreated to his hide in an old electricity substation buried in a huge patch of overgrowth in an out-of-the-way part of the Parish and tried to work out what to do. In one of the little brick-built sheds he propped the head on top of an equipment cabinet and slumped in a corner. He had, for a time, felt invulnerable, all-powerful. He moved like a ghost and his one-time neighbours had been unable to defend themselves against him. Now he was just an emaciated, ragged remnant of a man who didn't dare show either of his faces.

"You cut my fucking head off, you cunt," said the head from the other side of the shed.

"Shut up," Morty said, and his voice sounded croaky because he'd barely spoken to anyone since he killed his wife and her lover and her lover's entire family. "I'm trying to think."

"What the fuck did you do that for?" the head whined. "What did I ever do to you?"

"I said, shut up," said Morty. "Or I'll cut off your ears. And maybe your nose."

The head had once sat proudly on the thick neck of Albie Dodd, who had ridden to the Parish in command of a group of armed Enforcers from Margate in search of Adam Hardy, who had stolen his boss's prized sniper rifle. Albie and the Enforcers were used to getting their own way, and they had been enraged to discover that the locals were too busy with their war to pay them much attention. This had caused them to make several critical errors, culminating in riding into the middle of the final battle outside Harry Lyall's compound. Most of them had been killed, and Albie had been in the process of fleeing when he met Morty.

Morty didn't know any of this, of course. There hadn't been time for conversation while he was cutting Albie's head off. All he'd seen was a man on a horse with a good-looking shotgun, and he'd reacted accordingly. Now he was stuck with the head, and the head kept muttering to him.

"Miserable little twat," the head told him. "Hiding in a corner pissing your pants. No wonder your wife was fucking Big Keith."

"I said, shut up!" Morty screamed, throwing a rusty wrench

at the head and knocking it off its perch. He sat back in the corner and wrapped his ragged, filthy clothes around himself, breathing hard.

The thing was, the head was right. He'd been weak and pathetic and useless. And then he'd shaken that off like a snake shedding its skin and he'd killed Karen and Big Keith and Big Keith's repulsive family, and he'd gone on killing and he'd become a force of retribution. And now he was back to the beginning, weak and pathetic and useless, and if he didn't do something about that he was going to die.

As it sometimes did when he was under stress, Morty's mind blanked out for a while, and when it came back his hiding place was in an even worse state, stuff thrown all over the place, things broken. His fists hurt. The head was back on its perch, but it was missing an ear.

"What the fuck did you do that for?" it moaned.

"Serves you fucking right," Morty said, but he said it with a smile, because he suddenly had a plan.

AT SOME POINT during the war, Morty had become aware of a stranger in the Parish. Pretty much everyone in the Parish was a stranger to him, despite having lived there for some years, but he had a sense that this one was not a local. Like him, the stranger was killing his way through the local population, but where Morty simply cut down anyone he came across, the stranger was more purposeful, almost elegant. He wasn't just killing the locals, he was *punishing* them. He was an artist, a genuine predator.

They'd only met once, when Morty had tried to give the stranger some of his souvenirs as a tribute, and the stranger had rejected him. That had hurt, in a place deep down where he hadn't thought he could be hurt anymore, but it seemed to him that the predator never did anything without a reason and he thought he detected a deeper purpose, something intended to save them both. It felt as if the stranger was protecting him.

Which was why, he reasoned, he needed to speak with the stranger now. They were both in the same situation, unable to do their work freely, exposed to possible capture. It made sense to pool their resources and expertise, find a way out of the trap.

There were a number of obstacles standing in the way of this plan, but he had grown used to either overcoming obstacles or going around them altogether. The first was that, even in his present state of mind, it was obvious to him that he couldn't be seen in public looking the way he did at the moment. The second was, he didn't know where the stranger was.

The first obstacle was easy enough. He hacked away at his long, greasy hair with a knife, and washed his face as best he could in a puddle. He couldn't do anything about his clothes right now, and he'd long ago stopped being aware of how bad he smelled, but when he'd finished, he felt confident that he wouldn't look too out of place.

AND ACTUALLY, HE wasn't far wrong. The Parish was full of pitiful, ragged figures wandering from place to place, their homes and families destroyed. So long as he didn't get too close to anyone, he didn't attract a lot of attention. But after a couple of days, he still hadn't spotted the stranger, or seen any sign of his work, and he realised that he was going to have to try something else.

One night, Morty set out from his hiding place and made his way quietly and carefully to the remains of a little village some miles away across the Parish. The village was just a few ruined houses and the shell of a pub arranged around a lake which had once been a little duckpond. Here, Morty had watched the stranger, with a single shot, set off a firefight which had accounted for many lives. It had been a beautiful piece of work, something Morty could only ever aspire to. And even more important, the stranger had left his mark here.

Morty made his way into one of the derelict houses and went upstairs to the room where the stranger had taken his shot. The room was damp and full of rubbish and warped furniture, but it only took Morty a few moments to retrieve a section of wooden board from the place where he had hidden it in case someone else came along. Carved deeply into the wood was a single word. Morty didn't know what it said because he couldn't read, but the stranger had left it here, so it had the weight of a religious relic. He traced the letters with a fingertip and thought they felt warm, charged with power and significance.

When he got back to his hide, he held the board up in front of the head, but the head didn't respond. Either it couldn't read, or it was sulking at the loss of its ear. This didn't deter Morty, though. He hadn't seriously expected any help from that direction.

The next part of his plan, though, was freighted with risk and required him to be patient, something he had learned to do in his former life. He set out, and over a period of several days, staying out of sight as much as possible, he kept a cautious watch on the routines of the invading soldiers, the ones in the black uniforms, and after a while he noticed two things he hadn't quite appreciated before. First, the Parish was a lot bigger than he'd realised. And second, there were fewer of the invaders than people thought. If they seemed to be everywhere, that was because they were well-armed and well-organised and everyone was afraid of them, but their patrols were actually quite thin on the ground and, while they patrolled in twos and threes out in the more distant parts of the Parish, closer to the compounds where they had made their bases they occasionally patrolled singly. That presented an opportunity, but it was a risky one.

"You don't fucking dare," the head told him as Morty sat sharpening a knife. "You haven't got the balls."

"You're a fine one to talk about not having balls," Morty said, and he made a braying noise that was the closest he had ever come to laughter.

"Yeah," said the head, "you fucking laugh. You won't be laughing when they're hanging you."

That was true enough; Morty had watched, from hiding, as the invaders hanged people in twos and threes and fours, and on one memorable occasion in a group of seven. He understood why they were doing it, they were scaring the locals into obedience, but that didn't change the fact that he wanted to avoid it happening to him.

"I'll be careful," he said, and the head laughed. Its laugh was a lot like his.

And Morty *was* careful, a lot more careful than he really wanted to be because every day that passed was another day that the stranger might have left the Parish. He moved through the deserted and little-used spaces, and he started to feel a little of his power return. He was everywhere, he was invisible, he was Death. Even when he did break cover, he was just another lost figure wandering in the landscape. He didn't carry a gun – he'd seen the soldiers disarming people – but he kept a couple of knives hidden about his person. He even – and this took reserves of nerve that he hadn't known he possessed – visited one of the free food kitchens the invaders had set up, queued for a bowl of stew and a mug of tea, didn't notice when people moved away from him when he sat down to eat. He watched the soldiers and waited for his chance.

And, miraculously, when it came, it came out of nowhere.

He was moving through the undergrowth one morning a mile or so from his hide when he heard someone walking along the path off to his right, a slow, steady tread crunching twigs. He stopped and listened, and heard the crackly, abrupt voice of one of the little boxes the soldiers carried.

Moving carefully, he went to the edge of the path and looked out, saw one of the soldiers walking along a few yards ahead of him, completely alone and completely unaware that he was there. It never occurred to him that the soldier was upwind of him, otherwise what happened next might have turned out very differently.

Morty felt a sudden thrill of anticipation so powerful that it almost made him giddy. He searched the ground about his feet, found a fist-sized stone half buried in the soil and prised it up. He leaned out of the undergrowth again and looked around. There were no farms nearby, and the path the soldier was using was not very well-travelled. There was nobody nearby. Morty moved, all of a sudden.

He was unnaturally fast and light-footed, but even so the soldier heard him at the last moment and half turned, and the stone in Morty's fist caught him on the temple instead of the back of the head and he crumpled over to one side.

And that was it. Simple as that. Morty stood over the stunned soldier for a few moments, looking about him, in case somebody came along. Then he went to work.

All the soldiers carried short lengths of cord to tie up people who displeased them, and Morty bound the soldier's elbows and wrists behind his back and tied his knees and ankles together. While the soldier groaned and writhed on the ground, Morty searched him quickly, shouldering his automatic rifle and putting his sidearm and knives in various pockets. There was a sort of handle on the front of the soldier's ballistic vest, and Morty took hold of it and dragged him off the path and into the undergrowth. By this time the soldier seemed to be coming round, so Morty dropped him to the ground and hit him again. This time he tied rags around his mouth and eyes.

Another quick search. He plucked the talking box off the soldier's uniform and smashed it to pieces with the butt of the rifle. There were other things on the soldier, fat little cylinders attached to loops or in pockets. Morty didn't know what these were, so he buried them with the pieces of the radio, picked up the soldier again and moved on. It took a while, because he didn't go straight back to his hide. He went in the opposite direction for quite a distance, then slogged through a patch of bogland, across another path, then back through the bog. Morty looked as if a light breeze would snap him in two, but years of trying to keep his farm going on his own had put surprising layers of muscle on him and his time roaming around the Parish had increased his stamina way beyond that of the average local. By the time he turned for home he could hear people crashing around in the woods, far away. At some point, the soldier recovered consciousness and tried briefly to struggle free, but by then it didn't matter.

MORTY HAD TWO faces. He had the Morty Face, which was the face that he showed to the rest of the world: harmless, cheerful, always ready to help no matter how bad things were. And then he had the other face, the one his victims saw in the moments before their death, if they saw him at all. He dumped the soldier in a corner of his shed, squatted down in front of him, removed the blindfold, and composed his Morty Face.

The soldier, who was actually a Marine Warrant Officer named Watkins, opened his eyes and blinked about him. He was sitting in a small, filthy, brick-walled room lit by a single candle stuck to the top of a low metal cabinet. He'd already figured that he'd been captured by one of the locals, and he'd been silently cursing himself the whole time he was being dragged through the woods. He'd done what he always advised young recruits not to do: he'd got sloppy. He'd thought the locals had been subdued and that it was safe to patrol around the area alone and now here he was with a colossal pain in his head, arms and legs bound, sprawled against a wall in near darkness. The place absolutely stank, but that wasn't the worst of it. The worst was the stick-thin rag-clad figure crouched in front of him, its head nearly bald in some places and tufted with hair in others. It was staring at him with a bizarre simpering look on its filth-streaked face. It had a rusty wrench in one bony hand.

"Can you read?" it asked in a squeaky voice.

"Can I what?" Watkins said, surprised.

The ragged man tipped his head to one side, but that sickly-sweet fake smile didn't waver. "Can you read?"

Watkins took a deep breath and yelled at the top of his voice, "*Here! Over here!*" and the ragged man lashed out with the wrench and struck him on the side of the head.

When Watkins could see properly again, there was a ringing noise in his head that wouldn't stop no matter how much he tried to shake it away.

"You stupid cunt," said the ragged man in a quite different voice, lower and growly, although his horrible expression didn't change. "You've got yourself killed for nothing and it fucking serves you right."

The ragged man glanced over his shoulder and looked into a corner of the shed. "I told you to shut up while I'm working," he said in his squeaky voice.

"You wouldn't know work if it came up and bit your balls off, you pathetic twat," he said in the growly voice.

Watkins tried to focus on the corner, saw something sitting on the cabinet next to the candle. It was hard to make out, but was that somebody's *head...?* No. That was ridiculous. Wasn't it? He looked at the ragged man and more or less completely abandoned any hope of getting out of this alive.

"Can you read?" the ragged man asked again.

"Yes," Watkins said. "I can read."

The ragged man's smile widened horribly. "I thought so," he said. "You're not like people round here. You're educated."

"Who the fuck are you?" Watkins asked.

The ragged man didn't answer. He picked up a length of board and held it up. "What does this say?"

"What?"

The ragged man thrust the board closer. "What does it say?"

Watkins saw marks on the board, but he couldn't make them out properly. "I can't tell," he said. "It's too dark in here."

The ragged man tilted the board so it caught the light of the candle, and Watkins saw that the marks were letters, although they made no sense. "What does it say?"

"It says 'Fuck your mother'," Watkins said.

The ragged man lashed out with the wrench again, and this time when his head cleared Watkins found that the ringing in his ears was louder and one of his eyes wouldn't look in the right direction. He felt sick. The room seemed to be seesawing.

"What does it say?" said the ragged man.

"'Wayland'!" Watkins shouted. "It says 'Wayland'!"

"Wayland," said the ragged man. He laid the board aside and said it again, tasting the word. He looked at Watkins and showed him his true face.

"Fucking *hell*," Watkins said.

FOUR

"WELL," SAID DETECTIVE Sergeant Wallop, "this is a bit of a mess."

"It is," Mellow said, looking around the warehouse. "Well spotted."

If Wallop detected any sarcasm in her voice, he gave no sign. "Who do you think did it, boss?"

"That," she said carefully, "is our job to find out."

They were in the north of the city, on a derelict old industrial estate tucked away out of sight off the Banbury Road, a little complex of rusting metal-sided buildings on an expanse of cracked and weed-choked asphalt. Before The Sisters, it had been the home to half a dozen or so little businesses. On the way in, Mellow had seen faded signs for a light engineering firm, a frozen food importer, and a footwear supplier, but most of the units had been stripped of anything useful long ago, and the only sign there was anything out of the ordinary was the little group of officers from Sunnymead police station hanging around outside one small warehouse trying not to look useless.

"Who found it?" she asked.

Wallop consulted his notebook, tilted it to catch the weak daylight coming through the filthy skylights. "Scrap metal merchant," he said. "Name of Harris." He indicated the rows of metal shelving that ran the length of the warehouse, from the floor almost to the corrugated roof. "Says he has a contract to reclaim stuff on the site. He's at the local nick waiting for us to talk to him."

Mellow nodded, wondering what the unit had been used for, when it was still being used. Not manufacturing, certainly; there was no sign of machinery, just the rows of shelves. Generations of scavengers had passed through and taken away whatever had been stored here. The place was cold and damp and smelled of wet concrete and rust and animals that had taken shelter here, and a faint scent of burned meat.

She stepped forward down the aisle between two rows of shelves until she reached the body, stopped a few feet away, looking at the floor. There were footprints everywhere in the dust and muck, the majority of them from police issue boots, overlapping and smudging each other until it was impossible to make out one from another. Oxford's finest, coming to sightsee.

The boot prints were heaviest around the body, of course, which was where she least wanted them. The body lay on its back in the middle of the aisle, an adult male of average height and build wearing jeans and a sweater. His hands were charred clusters of sticks, and it looked as if his face had been blowtorched off and smashed with a hammer, although it wasn't possible to tell in which order. The concrete around his head and hands looked scorched. A four-foot length of rusty rebar stuck straight up from his chest. Scuff marks around his feet suggested that at least some of this had been done while he was still alive. Trying to avoid the pool of blood which had seeped out from under the body, Mellow took another step forward, reached out, and touched the rebar with a fingertip. She pushed gently, then harder, but it didn't move. It had been driven entirely through his body and into the floor.

"It could," she said, "be a particularly complicated form of suicide."

Wallop stared at her. "Boss?"

Mellow shook her head. "Joke."

It took Wallop a moment to catch up, and when he did his face took on a faint look of disgust. "Yes, boss," he said.

Mellow sighed. A few feet away, a little puddle of sick marked where one of the local constables had regretted coming to look at the body. "I want the place sealed until Forensics get here," she said. Which was pointless, she knew, because the scene was already contaminated. "Get a couple of people from headquarters. I don't want the local plod on guard; they'll probably sell tickets to their mates."

"Boss." Wallop made a note.

Mellow retraced her steps until she was standing beside him again. She looked around. "I don't see any drag marks," she said. "Which suggests he was either walked in or carried in."

Wallop made another note.

"And I want you to go to the Chancellery archive and see what you can find out about this place."

Wallop glanced at her.

"It's off the beaten track in what used to be an affluent residential area," she told him. "You wouldn't know it was here unless you were a local. See if you can find out what this warehouse was used for, who owned it. That kind of thing."

He made another note and said, "Boss," grudgingly.

Mellow headed back for the door, Wallop trailing in her wake. "And stay here until Forensics arrive," she said. "I don't trust the locals to keep the scene secure."

This time Wallop didn't answer.

Outside, it was raining heavily again. Mellow pulled up the hood of her coat. "Close the door and stay here until you're relieved," she said. "Then come and meet me at the local nick." She nodded at the little group of local police. "One of these laughing boys should be able to give you directions." She walked off towards where her bike was secured to a fence, and Wallop glowered after her.

Wallop was young and he was keen, but that wasn't why Mellow didn't like him. She didn't like him because he was *new*. According to his Personnel file, he'd only joined the force a year ago, and after just eight months on the beat in Cumnor – not the most crime-ridden part of the city – he'd been promoted to the CID. Mellow wasn't an excessively suspicious person, as police officers went, but it had taken her the best part of ten years to get into plain clothes and she felt more comfortable if Wallop was doing something harmless. And you never knew, he might turn up something useful.

As she cycled over to Sunnymead nick, she took a good look at the area. It had, as she'd pointed out to Wallop, once been quite a well-to-do part of the city, big, detached houses and little blocks of flats and nice curving streets, but it was now dilapidated and overgrown and more or less abandoned, although she spotted a few houses with wind generator masts in their gardens, which indicated some people at least were still living here. The industrial estate was down several little streets off the main road, not immediately obvious to anyone who didn't know the area. On the other hand, it was a nice private place to torture and murder someone. You could scream for hours, and nobody would hear you.

The police station was in a former hotel on the Banbury Road, three neat and clean one-storey buildings set among gardens which had been dug up to grow vegetables. Fifteen years before, during a brief period of rioting, it had been firebombed by a mob, but there were no marks of violence now. There was a big sign outside; Mellow chained her bicycle to it and went in and showed her warrant card to the young constable manning the front desk. A minute or so later, at the summons of another constable, a uniformed inspector emerged.

"Detective Inspector Mellow," Mellow introduced herself, putting her hand out. "I don't think we've met before."

The inspector, a tall, dour-looking woman in early middle-age, didn't shake her hand. "Inspector Kelly," she said. "I assume you've come to speak with the witness?"

"That was the plan, yes."

Kelly sniffed. "He could have been taken to headquarters," she said. "He's been taking up one of my interview rooms all morning."

"I thought it best if he was got out of the way as soon as possible, ma'am." In police etiquette, Kelly outranked her because she was in uniform. "It limits the chances of contaminating his evidence."

Kelly sniffed again.

"And speaking of contaminating evidence, ma'am," Mellow added, "you might want to have a word with your officers about protocol when attending a crime scene."

Kelly favoured her with a cold look. "Are you accusing my officers of destroying evidence, inspector?"

Mellow found herself regretting opening her mouth. "Not deliberately, ma'am, but the scene looks like a herd of sheep went through in hobnail boots."

"I think you'll find that wasn't any of my men," Kelly said crisply.

"Yes, ma'am," Mellow said.

"More likely to be *your* colleagues," Kelly went on.

"Yes, ma'am."

Kelly tipped her head back slightly and looked down her long, straight nose at Mellow. "You might consider that, the next time someone from headquarters comes out here wanting our cooperation."

The last time Mellow had looked, they were all working for the same organisation, but she nodded. "Absolutely, ma'am."

"Are you taking the piss, inspector?"

Mellow was rescued from having to answer this by a beeping from her pocket. "Excuse me, ma'am," she said. She backed off a couple of steps, took out her radio, held it to her ear, and pressed the talk button. "Yes?"

"Mellow?" The voice of her immediate superior, Superintendent Todd. "Where are you?"

"Sunnymead police station, sir," she said. "Just introducing myself to the station inspector."

"Ah," Todd said. "You picked up that job, did you? How does it look?"

"Pretty bad, sir." Mellow glanced at Kelly and gave her a brief smile. Let her wonder what she was talking about.

"Hm. Look, why isn't Fleet with you? I just looked into the squadroom and he's sitting there with a pile of paperwork."

"He's a bit behind with his reports, sir," she told him.

"We can't have our officers just sitting around writing reports, Mellow. We're undermanned as it is."

"There's a good reason, sir. I didn't see I had any choice."

There was a brief silence, at the other end of the radio link. "Is this something I'd rather not know about?" Todd asked.

"I don't know, sir. The chances are probably good, though."

Another silence. "Right. I'll see your report about this murder? It *is* a murder?"

Mellow gave Kelly another brief, chilly smile. "It looks that way, sir. I'll have my report with you tomorrow morning at the latest."

"Good." The link went dead.

She put the radio back into her pocket and turned to Kelly, who was looking less certain of herself now. "If I could see the witness now, ma'am?" she asked gravely.

THE WITNESS WAS a broad-shouldered man in his early sixties with thinning curly ginger hair and freckles across the bridge of his nose. He was wearing work clothes and looking anxious.

"Mr Harris?" Mellow asked as she stepped into the interview room. It was always best to check; there was a story of some long-ago officer who had spent an hour interviewing a particularly stubborn suspect before it dawned on him that the suspect was stubborn because he was in the wrong room and talking to the wrong person.

"Am I in trouble?" Harris asked.

"I don't know," Mellow said brightly. "Are you?"

"I didn't do anything."

"Oh, come on, Mr Harris," she said. "Everyone's done *something*." The colour drained from Harris's face. "I'm sorry," she told him. "That was a joke."

Harris scowled at her. "Pretty fucking stupid joke, if you ask me," he muttered.

"Quite." The room was tiny, with just room enough for a table and three chairs. Mellow sat down and looked at him across the table. "Haven't they given you anything? Not even a cup of tea?"

Harris shook his head.

She got up and went to the door and looked out into the corridor beyond. "You," she said, showing her warrant card to a constable who happened to be passing. "Two teas in here, please."

The constable looked at her, looked at the card, looked at her again. "I'm busy," he said.

"Yes," Mellow told him. "You're busy making two teas and bringing them in here. Otherwise, you'll be busy on patrol in Cowley."

"You can't do that," the constable said, but he stood up a little straighter.

"You have not the faintest idea what I can do," Mellow told him seriously. "Two teas. In here. Quick as you like."

The constable headed off down the corridor and Mellow closed the door behind her and went back to the table, where

Harris was looking bemused. "Well," she said, sitting down again and rummaging in her knapsack, "you and I seem to be having a bit of a *day*, Mr Harris."

"I'll say."

Mellow took a notebook and pen from the knapsack. The third chair in the room was for someone to sit and make notes of interviews, but Kelly hadn't offered anyone and Mellow didn't think she could trust anybody from this police station to make accurate records. She opened the notebook to a fresh page, wrote the date and time at the top of the page. "I'm Detective Inspector Mellow, Thames Valley CID," she told him. "Could we start with your full name, please?"

"Alfred Brian Harris."

Mellow wrote it down. "Do you prefer 'Fred', or 'Alf'?"

"Al," said Harris.

"Okay. What's your address, Al?" He told her an address a couple of miles from there. "And what do you do for a living?"

"I'm in reclamation," he said. "Scrap metal, mostly. It's just a small business."

"I bet you keep busy, though. Do you have a licence for that?"

Harris reached into an inside pocket of his jacket and took out a wallet, from which he removed a folded sheet of paper. He handed it across the table. Unfolding it, she saw a Department of Reconstruction letterhead. Alfred Harris, address such and such, licenced to carry out such works as directed. Issued three years ago and stamped at the bottom with the Chancellery stamp.

"We'll keep this for the moment," she told him, folding the paper and tucking it at the back of the notebook. "I'll make sure you get it back. Could you tell me what you were doing at the industrial site off Morton Street this morning?"

Harris looked at the notebook as if already regretting handing over his licence. "I've been subcontracted to clear the site of scrap."

"Subcontracted by whom?"

"The Foxes."

Mellow had to fight hard not to raise an eyebrow. "Effie Fox?"

He nodded. "They've got all the major contracts more or less sewn up, but sometimes they'll farm work out, if they're busy. They get the fee, and they pay me a flat rate, so much per hundredweight of scrap plus manpower." He added, "I've never dealt with her, only her son. Doug. Not the other one."

"Do you do much work for them?"

He shrugged. "Now and then. Mostly we strip old wiring out of houses that are too far gone to be refurbished. For the copper. Some of the really old houses have copper piping, too, and we take that as well. Deliver it to the Reclamation Department yard on the old Western Bypass. After that it's taken away to be melted down. Occasionally Doug comes round and asks if we need some extra work."

"And do you?"

"We can always use the work."

Mellow stopped taking notes and looked at him. "What are they like to work for, out of interest? The Foxes?"

"They've always been straight with me," he said with a shrug. "They pay fairly, and they pay on time. I don't know about any other stuff they do."

"Hm." Everybody knew about the other stuff the Foxes did. The difficult thing was proving it. She said, "When did you get the contract?"

"Yesterday. Doug came round in the morning, asked if we fancied taking the job on." He shrugged again. "Work's been a bit slow lately."

"And Doug said they had a contract from the Department to clear the site?"

Harris nodded.

"Had you ever seen the site before?"

He shook his head. "I didn't even know it was there."

She looked across the table at him. "You took the job on without having seen it?"

"They weren't asking us to do anything we weren't capable of," he pointed out. "And like I said, work's been a bit slow. We could use the money."

Mellow nodded and made a note. "So, you went out there this morning?"

"Yes. I wanted to have a look at the place, get a better idea of how long it was going to take us."

"And you went alone."

"Like I said, I was just going to look."

"What time did you get there?"

Harris thought. "I didn't check. I left home after eight, so I suppose it was around nine."

Mellow wrote it down. "Did you see anyone else about?"

Harris shook his head. "Not a soul."

"Anything out of the ordinary?"

"Nothing that leapt out, no." Harris thought again. "It's just a little industrial estate. Mixed use, half a dozen units. Didn't look like anyone had been there since The Sisters came down."

"Did you look in any of the other units?"

Harris shook his head again. "I went to that one first. The door was open."

Mellow looked up from her notes. "And you don't think that's unusual?"

Harris scratched his head. "Well, no, not really. You'll be lucky to find anywhere in Oxford that hasn't been looted at some point in the past hundred years. Mostly they'll have taken anything they thought was useful and missed the really valuable stuff. They didn't usually lock up behind them. There's about a quarter of a mile of metal shelving in that unit; that's a lot of scrap that can be reclaimed and made into other things."

The reclamation and refurbishment of the city had been going on for years, but it had accelerated lately, for reasons nobody had seen fit to explain to Mellow. She said, "Were the doors of the other units open?"

"I don't know," he said. "I didn't notice. I saw that door open when I arrived and decided I'd look in there first."

"And what happened then?"

Harris shook his head. "That poor bastard. Did you see what they–" He stopped. "Of course you did. Sorry."

"No, I'm sorry, Al," Mellow said gently. "But I have to know what you saw."

He nodded. "I saw him straight away, lying on the floor with that thing sticking out of him. I went over and had a look at him, but it was obvious he was dead. I mean, the state of him…" He took a long breath. "So I scarpered, got on my bike and came over here to report it."

"And you came straight here? Didn't stop off to talk to anybody on the way?"

"Straight here. Didn't see anybody."

"Did you notice anything unusual in the warehouse?"

He gave a mirthless chuckle. "You mean apart from the chap with his face burned off? No, but I wasn't really paying any attention to anything else by then."

"And what happened when you got here?"

"I told the lad on the front desk what I'd found and a couple of minutes later some coppers got me to take them back to the site and show them where the body was. Then one of them brought me back here and I've been waiting for you ever since."

"Yes, I'm sorry about that." Mellow paged back through her notes. "Did nobody come and talk to you? Get any details?"

"No."

"Hm." Mellow closed the notebook and put her hand on it. "Right. I'll get these notes typed up and if you could come into headquarters tomorrow you can read and sign them. Apart from that, I think we're done here."

Harris raised his eyebrows. "That's it?"

"We might need to get in touch, just to clear up some points, and if this ever gets to court, we'll expect you to give evidence, but yes, Al, that's it. Thank you."

While she put her notebook and pen away, Harris got up from his chair. "What are the chances of it getting to court?"

"Now that I can't tell you," she said. "We will do our best."

He nodded. "We never did get that tea, did we?"

"No." Mellow looked at the door. "No, we didn't."

BACK AT MORTON Street, the site was deserted. Sunnymead's constables had made themselves scarce, and Wallop was nowhere to be seen. Mellow propped her bike against the side of one of the other units and went over to look through the open door. Inside, two figures in blue overalls were standing over the body.

"I heard you were here," said one of the figures.

"Afternoon, Reg," said Mellow. "Liz. Where did everyone go?"

"Fucked off when we got here," said Reg, still looking down at the body. He was a burly man with a bushy moustache. "That creepy little shit handed the scene over to us and said he was going back into town on an errand for you."

Wallop, making sure he'd made his point. Still, it was gratifying to discover she wasn't the only one with a low opinion of him. "So," she said, "what do we think?"

"We're not paid to think," Reg told her. "All we do is collect evidence; we leave the thinking to you. What do *you* think?"

"I think someone *really* didn't like this chap."

"He probably died very quickly," said Liz, a tall young woman with her dreadlocks tied back and tucked down inside the collar of her overalls. "The stake pierced his heart."

"And then they burned his hands and face off to conceal his identity?"

"Like I said, we don't do the thinking," Reg said.

Mellow looked around the warehouse, wondering again what had been stored there. "Is anyone else coming, or is it just you two?"

"The photographer's on her way," said Liz. "And a couple of the lads. We could maybe use an officer or two outside, to make sure we're not disturbed."

Mellow nodded. She'd have to get someone up here from headquarters; there was no way she was going to trust anyone from Sunnymead nick, and she had a feeling Wallop would have contrived to forget to send anyone. "The scene's contaminated."

Reg grunted. "We noticed. It looks like half the plod in Oxford have been trampling through here. Has anyone touched the body?"

"I don't know. I touched the stake." She held up her finger.

Reg heaved a huge sigh and looked away along the ranks of shelves.

"It's not on, Leonie," said Liz. "If *we* were this unprofessional, we'd never hear the end of it."

"I know," Mellow said. "Do your best. How long?"

Reg and Liz exchanged glances. "Another couple of hours and we can release the body to Professor Solomons," Liz said. "It'll be this time tomorrow before we finish with the scene."

"Or we can just throw up our hands and give up now," Reg added.

"No, don't do that." Mellow turned to leave. "I have to go and write up a preliminary report. I'll call for some willing hands to secure the area."

"Better late than never," Reg said without very much enthusiasm.

Mellow turned back and looked at the body. "Have you ever seen anything like this before?"

"I told you," Reg said. "We just collect evidence. We don't–"

"It's not our job to interpret," said Liz. She thought about it.

"I haven't seen anything quite like this, but do you remember the riots?"

Mellow had still been in training at the time, but every copper who had been in the city back then remembered the riots. "I wasn't involved in that operation," she said.

"I know," Liz said. "But there was something *performative* about some of those killings. They were meant to be warnings, demonstrations of power. This reminds me of that, sort of."

"You didn't hear that from us," Reg said sternly. "We're not supposed to influence your investigation."

"You're talking about Leviathan, aren't you?" said Mellow.

Reg sucked his teeth and turned away and walked off down the aisle between the shelves.

"Leviathan was a myth," Mellow went on. "A *joke*. There was never any evidence that a single person committed all those murders."

Liz held up her hands. "You asked. Leviathan doesn't have to have been real for someone to maybe copy his style."

"Jesus," said Mellow. "That's all we need."

"You see what happens?" Reg called from the back of the warehouse. "We've put ideas in your head, and you'll miss stuff now because you're too busy thinking about a bunch of old killings."

"Reg is a bit of a purist, where evidence is concerned," Liz said.

'Fanatic' was perhaps a better word. How was she supposed to do her job if she didn't ask people's opinions? "Purist isn't such a bad thing to be," she said.

"No, it's not," Reg told them, coming back from his little walk. "Now you go and write your report and let us do our job. We'll have some notes for you by the end of the day."

FIVE

WITH THE FIRST part of his plan complete – rather splendidly, he thought – the second part almost wound up getting Morty caught.

He stripped Watkins's body and buried it in several places over a wide area, then he collected his weapons and his souvenirs, and he abandoned his hide and moved several miles south to a burned-out farm on the far edge of the Parish. He'd set fire to the house on the day he set out to kill his wife and Big Keith, and it was completely ruined. Which made it one of the few things he'd ever done on the farm which had actually worked.

He poked around on the ground floor, kicking at charred furniture and broken crockery, and he found he couldn't clearly picture what the house had been like before. It had never been much of a farm – it was so worthless that nobody had even bothered building a wall around it. The soil here was poor, for reasons nobody knew, and the few animals they'd owned had refused to thrive. He'd worked his heart out to make a success of it for Karen, and it had taken years for him to realise that she had been hoping it would kill him.

Outside, he stood almost ankle-deep in mud in the yard. The woods and undergrowth over to one side of the farm were already starting to encroach on the property; ten years or so from now it would all be gone. There were a couple of fields behind the house – big vegetable gardens, really – but what produce he'd managed to grow had been stunted and tasteless, and they were now knee-deep in weeds and brambles. He'd always suspected that Nature had just been waiting for his back to be turned before it reclaimed the farm, and here it was.

As he stood there, a sheep came out of the woods and stopped a few yards away. It was thin and its overgrown fleece was filthy and matted. He wondered if it was one of his sheep, one of the sheep he'd taken to sell at the market in Goring and then had to bring back again because nobody was mad or desperate enough to buy it. He took Watkins's pistol from his pocket, cocked it, and levelled it at the sheep's forehead, but it just stood there looking at him, chewing slowly, and finally he lowered the gun and made it safe. The sheep had never done him any harm. Unlike people, there was no malice in a sheep. It gave him one last look, then turned and wandered unhurriedly back into the woods.

Looking about him, he thought it would be a reasonable place to hide out for a few days. Hardly anybody had come here, even when it had been a working farm. He doubted most people even knew it existed; it was a couple of miles west of the wagon road across the Downs towards Newbury. The nearest farm was almost a mile away, and he'd burned that one, too. Unless somebody deliberately decided to check on how the old Roberts's farm – just thinking about the name caused a pang – was doing, he wasn't going to be disturbed.

Still, there was no sense in tempting fate. He set up camp in the woods not far from the farm, hiding his weapons where he could retrieve them quickly, and when he was satisfied it wouldn't be discovered by anyone, he set out into the Parish again.

The mood of the invaders had obviously darkened since Watkins disappeared. Now they were all patrolling in threes and making no effort to conceal the fact that they were here as conquerors. He went past the place where he had captured Watkins and saw that the undergrowth had been cut back for a considerable distance into the woods, the ground churned up by a large number of booted feet. He didn't bother checking to see if his original hide had been found; either it had or it hadn't, and if it had they might be watching to see if someone returned to it.

The invaders' food kitchens were still operating, but the atmosphere inside was tense. Morty queued for stew and tea, sat alone in a corner eating, noting the armed guards by the entrances, the resentful looks of the locals. He felt rather powerful, sitting there right under their noses. If he'd taken Watkins's rifle with him and been able to smuggle it into one of the big canteen tents, he could have killed everybody there and been gone before the invaders could react. Of course, he wouldn't have lasted long afterward, but just knowing he *could* do it gave him strength.

Leaving one of the canteens one day, he saw a group of locals standing nearby and he went over to them. He carefully composed the Morty Face so as not to alarm them, but they still took a couple of steps back as he drew closer.

"Morning," he said, in what he believed was a cheerful tone of voice. "How's it going?"

The men just looked at him as if they couldn't quite understand what they were seeing, and even if they did understand it, they didn't believe it was happening.

Morty jerked a thumb towards the tent. "I'll say one thing for them," he told the little group, "they make a good stew in there."

He saw a couple of the men snigger. Others just muttered and shrugged and drifted away. It was the same reaction Morty had been getting his whole time in the Parish, people either laughing at him or ignoring him altogether. *Kill you all*, he thought, before remembering that he couldn't do that now without putting himself in danger. Still, he made note of the faces, just in case an opportunity presented itself later.

He said, "Anybody heard about Wayland?"

That got their attention. "What the fuck's he done now?" asked one.

"I don't know," said Morty. "Just wondered if you'd heard anything."

The remaining men shuffled back another half step or so. "Are you sick or something?" asked the first one.

"Sick in the fucking head," said another.

"What do you want to know for?" asked a third.

Morty belatedly realised the situation was sliding out of his control. He ratcheted up the Morty Face, and the men took another step back. "I didn't mean anything by it," he said, holding out his hands. "Just asking."

"Fuck off, you weird cunt," said the first man. "Go on, fuck off."

Morty glanced to one side and saw one of the guards outside the tent starting to pay attention to them. He took a few steps back, holding up his hands and bobbing his head in a little bow. "Of course," he said. "No offence meant."

"Get out of here, you sick bastard," said another of the group. "And don't come back."

Morty was already turning away, face burning with embarrassment and heart pounding. Every step he took away from the men he expected to hear booted feet running after him, but they never came. He reached the edge of the clearing where the tent had been pitched and looked back, and saw the guard and the men in conversation. One of the men pointed in his direction, and the guard looked and hefted his rifle, but by then Morty had slipped away into the trees.

* * *

HE MOVED CAMP four times in the next three days. The invaders were quick on their feet, increasing their patrols again for a few days, and he had a couple of close calls, but in the end there were too few of them and he knew the secret places of the Parish too well.

There was no sense in pushing his luck, though. Morty's relationship with reality was a little thin in places, and it had seemed perfectly reasonable to him that all he had to do was ask the locals if they had any news of Wayland and use that to locate him. That obviously wasn't going to work if the locals didn't want to talk about Wayland, so he needed to think of something else.

While he did that, there was something else he could be getting on with. On one of his excursions into the Parish he noticed the man who had pointed him out to the invaders. Trailing the man back to his farm was fairly straightforward, and Morty was gratified to note that the front gate had been broken down during the recent war and only poorly repaired. He was even more gratified to see it was in a part of the Parish which the invaders hadn't yet swept through in their search for the widely distributed Watkins.

A couple of days later, Morty sneaked into the farm compound and buried Watkins's pistol in a spot where it would easily be found but still look as if someone had made an effort to hide it. Then he sneaked out of the compound again and went back to his latest camp to wait.

He didn't have to wait long. A few days after he buried the gun he was watching from cover as the invaders hanged the man and three other locals from the gallows they'd set up in one of the bigger clearings in the centre of the Parish. At the beginning, they'd forced as many locals as they could round up to witness the executions, but that had only caused more resentment, so today it was just a few soldiers standing in the rain to watch, and even they didn't seem particularly enthusiastic. Morty was rather thrilled, though, to discover that if he did things right, he could kill people by remote control. It opened up huge areas of possibility.

He was thinking about this and watching the bodies swing slowly in the gusty wind when one of the soldiers turned away from the gallows, and he got a brief look at his face. His hair and beard were shorter, and he was wearing clean clothes and there was a sour expression on his face, but Morty immediately recognised Wayland.

For a few moments, Morty's mind struggled with this image. Why was Wayland with the soldiers? Had he always been with them? Working undercover to pave the way for the invasion?

And then the picture sorted itself out in Morty's head. Of course Wayland was undercover. He was hiding in plain sight among the invaders, and that was incredibly brave. They could be looking everywhere for him and there he'd be, right under their noses. It was something Morty would never have dared to try, even if he'd thought there was the slightest chance of getting away with it. His heart swelled with renewed admiration for Wayland.

And actually, now he thought about it, his plan had worked perfectly, just not in quite the way he had expected. If he hadn't approached that group of men last week, he wouldn't have wound up framing one of them for the disappearance of Watkins, and he wouldn't have been here today at the hanging to spot Wayland. It was beautiful.

Anyway, now he'd located Wayland the question arose of when to approach him for advice about what to do next. Clearly, he couldn't just walk up to him in public because that would blow his cover. And he couldn't do it secretly because careful observation revealed that Wayland was living in a tent in the largest of the compounds the invaders had occupied, and he was surrounded by soldiers. There was nothing for it but to keep an eye on him and take advantage of any opportunity that presented itself.

Unfortunately, the opportunity did not present itself. Wayland spent most of his time in the compound, and when he did go out he was always accompanied by one of the soldiers. That briefly raised the possibility in Morty's mind that he had actually been taken captive by the invaders and was under constant guard and therefore in need of rescue. That in turn sparked off an examination of possible scenarios in which he accomplished this, but they all ended with him being dead.

And they weren't necessary, anyway. Further observation convinced him that Wayland was not a captive. Indeed, he seemed to have convinced the invaders to give him one of their soldiers as a bodyguard, which to Morty's mind was an act of genius.

It didn't, though, solve Morty's original problem, which was how to contact Wayland. Without him quite noticing, it had grown from a possible course of action to an obsession, and as the days went on, he became increasingly despondent about ever managing it. He caught himself, late at night, almost surrendering to the urge to simply storm the invaders' camp, whatever the consequences.

In the end, though, the problem solved itself. He was keeping watch on the invaders' camp one morning when he saw Wayland and his escort emerge from the front gate. Morty's heart lifted when he saw that Wayland was kitted out for travel. He was wearing a long, hooded coat and carrying a big, heavy-looking rucksack, and he had a shotgun and a long thin bag slung over his shoulder.

With a sense that something seismic was happening, Morty rushed back to his most recent hiding place. He dressed hurriedly in Watkins's uniform and body armour, put a ragged coat on over it, dithered a few moments over which of his souvenirs to take with him, then grabbed a sack and slung it over his shoulder.

"What the fuck are you doing?" the head demanded from inside the sack.

"Going on an adventure," Morty said, trying to decide which of his guns to take. He wrapped Watkins's rifle in rags and hoped nobody would stop him.

"Fuck that," said the head. "Put me down."

"Oh no," Morty said. "You don't get away that easily."

With the head periodically complaining, he made his way back through the woods and undergrowth in the direction he'd last seen Wayland and his bodyguard taking. He emerged from the trees onto a road that led away north and south just in time to see Wayland, alone now, trudging away into the distance. And then Morty paused, uncertain.

Wayland was obviously sending him a message in the only way he could. They couldn't stay in the Parish and continue their work, so they had to move on, find another place in which to hunt. But did Wayland mean they should go together, or separately? Was the message *Follow me* or *Go your own way*? Morty didn't cope well with ambiguity.

"You're completely fucking useless," said the head while Morty stood in the middle of the road trying to decide what to do next. "You're going to get us both killed."

"Shut up," Morty said, looking one way and then the other along the road.

"I mean, you're going to get *yourself* killed," the head went on. "I'm already dead, on account of you cutting off my fucking head."

"I said, shut up," Morty muttered. Wayland had already disappeared over a rise. What to do?

"Make your mind up, make your mind up," the head urged.

Morty made a snap decision and turned in the direction Wayland had taken. He could always change his mind later if it turned out he was wrong, he thought.

SIX

ADAM HAD BARELY descended from the Hills and started to slog his way north when a series of storms began to howl along the Vale of the White Horse, hiding the landscape behind driving curtains of rain and sleet and hail. It was just bad weather – the genuine misery of the autumn monsoon season was still some weeks away – but he still pondered turning back for the Parish and waiting it out.

In the end, he elected to carry on – he had started, after all – but he found himself regretting every step he took. The going would have been difficult enough without the storms; the terrain was marshy and overgrown and flooded in many places, roads crumbled and overwhelmed by vegetation or washed away altogether by the weather decades ago. There only seemed to be one usable road across the Vale, leading northeast from Wantage. He'd seen people in Wantage, clearing the road little by little late at night, and nobody in the Parish had even been aware of it, let alone able to suggest who was doing it. Chrissie was of the opinion that it had been Father John's people, preparing the way for an advance into the Chilterns, and from there... where? Across the Downs to Newbury and from there to Winchester? Spread out along the hills and take Goring and the Thames crossing? Not his problem, for the moment, but he didn't want to bump into anybody until he was closer to Oxford, so he gave the road a wide berth and trudged on across the sodden landscape some miles to the west.

Towards the end of his first day, not much more than four miles from the Hills, he came across a little farm sitting on a low rise above the marshland. It was surrounded by a low stockade of wooden stakes, and its front gate was wide open. He was half minded to ignore it and carry on his way, but something about the farm bothered him, and instead of passing by he found himself a place to hide in a patch of bushes on a knoll half a mile or so away and spent some time watching the compound through his binoculars. Then he spent some time considering what to do next.

Finally, he stashed his rucksack in the bushes, left cover, and made his way carefully across the intervening ground until he reached the wooden fence. It barely came up to the top of his head, just about adequate for keeping animals out but not enough to stop a reasonably determined gang of bandits, and he wondered about that. The little farms of the Chilterns were surrounded by high brick walls or rings of old shipping containers, but whatever hazards they had been built to resist didn't seem to apply down here. Maybe it was such an awful place that no one in their right mind could be bothered to attack the scattered farmsteads in the Vale. It was certainly hard to understand how anyone in their right mind would choose to live here.

He stood for a while by the fence, listening, but he couldn't hear any activity on the other side, so he walked around to the open gate and looked in. The fence enclosed a single two-storey house and a few outhouses and animal pens. There was not a single sign of life. He cautiously stepped into the compound, paused in the gateway looking about him. All the animal pens were empty, and the door of one of the outhouses was open and moving back and forth in the wind. The front door of the house was open, too. The ground inside the compound looked churned up, as if a lot of people had been walking around at some point in the past, but there was so much water puddling in the yard, and so much mud, that it was hard to be sure. He could see nothing that presented as a recognisable footprint or a cart track, anyway.

He walked slowly around the house, checking the outbuildings and finding them all completely empty. Around the back were some more empty pens, and a deserted henhouse. He peered through the ground floor windows of the house, but it was so dark inside that he couldn't make out any details. Coming back round to the front, he stood against the wall to one side of the door and pushed it slowly open with the barrel of his shotgun. When nothing happened, he moved quickly inside and crouched in a corner where he could cover all the entrances and exits.

He might as well not have bothered. The house was empty. Not just empty; it had been stripped. He moved slowly from room to room, and everything was gone. All the furniture and fittings, all the clothes and bedding, all the personal possessions. There was not a single pot, pan or fork left in the kitchen. There were even pale patches on the walls where paintings or mirrors had once hung. Whoever had once lived here, they were simply gone, and all their possessions with them.

The house might have been deserted, but it was not derelict. The windows were still intact, and damp was only just beginning to take hold. Whatever had happened here, it had happened fairly recently. He stood at one of the bedroom windows and looked out into the yard in the failing light. This would have been a good place to lay up for the night, but the house gave him a bad feeling. There were no signs of violence, or even a struggle, but he left the farm, retrieved his rucksack, and tried to put as much distance between himself and the house before it was too dark to see. He wound up pitching his tent among a stand of stunted trees on a little patch of dry ground.

THE FOLLOWING DAY was more of the same. He came upon three houses, all within half a mile of each other, which were in a good state of repair and showed signs of recent occupation – the outside woodwork of one had been repainted in the not-so-distant past – but which were deserted and stripped of everything they might once have contained. Again, there were no signs of a disturbance. It was as if the occupants had suddenly taken it into their heads to pack up and leave, taking every item of personal possessions with them. Adam thought that if he had somehow wound up living in this awful place, he would be strongly tempted to do the same, but something felt wrong about the whole situation. Had everyone in the area apparently decided to up sticks at the same time? Why take literally *everything*? It was hard enough for him to make his way across country with a rucksack and a couple of guns; he couldn't imagine being crazy enough to take a bed with him. And where had they gone?

They had given him a month or so in the Parish to recover and to receive briefings about his mission. A lot of it was guesswork and rumour, which was par for the course – if the Bureau had all the intelligence it wanted, they wouldn't have sent him north in the first place – but he knew there had been sightings of what appeared to be flatboats moving along the flooded lanes and roads down here in the Vale, full of people and cargo. So what was it? An exodus? An abduction? Either would imply a level of resources and organisation he simply hadn't seen in this part of the country.

He started to walk in cover as much as possible, which wasn't difficult because the parts of the Vale that weren't flooded or impassibly marshy were wildly overgrown, but it slowed him down. And the weather kept getting worse. The weather was an important consideration for the Navy, and Guz had a well-staffed and experienced meteorological bureau. They were of the general opinion that the weather, thrown into chaos by the impact of hundreds of comet fragments, was finally settling down and that the Long Autumn was coming to an end. Adam found he was of a mind, when his present assignment was over, to bring a couple of those meteorologists back here around this time of the year and see if they still felt the same way.

In the end, it became impossible. The rain and sleet were so heavy that he could barely see a hundred yards ahead of him, and he found himself making less and less progress every day. He found a ruined house on the edge of a little village and camped out there until the weather eased off. If it was ruined, it was at least honestly ruined, abandoned decades ago, and it didn't give him a creeping sense of doom the way the more recently vacated houses did. There was enough of the roof left to keep the worst of the rain off, and he pitched his tent in the corner of what had once been a bedroom, set up a stove, and heated a pack of field rations.

The stoves came in flat packs of five, sheets of compressed cardboard that you folded into a stove shape, pulled a tab, and shook to mix the chemicals. They stayed hot for about forty minutes, which was long enough to cook a meal and make a brew, and warm for another hour or so after that, so you could pop them in your sleeping bag to keep you cosy. He only had one pack, though; they were meant for occasions when it was impossible to make a fire.

The food was stew. It was always stew.

When he'd finished eating, he walked to the other side of the room with his mess tin and held it out of the window, where it filled almost instantly with rainwater. He swilled it out and dumped the water into the overgrown garden below, then he stood looking out into the pounding rain.

A year ago, as near as he could judge, he had been in Wales, where he had come across a little community of farmers, no more than a hundred strong, desperately clinging on to survival on a valley hillside. None of them had ever travelled more than a couple of miles from home, and until he walked up to their farmstead, they had believed that they were the last surviving people on Earth.

He'd argued that Guz should evacuate them, take them in and put them to work, but Guz wanted them left in place, for much the same reason that they wanted the people of the Parish to remain where they were. They wanted to establish a foothold in the Welsh valleys. It had always been plain to Guz that the end of the Long Autumn, if it ever came, would be a dangerous time. People would travel further afield, communities would make contact and form alliances, the question of who was actually running things would arise for the first time in almost a century. So it had been decided that Order would have to be imposed, and to do that Guz needed outposts everywhere.

This was by no means straightforward. Guz wasn't the only large population centre in the South; in Kent a man named Frank Pendennis was ruling what was basically a private fiefdom of several thousand people. Adam had been sent to take a look at that and had barely escaped with his life. He'd almost immediately been sent to the Chilterns, where he had ridden into the middle of the Parish's stupid little war, and at some point he had simply snapped.

"What you have to watch out for, sir," a long-ago trainer had told him, *"is the Monkey. Sooner or later, you're going to find yourself doing something you don't like, there's no avoiding it. That's the Monkey, and it'll do your head in if you let it. You have to learn to put it in a box and close the lid and bury the box somewhere and get on with the job."*

Which was all very well when you were sitting in a nice, warm, dry classroom. It was something else when you were hiding in a derelict house somewhere in the arse end of nowhere in the middle of a storm and you'd either killed or caused the deaths of dozens of people. After the Marines had ridden in and ended the war, he had, briefly, tried to put it in a box and he'd written *Wayland* on the lid, but somehow the lid kept coming off.

As well as a pouch of stew, the ration pack contained a packet of mints, a little box of waterproof matches, strips of dried meat, packets of dried apple, water purification tablets, a couple of teabags, and sachets of sugar, salt and pepper. Although he had rarely ever used them, there was also, lurking somewhere at the bottom of the pack, always a packet of fishhooks and fishing line, and a little sewing kit. He boiled a tin mug of water on the stove, dropped in a teabag, and while it was brewing, he took his radio from the rucksack, wound the little handle on the side a few times, then pressed the transmit button.

"Hello," he said.

"You're ahead of schedule," Chrissie said almost immediately. "You're not due to check in for another two days."

"I might as well do it now," he said. "I'm not going anywhere for a little while."

"Is it bad where you are, too?"

"It's pretty bad, yes," he said.

"Fucking place," she grumbled. "Who in their right mind would want to live here?"

"Don't blame me; I didn't tell you to come."

"Hm. Betty sends her regards, by the way."

So she was at Blandings, Betty Coghlan's fortified stately home and weapons shop near Wallingford. The two of them had discovered they were kindred spirits, Betty having engineered Guz's intervention in the Chilterns in order to protect them from whatever was happening further north.

He said, "Tell her we were right. It looks like someone's been moving people out, I don't know why yet."

There was a silence at the other end, then Chrissie said, "Okay.

Any sign of the opposition?"

"I don't think there's anyone down here at all."

Another silence. "Right. Well, be careful all the same. And stick to your schedule."

"Will do."

"Are you okay? You sound weird."

"It's the weather," he told her. "It messes with reception."

THE WEATHER HAD eased off the next morning, and he was able to make reasonably good progress north. He reached the Thames late in the day, but there was no way across. The river had broken its banks decades ago and, in some places, it was a quarter of a mile wide. All the old bridges were long gone. Still, he walked west a couple of miles just to make sure, and as the light was beginning to fail, he came upon a ferry.

He found some cover and observed it as best he could in the rainy dusk. It was just a big flatboat, hauled back and forth across the river by steam engines on both banks, like the ferry at Goring. On this side there were a couple of one-storey wooden buildings, little more than shacks, and through his binoculars Adam could see a number of armed figures patrolling outside. An old road, leading south towards Faringdon, had been painstakingly banked up until its surface was above the marshland, but everything felt wrong. If this was the only crossing for several miles, it should have been as busy as the one at Goring, even this late in the day, but the ferry was currently moored on the far bank, and there was no smoke coming from the chimneys of the enginehouses, which suggested the winches weren't fired up. The only people he could see were the guards. He wasn't going to cross the river here; this was a strictly private ferry. He turned east again.

Over the next couple of days, as he followed the river eastward at a careful distance, he came across three more ferries, all of them guarded and all of them inactive. Once, he spotted a flatboat being poled southward along a sunken flooded lane by a dozen or so people. No one saw him, though. The landscape was huge and choked with overgrowth and it was easy for one man to lose himself in it completely. And apart from that one boat all the patrols seemed to be clustered around the ferry stations. He couldn't decide whether that spoke of confidence or sloppiness. Certainly, these people, whoever they were, controlled this part of the river, and by extension the country on either side.

As he came closer and closer to Oxford, he began to see more signs of habitation. Around Cumnor the old A420 started to climb out of the sodden landscape, and from a distance he could see smoke coming from the chimneys of some of the houses, and people moving around. It was hard to tell at this distance, even through the binoculars, but few, if any, of them seemed to have guns. He sat watching them for some time, trying to decide whether to commit now or spend more time getting a sense of the territory. There was always a point where you had to take that step forward, the one you couldn't take back.

In the end, he chose caution and withdrew south a couple of miles, off the higher ground and into the floodlands where there was less chance of someone happening by. He found a row of abandoned houses on the edge of a little village and forced his way into one of the middle ones. The downstairs was a waterlogged wreck, but upstairs was still intact. He set up his tent on the landing, used the fishing line from one of his ration packs to set up tripwires on the stairs, and made himself some stew before turning in for the night.

Some time later, he started awake with the sudden conviction that someone was in the house with him. He pumped a round into the shotgun, left the tent, and crouched in one of the bedrooms for the rest of the night, but he didn't hear anything, and the next morning his tripwires were undisturbed, but there was a terrible smell lingering in the air, as if a large carnivore had passed through during the night.

SEVEN

THE COLLEGES HAD played a very large part in the survival of Oxford as a community after the fall of The Sisters, and they had spent the intervening years not letting anyone forget it. Many staff and students had fled, with a large percentage of the population, in the very early days of the catastrophe, but many had stayed behind. For some of them – those from overseas or from parts of the country that were now impossible to reach – there was no choice; there was nowhere else for them to go. Others had stayed because they had decided that preserving their research was more important, which Mellow sometimes had a hard time understanding. Some had stayed because they thought it was entirely possible that they were the only people left alive in the country – communications were basically impossible back then – and they believed it was important to preserve what they could of human knowledge. Whatever their reasons, the city had wound up with a hard core of people with useful knowledge – engineers, chemists, doctors, biologists, botanists – as well as people the usefulness of whose knowledge might one day become apparent, such as mediaevalists and philosophers.

They opened their doors to the remaining people of Oxford. They fed them and, where necessary, housed them in former student accommodation. They set up schools for the children – everyone in the city could read and write and do at least basic maths – and clinics. Along with the remains of the local police and some units of the Army which had turned up from who knew where, they began to organise. They basically kept a battered and fearful kind of civilisation going, when things were at their worst. Under their patronage, Oxford had encysted itself for its own survival. For decades, few people travelled more than a few miles from the city.

When it became apparent that there was no civilian authority – no authority of any kind, really – anywhere in the country, the Colleges had set up an ad-hoc civil administration intended to run Oxford until the country could get back on its feet. It was still, technically, a temporary arrangement, but everyone had long since stopped kidding themselves that anybody was coming to help them, and Chancellery had evolved into a little government years ago.

All of this was ancient history as far as Mellow was concerned. It was just the way everything had always been. Stories of her great-grandfather's day – of the time when the Thames Valley Force covered a huge operational area and had at its disposal motor cars and helicopters and all kinds of technological miracles – handed down to her grandfather and her father and, duly, down to her, might as well have been about the Tudor monarchs for all the relevance they had to her day-to-day life. The stories had seemed strange and exciting when she'd been young, but now thinking about them just made her feel rather sad, because those days were never coming back.

"Penny for them?" asked Professor Solomons.

Mellow blinked. "Sorry," she said. "Miles away."

Solomons regarded her from behind his desk. "You look tired."

"It's been that kind of week," she said.

"It's only Tuesday," he pointed out.

"Well, yes." She sighed and took her cup and saucer from where they sat on a corner of the desk, taking a sip.

"Surely you have some leave due to you?"

"We're the Thames Valley Force," she said. "We don't do *leave*."

He took a sip of his own tea, a small, neat, round man in a suit and tie. "Well, I'm not your doctor, obviously," he said, "but I am *a* doctor, and I'd be remiss if I didn't mention that you'll only wind up becoming ill if you don't get a break."

"Consider me told." There was a strain of macho running through certain detectives, almost certainly from reading too many old crime novels, which dictated that they had to attend autopsies. Mellow had never had time for that. There was no need to stand in a freezing mortuary watching a pathologist removing some poor sod's lungs and putting them in a bucket when she could get the same information from a well-written report and an informal chat here in Solomons's book-lined rooms at Christ Church. She nodded at the folder which lay on the desk between them. "Thanks for doing this so quickly, Michael."

He shrugged. "We weren't busy. It's only a preliminary report, of course. Some of the tests will take a day or so to come through. Anyway, adult male, about forty years of age. Average height and build, no identifying marks or deformities, no obvious medical conditions. He hadn't eaten for several days. When he arrived here, he'd been dead for between eighteen and twenty-four hours."

Which put the time of death sometime during the night before the body was found. "How did he die?"

"Oh, that's easy. Single large puncture wound to the heart." He held up his hand, thumb and forefinger about a quarter of an inch apart.

"So the other injuries were postmortem."

"Oh yes, just like Reg and Liz said." He sipped some more tea. "They're very good; I keep asking them to come and lecture here. Reg won't, but I have hopes of Liz. Yes, that was the cause of death. The poor chap had been in the wars before that, though. Ligature marks on his throat and legs and elbows, as if he'd been trussed up for a period of time. There's a fracture at the back of the skull, too, blunt-force trauma. Not enough to be immediately fatal, but certainly debilitating. He may only have been semiconscious when he was killed."

Mellow looked out of the window. Out in the gathering gloom, she could see the huge lake where the confluence of the Thames and Cherwell had eaten away and finally inundated Christ Church Meadow sometime before she was born. "What about his face and hands?"

"Yes," said Solomons. "Haven't seen anything like that before. A very intense and directional source of heat. The bones at the front of his head were quite deeply charred and the hands were all but destroyed, but the back of his head was untouched. If I were to speculate, I'd say it was something like a welding torch."

"To destroy his identity?"

Solomons smiled. "As Reg would say, it's my job to provide you with evidence, not steer your investigation. I would note that, whatever the reason, what was done to him did, in fact, quite efficiently render him unidentifiable. No face, no fingerprints. His teeth and lower jaw have been more or less destroyed. With a hammer, I think. Again, if I were to speculate, I would say there may have been something distinctive about them." He put his cup back on the desk. "And there are punctures through his wrists. Here." He held up his own wrist and pointed. "Liz spotted them when the body was being moved, which was very sharp of her; they're quite hard to see because of all the charring."

"Any... speculation?" Mellow asked.

"Well." Solomons sat back in his chair and clasped his hands across his stomach. "There could, of course, be other explanations, but if you were going to crucify someone, that's where you'd hammer the nails."

For a little while, the only sounds in the room were the patient ticking of the grandfather clock in one corner and the knocking of the radiators. Finally, Mellow said, "And you couldn't have mentioned that first?"

Solomons smiled sadly. "I admit it," he said. "I've become a drama queen."

Mellow picked up the folder and leafed through the half-dozen typed pages inside.

"There will be photographs, of course," Solomons told her. "But they're still being developed. I'll have them biked round to you tomorrow, together with the test results."

"You don't say anything about crucifixion here," Mellow said, looking up from the folder.

"Oh, absolutely not," he said. "It's one thing to sit here thinking out loud, it's another to put it down in black and white where someone might bring it up at a departmental review."

Mellow thought about that. "Are you in some kind of trouble?"

Solomons shrugged. "Academics," he said. "Always plotting against each other. It'll pass."

"Anything I can do?"

"Good lord, no. Most of my colleagues regard the police as a lower form of life. At best they'd only laugh at you."

"But you'd let me know," she said. "If there *was* something."

"Yes," he said, obviously not meaning it. "You'll be the very first to know."

She looked at him for a few moments longer, then down at the report. "It'd be hard for just one person to do all this," she mused, putting the sheets back in order and studying the top page.

"That's a determination for you to make, I'm afraid," he told her. "If we're thinking out loud, I'd say difficult, but not impossible."

Mellow thought about the warehouse, the absence of drag marks on the floor. "Would he have been able to walk after the head injury?"

Solomons considered it for a few moments. "Possibly, but it's likely someone with an injury like that would need help to stay on their feet."

She closed the folder and looked across the desk. "I'd better go," she said. "I've taken up enough of your time, and Dad's doing us a roast chicken tonight."

Solomons nodded. "Give your father my regards. How is he?"

Mellow put the folder into her knapsack, did up the straps. "Physically, he's okay," she said. "He doesn't get out as much as I'd like, though. He potters about the garden when the weather's not too bad, but mostly he just sits in his room reading."

"It's hard for someone like that, suddenly confined to a wheelchair, reliant on other people for things he used to be able to do for himself." Solomons held up a hand. "I know it's been five years now, but there's no time limit on stuff like that. You should bring him over one evening. Come and have dinner with me."

Something like that had never occurred to Mellow, and she kicked herself mentally. "I'll mention it to him," she said. "Thank you, Michael."

"I always enjoyed chatting with him. More than with most police officers, anyway. And Leonie?"

Mellow had got to her feet and was standing by her chair. "Yes?"

"Try to get some rest."

"Do you remember Leviathan?" she asked later over dinner.

Her father looked up from his plate. "Why do you ask?"

She shrugged. "The name came up today. Michael Solomons said to say hello, by the way."

"You were talking to the Prof about Leviathan?"

"No, somebody else mentioned him."

Jack sat back in his wheelchair and looked at her. "Leviathan was a long time ago," he said. "The year before you joined the force."

"I know it was a long time ago, Dad."

He thought about it for a little while. He ate some chicken and vegetables, then he sat back again. "What people forget is that Leviathan was never a *him*. We never thought it was one person. Leviathan were a gang, just like the other gangs. A bit crazier than the others, but just another gang."

Mellow carried on with her dinner. She could have gone down to Records and requested the file on Leviathan, but she didn't want to start rumours. She said, "It wasn't the year before I joined the force; it was the same year. All the cadets were terrified the force was going to send us out to Cowley and the Leys as cannon fodder, but that never happened."

He looked at her. "Was it the same year? I suppose it must've been, now I think about it." He shook his head. "Memory's starting to go."

"Your memory's better than mine is; you know very well what year it was. You were trying to catch me out, you mean old sod."

Jack smiled. He laid down his knife and fork and dabbed at his lips with his napkin. "We almost lost control of the city, you know."

"I know, Dad. I was there."

He smiled and looked away into a corner of the kitchen. "There wasn't a lot of crime in the early days, according to my dad," he said. "Oh, there were some arseholes, there always are, but mostly people were just terrified that the world was ending, and they were all pulling together to survive. It wasn't until they realised they weren't all going to die that proper criminality started. Theft, hoarding. Some people didn't take to the idea of Chancellery and wanted to set up their own little independent areas. We started to get little gangs, and they got bigger, and for a long time there was, what do you call it, *equilibrium*. They did crime, we arrested them, they did more crime. We couldn't stop them, they couldn't stop us."

"The Old Families," she said.

"Well now," he said, "I never liked calling them that, because *we're* an Old Family; we've been in Oxford since the Year Dot. But yes, some of the gangs started out like that. You'd get one family who decided they had to have more than everybody else and didn't much care how they got it. People who wanted *respect*." He picked up his knife and fork and went back to his meal. "We heard a lot about *respect*, back then."

They ate for a little while in silence.

"I suppose you could say the police started it," Jack said. "Maybe it would have happened anyway, sooner or later, but word came down from the top that some of the gangs had started to take liberties and we were to begin cracking down on them. We knew that would cause trouble, but orders are orders. So there were some raids and some arrests, and the gangs didn't like that." He looked into a corner of the kitchen. "And then it just seemed like we were at war, all of a sudden. Just like that. There were riots everywhere: in Cowley and Blackbird Leys, in the centre of town, even up in Sunnymead."

"I was up there today," Mellow said.

Jack nodded. "There's more people there these days, but back then it was just a couple of hundred people keeping themselves to themselves, and one night they had a mob of about thirty arseholes firebombing the local nick. They broke in and dragged the officers out and killed them in the street. It was like the whole city had lost its mind."

She hadn't noticed any marks of violence at Sunnymead

police station, but as her father had pointed out, it was a long time ago. "Could they have taken over?"

"Oh Christ, yes. We were overwhelmed. The Colleges shut their doors. Chancellery were making plans to get out of the city."

"I didn't know that."

He nodded. "There was talk of them moving to Abingdon. Abingdon was a shithole back then, but at least there was no violence. If they'd gone, that would have been it; we might as well have abandoned the city."

"So, what happened?"

Jack looked at her. "You know what happened."

"Leviathan."

He snorted. "We started finding bodies that had been *completely* messed up. Mutilated beyond anything you could imagine. There was a chap with his face cut off and his heart missing, just dumped in the street outside force headquarters. Another one hung up by his own entrails on a fence outside the Ashmolean. Someone found a dozen feet lined up on the pavement in Summertown, just standing there, but they were all left feet. Nobody ever found the rest of them. It was butchery, pure and simple." He shrugged. "Took us a little while to twig that all the victims were gang members, some of them gang leaders. That's what happened to Effie Fox's dad, and her brother." He looked thoughtful. "I liked old man Fox. Not so keen on Courtenay."

They were quiet for a little while. Jack didn't often talk about Effie Fox, and he seemed a little surprised that he'd mentioned her now.

"Anyway," he went on, "the rioting started to die down. Some of the gangs sent people to talk to us, asking what we were doing. They thought it was us doing the killing, you see. Which it wasn't," he added. "Susan Bates, who was chief superintendent back then, went out to Cowley with Jimmy

Pickard, who was her superintendent, and she met with the gang leaders. Bloody brave thing to do, that. That's when we first heard about Leviathan. The gangs had come to the conclusion it was another gang, someone using the chaos to try and take over. They called them 'Leviathan' because it didn't seem like anything could stop them."

"And was it?" she asked. "Another gang?"

Jack shrugged. "We never found any of its members. Nobody who'd admit it, anyway. Everything calmed down, though, and the killings stopped. And everyone lived happily ever after."

If only. "I've only heard about this in bits and pieces, you know," she said. "Nobody who was there really wants to talk about it, and the people who weren't there just have all these weird rumours."

He grunted. "No great surprise; it was hardly our finest hour. The whole thing lasted about three weeks, and I spent most of that in Blackbird Leys with a riot shield and a shotgun, with various arseholes chucking bricks and firebombs and taking pot-shots at me. I was just glad it was over."

"What happened to Bates and Pickard?"

"Susan retired not long after," he said. "Outstanding copper, Susan Bates. Don't know what happened to her after that. Jimmy took over as chief super. The rest of recent history, you know."

She did indeed, a diminishing quality of superior officers. The best you could say about Todd was that he was adequate; she found it best to keep her thoughts about Maxwell to herself. "Have you finished?" she asked, nodding at the table.

"I'll do it," he said.

"No, you cooked." She got up and collected the plates and took them over to the sink. Scraping the leftovers into the bin, she said, "Was that the last anyone heard from Leviathan? Nothing else like that since?"

"Not that I ever heard of, no." Jack unlocked the wheels of

his chair, rolled it back from the table, and turned it so he could see her at the sink. "Until now, maybe."

Mellow put the plates in the sink and ran hot water over them. "I told you, the name just came up today."

He sighed. "Leonie."

"A body turned up in Sunnymead," she said. "It was pretty messed up."

"Messed up how?"

She put the plug in the sink, added detergent. "Very badly mutilated. Left on an industrial estate." There was a silence behind her, and it went on so long that she turned from the sink, and for a moment she thought her father had fallen asleep. He was sitting in his chair with his head tipped forward, chin against his chest. "Dad?"

Jack took a deep breath and raised his head and smiled at her. "And you thought of Leviathan?"

"Reg Campbell and Liz Howell brought it up. I told them it was ridiculous."

He didn't stop smiling, but now she thought there was something bleak about it, and she cursed herself for bringing up the subject. Jack didn't normally dwell on the past, but in odd moments she caught him with a distant, thoughtful look on his face, and she knew he was remembering the days before he'd been injured, and hating the way he was now. "You'd better hope it is," he told her. "Because if they're back we're in a lot of trouble."

EIGHT

A COUPLE OF years before Adam was born, a compact expeditionary force – Marines and scientists and cartographers – had set out from Guz. For over half a century, the city had more or less kept itself to itself; the weather was too awful and the terrain too sodden to do much in the way of adventuring and nation-building, and the Bureau had not yet developed its policy of sending lone scouts out into the countryside to see what they could see. The Committee which ran Guz had been occupied with nation-building at home; agriculture was – just – possible in England's awful new climate but there were many mouths to feed, and in the early days more arrived regularly from the communities of the south-west and even further afield. There was a huge amount of work necessary on infrastructure. And there was the ever-present need to maintain Order. The Navy liked Order, and HMS Drake, Plymouth's naval base, had more than enough manpower and weapons to impose it.

Still, all this was a full-time project, and for years the Committee had found its focus more at home than further afield. Smaller patrols had gone out down the years, west towards Cornwall and up to the north Devon coast, and when the weather allowed boats had managed to struggle along the coast as far as the Solent, where Guz's sister, the naval base at Gosport, had taken a direct hit from one or more Sisters and was a rusting ruin, but the situation in the wider country was a bit of a mystery.

The expeditionary force left Guz at the beginning of what passed, in those days, for summer, a hundred people on horseback and in wagons, and it picked its way patiently eastward along roads which were either choked with abandoned vehicles or almost overgrown or washed away entirely. At Exeter, where it found a couple of thousand people still eking out a kind of survival in the ruins of the town, it picked up the old A30 and made its way into Somerset.

This was already further overland than anyone from Guz had travelled since the fall of The Sisters, and what they found was an almost-deserted, waterlogged country dotted with tiny communities and farms which had, down the years, fortified themselves against the weather and intrusions by people wanting the supplies they had. The Somerset Levels were virtually an inland sea, and it took them weeks to find a route up into the Mendips, where they came upon several communities which were doing relatively well for themselves and didn't want anything to do with outsiders. They discovered that a Sister had come down in the Bristol Channel, destroying Weston-Super-Mare and inundating Bristol, and that the resulting tidal wave had travelled up the Channel and scoured both banks clean of life before flooding Gloucester.

They turned east again, and found that another Sister, quite a large one, had struck a little east of Warminster, and the land beyond that was a flooded, boggy mess. It was here that they found a small group of people who were barely surviving on a small patch of dry ground.

It was probably going too far to call it a 'community'. There were no more than thirty people, living in a collection of wagons and rough shelters, hunting and foraging and slowly succumbing to hunger and illness, and Adam didn't know the details of what happened next because that part of the report of the expedition's commanding officer was still classified some distance above his security clearance, as was much of what followed.

Whatever his reasons, the commanding officer – his name and the names of all the other members of the group had also been redacted from the report – had decided to call a halt to the expedition. That wasn't really a great mystery; they had been out in the wilds for three months and his men were no doubt exhausted. It was what he did next that was a bit of a puzzle, because he elected to take the little community from Wiltshire with him when he returned to Guz. There may have been some puzzlement when the expedition arrived back at HMS Drake with thirty more bodies than it had departed, but in those days the policy of the Committee had not yet hardened towards outsiders and the refugees had been made welcome.

For a while, all had been well, then the newcomers, led by a young man who called himself Father John, began to quietly spread sedition. They did it so quietly that the coup, when it came, caught the authorities unawares and they had no choice but to respond by putting the attempted rebellion down with extreme prejudice. A lot of people died, but when the dust finally settled Father John and a handful of his people were unaccounted for. The Commodore of the time had sent Marines out in pursuit, but the West was a big place and the weather was far worse back then, and it was easy for a few people to lose themselves. The hope was that they had starved or died of exposure or disease, or fallen prey to roving groups of bandits. There were certainly not enough of them left to pose a threat.

It was a salutary lesson, and one for which, Adam thought, a lot of struggling little communities had suffered in the following decades. Guz had effectively walled itself off from the world, and any survivors it encountered were mostly left to stand or fall on their own. It was only in the last ten years or so that Guz had emerged from its exile and, as if making up for lost time, had set out to dominate the southwest and make plans for the rest of the south of England.

Quite when the subject of Father John had arisen again, Adam had no idea; the Bureau only told him what it thought he needed to know, which was usually barely enough. Betty Coghlan, not someone prone to panic, had been concerned enough about whatever was going on in Oxfordshire to barter the independence of the Chilterns in return for Guz's protection, but she didn't know who was behind it. Had Guz suspected something even before Chrissie and the Marine expeditionary force had encountered Father John's followers in Wiltshire? Sometimes it felt as if he spent more time trying to second-guess his superiors than actually doing his job.

If it *was* Father John, he and his followers had been busy in the years since they fled Guz. The higher ground around Cumnor was densely populated, by present day standards, and it was well-guarded. There were checkpoints on all the cleared roads in the area, and roving patrols of armed people on horseback. Adam emerged from his hide at dusk and observed the community from a distance. As it got dark, lights came on in the houses, which meant they were secure enough to spare the time to build wind generators. Most communities couldn't; electricity had been a long way down Frank Pendennis's list of priorities in Margate.

Clearly, what intelligence he had been given about Oxford was out of date and inaccurate. He'd been led to expect a reasonably well-organised community of a few thousand people who had managed to survive quite well on the leftovers of pre-Sisters society, stripping supermarkets and department stores for supplies until they were able to support themselves.

This felt different. He had a sense that the population of the city was much larger, and was doing considerably better, than he'd been led to expect.

Fine. Intelligence was a constantly evolving thing, and he had been sent here to provide up-to-date information, but it had implications for his approach to the city. Judging by the checkpoints, it was going to be impossible to just walk openly into Oxford. It should be relatively straightforward to avoid them and slip into the city unseen, but that had its own drawbacks – he was going to be a stranger, an outsider, and the moment he asked someone a simple question he was going to give himself away.

Still, it was worth testing out the defences. Maybe he could get away with it. One morning, he stashed everything that could be identified as military issue – his rations, the stoves, the tent, the radio – in the roof space of the house, and after some thought he left Gussie there, too, the sniper rifle he had stolen from Frank; it would only attract attention. He left the house wearing clothes and a coat sourced in the Parish, and set off north.

By early afternoon he was walking up Cumnor Hill, just another weary traveller looking for a place to rest and maybe pick up a few days' work. He was fairly certain that he had been observed long before he reached the checkpoint that barred the road into Oxford.

It was quite a professional checkpoint, a counterweighted pole across the road, and to one side an old garden shed for the guards to shelter in. Coming up the hill towards it, Adam saw two armed people standing at the pole, and he mentally added another one or two in the shed where he couldn't see them.

As he approached, the people in the road unslung rifles and shotguns, but more out of routine than as a threat. One moved to the side of the road to keep an eye on him, leaving the other standing behind the pole in the middle.

"You can stop there, thanks," she said when he was a few yards from the checkpoint.

Adam took another couple of steps forward and stopped and looked about him. Nobody was quite pointing a gun at him, but he didn't feel welcome.

"What do you want?" the guard asked. She was a tall woman wearing a rain poncho and carrying an old British Army assault rifle, of which, Adam felt personally, there were altogether too many floating about the countryside.

He and Chrissie had worked out what they thought was a reasonably convincing backstory, something it would be difficult to prove or disprove. "I'm looking for work," he told her.

"We've been expecting you," she said.

That stopped him in his tracks. "You have?"

"Oh yes." She looked towards the shed, where a third guard had emerged and was holding a radio to his ear. Adam kept a straight face. None of his briefings had included the information that the people in Oxford had radio.

"Okay," he said.

"You're to wait here," she said. "Someone'll be out to get you presently."

"Right."

"I'll have your gun."

"You will not," he told her.

"Oh, don't be such a weakling," she said. "You'll get it back, probably." She made a gimme gesture. After a couple of moments, he carefully unslung his shotgun and held it out. She took it, gave it a quick look, then slung it over her own shoulder. "Is that all you're carrying?"

He nodded. He'd left his sidearm with his other gear.

She nodded to the guard at the side of the road, who stepped forward and gave Adam a brisk frisking, during which he found both his knives. "They're tools," Adam said, as the guard handed them over to the woman.

"Well, today they are," she said. "But who knows what they'll be tomorrow?" She jerked her head towards the shed. "You might as well go in and get out of the weather. No point standing around in the rain."

He looked around. "I like standing in the rain."

"Oh, don't be daft," she said cheerfully. "Get inside. Take the weight off your feet."

He looked through the door, saw some old kitchen chairs and a table with a couple of thermos flasks and some mugs. He went in, put his rucksack in a corner, and sat on one of the chairs.

"Fancy a cuppa?" asked the guard who had frisked him.

Adam shook his head.

"Ah, go on," said the guard. "We've got sugar today."

"Well." Adam pulled back the hood of his coat. "If you put it like that…"

The guard filled a mug from one of the flasks, found a little bag of sugar lumps, dropped one into the tea, and stirred it. "There you go," he said, putting it on the table in front of Adam. "Sit tight. Be back in a bit."

Well. It would have been no surprise at all to discover that he'd been spotted coming up the road, but being *expected* was different. Presumably, the guards had mistaken him for someone else and the error would be realised before very long, but in the meantime it seemed that it would serve to get him into the city, and he could wing it after that. The guards didn't seem openly threatening, although they didn't seem inclined to much conversation either. Adam sipped some tea and looked out through the shed's grimy window. In the distance, two horses were pulling a cart up the hill. The cart's load was covered with a tarp, but judging by the way the horses trudged along, it was heavy. They stopped briefly at the checkpoint and the driver and one of the guards had a brief conversation. Then another guard put his weight on the end of the pole and tipped it up until the cart could pass through. Adam watched the horses plod past the open door. He drank some more tea.

At one point, he got up and stood in the doorway. Nobody tried to stop him, but one of the guards was standing by the shed looking alert. They looked at each other for a few moments, then Adam went back inside.

After about half an hour, he heard the sound of hooves on the road. He got up again and went to the door. Another cart was pulling up outside, this one smaller and pulled by just the one horse. The woman was coming across the road. "Grab your stuff," she said. "Your ride's here."

"Where am I going?" he asked.

"Don't know; I was just told to keep you here till somebody came to get you." She smiled brightly. "Maybe they've got some work for you."

He looked at the cart. Two men were sitting on the front seat. "Can I have my gun back?"

"Nope," she said. "That'll follow you along presently. Same with your... tools."

He thought about it, but really there was no choice. He went back into the shed for his rucksack, carried it over to the cart, and threw it in the back.

"Hop on, then," said the driver's mate. "We haven't got all day."

Adam climbed up beside his rucksack and sat down on a wooden box behind the driver and his mate. The driver got the cart turned round and the horse started to pull them up the hill. Looking back, Adam saw the woman at the checkpoint smirk and wave.

"Let's see your hand a second," said the driver's mate.

Adam said, "What?" and held his hand out without thinking, and the driver's mate reached over and Adam felt something hard close around his wrist. When he looked, he saw that he had been handcuffed to one of the metal braces that attached the driver's seat to the cart.

"It's for your own safety," the driver's mate said, turning back to look ahead.

"Don't want you falling out and hurting yourself," added the driver.

"And I know what you're thinking," his mate went on, "but we haven't got the key. That's at the station."

"So just make yourself comfortable and enjoy the ride," the driver said.

Adam hadn't been thinking about the key. He didn't want to escape; nobody had threatened him yet and he was being taken into Oxford, which was where he wanted to go. Besides, there was at present no way to get out of the cart without attracting attention. He took the driver's advice and tried to get comfortable on the box as the cart reached the top of the hill.

They didn't seem to be in any hurry. Just outside Cumnor village, they turned off the main road and passed through an area of big, once-expensive houses that were now derelict and almost overwhelmed by vegetation, though the road itself had been kept clear and any abandoned cars had been dragged away and dumped down side streets. They passed a couple of showrooms, their huge windows shattered long ago and the cars inside sitting rusted and useless, even if there had been any petrol to run them. There seemed to be a lot of people out and about; they passed a lot of carts and wagons and people on bicycles.

Eventually they came to a line of wagons pulled up in the road, loaded up with produce. Adam leaned out as much as he could and saw a broad river, and beyond that an old railway embankment. "Pull past them," the driver's mate said to the driver. "We'll be here all day otherwise."

The driver pulled out to the other side of the road, and they drove along the line of carts and wagons, raising shouts and complaints from their drivers. At the end of the line was a ferry crossing, and passengers and carts boarding a big broad flatboat. There was a squat brick building beside the road, with smoke pluming from its chimney, and a similar one on the other side of the river. The driver's mate hopped down and went over to talk to one of the ferrymasters. There was some gesticulating, and Adam heard raised voices, although he couldn't make out what was being said. Finally, the ferrymaster threw up his hands and stomped away, and the driver's mate returned to the cart.

"Go on," he said.

"I have to use this ferry every day, you know," the driver said.

"It's me he's angry at," said his mate, who Adam was beginning to suspect wasn't his mate at all. "Go on, get aboard."

They drove onto the ferry and a couple of minutes later Adam heard the sound of steam-powered winches and they were pulled across the river. Halfway across, he could see how it had undermined and eaten away the bank they had come from over the years. Rubble and the upper floors of a row of houses broke the surface upstream, and downstream it flowed through a huge area of floodland.

It took five minutes to cross the river, and on the other side they passed into a maze of rain-wet streets. Here were more carts, and people on horseback on bicycles, and even more on foot. As they passed by, he saw work going on in some of the buildings. What he didn't see was anyone obviously carrying a weapon, although he did spot a number of people wearing what looked like uniforms, black trousers and black coats with some kind of badge on the breast pocket.

The cart finally pulled up outside an office building. There were more of the black-uniformed people going in and out, but they didn't pay the cart any attention. The driver's mate turned and reached back and unlocked the handcuff around Adam's wrist.

"No offence," he said, acknowledging his lie about the key.

"None taken," Adam said. His attention was occupied by the

big wooden hand-painted sign mounted beside the front door of the building. It said THAMES VALLEY POLICE. "You have police?"

"We do," said the driver's mate. "Detective Sergeant Fleet, at your service. Come on, my boss wants a word."

They went into the police station, where a big front desk had been installed in the foyer of the old building. Fleet and the uniformed policeman behind the counter had a quick conversation, then Fleet beckoned to Adam, and they went up a flight of stairs and down some corridors until Fleet opened a door.

"Can I trust you not to do anything silly?" he asked.

"You mean apart from coming here looking for work?" Adam said, peering inside.

Fleet grinned. "Make yourself comfortable. The boss won't be long."

The room was windowless and completely bare apart from a table and two chairs. On the other hand, it had electric light and it was relatively warm and it didn't smell too musty. Adam sat down on one of the chairs and Fleet closed the door.

So, he might as well abandon all the briefings he'd had about Oxford. There were obviously far more people here than he'd been told, and they were fairly advanced technologically. In fact, from what he had seen so far, the city didn't look dissimilar to Guz. The people looked relatively well-fed and well-organised, and they seemed to be working comparatively enthusiastically without supervision. In Margate, most of the work gangs had been overseen by armed enforcers. Adam looked about the room. *How could we not have known about this?*

NINE

MELLOW'S DAY BEGAN with a packet of autopsy photographs from Professor Solomons. She made herself look at them, even though it was too early in the day for that kind of thing, and made some notes. Then she held a case conference for half a dozen detectives to brief them about the Sunnymead murder. Sergeant Wallop did not attend, but he sent a rather pointed note saying he was still working his way through the archives, and Mellow realised she was going to have to wind herself up to having a stern word with him, despite the possible consequences.

Then it was downstairs to the first floor for her weekly discussion of her caseload with Superintendent Todd. This usually involved her giving him a quick rundown of what was going on and him nodding absently, but today he interrupted her recitation of the most recent item on her list and said, "It's not that hard to make someone disappear in Oxford."

Mellow paused in the reading of her notes and said, "Sir?"

"I'm just thinking out loud," he said, turning his chair until he could look out of the window. It was drizzling outside.

"Doesn't it strike you as a rather... *extravagant* way of killing someone?"

She looked at her notes, back at him. "Well, yes, sir."

"I mean, you could just shoot them or stab them and dump the body in the river and probably nobody would see it again until it reached Goring."

"Yes, sir."

"It's as if whoever did it was making a point," Todd said to the drizzle. "But they did it somewhere the body was unlikely to be found."

"That's not quite true, sir," Mellow said, sorting through her notes. "The site's scheduled to be cleared of scrap metal, so someone would have found the body eventually."

"So perhaps the killer knew that." Brian Todd was a mild, inoffensive man who her father had once described as having ridden to his present position in the wake of far more competent superiors.

To be fair to Todd, that was something that had crossed Mellow's mind. "I spoke with the man who found the body," she said. "He was subcontracted to clear the site."

Todd nodded. "Subcontracted by whom?"

"The Foxes," Mellow told him, all of a sudden knowing where this conversation was heading.

He rotated his chair until he was looking at her again. "The Foxes, eh?" he said.

"Yes, sir." She wanted to caution him not to jump to conclusions, that in all probability this was much more complicated, but he was smiling at her.

"Well," he said, "there you are. Get Effie and her idiot boys in here."

He might as well have been telling her to make it stop raining, but she nodded. "Yes, sir." Actually, it might have been easier to make it stop raining; it would certainly involve a lower body-count.

He looked smug. "It'd be good to get Effie for something. She's been a pain in this force's arse for years."

Mellow didn't quite sigh, but it was an effort. "Sir."

Todd beamed. "Was there anything else?"

Mellow hesitated but decided she had to do it. "Sunnymead nick, sir."

"What about it?"

"I was up there yesterday and they were... unhelpful. Obstructive, actually."

"Oh, nonsense." Todd sat back in his chair. "Who's the inspector up there?"

"Inspector Kelly, sir."

"Of course. I was talking with him the other day; he's an exemplary officer."

"She, sir."

"Quite." Todd hurdled the obstacle effortlessly. "An exemplary officer. I'm sure you were just imagining it. You have to learn not to be so thin-skinned."

Well, at least she could say she'd mentioned it. "Sir."

"Now, what about Fleet?" he asked. "Is he still confined to headquarters?"

"Sir." Fleet was up to date with his paperwork now and had begun doing other people's. She'd caught a long-suffering look from him earlier in the squadroom.

"Well, that's no good, Leonie," he said. "You've got at least two investigations going on; you need everybody out on the streets."

"Yes, sir."

"Get Fleet out there, and get me some results, Leonie. Chief Superintendent Maxwell says we don't have enough results."

It seemed to Mellow that, of late, the prime motivator of the Thames Valley force was to make its superiors happy rather than doing a good job. She made Todd happy, Todd made Maxwell happy, Maxwell made Chancellery happy. Mellow had been brought up to believe that results were measured by quality, not by weight.

Midmorning, Al Harris came in to headquarters to review and sign his statement and get his scrap metal licence back. She gave that job to Fleet, who looked suitably grateful to be doing something involved with an investigation. While he was doing that, Mellow got her bike and went to take the ferry back over to Headington.

There was a joke – not to be mentioned within earshot of its subjects or anyone who knew them – that one of Effie Fox's sons was an imbecile, but it was impossible to tell which one. Mellow thought it was a lazy joke, and more to the point it wasn't true. Doug wasn't stupid, he was just quiet. And Archie... was Archie. They were both, anyway, best avoided, as was the rest of their large extended family. Which made the fact that they lived three streets away from her something of an issue, and even more so since she had joined the force. There were those who accused the Foxes of hiding in plain sight, virtually on the doorstep of Headington police station, and others who took it as a provocation, but the truth was that the Foxes and the Mellows had been here long before Headington nick.

Effie and her sons lived in a big but not especially notable house that sat cater-corner on a bend in the street, which gave them a clear line of sight in both directions. It was neat and freshly painted, and unusually for Oxford its little front garden and big high-walled back garden were planted with shrubs and rockeries rather than vegetables.

Mellow took it for granted that she was being watched as she pedalled up the street; there was always someone keeping at least half an eye on what was going on in the street outside the Fox house. She stopped outside, dismounted, and wheeled her bike through the gate and left it leaning up against the hedge – it was probably the safest place in Oxford to leave it; it was more likely to be stolen at headquarters – and by the time she was halfway up the path the front door was opening and Doug was standing there.

"Leonie," he said amiably as she reached the door.

"Douglas," she said. "Is your mum in? I'd like a word."

Doug was a couple of years older than her, a short, stocky, well-dressed man with brown hair and a big bushy moustache. Most people tried to avoid him if they saw him out on the street, but he'd never been less than courteous towards her. "Of course," he said, casually checking the street, just in case. "Come on in." He stepped aside to let her into the hall.

Inside, the house was warm and cosy and immaculately clean and tidy. Mellow stopped at the door and took off her boots, spent a couple of moments sorting through the little wooden box by the wall of the hallway to find a pair of slippers that fit her.

"Mum's in the study," Doug told her. "Can I get you some tea?"

Not really, but it was best to be polite. "Tea would be lovely, thanks."

He smiled. "Go on through, I'll bring it in to you."

The study was at the back of the house. On the way, Mellow peeked through open doors into the living room – furniture and carpet that looked brand new, a tall glass-fronted cabinet against one wall with little porcelain figures arranged on its shelves – and the dining room – big, polished table with ten matching chairs and a long waist-high cupboard for cutlery and crockery. As she reached the study, she thought she saw a tall, thin figure all in black move out of sight behind the half-open door of the kitchen at the end of the hall. If she had been forced to put money on who in this house was capable of burning a man's face off, she would have put it on Archie. That didn't mean he'd done it, though.

The study was lined, floor to ceiling, with shelves on which there were dozens of box files, and in one corner there was a little table with a typewriter on it. On the other side of the room, under the window that looked out into the back garden, was a big desk with lots of drawers, and an office chair, and it was from the office chair that Effie was just standing up to greet her.

She walked right up to Mellow and gave her a big hug. "Leonie," she said. "It's been too long."

"Hello, Effie," Mellow said, trying to radiate harmlessness while making it obvious by body language that it might not be entirely appropriate for a serving Oxford police officer to be hugged by the head of one of the city's most notorious crime families. It had never worked before, but one day the message might get through. "It's not a social call, I'm afraid."

"Yes." Effie let her go and took a step back, a compact, stocky woman in middle age, wearing jeans and a plain grey shirt. "I heard about that." She indicated a little sofa which stood against the wall by the door. "Sit down, please. Do you want some tea?"

"Douglas is taking care of it," Mellow said, sitting down.

"How's your dad?" Effie asked, sitting beside her.

"He's doing all right, thanks."

"I keep thinking I should pop round and see him," Effie said, although they both knew that was never going to happen. "I haven't seen him since it happened."

Improbably, Effie and Mellow's father had been at school together. Even more improbably, as teenagers they had for a time been sweethearts, to the disapproval of both their families. Mellow said, "Morton Street industrial estate."

"It's not really an industrial estate," Effie mused. "Half a dozen sheds." She thought about it. "Not sure what you'd call it, though."

"Let's just call it an industrial estate, until someone comes up with something better. I understand you have the contract to clear it of scrap metal."

Effie nodded and got up and went over to the shelves. While she was searching for the right box file, Doug came in with a tray on which were two cups, a teapot under a knitted cosy, a sugar-pot and a little milk jug. He put them down on a little table by the sofa. "Everything all right, Mum?" he asked.

"Everything's lovely, Douglas, thank you," she said, still scanning the shelves, although Mellow strongly suspected she knew exactly which file she was looking for. "Close the door on the way out, would you? Leonie's here on business."

Doug gave Mellow a brief, level look before favouring her with a charming smile and leaving the study. Effie said, "Would you be mother, please, dear? I'll find this thing in a minute."

Mellow poured tea for both of them, added milk and a lump of sugar to hers, and she was stirring it when Effie selected a file and brought it back to the sofa.

"Morton Street," she said, opening the file and leafing through the documents inside. "Yes." She selected one and handed it over. Mellow looked at it, a contract on Reclamation Department headed notepaper employing Fox & Sons to clear the structures at Morton Street of any recyclable metal and transport same to the municipal recycling yard. Dated three weeks ago, signed by the Clerk of Works, and stamped with the familiar Chancellery stamp.

"You subcontracted the work," she said.

"That's right." Effie poured a little milk into her tea. "We're a bit stretched at the moment and the Department were being stingy about the payment. It was hardly worth the effort, and I'm more than happy to put some work the way of other contractors."

"Just out of interest," said Mellow, "why *are* there any other contractors?"

Effie frowned. "Don't know what you're getting at, dear."

"There's you, and there's a bunch of little outfits. I don't understand how they're able to survive."

Effie broke into a wide smile. "Competition's good for everybody, Leonie. It would look awful if there was just one firm; we might as well just be part of Chancellery then."

"Hm." Mellow handed the contract back. "Did you know the site was there? Before the Department offered you the contract?"

Effie shook her head. "I don't know Sunnymead all that well. No real call to go visiting over there."

"What about the boys?"

Effie took a sip of tea. "Now I know you're not accusing Douglas and Archie of having anything to do with this horrible thing," she said, in a tone which was not quite a warning. "I have no idea whether they'd heard of it before, you'd have to ask them. Douglas went over there to take a look, when we were offered the job, to see if it was worth our bother."

Mellow stirred her tea some more. "Did he take anyone with him?"

Effie thought about it. "I think he went on his own, but you'd have to ask him. He was only going to look, after all." She looked at Mellow. "Maybe you're obsessing about who knew the site was there," she said. "It's not against the law, you know."

"It's how I do my job," Mellow told her. "Obsessing about things."

"You're going to stir a hole right through the bottom of that cup, you know."

Mellow sighed, stopped stirring, laid the spoon in the saucer and drank some tea.

"Listen," Effie told her. "I really doubt we're the only people who knew those sheds were there. The locals would know, for instance."

"We're talking to them." Unwilling to trust officers from Sunnymead nick to do the job, Mellow had sent out a couple of detectives from headquarters to do a house-to-house in the streets around the industrial estate. She didn't think it would take very long. "Have you any idea why there's so few people living there? It's not a bad area, really."

Effie shrugged. "Like I said, I've never got over there much."

"Did the Department give you any indication who owned the site?"

Effie laughed. "The city owns it, dear. Like it owns everything."

"It doesn't own this house, I'll bet."

"You know what I mean. The city owns all the commercial property and all derelict housing stock, by default. Maybe there's a property deed for Morton Street somewhere, but I wouldn't hold your breath; a lot of records went missing after The Sisters." She looked at Mellow. "And before you start getting all suspicious again, it's just one of those things; nobody was particularly interested in saving bits of paper, it's a miracle anything survived at all." She drank some more tea.

Mellow thought about it. "Have you heard anything at all about what went on there?"

"Al Harris was round here last night, shouting the odds and blaming us. That's the first I heard of it. I had to sit him down with a couple of drinks and get him to calm down."

"Why would he blame you?"

"Same reason you're here. We gave him the work. And because of who we are. Listen, Leonie," she said seriously. "We don't do that kind of thing anymore."

Mellow glanced at the window, to check if any pigs were flying by.

"I've spent the last fifteen years since Dad and Courtenay died trying to make this a proper legitimate business," Effie went on. "We've got a good relationship with Chancellery and the Department, it's less fuss and bother, and nobody gets hurt; we'd be insane to do anything to jeopardise that."

Mellow hadn't known Frank Fox very well. She remembered seeing him out and about, a big man with tattoos and a shaved head and a surprisingly dandyish cane. His head had been found spiked on a set of railings on the edge of Jericho; his heir apparent, Effie's brother, had never been found at all. Officially, he was still regarded as missing rather than dead.

She said, "Leviathan's name came up."

Instead of dismissing it, the way everyone else did, Effie just nodded. "Crossed my mind, too. We looked for them, at the time, believe me. We looked *very* hard. But we never found any sign that they even existed. And if they did, where have they been all this time? And why would they come back now?"

"So, if Leviathan didn't exist, who did all the killings?"

"My dad thought it was the police."

Mellow raised an eyebrow.

"He said Chancellery was trying to put the fear of god into the gangs, get them to stop rioting. The police would arrest someone quietly, take them somewhere out of the way and fuck them up in some spectacular fashion, then leave the body where it would be found. As a warning."

Mellow shook her head tiredly. "No."

"Well," Effie said, topping up her cup, "Dad found out whether he was right or not eventually." She put the teapot down and popped the cosy back over it. "Too bad he couldn't let us know, eh?"

They were silent for a little while. Mellow heard someone moving about in the kitchen, but otherwise there wasn't a sound in the house. Finally, she said, "My superintendent wants me to bring you and Douglas and Archie in for questioning."

Lost in thought, Effie gave a little snort at the thought of that.

Well, quite. Mellow was about to say something when her radio beeped. She took it from her pocket and pressed the talk button. "Mellow."

"Headquarters here, inspector," said someone in the comms room, a male officer, not a voice she recognised. "The chief super says your visitor's arrived."

It took her a moment or so to work out who he meant. "Oh.

Do we know where?"

"He's being held at the Cumnor checkpoint, the chief super says."

Mellow thought. "Right. Get Peter Fleet to go out there and bring him back to headquarters. Put him in an interview room. I'll be back as soon as I can."

"Message received," said headquarters, and the link went dead.

"Sorry, Effie," she said, pocketing the radio and gathering her knapsack from beside the sofa. "I've got to go and deal with something."

"Anything important?"

"Somebody thinks it is." She stood up. "Look, if you do hear anything about Morton Street, could you let me know?"

Effie stood up with her. "You want the boys to ask around?"

Mellow shook her head. The last thing she wanted was to owe the Foxes a favour, or even to look like she owed them a favour. "Just if the subject comes up in conversation or something. It wouldn't be like snitching," she added. "Just a legitimate businesswoman helping the police with their inquiries."

Effie grinned. "Always happy to help," she said.

IT TOOK HER longer than usual to get back to headquarters. One of the steam winches that hauled the ferry back and forth across the Cherwell had broken down, and she had to stand along with an increasingly grumpy crowd of passengers for almost an hour while it was fixed.

When she finally got back, she almost ran upstairs to the squadroom, where Fleet was sitting having a mug of tea. "We just got here," he said. "He's in Interview Two."

"Right." She rummaged in a cupboard for a pencil and some paper, popped them into a folder. "What's he like?"

Fleet shrugged. "Doesn't talk much. Can't see what's so special about him."

"Okay. Right. You'd better do a report for me; leave it on my desk. When you've done that, pop up to Sunnymead and join in with the house-to-house."

Fleet smiled with relief that he was finally getting out of the building again. "Will do, boss."

Down one flight of stairs, and approaching Interview Room Two at a fast walk, she saw the door open and a man poke his head out into the corridor. "No no no," she called. "No wandering about. We don't do tours, and even if we did, you've missed them."

He blinked incuriously at her and withdrew back into the room. By the time Mellow got there, he was sitting on one of the chairs at the table, hands clasped loosely in front of him. She closed the door behind her, sat down opposite him, and gave him a long look.

"So," she said. "I'm Detective Inspector Leonie Mellow."

"Adam," he said. "Adam Hardy."

"Wait, wait, wait." She took some paper and the pencil from the folder, scribbled the date and time at the top of the first sheet, wrote his name, and looked at him again. He was a lean man in his thirties, of a little less than average height, with a nose that had been broken at some time in the past and not very expertly reset. He seemed perfectly relaxed sitting there across the table from her. His clothes were dirty and – there was no way around it – smelly, and his hands were raw and cracked and there was dirt packed under the nails. He gave every appearance of having spent some time living rough, but Mellow thought his hair and beard showed the signs of having been trimmed in the not-so-distant past, and trimmed properly, not by hacking at them with a knife.

"Hello, Adam Hardy," she said. "Just out of interest, could you tell me why you're sitting here talking to me?"

He frowned at her. "You don't know?"

"I don't."

He watched her face for a few moments. "Sorry," he said. "I'm a bit confused. You've arrested me and you don't know why?"

"You haven't been arrested, you've been detained," she told him.

He thought about that. "So I can walk out of here whenever I want?"

"No."

"So how is that different from being arrested?"

"I promise, you'd know if you'd been arrested. No way to mistake it for anything else." Mellow made a note and looked at him. "What are you doing in Oxford, Mr Hardy?"

He shook his head, baffled. "I'm just looking for some work."

"What kind of work?"

"I've been doing farm work lately," he said. "But I can turn my hand to most things. Maybe I could be a policeman."

She looked up from her notes, but he was just looking at her deadpan. "Where are you from?" she asked.

"Southampton."

"That's a long way away."

He blinked at her. "Look," he said, "could we start this again? Do you do this to everyone who comes to Oxford?"

Mellow sighed. "For the avoidance of doubt, Mr Hardy, I'm the police officer here. I do the questions, you do the answers. I've found that works pretty well."

He shook his head. "I honestly don't understand what's going on here," he said. "I only came here looking for some work. I didn't expect to be arrested."

"You haven't bee—"

He raised a hand. "Yes, I get it. I haven't been arrested but I was picked up and brought here in handcuffs and I can't leave. Yes." He rubbed his eyes. "Yes, Southampton is a long way away. I've been working my way from place to place for the past eighteen months or so. No, I didn't plan to come here, somebody in Abingdon said there might be work and I thought I'd give it a try. Yes, I am regretting it."

She stared at him. "Are we done?" she asked finally.

He shrugged and looked helplessly around the room. "Look," he said, "if there's no work here, just take me back to the road and I'll go somewhere else." Mellow didn't say anything. "You don't even have to take me back to the road. I can walk."

"Are we *done*?"

He blew out his cheeks and settled his hands in his lap.

"So," she said. "You don't know anyone in Oxford?"

"No," he said. "Never been here before, never met anyone from here, don't particularly like the place, to be honest."

He was, Mellow thought, doing a rather good job of presenting as a somewhat annoyed and confused agricultural worker caught up in a situation he didn't understand, but beneath that she had an uncomfortable sense that, without quite seeming to, he was paying attention to *everything*. Her, the clothes she was wearing, the paper, the pencil, the room itself. Most suspects she interviewed were so concerned about their own miserable situation that they couldn't have told you what colour the walls were, but she had a feeling that Hardy had not only made a note of this but estimated the room's dimensions as well.

"Where's my rucksack, by the way?" he asked. "Someone took my gun and someone else has taken my rucksack."

Mellow had no idea. "You'll get your rucksack back presently," she told him. "I'll have to ask after your gun. You won't be allowed to carry it in the city, anyway."

He opened his mouth to say something, but the door opened and Maxwell came into the room. Mellow closed her eyes momentarily and sighed almost inaudibly.

"So," said Maxwell, standing at her shoulder. "This is our friend from Cumnor, is it?"

"Adam Hardy, sir," Mellow said without looking at him. "He

says he's looking for work." Then to Hardy, "This is Chief Superintendent Maxwell."

Hardy looked at Maxwell, and again Mellow got that sense of *attention*. He didn't appear unduly impressed by what he saw.

"So you're here looking for work, eh?" Maxwell said.

"Yes," he said.

Maxwell peered at him the way people who pride themselves on being able to sum someone up at a glance sometimes do. "Well, there's no work here."

"No," Hardy said.

Maxwell looked at him a little longer, just to make a point, then he said to Mellow, "I'll leave this to your discretion, inspector."

"Yes, sir," Mellow said. "Thank you, sir."

Maxwell gave Hardy one last look and left. He closed the door with more force than was strictly necessary, to make sure everyone knew he had been there. Hardy looked at Mellow and tipped his head to one side. She scowled.

He said, "I don't know what's going on here, but I'm starting to think you have the wrong bloke."

Mellow didn't know what to think. The memo she'd seen had said that someone was coming to Oxford and that they were to be allowed through the checkpoints. It didn't give any instruction about what was to happen next. It was Maxwell who had wanted the visitor detained and questioned, not Chancellery, and that was only because he was pissed off about being left off the decision tree. And after all that, he'd washed his hands of the whole thing by telling her to use her *discretion*. Meanwhile, there was an unidentified body on a shelf at the mortuary at Christ Church with its face burned off and she could have been spending this time doing something about sorting that out.

Suddenly aware that Hardy was watching her, she said, "So,

you don't know anyone in the city, you don't have anywhere to stay, and you don't have any money."

For a fraction of a second, she saw a look of surprise cross his face. He said, "Money?"

"To pay for things."

"I know what money is," he said. "I just never heard of anyone using it before."

"Well," Mellow said, looking down at her notes, "we do things differently here."

"You're not kidding," he said, half to himself.

Mellow came to a decision. "Can you fix roofs?"

That took him by surprise, too, she noticed. "What?"

"Leaky roofs," she said. "Can you fix them?"

"I have fixed leaky roofs," he said cautiously.

"Fine," she said, stuffing her notes into the folder. "If you want work, you can come and fix my roof, because it leaks like a colander."

TEN

Mellow led the way back downstairs, stopping off on the way at an office to pick up her coat and a big old leather knapsack. His rucksack, it turned out, was tucked behind the front desk, and he picked it up and shouldered it.

"Wait here," she told him. To the uniformed officer behind the desk, she said, "Don't let him wander off."

"Will do, inspector," said the officer. He and Adam gave each other appraising looks while Mellow went off down a corridor towards the rear of the building.

"At least it's stopped raining," Adam said when she was gone.

The officer behind the desk looked towards the front doors. "Aye," he said.

"I'm Adam, by the way." He put his hand out.

The officer looked him up and down. "Aye," he said. But he did at least shake hands.

"I'm a friend of Chief Superintendent Maxwell."

The officer gave him the once-over again, and this time he smiled wryly and shook his head. "Aye," he said. "Right."

Mellow reappeared on the pavement outside, pushing a bicycle with a wicker basket mounted between the handlebars and beckoning through the glass doors. "Great to meet you," Adam told the officer.

"Aye," the officer said, smiling and shaking his head again. "Aye."

Outside, Mellow said, "This way," and led him a short distance along the street, to where a couple of carts were parked, their drivers waiting in a wooden shelter on the pavement. Mellow took something from her pocket and showed it to them, and one of them got up and climbed up onto the driver's seat of the first cart.

"Here," Mellow said, pushing the bicycle at Adam. "Put this in the back and get in with it. Can I trust you not to do anything stupid?"

"I'm afraid past experience suggests I can't rule that out," he told her. "But I won't try to run away, if that's what you mean."

She looked at him for a moment. "Hm," she said. "Okay, let's go then. Try not to bend the bike; I can't afford a new one."

Adam threw his rucksack into the cart, manhandled the bicycle in after it, and finally climbed up and sat down with his back against the sideboards and his knees drawn up to his chest. Mellow got up and sat beside the driver and said something to him, and he nodded and flapped the reins and they set off.

How could we not have known about this? Oxford city centre looked in pretty good shape. Adam had been in towns that were completely derelict, burned out by long-ago fires or half-demolished by the blast from nearby comet strikes or simply abandoned and left to become overgrown. Here, though, the buildings were in good order and many of them seemed to be in use. The streets were busy with pedestrians and people on bicycles and horseback, carts and wagons hauling building materials to work gangs or taking away rubble. Many of the old shopfronts were boarded up to protect them from the weather, but a lot were not, and he saw produce and clothes and other items displayed in their windows. It was probably not even a fraction of what had been available before The Sisters, but these days it was a bustling metropolis.

What it reminded him of most was Guz; there was a similar energy there, of people pulling together and getting on with their lives and making things better. It had a police force and some kind of presiding authority. It had *money*, which he'd never encountered before. The guards at the checkpoint had radios, and he assumed they weren't the only ones, which spoke of a technological sophistication absent from pretty much all the communities he'd ever visited.

They crossed a river on another chain ferry, and then the cart was making its way along streets that were not so busy. There were fewer office buildings, more houses, and judging by the look of them the majority of the houses were occupied. The main streets – and a lot of the side streets, by the look of them – were in good condition and clear of weeds and vegetation and abandoned vehicles, which spoke of a large and well-motivated workforce. There were a lot of people in Margate, but nobody could have accused them of doing anything but the absolute grudging minimum in order to get a bowl of watery stew and avoid a beating from the Enforcers.

The streets grew quieter until he was only seeing the occasional cyclist or cart, and the street where the cart finally drew to a halt was deserted save for a single tall figure wearing an ankle-length black coat with its hood pulled up, striding long-legged along the pavement in the distance. Instead of getting down immediately, Mellow sat where she was for a few moments, and Adam got the impression she was watching the black-clad figure as it walked away from them.

"Who's that?" Adam asked.

Mellow seemed to startle awake. "Neighbour," she said. "Come on, let's get inside."

The cart had pulled up outside a big, detached house with neat paintwork and unbroken windows and a little garden at the front which had been dug up and planted with vegetables. Adam handed the bicycle down to Mellow, and as he got down himself he peeked along the side of the house and saw the mast of a wind generator in the back garden.

"Nice house," he said.

"Thank you," said Mellow.

He looked up at the roof and saw that there were, indeed, some loose tiles. He said, "I'm going to need a couple of ladders and some tools."

"It'll start getting dark soon," she said. "It can wait till tomorrow. Come on in."

They walked up the path and Mellow wheeled the bicycle around to the back of the house and returned a few moments later to unlock the front door onto a wood-floored hallway. "We're back!" she called, taking off her coat and hanging it on a hook by the door while Adam looked about him.

"Who's 'we'?" called a man's voice from another room.

"I brought a mysterious man home."

A big, broad-shouldered man in a wheelchair emerged from one of the doorways off the hall. "Well, life is always more interesting with men of mystery," he said. He was in his late fifties, with thick grey hair and a craggy face. His arms and upper body were massively muscled, but his legs ended in smooth nubs just above the knee, the legs of his trousers tucked neatly out of the way. "Jack Mellow," he said, wheeling himself up to Adam and putting out a hand.

"Adam Hardy," said Adam. Jack didn't try to crush his hand, but he applied just enough pressure to put him on notice.

Mellow bent down and hugged him. She kissed him on the top of the head. "How was your day?"

"It was the same as yesterday," Jack said without looking away from Adam. "And the day before that. And–"

"Yes, Dad, we get the idea," she told him. "Mr Hardy's going to be staying the night and he'll fix the roof tomorrow."

Jack raised a bushy eyebrow. "Well, if he's going to fix the roof, I think I'll call him by his first name, if that's all right."

"It's all right by me," Adam said.

Mellow looked at them. "Did you make soup?" she asked.

Jack nodded. "It's cooking," he said. "Could use a little longer, probably. I didn't expect you back so early."

"No, that's okay," she said. "It'll give Mr Hardy time to clean up." To Adam she said, "Come on, I'll show you where everything is."

He followed her upstairs, where she opened a door off the landing. "You'll be in here," she said. Adam looked in, saw a neat little room with a single bed and a chest of drawers. "And the bathroom's down here." Along the landing was a tiled bathroom with a shower. Mellow didn't explain any of the other doors on the landing, but she opened one and it turned out to be a cupboard. She took out a couple of fresh towels out and handed them to him. "The shower's a bit weedy because the pump's not very powerful," she said. "But there's plenty of hot water. I'll be downstairs when you're done."

"Thank you," he said.

"I'll see if I can find some old clothes of Dad's that'll fit you," she said. "Those you've got on are a bit stinky."

"I stopped noticing," he said, because he had.

"Yes, well, trust me, they're stinky."

"This is quite an unusual way of doing things, if you don't mind me saying."

Mellow shrugged. "Nobody's told me what to do with you," she said. "The alternative's locking you up in a cell." She turned and walked away towards the stairs. "And I want my roof fixed."

As ADVERTISED, THE water pressure wasn't very great, but it was very hot and there was a lot of it. Adam soaped himself and rinsed, watched a lot of grime go down the drain of the shower, repeated the process. While he was drying himself, he opened the door of the bathroom cabinet and peeked inside, but all it contained was a couple of wrapped bars of soap, a razor, and a toothbrush.

In the bedroom, there was a little pile of neatly folded clothes on the bed, underwear, jeans, a black t-shirt and a sweater. The jeans and sweater were a little too big, but they were clean and fresh and he wasn't going to complain.

He went back downstairs and followed the sound of voices down the corridor to an airy kitchen with a big range and lots of cupboards. A big saucepan was simmering on the range. Mellow was sitting at a table in the middle of the room, talking to her father, and they looked round as Adam came in.

"Well, that's an improvement," Jack said. "Come and sit down. We were just talking about you."

Neatly lined up on one of the worktops were a belt holster with a small automatic pistol, a little leather wallet, a bunch of keys, and a radio of a design he was unfamiliar with. The gun was so obviously a test that Adam didn't even consider making a grab for it. He walked across the kitchen to the table, pulled up a chair, and sat.

"It looks like you've caused my daughter a bit of a problem," Jack told him.

"It's not his fault, Dad," Mellow said. "Leave him alone."

"I didn't mean to cause anyone any trouble," Adam said. "I was only looking for work."

"And I'm sorry you didn't get a better welcome," Jack said. "We weren't always like this."

"Dad," Mellow sighed. She got up and went over to the range and lifted the lid of the saucepan.

"Well, I'll not turn you away," said Jack. "You're welcome in my house."

"Thank you," Adam said. "You're very kind."

Jack waved it away. "Can you think why they let you through the checkpoint?"

Adam looked at him, at Mellow, who was stirring the soup, back to Jack. "I don't know," he said. "Is that unusual?"

"I'll say. We haven't let any outsiders into the city for... how long is it, Leonie? Two years? Three?"

"Closer to two," she said, without looking round.

"Why not?" Adam asked.

Jack pulled a sour face. "Chancellery says we're *full*."

"We're not remotely full, Dad," Mellow said. "It's about resources. They say we can't support a larger population at the moment."

"*They* say," Jack muttered.

Adam said, "The people at the checkpoint said you were expecting me," and he saw Mellow's shoulders move as she sighed.

Jack looked over his shoulder at her. "Haven't you told him?"

Mellow didn't say anything, just went on stirring the soup.

"Told me what?" Adam asked.

"I think this is ready," Mellow said, moving the pan to the edge of the range, away from the heat. "Do you want to eat in here?"

"No," Jack said after a moment. "Let's use the dining room for a change. I'll set the table." He wheeled himself out of the door and into the hallway.

"Told me what?" Adam asked again.

Mellow took a ladle from its hook beside the range. "There's a tureen in that cupboard," she said, gesturing. "Could you get it for me, please?"

Adam got up from the table, opened the cupboard, found a big white pottery tureen with a lid. He took it out and put it beside the pan.

"Thank you," Mellow said.

"Told me what, inspector?"

She sighed and laid the tureen lid to one side, started ladling soup into it. "On Monday we got a memo from Chancellery that someone was coming to the city and they were to be let through whatever checkpoint they turned up at. My boss decided he wanted to know what that was all about, so he told me to have whoever it was detained and questioned." She shrugged. "Now you know as much as I do."

Adam thought about it. "You've definitely got the wrong person," he said finally. "I have no idea about any of that."

"Hm. Well, here we are, anyway. Carry this through for me, would you? I'll bring the bread and butter."

By the time they got to the dining room, Jack had laid out three places at one end of the dining table and had managed to transfer himself from his wheelchair to a chair at the head of the table. Putting the tureen on the table, Adam looked around the room. Through a pair of French windows at the end, he could see rain lashing down on the back garden in the growing dusk. There was a big dark wooden sideboard against one wall, with a pair of silver candlesticks on it, and on the wall above that were two dozen or so framed photographs, all of them of men and women in various versions of police uniform and some of them very old.

Jack saw him looking. "There's been Mellows in the Thames Valley force for over a hundred and fifty years," he said. "Although Leonie's our first senior officer."

"Senior," Mellow snorted as she began to ladle soup from the tureen into bowls.

Adam looked along the rows of photographs and finally spotted a younger version of Jack in a uniform quite different to the one being worn by the Oxford police these days.

"I'm sorry it's just soup," Jack said. "If you'd turned up a day earlier you could have had some roast chicken."

"Don't apologise," Adam told him, coming back to the table and sitting down. "It looks great." And it did; there were pieces of chicken and bacon and carrot and potato and peas floating in it, and it smelled wonderful. "I can't remember the last time I had a proper sit-down dinner." He supposed it had been at Betty

Coghlan's house, the evening before he left for the Parish, the last evening of a better, more innocent time.

"So," Jack said, "what's Southampton like?"

"Just getting by," Adam said, sticking to his story because he still wasn't sure about the Mellows. He'd spent some time in Southampton a couple of years before, so at least he could make it sound convincing. A thousand or so people had settled in the eastern outskirts of the city. Some of them farmed, but most of them scratched a living salvaging building materials and trading them with communities further along the coast. The Bureau, he was sure, had noted them for future plans. "Everyone's just getting by."

"Is it all like that south of here?"

"A lot of the smaller places are doing all right. I've been to Brighton a couple of times, there's not a lot of people there but they seem to have their act together. They say there are people in Kent, but I don't know about that."

"How did you come to be here, then?"

Adam shrugged. "I thought I'd see what things were like inland and I just kept on moving north. I've done a lot of farm work." He filled a glass from a jug of water on the table. "I was in Newbury for a while, doing odd jobs. Newbury's all right, they've got things pretty well organised there."

"How about the Chilterns?" Mellow asked casually, cutting herself a slice of bread from the loaf.

He was on safe ground making up stuff about his supposed work in Hampshire and the Downs, less so as he got nearer to Oxford. "I went through Streatley," he said. He took a drink of water. "Didn't stop."

"Abingdon?" asked Jack.

"I wasn't there long. They didn't seem very friendly."

Mellow snorted. "That's Abingdon for you."

Jack scratched his head. "Well, it's a long way to walk to wind up being arrested."

"He's not been arrested, Dad. He's sitting here eating dinner with us."

"I was handcuffed for a while," Adam reminded her.

Mellow shook her head. "Not the same. I keep telling you."

They ate quietly for a while, the only sound the rain pounding down outside. Adam asked, "What's this 'Chancellery' everyone keeps talking about? The people who run Oxford?"

Jack snorted. "They like to think they do."

"Do you always turn up at a strange town without doing your homework first?" Mellow asked.

Adam shrugged. "There's usually someone who'll know if there's work in the next place."

"And somebody in Abingdon told you there was work here?" Jack chortled and shook his head. "I think someone was pulling your leg, son."

"Obviously." Adam finished his soup, looked at the bowl, and said, "Is it okay if I have some more? I'm starving."

Mellow waved her spoon at the tureen.

"Anyway," he said, ladling more soup into his bowl. "All I ever wanted was a couple of weeks' work. Whose business is that?"

"I don't know," Mellow said. She beamed at him. "Maybe tomorrow they'll change their mind and they'll tell me to arrest you properly."

WHEN DINNER WAS finished, Adam and Mellow did the washing up and then she went to get her father settled in his bedroom next to the dining room.

"It used to be the study," she said, "but he doesn't do stairs anymore."

While she was doing that, Adam went back into the dining room and took a closer look at the photographs on the wall. None of them was dated, but if Jack had been telling the truth the oldest-looking ones must have been at least a century and a half old, generations of young police officers standing stiffly in their uniforms, sometimes in groups, sometimes singly, and staring seriously into the camera. If these were all Mellows – and the family resemblance was so marked that he could spot them even in class photos – they had been a mainstay of the Oxford Police for decades.

He leaned in close to look at the photo of Jack, a tall, gawky youth in a uniform that looked as if it had been put together from military surplus. His hair was cut short, and he was carrying a pistol in a holster on his hip, looking out from that distance of, what, thirty years? forty? with an expression of determination which Adam was learning to recognise.

"I'm going to turn in," Mellow said from the doorway. "I've got an early start tomorrow. Nothing to do with you."

"Yes," he said. "Me too."

"There are tools in the shed and there's a little pile of spare tiles I managed to find. Dad'll show you where everything is." She looked at him. "I'm going to trust you not to do anything stupid. All the main roads out of town are guarded, and all the minor roads are blocked and there are patrols, but it's not hard to slip by if you make a bit of an effort."

"But if I did that, you'd be in trouble with your superiors."

"To be honest, I don't know. But let's proceed as if I would be, yes?"

Adam smiled and looked at the photos again. "Why isn't there one of you here?" he asked.

"Never had time," she said, a little too carelessly. "I'll get round to it eventually. Goodnight, Mr Hardy."

"Goodnight, inspector."

He heard her walk down the corridor, and then up the stairs. He went quietly into the kitchen. The gun, keys and radio were gone, but the little wallet was still on the worktop. He lifted it open with a fingertip. Inside was a metal disc with a crown and the number 1072 stamped on it. Did that mean there were more than a thousand police officers in Oxford? Pretty much everywhere else in the country, a thousand people was a potential army.

Upstairs, he undressed and got into bed. It was the first real bed he'd been in in weeks and he should have fallen asleep almost immediately, but he lay staring up at the ceiling.

How could we not have known about this? Well, the answer was, of course, *we did*. The authorities here used radio. Guz had a radio unit staffed twenty-four hours a day, scanning frequencies for news from the rest of the world and keeping in touch with its fleet of boats. The Bureau had a similar, smaller unit to stay in contact with its people out in the field. Oxford's radios might not have been powerful enough to be picked up in Devon, but Betty Coghlan was only a few miles to the south and he knew she had a radio setup. It seemed absurd to think she hadn't been listening in to the transmissions of the Oxford police, and absurd to think she hadn't told Chrissie about them. That Chrissie hadn't told *him* was so normal that it wasn't even a surprise.

The business about the authorisation to let him – to let *somebody,* at any rate – into the city was a worry. The Bureau's radios were scrambled, but if someone was able to unscramble the transmissions, they would have heard him reporting to Chrissie and known he was coming. So, was it a coincidence, or had his cover been blown before he'd even arrived? And if it had, why make an exception for him and let him through the checkpoint?

Still, however confusing it was, he had been in Oxford for less than a day and he'd already made contact with the authorities and begun to get a sense of how the place was organised, along with a large amount of incidental intelligence, which he thought was not a bad day's work.

And there was also, he thought as he finally started to nod off, the fact that he had never, not once, seen a photograph taken after the fall of the Sisters.

* * *

THE NEXT MORNING, he followed the smell of frying bacon downstairs to the kitchen, where he found Jack making breakfast.

"Bacon and eggs?" Jack asked.

"Yes, please. Can I help?"

"No, I can cope. Sit down."

Adam pulled out a chair and sat at the table. Through the kitchen windows, it looked as if it had stopped raining for a while.

"Leonie had to go out early," said Jack.

"Yes, she mentioned it last night. Nothing serious, I hope."

"She's busy with a couple of investigations."

There was a teapot under a cosy on the table. Adam put his hand against it and felt the warmth. "Do you have a big police force?"

"Bigger than it used to be. Come and get this, would you?" He put bacon and a couple of fried eggs on a plate and held it out. Adam got up and took it back to the table. Jack filled another plate, put it on his lap, rolled backwards down the ramp in front of the range, and wheeled up to the table. "How many police do you have in Southampton?"

In Guz, each area of the city had a small group of civilian constables, to enforce the curfew and deal with minor crime. For anything more serious, there were Marines, of which there were many. "We don't have any police at all," he said. "We sort things out among ourselves."

"Well, that's no good, is it?" Jack said, tucking into his breakfast. "That's just asking for trouble."

Adam thought about the Parish, where the presence of some kind of authorities might have stopped things before they went too far. "We manage," he said.

"There were five or six thousand officers back before the Sisters," Jack went on. "But the force covered a much bigger area back then. Afterwards, well, it was every man for himself. I expect it was the same where you're from."

Thinking about it now, the discipline of the garrison at HMS Drake must have been fearsome, keeping order in Plymouth when the world was falling apart. They'd never quite got out of the habit. "I expect it was the same everywhere," Adam said.

Jack took the cosy off the teapot and poured tea into two mugs. "Can I give you a bit of advice?"

Adam looked up from his breakfast. "Of course."

"When you get a chance, leave. Go back to Southampton, maybe."

"Why?"

Jack shook his head. "You'll see, if you stay long enough. You already attracted someone's attention, and that's never good."

Adam thought about it. "I don't seem to have a choice, right now."

Jack looked at him. "You know, I was a copper for nearly thirty years, and I've seen a lot of people. Most of them were just confused or desperate or angry. Some of them were bad. Properly bad. You?" He went back to his bacon and eggs. "You, I can't tell what you are."

"Mostly confused."

Jack smiled. "I don't think you're confused at all."

"I'm just looking for work," Adam said.

"You keep on saying that," said Jack. "And I keep on not knowing whether to believe you or not."

There was a silence, while they got on with breakfast. After a while, Adam said, "What happened to your...?" He gestured at the stubs of Jack's legs. "If you don't mind me asking."

Jack considered answering. "That was one of the angry people I was talking about," he said finally. "Lad called Lawrence Marsh. He and his brother made a living stripping electrical cable out of old office buildings and trading the copper on. They had a row about something, we never found out what, and Lawrence hit his brother with a lump hammer, killed him stone dead. He was too dim to leave the city; we found him hiding in Cowley, eventually, and instead of coming quietly he decided to shoot me in the legs." He shrugged. "Maybe the little shit thought he was being kind not shooting me in the face. Anyway, he wound up hanged and I wound up with these." He tapped one of his stumps with the handle of his knife.

Medical care in Oxford must be outstanding; in almost every part of the country Adam had visited an injury like that would have been fatal. "I'm sorry," he said.

"I tried to carry on," Jack went on. "They got me a job at force HQ, sitting at a desk and doing paperwork, but *I* started to get angry, so I stopped going in to work." He looked at Adam. "Leonie's worked hard to get where she is," he said. "I wouldn't like it if someone did something to hurt her prospects."

"Well, obviously," said Adam.

Jack looked at him a moment longer, then backed his chair away from the table. "Leave your plate. I want to show you something."

They went into the dining room and Jack stopped in front of the wall with the photographs. He pointed at one, a water-stained and warped photo of a young man in old-fashioned police uniform. He looked about fourteen, but he was recognisably a Mellow.

"That's my grandad," Jack said. "Taken two years before The Sisters. He was about twenty-one; he'd been with the force for a year, straight out of university. My dad would have been a year old. Young man with a young family, just starting out on his career, then *wallop*."

"How did they survive?" asked Adam.

Jack shrugged. "We were lucky here. None of the Sisters came down anywhere near us, so at least the city was in one piece, but everything else fell apart. They say London was destroyed, is that true?"

Adam had never been to London, but he'd seen reports from people who had. "So I heard."

"Well, the government was wiped out, the regional authorities couldn't cope, there was no electricity, nobody knew what had happened. It was chaos. Looting, fighting. Like I said, every man for himself. A lot of people left; I suppose they thought they stood a better chance out in the countryside, Christ only knows why. Some of the old folks, they'll tell you it was their finest hour. Everybody stayed at home and looked after their neighbours and sang songs to keep their spirits up, and I don't doubt some of that did happen. But mostly it was awful."

Adam went over to the table, pulled out one of the chairs, and sat down.

"And that went on for years," Jack said, still looking at his grandfather's photograph. "Years and years and years. People died of disease or starvation or the weather or just because it never stopped." He sighed and tugged at his chair's wheels to turn it to face Adam, sat back and folded his hands in his lap. "One big advantage we had was the University. We had a lot of very very clever people here, people with practical knowledge, and not all of them left. Some of the Colleges fortified themselves, the ones that could. Eventually, the University authorities decided that if nobody else was going to take charge, they'd have to do it themselves, so they set up what became Chancellery. There were about two hundred police officers left by then, and some soldiers who'd come from Christ only knows where, and they started to organise. We still almost went under; at one point there weren't much more than two thousand people in Oxford."

"There's a lot more than two thousand people here now," Adam pointed out.

Jack looked at him and tipped his head to one side. "You're not from Southampton, are you?"

I can't teach you who to trust, sir, one of his instructors had told him, years ago. *You'll either know or you won't, and if you don't know it's best to stay schtumm. On the other hand, sometimes you just have to wing it.* Adam looked at Jack and didn't say anything.

Jack's face took on a sour expression. "Chancellery's not like it used to be. The city's not like it used to be. If you had any sense you'd go back where you came from, wherever that is, and you'd tell whoever sent you to stay well clear of us."

They looked at each other for quite a while without speaking. Finally, Jack heaved a sigh and looked at the window. "I'll show you where everything is, and you can take care of the roof."

"Yes," Adam said, wondering what the fuck was going on here. "Yes, let's get that done before it starts raining again."

As IT TURNED out, only a couple of the roof tiles were actually missing. The rest had just been shifted by recent storms, and it only took him an hour or so to reseat them and replace the missing ones.

He was just finishing when he heard the sound of horse's hooves on the street below, and when he looked down, he saw a cart driven by a uniformed constable pulling up outside the house. Mellow was sitting beside the driver.

"Get down here," she called up.

"I haven't finished yet," he told her, just to see what would happen.

"You have now," she said. "Get down here or I'll come up and get you."

He was tempted to stay where he was, just to see her do that, but instead he got the tools together and climbed down the ladder and stood looking at the cart.

"Get in," Mellow said.

"Why?"

"Because I say so. Get in."

He held up the tools. "I'll just put these in the shed."

"Leave them there," she told him. "Get in."

Adam put the tools on the path beside the house, walked into the street, and climbed up into the back of the cart and sat down.

"Hand," Mellow snapped.

"What?"

"Hold your hand out. Do as you're told."

"What's going on?"

"Just hold your fucking hand out." Adam held out his hand, and Mellow handcuffed his wrist and snapped the other cuff to the seat bracket. She nodded to the driver. "Go."

They went back across the Cherwell and drove into the city centre, but they didn't stop at police headquarters. Instead, they carried on, across the Thames ferry and onto the Botley road.

"Where are we going?" Adam asked at one point, but Mellow just sat staring straight ahead and didn't answer. Adam gave the handcuffs an experimental tug, but he wasn't going anywhere without the cart, so he sat back and watched the city go by. Presently, it started to drizzle. Adam, who had taken his coat off because it was getting in his way clambering about on Mellow's roof, scowled up at the clouds.

By the time they were descending Cumnor Hill, he was wondering if they weren't going to throw him out of Oxford. Would they do that? Without a coat? Without giving him his rucksack back? He realised he couldn't guess; something weird and unpredictable was going on here. *How could we not have known about this?* Well, one reason could be that the community that had built itself in Oxford had isolated itself from the outside world, turning outsiders away. *The city's not like it used to be*, Jack had said. And someone had patiently, quietly, been depopulating the countryside to the south, creating a deserted buffer zone so there were no locals to spread the word that it was no longer like it was. Had they been doing that to the north and east and west, too? That was Guz-level planning, the kind of planning that other communities were just too busy trying to survive to even contemplate. Even Frank Pendennis, with his thousands of vassals down in Thanet, wasn't doing anything like this.

Eventually, they approached the checkpoint where Adam had come into the city the day before. Looking past Mellow, he could see a rope stretched across the road at chest height some distance from the checkpoint proper. The driver pulled the horse to a halt just before the rope, and Mellow climbed into the back of the cart, undid the handcuff from the seat bracket, and closed it around her wrist.

"Out," she said.

Together, they clambered awkwardly over the side of the cart and stood in the road. He opened his mouth to say something, but she ducked under the rope and marched off down the road, tugging him along behind her. Glancing back, he saw that the driver had also dismounted and was following at a discreet distance. Neither of them, he noted, were armed, but the people coming up the road towards them were. Not police, though, something altogether more dangerous. There were four of them, and they were dressed in black combat suits not unlike the ones Guz's Marines wore. They were carrying automatic rifles and they looked deadly serious. They stopped a few yards away and then moved to one side when Mellow flashed her badge at them and stomped by towing Adam.

There were things lying in the road around the checkpoint. They looked like piles of rags until Mellow and Adam got closer and he saw they were people. There was blood everywhere, being slowly washed off the road by the drizzle. Passing one body, Adam saw that the top of its head was a single raw wound. The face of another was a landscape of bloody meat and bone.

Mellow came to a stop, breathing hard. "Is this anything to do with you?" she said in a low voice.

"No," he said. "I don't know anything about this." There were three bodies in the road, another slumped over the threshold of the shed.

"Are you sure?" Mellow said. "Because you came through here yesterday afternoon and sometime during the night someone did this."

He shook his head. "I had nothing to do with this." He looked about him again. "They were all alive when I left here yesterday, and I've been with you ever since."

She was watching his face, trying to decide whether she believed him or not. "You know the worst thing I ever saw?" she asked, and Adam realised she was only keeping her voice level by an effort of will. "Man killed his wife and daughter. Beat his wife to death with a chair leg and smothered the little girl with a cushion and then he cut his own throat. We never found out why. That was the worst thing. Until Monday."

He glanced at her. "What happened on Monday?"

"Never you mind," she said tightly.

He walked over to one of the bodies and squatted down at the edge of the huge pool of blood in which it lay. It was a young man, and his throat had been cut so deeply he had almost been decapitated. There were two bloody holes in the front of his poncho. Adam said, "Have they all been shot?"

"Most of them," Mellow said.

He looked at the boy's body again. "He's been shot twice in the chest," he said. "There was no reason to cut his throat, too." He looked down the hill, remembering the Parish. "That one we passed was scalped. Whoever did this, they did it while these people were either dead or dying. As if just killing them wasn't enough."

Mellow looked down at him. "You're no wandering handyman," she said, too quietly for the watching militia to hear her.

"It doesn't matter what I am," he said. He put his weight on the handcuffs and hauled himself to his feet. "Something bad was here. You have a real problem, inspector."

She looked at him for a few moments, then she turned and started to walk back to the cart, pulling him along behind her. "Yes," she said. "Yes, I do."

ELEVEN

THIS TIME, THEY put him in a cell. The cells were on the top floor of police headquarters, repurposed offices with heavy solid wooden doors with multiple locks and no keyholes on the inside. They didn't remove the handcuffs, which he thought was overdoing it a bit. His cell was bare of furniture apart from a stained mattress on the floor and a metal bucket in one corner with a splash of disinfectant in the bottom, but at least it had a window, with bars mounted on the inside and the outside, through which he could look down on the rain pouring into the street. It would have been quite straightforward to escape, if he had been able to remove the bolts holding the bars on the inside with his bare fingers, smash the window, remove the bars on the outside, and climb five floors down the outside of the building.

They had taken his clothes and given him a pair of old blue overalls that were baggy in the seat but too short in the leg. They had fingerprinted him and plucked hairs from his head and beard, scraped under his fingernails and taken clippings. He had watched, fascinated, while someone took a blood sample. And then they had stood him against a wall and someone had come in and photographed him. He had never seen a camera before outside of old books; it was a piece of pre-Sisters technology which Guz hadn't managed to recreate, either because it lacked the requisite raw materials or because there were more important things to do. This one, a box on a tall tripod, looked bulky and overcomplicated and composed of spare parts from several other devices, but the technician who was using it handled it with all the reverence of a religious relic.

He stood at the window for a long time. From this height, he could see that all the buildings on the other side of the street had wind turbines mounted on their roofs, and as the afternoon wore on and dusk started to fall lights began to come on in their windows. It was full dark, though, before the light suddenly came on in his cell.

Eventually, he heard rattling sounds as the door was unlocked, and he turned from the window as someone outside opened it, a uniformed sergeant. "Come on," said the sergeant.

"Where?"

"Wherever I tell you, you cunt," the sergeant said. "Now move."

Adam walked over to the door and the sergeant retreated into the corridor. Adam looked out and saw two more officers, both armed with shotguns, standing a safe distance along the corridor. One of them gestured with his gun, and with the sergeant leading the way and the two armed officers bringing up the rear, Adam went down several flights of stairs and along another corridor to an interview room.

"Sit," the sergeant told him, pointing at one of the chairs at the table in the middle of the room.

Adam sat, and while one of the armed officers stood in the open doorway the sergeant unlocked one of the handcuffs and attached it to the chair. Then he straightened up and hit Adam in the face hard enough to snap his head to one side and make him see stars. Adam sat up straight and tried to blink the pain away, and the sergeant hit him again. Then he turned and left the room, closing and locking the door behind him. Adam reached up with his free hand and touched his face gingerly. He gave the handcuffs an experimental tug, but the chair felt solid, and he saw that it was bolted to the floor, as was the table.

He sat there for a long time. At one point, the door was unlocked and Chief Superintendent Maxwell stood in the doorway and looked at him for a minute or so without saying anything before closing the door and locking it again.

Again, he waited a long time. Eventually, he heard the door being unlocked, and when it opened a tall, thin man about his age came into the room carrying two tin mugs, one of them with a plate balanced on top with a sandwich on it. He had a cardboard folder clamped under one arm. Someone outside in the corridor closed the door behind him and locked it again.

"I thought you might want something to eat," he said, putting the mug with the plate on it in front of Adam. "I knew they wouldn't feed you." He put his mug down on the table, placed the folder beside it, and pulled out the other chair. "What happened to your face?"

Adam sat staring at him.

He leaned to one side and looked at Adam's wrist handcuffed to the chair, and a look of anger crossed his face. He got up from the chair and went over and banged on the door. When it was opened, he pointed at Adam and said to the constable standing there, "Who did this?"

The constable looked at Adam. "Did what, sir?"

The man grabbed the constable by his lapels and dragged him into the room. "This," he said, pointing again. "Who struck this man?"

The constable tried to step away, but the man had too firm a grip on him. "Don't know."

"Don't know what?"

"Don't know, *sir*." The constable looked as if he would happily punch him.

The man looked at Adam. "Did this officer strike you?"

Adam shook his head.

"Did another officer strike you?"

Adam looked at them.

"Right," said the man, bodily shoving the constable across the room. "Undo those handcuffs, we're not bloody animals."

Grudgingly, the constable took a bunch of keys from his pocket, selected one, and unlocked the cuffs from Adam's wrist and the chair.

"Now get out," the man snapped. When the constable didn't move, he shouted, "Out! Now!"

When the constable had left the room, and the door was locked again, the man resumed his seat opposite Adam. He seemed perfectly calm again. "They lost four of their colleagues this morning," he said. "That's no excuse, of course." It was, Adam noted, also not an apology. "I'm Richard Hob, by the way."

"And what do you do?" Adam asked.

Hob opened the folder in front of him. "Too bloody much, between you and me." He was clean-shaven and balding, his hair a close-cropped narrow fringe that ran around the back of his head from just above his ears. He was wearing jeans and a white shirt with the sleeves rolled up to the elbows, and he had a pinched, sour face. He sorted through the sheets of paper in the folder. "Well," he said without looking up, "the samples we took are still being tested, and that will take a little time. Detective Inspector Mellow is of the opinion that you weren't involved in today's... incident, though." He looked up. "You're not eating."

Adam stared at him.

Hob waved at the plate. "Eat. It's only ham and cheese, but it's better than nothing." When Adam didn't move, he reached over and took the plate. "Well, I didn't have any lunch." He bit into one of the sandwiches, then looked down and brushed crumbs off the top sheet of paper in the folder. "You're from Southampton, yes?"

"Yes."

Hob sat back in his chair and took another bite of sandwich. "You know, I don't remember anyone from the coast coming this far north before. What's the travelling like?"

"Some of it's not too bad," Adam said. "Some of it's rough."

"But you kept going. Through the rough bits. Obviously you did, or you wouldn't be here, would you?" He looked at the folder, turned over the top sheet, looked at the next one. "You know," he said, "we still haven't been able to find out who gave the order to let you through that checkpoint yesterday."

"Who's 'we'?" asked Adam, but he was beginning to get an idea.

Hob shrugged. "Colleagues." He looked at Adam. "Chief Superintendent Maxwell says he got a message that someone was coming and they were to be let through. From Chancellery, he says, but he doesn't know from who in Chancellery." He raised his eyebrows. "Any ideas?"

"Shouldn't that be 'from *whom*'?"

Hob beamed happily at him. He looked down and sorted through the sheets of paper in the folder again, extracted one and held it up by one corner. He showed it to Adam. "Official Chancellery notepaper," he said. "Everything set out properly. Signature's just a scrawl, but that doesn't matter because everything *looks* right. I'm afraid the chief superintendent's in the doghouse about this, rather. He should have checked before issuing any orders."

Adam shook his head. "It doesn't say anything about me; it could be about anyone."

"You're the only outsider who's tried to come into the city this week."

Now that was an interesting little piece of information. Even in Margate there were always people coming and going, mostly to trade. The ones who came looking for work or shelter tended not to leave again because Margate was basically a huge trap, but that didn't stop them coming.

"What's that?" Adam asked, nodding at a red smudge at the bottom of the sheet of paper.

"Chancellor's Seal," Hob said, turning the paper round and looking at it. "It isn't really, of course. The impression would be sharper if it was, but Chief Superintendent Maxwell didn't bother to look properly. He must be a *terrible* detective." He laid the paper back in the folder. "Inspector Mellow's in the doghouse, too, I'm afraid."

"She didn't do anything wrong," Adam said.

Hob looked at him. "She *took you home*, Mr Hardy. I can understand her not clarifying her orders – Maxwell isn't the kind of superior who encourages that kind of thing – but taking you home for the night?" Hob shook his head sadly.

"I got the impression nobody told her not to."

"Inspector Mellow's an experienced officer," said Hob. "She's a bit of a star, actually, between you and me. She should have known better."

"What's going to happen to her?"

Hob looked at Adam and smiled faintly. "Oh, nothing, I expect." He looked into the corner, as if to confirm this. "No, nothing. She's too good an officer to lose. I expect someone will have a quiet word with her, make sure it doesn't happen again, that kind of thing. How rough were they?"

"What?"

"You said some bits of the journey here were rough. How rough were they?"

Adam blinked at him. "Some of it was very rough."

"Not bad enough to stop you, though. Where was this? Which bits?"

"The country between Winchester and Basingstoke's hard going. It got better once I was on the Downs."

"Do you mind if I send someone to have a chat with you about that? Help us fill in our maps a little bit?"

Adam shrugged, wondering where this was going. "Go ahead."

"There was a big Naval base down there, wasn't there? Near Southampton?"

"Portsmouth. It's gone, a Sister came down on it."

"There must have been some things left, though. Equipment, weapons, ships."

"Maybe there was, but it was all looted years ago. There's nothing left there now but scrap metal."

"Still, that's useful, isn't it?" Hob sat back and rubbed his eyes. He looked at the remaining sandwich. "Are you sure you don't want that?" Adam shook his head and Hob picked it up and took a bite. "I keep thinking we ought to send someone down there, have a look at what's left of Portsmouth."

Adam wasn't sure that would end well for the people still living in Southampton, or anywhere in between. He said, "I never had much to do with the place, myself."

"I've never seen the sea, you know. I think I'd quite like that."

"It's just a lot of water. Nothing special."

"Can you see France from there?"

Adam shook his head.

"What do you think's going on over there?"

In recent years, Guz had started cautiously making landings on the French coast between Roscoff and Saint Malo, and all they had found was a string of derelict towns ruined by flooding and the weather. If anyone had survived the Sisters, they had all withdrawn inland. He said, "If it's as bad as over here, they're barely getting by."

Hob looked at him. "We're not 'barely getting by'," he said. "Maybe you are down in Southampton, but I think we're doing pretty well here, under the circumstances."

"You all look well-fed, it's true," Adam said.

Hob looked at the sandwich in his hand, put it back on the plate. "Oxford is an island, Mr Hardy," he said. "Everyone here can read and write, we have industries manufacturing everything from socks to wind generators, we're reclaiming and rebuilding the city." He gestured at the door. "What have you got out there? A few illiterate farmers who can't even count to ten without using their fingers. This is already the biggest city in the country; in ten or twenty years it'll be the capital of England."

Adam's view was that 'England' had ceased to exist one summer day almost a century ago. Certainly as something that needed a capital, anyway. He said, "I've met a lot of illiterate farmers, and not one of them ever arrested me."

Hob sucked his teeth. "What do you think happened at that checkpoint?"

"I don't know what happened."

"You said to Inspector Mellow..." Hob leafed through the folder until he found the sheet of paper he wanted. "...'Something bad was here.' Why did you say that?"

"I'd have thought that was obvious."

"How many people do you think were involved?"

"I have no idea."

"Come on, you must be able to make a guess." He looked at Adam. "There were four well-armed and well-trained people at that checkpoint and they're all dead. Butchered. How many people do you think it would take to overpower a group like that?"

Adam shrugged. "I have no idea."

Hob sorted through his pages again. "You'd think that was quite a gunfight, wouldn't you? People blazing away at each other. But some of the locals heard gunshots around dawn this morning, and more than one of them says it didn't sound like two groups firing at each other. They say it sounded more like one weapon, two at the most." He looked at Adam.

"I don't know," Adam said.

"Also, whatever happened, nobody at the checkpoint had time to raise the alarm. Nobody called in to ask for help."

They looked at each other for a while.

"Can I go now?" asked Adam.

Hob raised an eyebrow. "Go? God no."

"I only came looking for work."

Hob started to sort his papers into order. "Perhaps you did. Perhaps you're an innocent bystander and that forged order to let you into the city was a matter of mistaken identity. Perhaps the murders in Cumnor this morning were a coincidence." He put the papers into the folder and closed the cover. "But until we're sure, you're not going anywhere. And you're not going back to Inspector Mellow's either. I'd rather keep you here. For your own safety."

Adam wondered quite how safe that was.

Hob got up and went to the door. "There's another thing you said to the inspector," he said. "Something about her having a real problem. What did you mean by that?"

Adam looked at him, wondering how senior he was, how sophisticated the organisation he represented was. "Whoever killed those people, they're in the city now," he said.

Hob considered that. Then he started going through the folders in his hands. "That's a good point," he said, coming back to the table. "And while we're on that subject, do you know anything about this?" He took a photograph from one of the folders and put it in front of Adam.

Adam sat forward and looked down at the image. For a long moment, he couldn't work out what he was seeing; the picture was grainy and weirdly lit and there were no obvious points of reference. Then his mind suddenly sorted it out and he sat back involuntarily. "Jesus Christ."

Hob was watching him carefully. "Anything?" he asked.

"No. What the fuck is this?"

"Are you sure?"

Adam looked cautiously at the photograph again. It was an image of a prone figure, its face smashed and blackened, a long metal rod protruding from its chest. "What the fuck is wrong with you?" he demanded. "I had nothing to do with this."

Hob waited a couple of seconds, then he took back the photograph and returned it to its folder. "When those people were killed at Cumnor, you were tucked up at Inspector Mellow's home, so it seems unlikely that you were *personally* involved," he said. "But we found this poor sod a couple of days ago, when you were still unaccounted for." He hugged the folders to his chest and tipped his head to one side.

Adam glared at him. "Fuck off," he said. "Just fuck off."

Hob shrugged and went back to the door and thumped his fist on it. "I'll have someone come and chat with you about your trip from Southampton," he said as the door was unlocked and opened. "It might be a couple of days, though. Still, you weren't planning to go anywhere, were you?"

Adam stared at him, and after he was gone he stared at the door. He was still staring when they came to take him back up to his cell.

TWELVE

Morty's problem was that he didn't know for sure where he was.

It wasn't his only problem by a long way, but it was starting to nag him in a way that felt unfamiliar and somehow disorientating. He thought he might be in Oxford – it was certainly a big place – but his knowledge of the landscape to the north and the west of the Chilterns was sketchy and mostly based on bits and pieces of gossip he'd overheard in the Parish. Names like Oxford and Lechlade and Abingdon and Didcot were just meaningless words, no suggestion of what they were like, no way to tell them apart, no real idea of where exactly they were. He couldn't read any old road signs he came across, and asking someone was out of the question. He should have thought to ask his host, but it was too late now.

He knew what lay to the south of the hills, because he and Karen had come up that way from Southampton, and he had some idea of the east because he'd been to Goring on market day, on the odd occasions when his ruin of a farm had produced anything worth trading. Beyond that, places like Aylesbury and

High Wycombe were just names, and Dunstable might as well have been on the edge of the world.

"Stupid cunt," said the head. "You should have stayed where you were."

From his nest of blankets on the bed, Morty looked across the room at the little table on which he had set the head. "You talk too much," he told it. He was practicing speaking, because he suspected he was going to have to talk to people at some point, and it would be important to be convincing.

"Fuck you," said the head. "If it wasn't for me, you wouldn't be talking to *anybody*."

Morty had placed a candle beside the head, and when the flame flickered it made it look as if the head's lips were moving slightly, but it was an illusion that was getting harder to maintain. The head was starting to show signs of wear and tear, quite apart from the fact that it wasn't connected to a body anymore. The nose and jaw had been broken in the process of forcibly separating it from Albie Dodd, and one of its ears had gone missing, Morty couldn't remember how. It was going all manner of odd colours as it rotted, and liquefying flesh was falling off in places. Still, apart from his guns and the clothes he stood up in, it was the only souvenir Morty had from the Parish. He'd had to leave the rest of his collection behind; it was just too bulky to carry across country.

He got up from the bed and went downstairs to the kitchen. He'd made a casserole with a chicken and some vegetables he'd found in the larder yesterday, and there was still quite a lot left in the pot. He checked the range, then put the pot on the hob to heat up. Morty was actually quite a good cook; he'd had to be, because Karen had never once lifted a finger to do any housework. Morty didn't like to think about that time, and he was beginning to think he might have imagined it.

It hadn't been all that difficult to follow Wayland across the Vale of the White Horse, though the weather had been terrible and the terrain rough. In fact, at times he thought it was almost *too* easy. Wayland didn't seem to care whether anyone was trailing him, just plodded slowly along through the wind and the rain, and it wasn't hard to keep track of him because he was the only thing moving in the sodden, boggy landscape.

Morty would never have chosen to live down here; there were patches of bogland in the Parish, but in general the high ground was well-drained. People did live here, though. Or at least, they had. Wayland stopped at a couple of deserted farms and had a look around, and after he moved on Morty did the same, but they were just empty compounds and abandoned farmhouses. There were no supplies, no food, no useful tools.

Where there was no alternative, Wayland pitched a tent at night, and Morty found what shelter he could nearby. But his quarry mostly seemed to prefer sheltering in ruined houses. Not the deserted farmhouses, Morty noted, which were in good repair, but properly ruined houses, overgrown and half-collapsed. One night, Morty screwed up his courage and crept into one house and stood on the ground floor, just a few feet away from Wayland. The smell of cooking food still hung in the air, making Morty's stomach growl, but he didn't go upstairs. He stood stock still for what felt like hours, then turned and made his way out into the rain again.

Eventually, they came to a wide, slow-moving river with a ferry crossing like the one between Streatley and Goring. Wayland took to cover and spent a long time watching it, and so did Morty, although without binoculars he couldn't make out very much. He wasn't sure what he was going to do if Wayland decided to cross the river here, because he couldn't go with him without revealing himself. He might, at best, be able to follow later, although he had distant doubts about whether he would be able to talk his way onto the ferry. He supposed he'd have to cross that bridge if he had to, and he liked that joke so much that he told it to the head later and the head called him a sappy twat.

In the end, Wayland decided not to cross the river, but set out parallel to it a couple of miles inland, and gradually Morty noticed that the landscape was becoming marginally less marshy and boggy. Patches of relatively dry ground started to appear, and they came to a road which rose up out of the floodland towards a hill in the distance. Wayland found himself some cover and spent some time watching that hill.

Morty could see houses, and smoke from chimneys. It was the first sign of human habitation he'd seen since they left the Parish. And at this point he began to wonder just what Wayland was playing at, because instead of heading for the houses as a normal person would, he stayed back and seemed to be unable to decide. Morty had thought that the point of the difficult, unpleasant slog across the Vale was to go from one place to another, not sit out here in the rain. He'd become used to sleeping rough since he'd abandoned his home, but even he was tired of being outdoors. He was cold and wet and miserable and hungry, and the head kept telling him what an arsehole he was.

Finally, Wayland withdrew to another ruined house some distance away, and he stayed there for some time. Morty found another house, a little further up and on the other side of the overgrown street, so at least he could stay mostly dry while he kept an eye out for Wayland to finally do something.

This went on for a couple of days, while Wayland made occasional excursions without his gear to observe the community on the hill.

One morning, Wayland emerged with his pack and shotgun, but he was missing the long black nylon case he'd been carrying, and his pack looked lighter somehow. Morty followed him at a distance, and it wasn't until they drew quite close that he realised there was a barricade across the road and several people with guns manning it.

Morty took cover and watched with a sinking heart as

Wayland was taken into the shed by the barricade, and then was whisked away in a cart. He watched the cart disappear slowly into the distance and felt an almost physical sense of anger. He'd come all this way, all this miserable way, only to have Wayland literally taken away from him.

He could have sneaked past the barricade fairly easily – as indeed Wayland could, but Morty assumed there was some good reason why he had not – but that sense of anger kept growing for the rest of the day and all that night, and in the small hours of the morning he let it express itself on the people guarding the barricade. They were tired and bored, and they weren't expecting the storm of knives that erupted at them from cover, and once he got hold of one of their guns it didn't take long. After that, all that remained was to take some souvenirs and make his way into the city.

"YOU'RE NOT GOING to last five minutes here," the head told him from the sack slung over his shoulder. "Just look at the fucking state of you."

Morty was moving in cover, from garden to garden, following the road, but it was true, he was a bit of a mess and the increasing number of people he was seeing were not. They were even cleaner and better dressed than the people in the Parish had been before the war. He also noted that not many of them were carrying guns, and the ones that were seemed to be wearing some kind of uniform. Things here were obviously quite different, and he was going to have to be careful.

First thing, it was obvious that he couldn't just crash around this place, wherever it was, in search of Wayland; he had to get some idea of the community first, and to do that he was going to need to fit in, which meant some new clothes. He was also going to need somewhere to hide out for a while. And food.

Which brought him, after a couple of days of careful

consideration, to this little house whose single occupant had not caused him any trouble. He'd cleaned himself up and replaced his clothes and in the mirror in the bathroom he looked pretty good. Good enough, certainly, to venture out on the streets and look for signs of Wayland. It shouldn't be too hard; all he had to do was follow the trail of dead.

Meanwhile, he thought as he finished his casserole, there was nothing to stop him leaving some signs of his own.

BUILDING A BETTER ENGLAND

THIRTEEN

THE DAY AFTER the murders at Cumnor, Mellow experienced a small and increasingly rare victory when an anonymous tip led her and a team of officers to a derelict house on the edge of Cowley, where they found the dismantled components of a still and a stock of just over a hundred bottles of 'vodka' so powerful that it could have been used to strip paint. Enquiries among the few people who lived on the street turned up nothing. No one knew who the house belonged to, if anyone, and nobody had seen anything. Which wasn't a great surprise – the police weren't exactly popular in the area – but it meant that whoever was making the vodka was still at large and free to set up shop somewhere else.

Still, they'd taken a lot of stock off the streets and at least inconvenienced the unknown distillers, which was something.

"Although," said Detective Sergeant Fleet as they stood on the pavement and watched officers chucking coils of copper tubing and pressure vessels and metal saucepans big enough for a five-year-old to sit in into a wagon, "if the stuff didn't kill people we probably wouldn't be bothering."

Mellow turned and looked at the house. Half its roof was missing and all the windows were broken. The front door lay in the overgrown garden, although whether it had already been like that or had been energetically removed by the police, she didn't know. When she and Fleet arrived, she'd found a squad of constables already busy inside and Wallop standing on the front path with a smug look which even an admonition to wait for his superior officer next time didn't wipe off his face.

"He seems popular, anyway," Fleet said, as Wallop emerged from the house laughing and joking with four constables, each of whom was carrying a wooden case containing bottles of vodka.

"Hm," she said. "Do you know any of those officers, Peter?"

Fleet shook his head. "I don't recognise half the coppers at HQ these days, boss, let alone at the stations out here."

Wallop came over, still smiling. "That's the lot," he said.

"Are you sure?" Mellow asked.

"I've been through that place three times," Wallop told her, a defensive tone creeping into his voice.

Mellow looked at the house again. "All right, sergeant," she said. "Get it all back to headquarters and sign it into the evidence store."

"Maybe tell them not to smoke around it," Fleet added.

The smile was slowly fading from Wallop's face. "Right," he said.

Fleet and Mellow watched him climb up beside the driver of the wagon, and after a moment the horses began to pull it along the street towards the main road. Fleet sucked his teeth as he watched them go.

Mellow turned to the little group of constables, who had gathered on the pavement sharing cigarettes and generally loafing. "All right, you lot," she said, walking over to them. "You can go back to your nick now. Thank you for your participation; I'll be dropping a note to your inspector presently." They gave her sullen looks and started to drift off in twos and threes.

"Friendly blokes," Fleet commented when they were out of earshot.

"Hm," Mellow said, and she turned and walked up the path and into the house.

Inside, the place stank of damp and mould and animal piss. The front door opened onto a short, dark hallway with three doors off it. The first led into the front room which must once have been nice and cosy but was now a ruin, the furniture and carpet rotted and mould all over the walls and ceiling. On one wall there was a bracket for a big television, which Mellow presumed meant the house had been the target of looters in the very early days of the Long Autumn, and she briefly wished them joy of their loot because there hadn't been television anywhere in England – and probably the world – for almost a century. She gave one rotten armchair a kick and it seemed to settle wetly in on itself.

It was harder to tell what the back room had been used for, because all the furniture had been removed and decades of damp had blown a lot of the plaster off the walls to reveal brickwork. One side of the room was a wall of vegetation where weeds and overgrown bushes had invaded through the broken window. The floor was littered with lengths of copper piping and metal vessels of varying sizes, and there was a little wooden box of tools by the wall, wrenches and spanners and screwdrivers and a hammer. Wallop and the local constables had evidently not done as thorough a job of clearing the scene as they'd claimed.

"Have I ever told you how much I hate slapdash work, Peter?" Mellow asked.

"Once or twice, boss," Fleet said, looking around the room. "What do you want to do?"

What she *wanted* to do was go back to headquarters, tear Wallop off a strip in front of his fellow officers, then issue formal reprimands for him and the constables who had helped with his supposed search of the house, but she didn't see what good it would do. It would only cause antagonism between her and whichever local police station the constables had come from, and Wallop would just ignore it.

She puffed out her cheeks. "Check upstairs to see if they missed anything else," she said. "I'll have a quiet word with Wallop later." Fleet glanced at her. "Don't look at me like that, Peter," she told him. "We've got two murder inquiries and a bunch of other stuff running, I don't have time for disciplinary admin."

Fleet didn't make a thing of it. He said, "Boss," and left the room, and a moment later she heard him going up the stairs. She put her hands in her coat pockets and nudged one of the metal vessels with her foot.

The kitchen was a ruin. Here, at least, it looked as if Wallop and his pals had made a bit of an effort. All the cupboards were open and their contents – crockery, tins rusted almost beyond recognition, jars and bottles – were strewn across the stained and brittle flooring. Some of the doors had come off altogether, although whether they'd been actively pulled off or had fallen off their hinges when the attempt was made to open them would have to remain a mystery. Mellow stirred the rubbish about with the toe of her boot, feeling rather flat. Wallop would get the credit for the discovery, because the tip-off had come to him, probably from one of his snitches. Mellow had been a detective for long enough not to be all that bothered about who got the gold stars, the point was to get the job done, but the fact that Wallop had done it so carelessly – just grabbed some bits and pieces of evidence and left the rest – annoyed her. She didn't think anyone deserved credit for doing the job like that.

Bending down, she pulled open the oven door. Inside on the shelf, three bottles of vodka lay on their sides, and Mellow couldn't work up the energy to even be surprised. Presumably one or two of the constables had decided to put some of the evidence aside for themselves and come back later to collect it, and she was tempted to let them. Other people who'd drunk this stuff had died or gone blind, and if they wanted that to happen to them, or their friends and family, that was their business. But in the end, she took the bottles out, uncorked them, and tipped their contents down the sink. Then she corked them again, put them back in the oven, and closed the door again.

There was a sudden sound of something heavy being moved upstairs, then a creaking, breaking noise. Mellow went out into the hall and stood at the bottom of the stairs. "Everything all right up there, Peter?" she called.

There was a moment's silence, then Fleet called, "Could you get one of those screwdrivers from that box, please, boss? One of the big ones?"

Mellow went into the back room and sorted through the box until she found a foot-long screwdriver with a wide head, and she took it upstairs, where she found Fleet standing in the bedroom at the front of the house. He'd shoved the bed over to one side, and he was holding part of a broken-off floorboard.

"Found a loose floorboard," he explained. "I tried to prise it up with my penknife, but the board snapped." He looked down at the hole in the floor.

Mellow went over and stood by him and looked into the hole. The light was better up here, but it was still hard at first to make out what she was seeing. It looked like a bundle of old clothes stuffed down between the joists. Then she changed position slightly and realised that staring up at her from the nest of rags were the empty eye sockets of a charred and blackened skull.

"Oh, my word," she said.

She and Fleet looked at each other, then they looked down into the gap in the floorboards again, and they stood like that for quite a while.

Finally, Mellow said, "Right. Contact headquarters, please, Peter. Get them to send some officers over here. People we know, not local plod. Ask for them by name, if you have to."

"You don't want to get the rest of the boards up?" Fleet asked.

Mellow shook her head. "No, let's preserve as much of the scene as we can. We're going to need Reg and Liz. And get someone to contact Professor Solomons. Pass on my apologies for disturbing him, but I think he's going to want to supervise this."

"Boss." Fleet put the broken floorboard on the bed and left the bedroom, and she heard him going downstairs and out of the front door to radio headquarters. Still clutching the screwdriver in her fist, she looked down into the hole.

"Oh, my word," she said again.

It took two days to remove the remains from under the floorboards of the bedroom. They set up lanterns to enable Liz and Reg and Solomons to work, and for the crime scene photographer to record the scene. Mellow and Fleet took turns to be at the house.

Wallop turned up on Saturday afternoon, but Mellow had instructed the uniformed sergeant guarding the front door not to let him in.

"You can't do this," he told her when she went downstairs.

"I'm your superior," she reminded him. "I can tell you to tap-dance, and you'll have to do it."

"This is my crime scene," he said.

"*Was*, sergeant. And if you'd bothered to search the premises properly it might still be. But you didn't. Did you even *go* upstairs?"

"Yes!" he almost shouted. "I did!"

"Yeah, right. Go home. You're not coming in." Beside her on the doorstep, the sergeant stared impassively into the middle distance.

Wallop's face grew red with anger. "You can't stop me."

Mellow leaned forward a little, as if listening hard. "I'm sorry, sergeant?" All the time, she was thinking, *go on, you little shit, threaten me with this officer standing beside me as a witness; I dare you.* But he didn't. He just stood there, clenching his fists, face suffused. "Go home," she told him again. "I've got police work to do." And she turned and walked back into the house without bothering to see if he went away.

On Monday morning, she went to see Adam Hardy, but when she handed over her request chit the custody sergeant slid a printed form across the desk at her.

"What's this?" she said.

"New regulations," the sergeant told her. "You have to fill in the form and then I'll get someone to escort you."

Mellow glanced down the form. There were little boxes for name, rank, date, purpose of visit. "What the fuck's this, Trish?" she asked. "And what do I need an escort for? Do you think I'm going to break him out of here?"

The sergeant looked uncomfortable. "Chief super's orders," she said. "If you don't fill it in, I can't let you up to the sixth floor, inspector." She added, "Sorry."

Mellow had had enough after the weekend. She borrowed a pen and filled in the little boxes. Where it said 'purpose of visit', she wrote *conjugal*. She signed it and handed it back, and the sergeant read it and raised an eyebrow, but she didn't comment, and a couple of minutes later Mellow was being escorted up through her own headquarters by an armed constable.

"Don't enter the cell, ma'am," the constable said as they arrived on the top floor. "Stay in the doorway and I'll be behind and a little to one side of you."

"Has this whole nick lost its mind?" she asked.

"Not for me to say, ma'am," he said. "I just do as I'm told."

They reached the door of Adam's cell and the constable pounded on the door. "You in there!" he said in a loud voice.

"Move away from the door!" Then he unlocked the door and pushed it open.

Adam was sitting on the mattress under the window, his back against the wall. He was still wearing the baggy overalls he'd been given on Thursday, but he looked relaxed, although the side of his face was bruised.

"Hello," he said.

"What happened to your face?" she asked.

He shrugged. "Walked into a door." He glanced at the window. "Have you made any progress on the killings?"

The past seven days had been so full of murders that it took Mellow a moment to work out which ones he was talking about. "I can't share details of that with you," she said.

"Am I still a suspect?"

"We're still working on that," she said.

"But I haven't been formally arrested."

"No," she admitted.

"And nobody's questioned me about them."

"I've had a busy few days."

He looked at the window again and said, "Well."

"I just wanted to see if you needed anything," she said.

He looked at her. "I need to be out of this madhouse."

She couldn't fault him for that. She was feeling a bit that way herself, today. "I'll be interviewing you later today, or tomorrow at the latest."

"It'll be the high point of my day."

She gave him a hard look. "If you do need anything, tell the guards and they'll pass a message on to me." She glanced over her shoulder at the constable. "Are there any new regulations about that?"

"Not that I'm aware of, ma'am."

"Okay." She turned to go.

"Who's Hob?" Adam asked.

Mellow stopped. "What?"

"He came to see me a few days ago."

"Hob was here?"

He nodded. "Didn't say who he was, though."

"Special advisor to the Chancellor," she said. There was more she could have added, but she was conscious of the constable standing behind her. "You're honoured. What did he want?"

"Mostly he seemed to want to know how I got here from Southampton."

"Did you tell him?" she asked archly, just to remind him what she thought about the whole Southampton thing.

"He said he'd send someone to talk to me about it, but nobody's turned up yet."

She stared at him. To her knowledge, Hob had never visited police headquarters; if he wanted something, Maxwell would be summoned to Chancellery, usually to return in a spectacularly bad mood. "Well," she said, "I'm sure someone will be along soon."

"He showed me a photograph."

"A photograph of what?"

"Somebody with a metal stake through their chest."

Mellow kept her expression neutral, but it took an effort. "Did he say why he did that?"

"He suggested I might be a suspect in their murder."

The possibility had briefly occurred to her after the Cumnor killings, but she'd mostly dismissed it – why go to the trouble of sneaking into the city, committing a very extravagant murder, sneaking out again, and then trying to come *back* into the city through one of the checkpoints? She said, "It's something we're looking at."

He sighed. "None of this has anything to do with me, inspector," he said wearily.

Mellow was inclined to believe him; she was more annoyed, right now, by the thought of Hob wandering around with crime scene photographs. But she wasn't about to let Adam out before she had some idea what was going on.

"Just let me do my job," she told him. "I'm sure this will all be cleared up soon." Although she had no confidence at the moment that it would.

The constable locked up the cell and escorted her back downstairs, despite her noting that the chances of her being attacked in police headquarters were probably quite close to zero. He left her outside the custody sergeant's office and went off to put his shotgun back in the gun room, while Mellow went in and signed out.

The custody sergeant compared the times on the form and said, half to herself, "That didn't take long, then," and in spite of everything that made Mellow smile. "Could you close the door a second, Leonie?"

Puzzled, Mellow pushed the door shut and went back to the desk.

The sergeant put Mellow's form in a folder and put the folder in a drawer of her desk. "Have you seen Ruth Sharpe lately?" she asked quietly.

Mellow had to think. "I looked in on her last week," she said. "Monday. Why?"

The sergeant nodded. "That was the last time I saw her, too. I don't think she's been in since; there's another officer in there now, someone I don't know."

Mellow thought about it. "Maybe her shift changed," she said. "Maybe she's off sick."

The sergeant looked at her. "The constable who took you upstairs? He's new, too. I never saw him before today."

It was an article of faith that the force was undermanned; it had been like that in her father's day. "There was talk about a new recruitment drive a while ago," Mellow mused.

"And that's great," said the sergeant. "But why am I seeing fewer old faces here and more new ones?"

"I don't know, Trish," Mellow said carefully. "There's probably a simple explanation. There usually is."

The sergeant looked at her a moment longer, then went back to some paperwork on her desk. "That'll be it," she said. "A simple explanation."

Mellow watched the sergeant, suddenly thinking it was safer to disappoint her, for the moment. "I have to go over to Christ Church now," she said. "But maybe I'll ask around."

"Yeah," the sergeant said without looking up. "That'd be good."

The comms room was just along the corridor from the custody sergeant's office. Mellow opened the door without knocking, as usual, and popped her head round the door. "Oh," she said.

A beefy-looking sergeant in a uniform half a size too small was sitting at the radio sets, a pair of headphones looking faintly ridiculous balanced on his big, shaven head. He looked at her. "What?" he said.

What, inspector? Mellow thought. She said, "I was looking for Ruth. Sergeant Sharpe. Wondered if she fancied lunch."

The man with the headphones looked at her a moment longer, then went back to staring at the radio. "Transferred," he said disinterestedly.

"Oh," she said, trying to radiate harmless bafflement. "I didn't hear about that."

He shrugged.

"Do you know where she's gone?"

He thought a moment, then said, "Jericho police station, I heard."

"Ah," Mellow said. "Okay, maybe I'll catch up with her there one of these days."

The man at the radio nodded.

"Okay," Mellow said. "Nice to meet you, anyway." When there was no answer, she closed the door and set off down the corridor towards the front desk again, thinking hard. Jericho was close to the river, and it was usually at least knee-deep in water. There was no police station there.

*　*　*

"WELL, AT LEAST you're keeping us busy," Professor Solomons said. "Not that I'm complaining. Busy is good."

"Hm," said Mellow.

He glanced at her. "Are you all right?"

"Got a lot going on," she said, forcing herself to concentrate.

"We can do this tomorrow, if you'd rather," he said.

She shook her head. "No, this is good. At least it's something I can understand."

They were in the mortuary at Christ Church, a big, tiled room with racks along one wall for trays supporting body bags. The racks were about half full, which was unusual; Oxford typically had one death a month which merited the attention of Solomons and his assistants. Sometimes months went by without a suspicious death; now they'd had five in a week. Six, if you included the remains lying on a metal table in the middle of the room.

"Well," said Solomons, pulling a trolley closer to the table. "If you're sure…" He selected a metal probe from the various tools on the trolley and turned to the table. "This is an interesting one. More of an archaeological recovery than an autopsy."

The body was mostly skeletonised, the bones stained. Some flesh still adhered in places, thin and leathery and dark, spotted green here and there with mould. The front of the skull was deeply charred, and so were the bones of the hands.

"He's an adult male, aged between twenty-five and thirty. He was five feet ten inches in height, slim build," Solomons said. "Cause of death is uncertain. There's a fracture in the skull" – he pointed with the probe – "but it might not have been fatal. As you may have noticed, both the skull and the hands have been subjected to intense heat, causing extensive charring and blackening."

"But the teeth were left intact," Mellow said.

"I'm afraid I'm not here to draw comparisons between different cases," Solomons said. He was wearing a pair of overalls and a stained apron, but his sleeves were rolled up to his elbows despite the chill in the mortuary.

"What would it have done to his face?" Mellow asked.

"Oh, he would have been quite unrecognisable when he was put under the floor. By the way, he was carefully hidden. The floorboards had been nailed down, but over the years some of the nails rusted away and the boards warped and lifted a little. That was how you were able to find him."

"I didn't find him," she said, staring down at the body. "My sergeant did."

"Credit where credit's due," Solomons said with a smile. "I always liked that about you." He moved along the table. "He doesn't seem to have suffered any more mutilations, and I can't tell you about identifying marks, of course, but he had suffered a broken leg some years before his death." He pointed again, at a spot on the lower right leg. "Possibly more than a decade before. It was quite a bad break, but the bone was set competently and it healed well. It would have left him with a limp, though. Probably not very pronounced and it wouldn't have caused him any difficulty in getting about, but it would have been noticeable if one were paying attention."

"How long was he under there?" Mellow asked.

"At least eighteen years," Solomons said, which was unusually precise. Before Mellow could comment, he moved over to another table, where a set of rotted clothes were arranged, a sweater, jeans, a shirt of some heavy material, socks, underpants, and boots. All of them had been carefully cut away from the body after its removal from the house.

"The clothes don't tell us very much," Solomons said. "They're too decayed to make any certain judgements, although the boots are well-made." He pointed. "You see the stitching here? That's professional work."

"Hand-made?" Mellow asked.

"In my opinion, yes. Although I wouldn't get too excited about that; they could have been made pre-Sisters and taken from the stock in an old shop. The clothes themselves are just ordinary working clothes, nothing notable. You'll see that the sleeves and neck of the sweater, and the cuffs and collar of the shirt, show signs of burning, which is of course consistent with his hands and face being subjected to intense heat. We've taken samples from the clothing, but I don't expect any great revelations." He straightened up. "Reg and Liz will no doubt mention this in their report, but while we were recovering the remains, I didn't see any signs of burning on the floorboards."

Not that it made any real difference where he was killed now. Mellow went back to the other table and stood with her hands in her pockets looking down at the remains. "While I'm here, have you managed to finish work on the bodies from Cumnor?"

Solomons looked at her for a few moments. "Are you still dealing with that?"

She turned from the table. "As far as I know. Why?"

"I got a memo from Chancellery this morning telling me I should report directly to them on that matter."

Mellow tipped her head to one side. "You did?"

He nodded. "I had my reports biked over to them shortly before you arrived."

All of a sudden, it seemed hard to arrange the day in her head. "Where in Chancellery?"

"Mr Hob's office."

Of course. Mellow looked at the racks of body bags and wondered what sort of game Hob was playing.

"I assumed you knew about this," Solomons said.

"It's okay, Michael," she told him. "Left hand not knowing what the right hand's doing. There'll be a memo waiting for me when I get back to headquarters, no doubt." Although there had been no memo this morning.

Solomons hesitated a moment, then he walked over to another trolley parked by the wall. "Anyway," he said, "forgive me for being dramatic, but there was also this." He took a cloth from a little china bowl and brought it over to her. She looked inside, saw a gold-coloured disc in the bottom with a fine gold chain curled up on top of it. "We found this under the body when we lifted it from beneath the floorboards," Solomons went on. "It's okay, you can pick it up. There won't be any forensics on it after all this time."

Mellow reached in, took the chain between her finger and thumb, and lifted it out of the bowl. The disc, a little smaller than a two-pence piece, dangled from it, dull and tarnished.

"I'm going to speculate now," Solomons said, "and you mustn't let that colour your judgement, but whoever killed him took great care to remove anything which might have identified him, including burning his face and hands off, and it seems careless of them to have missed this."

As the disc turned in the light, she saw that it was a St Christopher medal.

Solomons went over to a worktop, came back with a magnifying glass. "Judging by the position we found it in, I think the poor chap swallowed it shortly before his death. It would have been roughly here." He indicated a point just below his Adam's apple and handed the glass to Mellow. "My first thought was that he knew he was going to die, and either he didn't want anyone to take it, or he wanted to make sure there was some kind of identification on him."

Mellow lay the medal in her palm and turned it over. She could just make out some marks on the back. With the magnifying glass, she saw a date, eighteen years previously, and the words *To Courtenay, From Ma.*

FOURTEEN

THEY FED HIM twice a day. Breakfast was a bowl of groats which tasted of more or less nothing at all. Dinner was watery stew and a chunk of gritty bread. Bowls and spoons were ancient brittle plastic, useless as weapons or tools. Two constables delivered the meals, one of them armed. They shouted through the door for him to move over by the window, then they opened it and one put the bowl on the floor and swapped the bucket for a fresh one while the one with the gun kept watch. Neither of them was particularly interested in conversation, and after the first couple of visits he gave up trying to strike up a rapport.

Apart from that, he was left alone. Except for his encounter with Hob and Mellow's brief appearance, no one visited him, and despite Mellow's promise he was not interrogated. He spent a lot of time standing at the window, looking out at the rain and sleet and watching carts and horses and people pass by in the street. Sometimes, he gave the bars a tug, just in case they'd somehow loosened themselves since the last time he tried it.

He had a lot of time to think about the photograph Hob had shown him, and he thought about it a lot because it was something he *could* have done. It wasn't just a murder, it was intended to spread fear, to plant the idea that something awful was here, waiting to strike again. It was like some of the things he had done in the Parish.

There were a lot of gaps in his memory of his time in the Parish. Some things, things he'd put in the box marked *Wayland,* were incredibly, achingly sharp, others were foggier. Still others, appalling things which he had only learned about from speaking to the survivors of the fighting, were missing altogether. Sometimes he woke suddenly in the middle of the night with the near certainty that he had been screaming.

He sat against the wall under the window and went back over his journey to Oxford, step by step. Were there gaps there, too? Was there a day when he had crept into the city, slaughtered someone, and returned to his hiding place? A day he'd blotted out, simply refused to remember? It was hard to be absolutely certain, because one day hiding in a ruined house sheltering from the hail and the pouring rain was much like another, but he didn't think so. He hadn't been injured in a struggle with the victim, his clothes weren't bloodstained, he hadn't suddenly snapped out of it to discover that he was soaking wet because he'd been out in the rain all day. But there was still a tiny kernel of doubt, because it would have been *physically* possible. He could have done it.

Was that why Hob had shown him the photograph? To unbalance him? To make him doubt his memory? To trick him into some kind of confession? Because he wasn't a policeman, and whatever Mellow had said, he wasn't just a special adviser to the Chancellor. What Hob reminded Adam of the most was some of the intelligence officers in the Bureau, the senior ones who didn't go out in the field and spent their days in offices plotting instead. Which presented Adam with yet another problem.

The Bureau had more or less grown from HMS Drake's

base security and Naval Intelligence offices, and it had never encountered another intelligence organisation before. In all his classes and training sessions, not one had suggested what to do in a situation like this. Did he negotiate with them? Come to some kind of accommodation? Work to bring them down? There was no way to know how he was supposed to respond.

On the morning of the fifth day, instead of collecting his breakfast things, the constable without the gun said, "Get up."

Adam didn't move from the mattress. "Why?"

"Got anything better to do?"

Fair point. He got up and went out into the corridor. They were cautious – the one with the gun hung back out of reach – but they didn't handcuff him. They took him back down to the interview room, sat him down at the table, then locked him in.

A minute later, the door was unlocked again and a pudgy, untidy man in his fifties wearing a rumpled suit and a tie and carrying a briefcase looked in. He glanced around the room dramatically and said, "Adam Hardy?"

Adam nodded.

"Excellent!" He surged into the room with a grin that was part innocently happy and part sly, as if he was enjoying a private joke. "Thought for a moment I'd got the wrong room." He reached the table and put out his hand, but he'd stopped just a fraction short, so that Adam had to half get out of his chair and stretch to shake it. "Good to meet you," he said, slinging the briefcase onto the table. "My name's John; they've sent me to pick your brains."

Adam raised an eyebrow.

"About your rather marvellous odyssey from Southampton." John pulled out the other chair and sat down. "Mr Hob said you'd agreed to fill us in?"

Adam shrugged.

John blinked damp, pouchy eyes at him. "You're not terribly talkative, are you? Everything all right?"

"How much longer are you going to keep me locked up?"

"Me?" John protested. "*I'm* not keeping you locked up. Nothing to do with me, guv." He beamed at Adam. "Perhaps if you help out with this, they'll let you out. Quid pro quo. How does that sound?"

Adam had no idea what *quid pro quo* was, but it sounded like something to be avoided. He said, "I'm not sure I like the idea of telling you how to get to Southampton."

John sat back and spread his arms. Adam noticed what seemed to be bits of food on his tie. "It's pure research, Adam. Increasing our knowledge of the world. Surely you can't object to that?" When Adam didn't answer, he clasped his hands on the table in front of him and heaved a sigh. "Well, I must say I'm disappointed, Adam, I really am. It's not as if I don't have other things I could have been getting on with this morning."

"I want to see Mellow."

"Who?"

"Inspector Mellow."

John shook his head. "Don't know him. What you've got, here and now, is *me*, and I'm ready to work." He laid a hand on the briefcase. "I've got paper and pens and everything in here, and you *said* you'd help."

"I'll talk to Mellow."

John regarded him sadly. "Well," he said eventually, "I'll *ask*, obviously. But you'll have noticed that you're not really in a position to make *demands*."

"It wasn't my idea to be locked up."

"Oh, quite. Quite." John nodded enthusiastically. "And if it was my decision, you wouldn't be, believe me." He pouted. "Unfortunately, it's not my decision, and here we are."

"I'll talk to Mellow."

"What's Inspector Mellow to you?"

"I trust her. She didn't lock me up."

John thought about it. "I'll ask. But this is a really poor show, you know. Anyway." He stood abruptly and lunged across the table, holding out his hand. "Good to meet you, Adam."

Adam shook his hand without getting up. John grabbed the briefcase off the table and went and banged on the door. While it was being unlocked, he said, "If you change your mind, let us know."

"I'll talk to Mellow," Adam said again.

John nodded, gave him a sly smile, and left.

"I WANT TO see him," Effie said.

"Well," Maxwell told her, "to be fair, Mrs Fox, there isn't a lot left to see."

Mellow fixed her gaze on a point on the wall behind Effie and gritted her teeth, otherwise she would have run screaming out into the street. Maxwell was the very last person she would have wanted sitting next to her in any interview, but particularly not this one.

Effie stared stonily at him. "*Ms* Fox," she said tonelessly. "I never married."

There was a silence in the interview room.

"He's my brother," Effie went on. "I've got a right to see him."

Maxwell opened his mouth, no doubt to say something else crass, but Mellow got in ahead of him. "You do, Effie," she said. "You have an absolute right, and I hope you'll be able to see him soon. But you won't be able to recognise him, you do understand that, don't you?"

"I'm not stupid, inspector," Effie said stonily, although Mellow noted that she was being careful not to use her first name. "He's been dead fifteen years. I want to see what was done to him."

"It's not very nice," Mellow warned.

Effie looked at her. "When my dad was murdered, they called me down here to identify him. They let me into a room and his head was just sitting there on a table." She glanced at Maxwell. "I could hear them giggling behind me, they thought it was funny. So don't talk to me about *not nice*."

"I'm sorry that happened," Mellow told her. She almost followed up with excuses – it was a different time, things have changed now – but Effie wouldn't have believed her, and if she was honest, she wasn't sure she believed it herself.

Effie looked down at the tabletop, where the little St Christopher sat on its curled-up chain beside a small evidence envelope. "Ma got it for him for his eighteenth birthday, the year before she died," she said. "To keep him safe on his travels. Ma was always religious, Dad not so much. Fat lot of good it did any of us."

"It's not conclusive identification evidence," Maxwell put in. "It was only found with the remains." Mellow looked at him in disbelief. She had no idea what he was even doing here, unless it was just to be cruel. "But could you tell us, did he ever break his leg?"

If Maxwell had been a little more self-aware, the look Effie gave him would have kept him awake for the rest of his life. "When he was ten," she said. "He fell out of a tree. The doc said he'd always walk with a limp, but you hardly noticed."

Maxwell was writing in a notebook. "Well, that nails it," he said to Mellow.

Mellow looked bleakly at him, willing him to shut up or burst into flames or something. "Yes, sir," she said.

"Right," he said, closing the notebook and standing up. "I think we're done here. Show Mrs Fox out, Mellow." He looked at Effie. "Thank you for your help."

Effie didn't say anything.

When Maxwell was gone, Effie said, "Who killed him?"

"We don't know, Effie," Mellow told her. "We only found him yesterday, and that was just by accident. We've barely started looking."

"Where was he?"

"At a house in Cowley. An empty house. We don't know who it belonged to, if it ever belonged to anybody."

Effie looked at the St Christopher again. "Can I take this?"

Mellow shook her head. "It's evidence. I'm sorry. I'll let you have it back as soon as I can, I promise."

Effie picked up the medal, took a last look at it, then she put it back in the little envelope and slid it across the table to Mellow. Mellow put it in her pocket.

She walked Effie down to the lobby, where half a dozen officers were looking out through the glass doors at Doug Fox, who was standing on the pavement beside a horse and cart, completely unconcerned by the attention. It wasn't every day that the heads of one of Oxford's most notorious crime families visited the city's police headquarters.

"If you don't have anything to do, I can find something," Mellow told the officers. "And I promise you won't enjoy it."

The officers scattered and Mellow went outside with Effie. Doug nodded hello to her and climbed up into the driving seat of the cart.

"I want to know who did this, Leonie," Effie said.

"That may not be possible, Effie," Mellow told her. "You do understand that, don't you? It was fifteen years ago; we may never be able to find out."

Effie nodded. "You'll find out. You're a smart girl and you're good at your job, just like your dad." She looked up at the building behind them. "That cunt up there. Is that your boss?"

"Yes," Mellow said with a sigh. "Unfortunately. I'm sorry."

"No," Effie said, wagging a finger at her. "No, you don't ever apologise for the likes of him. He's not your responsibility. Do you remember Susan Bates?"

Mellow shook her head. "I was barely out of training when she retired."

"She was a good copper, was Susan," Effie said. "She had

some respect. When she heard how I'd been shown Dad's head she went ballistic, demoted a couple of coppers, fired some more. Then she came over to the house and apologised to me. Difference between her and you is that she *was* responsible. She was the boss, and she could do something about it." She smiled sadly at Mellow. "What can *you* do, apart from say *sorry*?"

"It matters," Mellow said.

Effie reached out and touched her elbow briefly. "You're a good girl, Leonie," she said. "But you're in the wrong job." She turned and got up onto the seat beside Doug. "You'll keep me informed about what's going on," she said. It wasn't a question.

Passing information to a known criminal, regardless of the fact that they were the next-of-kin of a victim of crime, could get her in all kinds of trouble. "I'll tell you what I'm able," she said.

Her careful tone didn't escape Effie, who smiled down at her. "He would have been about your age when he died," she said. She turned to Doug. "All right, Douglas. Let's go home."

Mellow watched them go for a while, as they drove off towards the Cherwell ferry, then she went back inside and up to the fourth floor, where Records, safely above any floods, took up almost the whole floor, a pair of huge rooms with ranks of filing cabinets and desks and chairs where officers could work, and a desk by the door for the librarian.

Records was regarded as something of a sinecure for retired coppers, somewhere they could earn a bit of money while keeping in touch with the job. Her father had been offered it, until he'd pointed out that someone would have to carry him and his wheelchair up and down the stairs, then they'd found him an office on the ground floor where he could shuffle paper, until the sheer tedium had driven him away.

The duty librarian today was a sixtyish veteran who'd been a sergeant on the beat when her father had been a constable. He looked up as she entered the room and smiled broadly. "Inspector," he said. "Good to see you."

"You too, Tommy," Mellow said, plucking a form from the box on the desk and bending down to fill it in. "Bit of a blast from the past today."

Tommy looked at the half-dozen names she'd written on the form. "Know this name, of course," he said, pointing at the first one. "Never had any dealings with them, though."

"You're lucky."

"Headington family, weren't they?"

"Still are, what's left of them. Legitimate businesspeople, now."

Tommy chuckled at the thought of the Foxes being legitimate. "I spent most of my time at Sunnymead nick."

She looked at him. "Yeah? Bit of a cushy number up there, I'd have thought."

He grunted. "It was till they started firebombing us."

Mellow thought for a moment, then said, "Morton Street. There's a little industrial estate there."

Tommy nodded. "Aye, there is. There's nothing there but empty sheds, though. Cleared out years ago."

"Shelves, Tommy," she said. "There's lots of shelves."

"Is there money in shelves, then?"

"So I'm told. Any idea who owned the land, back in the day?"

"Before the Sisters?" He thought about it. "Nah. I suppose the city owns it now."

"It owns everything else." Mellow started to turn away.

"Gateway to the North," Tommy said.

Mellow stopped. "Pardon?"

"That's what we used to call Sunnymead nick. The Banbury Road's the only main road in or out of Oxford that isn't properly blocked or doesn't have to cross a river."

She thought about it. "I suppose it is."

He looked at the form again. "These other names are all the way over at the back of the room, by the door," he said. "Do you want me to get them for you? Bring them over to you?"

"Nah, it's okay," she said, backing away from the desk. "I might not even have to check them."

"Okay," he said. "Well, if you do need anything, just give me a shout."

"Will do," she said, and she turned and walked down the nearest aisle of filing cabinets.

She found Courtenay Fox's file easily enough – the family had virtually a drawer to themselves – and took it over to a table near the back of the room, by a pillar which hid it from view, and she sat and started to leaf through a depressing progression of offences, from antisocial behaviour to theft to burglary to actual bodily harm, none of which Courtenay had somehow ever been convicted of. The file came to an abrupt end fifteen years ago with a brief but somehow gleeful missing persons report. Effie, she saw, had walked into Headington police station in the middle of the rioting to make the report. *Complainant was verbally abusive*, some long-ago sergeant had noted. Mellow opened her notebook and went back to the beginning of the file and started to make notes.

After about ten minutes, she heard Tommy's voice over on the other side of the room. "Inspector?"

She got up and went over to the desk "What's up?"

"Can you do me a favour?" Tommy asked, standing up. "Keep an eye on things while I go to the loo?"

"Sure," she said. "Tell you what, could you get me a sandwich and a mug of tea while you're out? I haven't had my lunch yet."

"Of course." Tommy was obviously pleased at the excuse to get away from the desk for a while. "Any preference?"

Mellow shook her head. "Whatever they've got. Not cheese, though. Milk and two sugars in the tea."

"Righto," he said. "Just make sure anyone who comes in completes a form. You can leave them on the desk; I'll file them later. If anybody's got a query, they'll have to wait till I get back."

Mellow looked around the room. They were the only people there. "I'm sure I can handle that. It doesn't seem busy."

"You'd be surprised how quickly that can change," he said, moving towards the door. "Won't be long."

"No rush," she told him, settling herself in his chair. "I'm only doing a bit of research."

When he'd gone, she counted to ten. Then she counted to ten again. Then she started pulling open the drawers of the desk. In the third one down was a little bunch of keys on a chain. She took them, closed the drawer, then got up and walked over to the locked door at the far end of the records room.

Ever since she was promoted to inspector, Mellow had had access to the Personnel files, but to get at them she had to fill in a request and hand it in to Superintendent Todd, which was not ideal at the best of times. With a final glance down the ranks of filing cabinets, Mellow unlocked the door and stepped through.

The Personnel room was identical to the criminal records room, more aisles of filing cabinets, some grey, some green, most of them metal but some of them wooden. Like everything else in Oxford, they had been scavenged from all over the city; it was something of a surprise that they hadn't run out of filing cabinets years ago.

She quickly found the S cabinets, and worked her way down the labels on the front of the drawers until she found the one she wanted. Ruth Sharpe's file was about halfway into the drawer. She pulled it out, balanced it on the open drawer, and paged through it. There was indeed a transfer form at the end, dated Tuesday last week, signed by Todd and countersigned by Maxwell. The name of the station she'd been transferred to was just a scribble, completely illegible. Mellow stared at it for a few moments, then she went back to the beginning of the file and found Ruth's address, put the file back in the drawer, and closed it.

As she was heading back towards the door, she had a thought. She stopped and backtracked a bit and moved into another aisle, and another, until she found the *K* cabinets and searched one drawer, removing files, checking them, and putting them back. It turned out that there were ten Kellys serving with the Thames Valley Police Force, but only two of them were women, and neither of those was of inspector rank and certainly not the inspector at Sunnymead police station.

She put the files back, closed the drawer, and left the room, locking the door behind her, and she'd just sat down at the front desk and returned the keys to the drawer when Tommy returned with a mug of tea and a ham sandwich.

"Thanks for that," he said. "Saved my life."

"Mine too," she told him with a smile, taking the mug and plate and going back to her table.

She did another twenty minutes with Courtenay's file, copying down names and addresses of known associates – most of them, depressingly, within about fifteen minutes' walk of her home but some in other suburbs – and then she packed up, signed out, left the file with Tommy to be returned to its cabinet, and went back to her office.

Someone had been in while she was away, and there was a memo and a long white envelope on her desk. She sat down and read the memo and felt her heart sink. "Peter?" she shouted.

A few moments later, Fleet came along the corridor and looked in through the open door. "Boss?"

"We've got a shout," she said. "Get a team together, if you can find anyone who isn't already working on a case." She scribbled an address on a piece of paper and held it out to him. "Botley nick have secured the scene but make sure whoever gets there first takes over."

"Right," Fleet said, taking the address.

Mellow opened the envelope, took out a sheet of paper, and read it. Then she read it again.

Already halfway down the stairs, Fleet heard her shout, "Oh, for fuck's *sake!*"

*　　*　　*

A few days after his interview with the plump clerk, Adam was taken down to the interview room again, and this time Mellow was sitting at the table, looking thunderous.

"What did I do to you?" she said as he sat down in the other chair.

"What?"

"I could have left you here," she told him. "I could have left you in a cell. But I took you home and I introduced you to my dad and I gave you food and a place to sleep, and now my life's completely fucked up."

He thought of reminding her that he had at least returned the favour by repairing her roof, but this was probably not the right time. "How have I fucked up your life?"

"Is it your idea of getting your own back because I wouldn't let you go?"

Adam sighed. "What's happened?"

Mellow got control of her anger with a visible effort. "I got a letter – a *letter*, not a memo – from Hob this morning ordering me to take a statement about your trip from Southampton."

"Oh," he said.

"Now, you've just been sitting around all week stuffing your face with food," she went on, "but I actually have *work* to do, and lots of it, and I really don't appreciate being sent here to write down your holiday memories."

"I'm sorry," he said. "I got tired of being pushed around."

"Well, we all get like that sometimes," she said. "*I* get like that sometimes. But I don't go round messing people up."

Adam suspected that Mellow wouldn't think twice about messing up anyone who got in her way. He said, "They sent some kind of clerk to talk to me about it, but I didn't trust him."

"You realise Hob could order us to keep you here for ever?"

she told him. "All he has to do is write out a chit and get the Chancellor to sign it and you'll never leave this nick again."

That wasn't so scary. Chrissie could do that, and a lot worse, and she didn't need the Commodore to countersign the orders. On the other hand, he and Chrissie had something resembling a working relationship, which he doubted was ever going to happen with Hob.

"Speaking of which, have you found out who faked that order to let me through the checkpoint yet?" he asked.

She sat back and crossed her arms. "Who says it was a fake?"

"Hob does. He says the stamp at the bottom's a forgery."

Mellow hadn't noticed, particularly, but she hadn't been paying attention to the stamp. "No one tells me anything," she said. "And it's none of my business anyway." She put a hand in her pocket, brought it out, and flipped something onto the table in front of him. He leaned forward and looked, saw it was a folded piece of brown card with a crown and the words CITY OF OXFORD printed on the front. Adam picked it up, opened it, found himself looking at his own face staring back in surprise.

"I'm to offer you a deal," Mellow said, nodding at the card. "You give Hob what he wants, you get that. You'll need it to get around."

The photograph pasted onto the card was in grainy black and white, but it was recognisably him, and he was looking surprised because that was how he had felt when he had seen the camera. There was a fancy-looking seal embossed on the lower right-hand corner of the photo, and on the other half of the card his name had been written in green ink. Spaces for date of birth and place of birth and address had been left blank. On the back, in tiny printing, was a list of rules which boiled down to the fact that he was required to produce the card if anyone in authority asked for it. Even Guz didn't have identity cards for the general population.

"I thought I was a murder suspect," he said.

"Not anymore, according to my superiors," Mellow said heavily. "Don't get too excited. You'll stay here at night. And you'll only be allowed out under supervision."

"Whose?"

The look on her face told him everything he wanted to know, even before she answered. "Have you ever," she asked, "thought about becoming a police officer?"

"YOU WON'T ACTUALLY *be* an officer," Mellow told him as the cart made its way through the city centre in the rain. "You won't get a badge. Officially, you'll be a consultant, but that's just an excuse for me to keep an eye on you during the day. I won't be asking for your opinion. And you won't be getting a salary."

"I wish you people would make up your fucking minds," Adam said. "First you let me into your city, then you lock me up, then you let me go, then you lock me up again and accuse me of murder, then you tell me I'm a policeman, but I'll be locked up at night."

"I told you, you're a *consultant*, not a policeman," Mellow said from the front seat of the cart. In the back, sitting across from Adam, Sergeant Fleet grinned.

It had taken him a little over an hour to recount his supposed route from Southampton to Oxford, Mellow taking notes and asking him to go back when she thought something wasn't clear. He'd felt bad about lying to Mellow, who seemed to be attempting to treat him decently even if it was obviously trying her patience, but he justified it by telling himself that he was actually lying to Hob; Mellow was just passing on the information. And she didn't believe a word he was telling her anyway.

They had given him back his coat and rucksack. It had obviously been searched, and a sweater and a couple of pairs of socks were missing, which felt more like spite than anything else, but at least they'd given it back. The chances of ever seeing his weapons again seemed slim.

Still, he was back in his own clothes, he wasn't handcuffed to anything at the moment, and after sitting in the interview room for a few minutes complaining about the food he'd been given while in the cell, he'd managed to annoy Mellow enough for her to have a bacon sandwich brought to him, so things were not entirely bad.

He thought, for a while, that they were heading back to the checkpoint at Cumnor, because the driver took the now-familiar route over the river on the ferry and through Osney, but they turned off the Botley Road onto a street that by some quirk of topography had escaped being flooded. Some distance down the street, Adam saw other carts, standing outside one of the houses, and several bicycles propped up against the hedges of neighbouring houses.

They pulled to a stop outside the house. "Don't speak unless you're spoken to, and don't touch anything," Mellow told him as they were getting down from the cart. "And don't get in my way."

The house seemed to be the only inhabited one in the street; the gardens of the others were massively overgrown, windows broken, front doors smashed down by long-departed looters, roofs damaged by decades of hail and snow. A bit further along, a couple seemed to have been partially collapsed by subsidence.

Number 32, though, looked in good shape. Its little front garden was neat and tended, and there were curtains in the windows. The front door was open, and a uniformed constable was stationed outside. Mellow and Fleet showed him their badges. "He's with us," she added, jerking her head in Adam's direction. Adam showed the constable his new identity card, and the constable looked unimpressed.

There was a terrible smell in the house. Adam smelled it

before they were even properly inside, as if the place was exhaling something awful from its open door. Once over the threshold it was powerful enough to make him cough. Mellow looked at him. "Are you going to throw up?" she said.

For a fraction of a second, it occurred to him to say yes and see if Mellow would tell him to wait outside. He wondered if he could outrun the constable by the door, and how far he would get. He shook his head. "No."

"Good. Don't."

Inside, the house felt small and cramped. The hallway beyond the front door was short and narrow. On the right, a staircase rose to a dogleg up to the upper floor of the house, and to the left there were two doors. At the end there was an open doorway through which Adam could see what looked like a kitchen. He heard people talking upstairs.

Mellow went to the first door and poked it open with a fingertip. She looked in for a moment, then moved on to the next one. Adam followed, glancing through the doorway as he passed and seeing a small, tidy living room. Sofa and armchairs, framed pictures on the walls, a little coffee table with a single mug sitting on it. A couple of steps along the hall, the second door opened onto what had probably once been a dining room but was now neatly stacked with boxes and various bits of furniture. A window looked out on a back garden that was less well-tended than the front; it was starting to grow a bit wild.

In the kitchen there was a small range, and a little table with a single chair. There was also a man in overalls standing in the back doorway looking closely at the frame of the open door. He seemed to know Mellow because he glanced up and said, "Got in this way, I reckon." He pointed to where a long chunk of wood had been split away from the frame. "Looks like they used a crowbar or something like that."

Mellow nodded and looked around the kitchen. Some of the cupboards were open, and there were bits of mouldy food on the floor. A pot sat on the hob, about a quarter full of congealed stew. Adam put his hand against the side, but it was cold.

"I told you not to touch anything," Mellow said. She said to the man at the door, "He touched that pot."

The man sighed. "Are his prints on file?"

"Yes."

"That's something, anyway. I'll make a note."

"Don't touch anything else," Mellow told Adam. "Our crime scene officers don't have my sense of humour."

The man at the door chuckled. "That'll be right."

Adam went to the sink and looked out of the kitchen window. The uncut lawn was surrounded by slightly overgrown flower beds. No generator mast. At the end of the garden was a thick, high hedge that would have been hard to get through, but on either side the fences that would have once separated the garden from its neighbours had either rotted away or been broken down by animals and it wouldn't be difficult to move from garden to garden. Still, why put in the effort to come in through the back when there were no neighbours, nobody to see you break open the front door?

He followed Mellow back into the hall, Fleet bringing up the rear, and they went upstairs. The smell was much stronger on the landing, and Adam saw Mellow grimace. The bathroom was the first place he'd seen in the house where there was serious disorder. There were filthy towels and bits of clothing on the floor and in the bath, the toilet was almost full of shit that hadn't been flushed away, and there were smears of what looked like old blood on every surface.

"Watch where you walk," Mellow said, and, looking down, Adam made out what looked like dozens of bloody bare footprints on the floor, as if someone had walked back and forth many times.

There were more footprints on the carpet on the landing, leading to the bedroom at the front of the house, but Mellow looked in the back bedroom first, and here again there was disorder, a pile of dirty sheets and blankets on the bed, clothes and plates crusted with old food all over the floor. It looked like an animal had been living here.

In the front bedroom, a wardrobe and a chest of drawers stood against one wall, opposite a double bed. Two more people in overalls, a man and a woman, were standing by the bed, leaning over what looked like a big pile of rotten meat sitting in the middle of a mass of gore-soaked blankets. There was blood everywhere, up the wall behind the bed, on the floor, even on the ceiling.

"Oh, hello," said the man without looking up. "You got here finally, then."

"Don't," Mellow said, going over to the bed with Fleet to take a look. "I'm having a day."

"It's not as bad as the day *this* poor chap's having."

"It's all a matter of perspective." Mellow looked down at the bed, and from where he was standing in the doorway Adam saw her scowl.

"Well," the man said, "I don't have any shattering insights for you yet, I'm afraid. He's a man aged about fifty. Multiple massive wounds from various sharp and pointed instruments. We still haven't found his head."

"We can't be sure of a cause of death yet," the woman said. "There are stab wounds in his torso, most of which would have been fatal. Wounds on his hands and arms suggest he put up a bit of a fight, but not much of one. He was probably asleep when he was attacked."

"His head was cut off," Mellow said. "That'll usually do it for you."

"That was done after he was dead," the man said. "The blood spatter would have been very different if he'd been alive. Not so sure about the disembowelling." He pointed to a shrivelled loop of intestine hanging off the end of the bed. "The dismemberment is definitely post-mortem, though. We were having a bit of a disagreement about that when you arrived."

"Reg doesn't think it was all done at the same time," the woman said.

"It's not done very expertly," Reg said. "Just brute force hacking. Whoever did it cut through the mattress over and over again while they were at it. It's a lot harder than you'd think to cut someone's arm off, if you don't know what you're doing."

"I don't know what kind of person could do that," the woman said. "Coming back again and again over a period of days to cut another bit off."

"You think this took days?" Fleet asked.

Reg nodded. "I think it was done over a period of days. Don't know how many, Professor Solomons might be able to help there. As well as the head, we're short a foot and most of the fingers."

"So when do you think he died?" Mellow asked.

Reg sucked his teeth. "What do you reckon, Liz?" he asked the woman. "A week?"

She nodded. "A day or so either way, maybe. We can try to be more exact when we've taken a better look at the remains. But yes, about a week."

"A week." Mellow glanced over at where Adam was standing, then she turned and looked at the wall. "What about that?"

From where he was standing, Adam couldn't see what she meant. He took a step into the room, saw smeared marks on the wall, but the angle was still wrong to make them out. He took another step, and the marks resolved themselves into big letters, written in blood across the wallpaper. They said *Wayland*. He felt the world grey out for a moment.

"No idea," said Reg. "You're the detective; we just do bodies."

Mellow looked at Adam. "You all right?"

Not remotely, no. He nodded, but she didn't look convinced.

"Who's he?" Reg asked.

"Consultant," Mellow said.

"Whose idea was that, then?"

She shook her head. "Don't ask."

"So, *consultant*," Reg said. "What do you think of all this?"

It was a physical effort to stop looking at the letters on the wall. "I don't know," Adam said.

"Well, you're no fucking use to anyone, are you?" Liz said.

Back downstairs, Mellow went into the kitchen again, where the same man in overalls was still looking at the frame of the back door. "Where's Lenny?" she asked.

"Gone back to the station to get some more people," he told her. "We weren't expecting anything like this."

"Tell him I want the whole house done, top to bottom," she said. "Do the attic, too, and the cellar, if there is one. Do the garden, and the gardens on either side. And I want all the houses on the street searched. On both sides."

"He said you'd say something like that."

"I'll send you more manpower for the house search. Any idea how long it'll take?"

"If you want it done properly? Days. Day after tomorrow, at the earliest."

Mellow nodded. "Do it properly, but drop me a note every day about how it's going."

"Would've done that anyway," the man grumbled mildly, going back to his inspection of the door frame.

They went back outside and stood on the pavement gratefully breathing fresh air. Mellow looked up and down the street, then turned to Fleet. "Peter, go back to the station and set up a case conference for five o'clock, would you? We'll hitch a ride back with someone in a bit."

"Okay, boss."

Fleet clambered up onto the seat of the cart, and Adam and Mellow watched him drive off up the street. When he'd gone, Mellow said, "You know, most of the crime we get is petty stuff. Theft, assault, drunk and disorderly, domestic violence. Sometimes we go months without a single murder. And you turn up and all of a sudden I'm ankle-deep in dead bodies." She started to walk away from the house, and after a moment Adam followed her. "Now," she went on, "you're going to tell me this is all a coincidence. You just happened to turn up a couple of days after someone forged an order to let *somebody* into the city, and the people who let you through the checkpoint just happened to be butchered by *somebody* the day after you arrived." She stopped in the middle of the street, out of earshot of the officers by the house, and lowered her voice. "And you don't strike me as someone who's easily shaken up, but something in there shook you up. What was it?"

He almost told her, but he was still trying to absorb that single word written in blood on the wall. He said, "It was pretty horrible in there."

She reached out and tapped him on the chest. "What's 'Wayland'?" she said. "Is it a person? A place? A gang?"

All he could do was shake his head helplessly.

"Something fucking bad is happening in my town, Mr Hardy," she told him. "And you may not be causing it, but you're definitely part of it."

"I don't know," he said. "What's happening?"

Mellow stuffed her hands in her pockets and set off along the street again. "I don't know, and it's starting to do my fucking head in."

"None of this has anything to do with me," he told her, but even as he said it, he was aware that he wasn't certain anymore.

"Hob thinks you're important," she said. "Thing is, I don't think he knows *how* you're important."

Adam shook his head. "I'm *not* important."

"Well, he thinks you are. That's why he's let you out on a short rope. To see what happens. And if something *does* happen, I'm going to be standing right next to it."

"I'm sorry," he said.

"Oh, please," she said. "You're not *remotely* sorry."

"I really am," he told her, and he was. He was slowly getting a sense that Mellow and her father might be the only people in Oxford he could trust.

They had reached the bottom of the street, where it dead-ended against a high railway embankment. They stood there in the drizzle looking at it, Adam thinking that it would be a good way to move quickly across country, above the flooded land. He wondered where it went.

Mellow said, "They've taken the investigation of the Cumnor murders away from me."

He looked at her. "Who? Chancellery?"

She nodded. "Hob's office, which amounts to the same thing. And you know what? They're welcome to it, except that I can't help thinking they're connected to this." She waved back up the street towards Number 32.

"Maybe they'll take this one away from you, too."

She looked at him, didn't quite glare. She walked over to the pavement and stood with her hands in her pockets looking at the last house in the row. Its roof had entirely collapsed, and the front was almost hidden by ivy and brambles and weeds. "Where are you from?" she asked. "Really?"

He didn't say anything for a long time. Finally, he shook his head and said, "Better you don't know."

She turned to face him and poked him in the chest again. "If you do anything that hurts my dad, I'll make you sorry you ever came here."

"I've been sorry ever since I arrived," he told her.

She seemed to run out of words all of a sudden. She shook her head and poked him in the chest one more time, then she turned and stomped away up the street. Presently, he followed her.

*　　*　　*

ON THE TOP floor of the ruined house, hidden from view by the vegetation that had overwhelmed it, Morty peeked out and felt a warm glow of satisfaction as he watched Wayland and the woman leave. He thought that had all worked out rather splendidly. He'd had shelter and hot food for a few days, he'd managed to clean himself up, he had fresh clothes, and he'd discovered that all he had to do to summon Wayland was use his name. That was going to simplify things a lot from now on.

He should move on, because the police would be searching all the houses in the street now, but he had one thing to do before he left. He'd left three sacks on the floor by the door. One of them contained little bits and pieces, food, spare knives. He opened one of the others and took out Albie Dodd's head, although it was no longer easily recognisable as Albie Dodd's head. He put it on the floor, and it fell over on its side with a squelching sound and some more bits fell off. Try as he might, he couldn't get it to stand up, so he left it where it was and took from the third sack his newest acquisition.

"Head from the Parish," he said, "meet the head from across the road."

"Hello," said the new head.

"Fuck off," said Albie Dodd's head. It sounded jealous.

FIFTEEN

WITH ADAM RETURNED to his cell, and the case conference over, Mellow went back to her office and tried to face the paperwork for her other cases.

She'd been working for twenty minutes when Fleet knocked on the door. "We've got an ID card for the chap in Botley," he said, holding up a little envelope.

"Well, that's something at least," she said. She took the envelope and took out the card. Harry Kay, aged fifty-three. "Of course, until we find his head, we can't be certain. Who is he?"

"Research assistant at Trinity."

They looked at each other. "Do you ever get the feeling we did something *very* bad in a previous life, Peter?" Mellow asked tiredly.

"My wife talks of nothing else, boss."

Mellow sighed and put the card back in the envelope. "All right, see if you can get us a meeting with Trinity's head of security. Tomorrow, if possible."

"Will do." But he didn't move.

"Something else to brighten my day?" she asked.

"I was thinking about Courtenay Fox," he said.

"Me too," she said, indicating the file on her desk. "Go on."

"Well, doesn't it feel like a bit of a coincidence that we get a tip-off about the still and the body just happens to be in that house?"

Mellow thought about it and sat back in her chair. "Okay," she said.

"We've been thinking we found Courtenay by accident because we got the tip about the still, but suppose that was the whole point?" Fleet said.

Mellow looked at the opposite wall of the office.

"I mean," Fleet went on, "it really is a hell of a coincidence, isn't it?"

"It's a coincidence either way," she said. She rubbed her face. "Okay, so somebody decides to tell us where Courtenay is after all this time. Why?"

"Bad conscience?"

"After fifteen years? No, I don't think so."

"Maybe whoever stashed the still in the house found him and decided to do the decent thing."

Sometimes, as a police officer, you had to remind yourself that people did occasionally do decent things, but she shook her head. "They would have moved the still first."

"Maybe someone found the body and spent a while trying to decide what to do, and in the meantime someone else hid the still in the house."

She smiled. "How many coincidences is that now?" She thought about it. "Did that floorboard look as if it had been disturbed?"

Fleet shook his head. "It was just sticking up a bit at one end and I prised it up for a look, just in case."

"Okay, so it probably wasn't found by someone else." Although she made a note not to dismiss it completely – life was full of coincidences. "So we're back to why anyone would want us to find Courtenay."

"Because they want us to know that the people who killed him are the same people who killed that chap at Morton Street."

And that was an interesting idea, and one that had been lurking at the back of Mellow's mind. "You'll have noticed that I've been cautious not to assume they're linked," she said.

"I know," said Fleet. "But how many other murders have we had where the victim's face and hands have been burned off?"

Mellow thought some more. "All right. So, we know word about the Morton Street murder has got out, because the witness told Effie Fox about it, and she probably isn't the only one he told. Someone who knows what happened to Courtenay hears about it and sends us a tip which leads us to find him. Why do it indirectly? Why not just say, 'Courtenay's under the floorboards'?"

"To disguise where the tip came from?"

Mellow looked at him. "Do we know where the tip came from, by the way?"

Fleet shook his head. "Anonymous," he said.

"Do we at least know what it said?"

"It was Matty Wallop's tip."

Mellow considered for a few moments, then she stood up. "Where is he?"

"No," Wallop said.

"Bit of career advice, sergeant," said Mellow. "Don't say 'no' to your superiors."

Wallop looked at Maxwell for support. "I don't have to reveal my sources, sir."

"You do if it's relevant to an investigation," Mellow told him.

This argument had been going on for the last twenty minutes. It had begun in the squadroom, where Wallop had refused to tell her the content of his tip-off, and it had raged up the stairs to Maxwell's office, where the chief superintendent was regarding his officers with the look of a man watching a pair of fighting dogs.

"Let's not be too hasty here," he said, and Mellow couldn't help giving him a hard stare. "If we all started exposing our sources, we'd have no snitches at all."

Mellow kept her eyes on Maxwell, but she could almost feel Wallop smirking beside her. "Sir," she said, "with respect–"

Maxwell raised a hand. "Is this really relevant, inspector?"

Mellow couldn't believe she'd just heard him say that. "If it connects two murders, sir, yes."

"Two murders fifteen years apart." Maxwell steepled his fingers. "It's a bit of a stretch, isn't it?"

"Sir, I don't think–"

Maxwell held his hand up again. "Sergeant," he said, "could the inspector and I have a moment, please?"

Wallop looked smug. "Yes, sir."

When he'd gone, Maxwell sat looking at Mellow. Finally, he said, "Did you have to browbeat the lad, inspector?"

"Sir, he was being insubordinate."

"An officer's entitled to protect his sources, you know."

"I gave him a direct order to tell me."

Maxwell waved it away. "Is this really so important?"

"I won't know until I know, sir. It might be."

"And it might not, and then all this unpleasantness will have been for nothing. Why didn't you take this to Superintendent Todd instead of bringing it all the way up here?"

"Superintendent Todd isn't in his office, sir."

"And it couldn't have waited until he returned?" Maxwell sat back and regarded Mellow across his desk. "I think you're blowing this up out of all proportion. I don't see what possible use it could be to you to know who sent in that tip."

Mellow was momentarily lost for words.

"I think your workload has become unsustainable," Maxwell went on. "I've handed the investigation into the murders in Cumnor over to the Transport Unit."

Had it taken away, more like. "So I gather, sir," she said dully. "From whom?"

"Professor Solomons said he'd been asked to send his autopsy reports to Chancellery."

Solomons, as a professor at one of the Colleges, was beyond Maxwell's reach. "Hm. Quite. Anyway, it'll give you time to concentrate on more important matters." He took a photograph from a drawer and put it on the desk. Mellow took a step forward and looked at it, saw the bedroom wall at the Botley murder scene, *Wayland* daubed on the wallpaper in blood. "Do you know what this is?"

There was an almost-complete set of *Encyclopaedia Britannica* in the squadroom, which some long-ago detective had found somewhere. Mellow had checked it when she got back from Botley. "Wayland is a legendary blacksmith in Norse legend," she said. "He's enslaved by a king, who cripples him to keep him captive, but Wayland creates a winged cloak and flies away."

Maxwell blinked. "What does that have to do with a murder in Botley?"

"I don't know, sir. There's a Stone Age tomb in the Chilterns that people call Wayland's Smithy."

Maxwell was obviously lost. "You don't think this could be a new gang?" he asked.

"I haven't ruled it out yet, sir."

"Well, I think that's a line you could be investigating, rather than harassing your sergeants."

"Harassing?"

"Yes." Maxwell seemed to come to a decision. "Yes, it really does feel like harassment, Mellow, and I won't have that sort of behaviour on my force." He tapped the photograph.

"Concentrate on this and leave Wallop alone."

It was really not worth losing her job over, but Mellow felt herself coming close to throwing her badge on the desk and walking out. "Sir."

"You won't have to put up with him much longer, anyway. He's being promoted."

Mellow felt her mind go blank, just for a second. "Sir?"

"He's being promoted," Maxwell said, putting the photo back in the drawer. "Back into uniform. He's going to be given his own station to command."

All Mellow could bring herself to say was, "Oh."

"We've done well here, Mellow," Maxwell said. "It hasn't been easy, but we've rebuilt the Thames Valley Force from almost nothing. We can't squander that achievement over petty squabbling."

Actually, it was officers like her father and grandfather who'd done the rebuilding; Maxwell was a political appointment, dropped into place by Chancellery. She didn't even know where he'd spent most of his career.

He shook his head. "Look, go and do your job, inspector. Concentrate on the work. And I want to know more about this 'Wayland'."

"Sir."

Mellow went back down to her office and sat at her desk and stared blankly at the wall until Fleet looked in. "Boss?"

"They're promoting Wallop to station inspector," she said without looking at him.

Fleet was silent while he tried to process this. "Wasn't expecting *that*," he said finally.

"No," she said. "No, me neither."

Another silence. "I got in touch with Trinity's security office," he said. "Commander Powell says he'll see you first thing tomorrow."

She nodded. "Good. Thank you, Peter."

"Was there anything else, boss?"

Mellow shook her head. "No, I don't think so," she said, still numb with what Maxwell had told her. "I think I'll call it a day and go home."

"Right. See you tomorrow, then."

"Yes," she said. "See you tomorrow, Peter."

SHE DIDN'T GO directly home, though. She caught the final ferry of the day across the Cherwell, but instead of cutting across the Iffley Road and into Headington she turned south. Ruth Sharpe lived quite a way out of the town centre, down near what had once been Florence Park but was now one of the city's many farms. It was dark and it was raining heavily, and the dynamo-powered lamp on the handlebars of her bicycle barely lit the way a dozen feet ahead of her, but she kept going, checking the signs until she found the right street.

Most of the houses on the street had wind generators in their back gardens and lights in their windows, but Sharpe's house was dark. Mellow carried on to the end of the street, did a U-turn, and cycled back the way she'd come. There didn't seem to be anyone else about, so she stopped, parked her bike, and went up the path to the front door. She knocked and waited, but no lights came on inside and nobody came to answer the door. She stepped over to the big front bow window and looked in, but she couldn't make out anything apart from darker objects that might have been furniture.

She wondered how far she could push it, one colleague coming to visit another who'd suddenly been transferred. Could she, for instance, reasonably break in? Knock up the neighbours and ask if they knew what had happened to Sharpe and her mother, who didn't get about very well these days because of a stroke?

Best not, she thought. She sensed that she was taking a risk just by being here, but she didn't know what she was at risk *from*. She was still angry about Wallop, and she was aware that she might let that cloud her judgement if she wasn't careful, but what was she worried about? Someone had been transferred and had moved house without telling her. So what? There was an inspector up at Sunnymead who didn't seem to have a personnel file. So what? She could think of half a dozen reasons for that, and none of them was in the least bit sinister. An officer who'd been in the force for about five minutes was going to be promoted above her. So what? Fuck that, that's what.

SIXTEEN

"CAN YOU RIDE a bike?" Mellow asked Adam the next morning, standing in the doorway of his cell.

"Yes," he said, and he saw that stop her in her tracks for a moment.

"All right," she said. "Come with me. We're going for a ride."

Downstairs, she led him down a corridor to the back of the building and pushed open a door and stepped out into a big walled yard. Three carts were parked neatly; to one side there was a stable block, and on the other side there was a big shed. Mellow opened the door of the shed and Adam saw rows of bicycles.

Mellow pulled her bike out of its rack and gestured towards the other end of the shed. "Those are for communal use," she told him. "Pick yourself one and let's go." Adam thought she sounded tense and brittle, even by her standards.

He took his time selecting a bicycle and wheeled it out into the yard, where Mellow was waiting and looking impatient. They pushed their bikes over to a big gate in the wall, a constable opened it for them and they rode off into the city.

"Where are we going?" Adam asked as they pedalled down the street. It was a little while since he'd last been on a bicycle, and he found himself having to concentrate on not losing his balance.

"I've got a meeting with someone," she said, "and because I'm not supposed to let you out of my sight, you'll have to come with me."

"I'm happy to stay in my room," he told her, although he wasn't, particularly. They'd stopped locking him in the cell, but there was no handle on the inside, so it didn't make any difference.

She shook her head. "Let's follow orders, for the moment," she said heavily. "We identified yesterday's murder victim. He was a research assistant at Trinity College, so we're going to see their head of security. I'll do all the talking. You just sit there."

"Okay."

"Back in the early days after the Sisters, the Colleges fortified themselves," she said, "but without them we wouldn't have survived."

"Your father explained it to me."

"He did? Okay. Well, even when things improved, they stayed fortified. The Colleges and the Chancellor's Office make up Chancellery, but otherwise they're independent. They each have their own little police force and we're not allowed inside without an invitation. In practice, we get on okay; in fact, I'm currently investigating some burglaries at Trinity because the suspicion is that somebody from outside is responsible, so I've been working with their security recently. The bloke we're going to see is all right, really, as it goes. But seriously, just sit and listen and let me do my job, all right?"

"All right."

"Who's Wayland?"

He's me. "I don't know," he said, not wrongfooted by the sudden right-turn in the conversation because he'd spent most of the night sitting on his mattress thinking about it.

"He's some sort of demon blacksmith in Norse legends," Mellow said. "Ring any bells?"

Adam didn't answer.

Mellow sighed. "How about I tell you a secret, and you tell me one?"

Adam thought about that. "How will I know what you tell me is a secret?"

"You'll just have to trust me."

He shrugged. "Okay. You first."

She pedalled on beside him for a hundred yards or so, thinking. "I'm terrified that if I'm not very careful, me and my dad will suddenly go missing one day."

Which was so unexpected that he looked at her and almost toppled his bike. "Why do you think that?"

She shook her head. "Doesn't matter."

"Come on, inspector, you can't just say something like that and not explain it."

She shook her head again. "Your turn."

He considered for a moment, wondering how to approach it. "Someone calling themselves Wayland killed a lot of people in the hills on the other side of the Vale of the White Horse," he said finally. "They were talking about it in Streatley when I passed through."

"That's not a secret," she said. "That's just you admitting you've been lying to me." She didn't sound disappointed, or even particularly surprised. "Which one are you? Red One, Red Two, or Red Three?"

"I don't understand," he said, so she told him about the radio transmissions the police had been picking up. Red One and Red Two would be Betty Coghlan and Guz, but Red Three sounded interesting, a distant and powerful radio transmitter he'd never heard of before.

"Do you think it could be France?" Mellow asked. "Ruth did."

He shook his head. "There's nobody in France. Not near the coast, anyway."

Mellow glanced at him and smiled. "Now *that*," she said, "is a secret."

He scowled.

They'd left behind the more modern city centre and were now riding through an area of far older buildings, stone-built with lots of spires and crenelations. Mellow nodded at one, a big round building with a dome. "That's Chancellery," she said. It wasn't really what Adam had imagined. "They couldn't agree which College to put it in," Mellow went on. "And they didn't want it in the city centre, so they stuck it here. Used to be a library. Do you think this Wayland is here now?"

"I genuinely don't know," he said.

"How many did he kill, up there in the hills?"

I lost count. "I don't know. A lot."

"And nobody tried to stop him?"

"There was a war going on at the time," he said. "All these farmers fighting each other. I don't think anyone really noticed."

"So how come people in Streatley were talking about him?"

"He signed his work."

Mellow thought about that. "Okay."

They were cycling now along a neatly tree-lined street. On their left was a stone wall that had been built up, first with more stone and then with courses of brick, until it was almost thirty feet high. They came to a gateway blocked by a solid-looking wooden door with the remains of an ironwork arch above it. "Trinity," said Mellow.

A head appeared looking over the wall beside the gate.

"Detective Inspector Mellow, Thames Valley CID," Mellow called. "To see Commander Powell."

Adam saw the figure on the wall train an automatic rifle at them. "Have you caught whoever's been nicking our stuff yet?" the guard called down.

"We're still making inquiries," Mellow said tiredly.

The guard snorted. "That sounds about right. You should let us do it."

"And if you can talk Chancellery into changing the rules and giving you jurisdiction in the city, I'll be happy to let you," she replied. "Now are you going to let us in or not, Richard? I've got things to be getting on with."

Richard pointed the rifle at Adam. "Who's he?"

"He's with me. For my sins."

Richard thought about it for a moment, then his head disappeared behind the wall, and a few moments later someone inside cranked the door open. Mellow dismounted and wheeled her bicycle through, and Adam followed.

Inside was another world. Ahead of them a path ran between neatly ploughed and planted vegetable gardens towards some old buildings in the distance. In the middle of one of the vegetable patches, held steady by a network of guywires, was a radio mast that must have been almost a hundred feet tall.

"You leave your bikes here," Richard told them, coming down a set of steps from the parapet. "You walk over to the security office. You don't enter any other building. You don't enter any of the workshops or classrooms or lecture theatres. When you're done, you come straight back here and collect your bikes. Unless they've been nicked."

"They'd better not be," Mellow told him, and if there had been a tone of reciting a well-worn set of instructions in Richard's voice, she sounded dead serious. She looked at Adam. "Come on."

They walked down the path towards the buildings, Adam trying not to stare at the radio mast. Mellow said, "Were there any murders in Abingdon?"

"What?"

"Abingdon. You said you came through there on the way here."

"Oh." That particular part of the story had slipped his mind. "No, I don't think so."

Mellow sighed and lowered her voice. "You can carry on telling Hob and my superiors this lovely little story about coming here from Southampton looking for work, and I won't stop you," she told him. "But if you have any information, anything at all, that could help me stop this person, I'd like to hear it. I'm not involved in the investigation into the Cumnor murders anymore, but I'm proceeding as if this *Wayland* was responsible for them, too. That's five people butchered, and I don't want any more."

"Did he leave his name at Cumnor?"

"Nobody reported seeing it," she said.

"He'd have put it where we could see it."

"There *is* no *we*, Mr Hardy," she told him crisply. "There's *you*, and there's the Thames Valley Police Force. Here we are."

The path ended in a courtyard surrounded on three sides by three-storied buildings of biscuit-coloured stone. They were the cleanest buildings Adam had ever seen. The whole of Trinity was the cleanest, neatest place he'd ever seen. If it wasn't for the pouring rain, he could have kidded himself that The Sisters had never happened.

Mellow led the way across the courtyard to a door, and then up a couple of flights of stairs to an office, where a young woman wearing olive-green trousers, a green shirt, and a green sweater with two pips on each shoulder was sitting behind a desk.

"Captain Marks," said Mellow. "I'm here to see the commander. I have an appointment."

"Yes, you do, inspector." Marks looked at Adam. "I'm not sure this gentleman does, though."

"The commander knows about it," Mellow told her. "Mr Hardy's consulting with us about this case."

Marks raised an eyebrow. "Well, if the commander knows about it," she said. "Go on through; he's waiting."

Mellow went over to another door, knocked, and opened it. "Commander Powell," she said. "Good morning."

The office beyond the door was well-furnished, with two leather armchairs and a leather sofa, desk, chairs, filing cabinets along one wall, a coat-tree beside the door. It had a big window looking out over the courtyard and the vegetable gardens beyond, and the man standing at it would have been able to watch them all the way from the gate.

"Inspector," he said, turning from the window and coming round the desk with his hand outstretched. "And the mysterious Mr Hardy. Good morning." He was a tall, trim man in his forties, with greying hair and a firm handshake. He was wearing the same uniform as the captain in the outer office, but instead of pips he had a little brass star on each shoulder. "Sit down, please."

There were some moments of low comedy while everybody tried to decide where to sit. Adam and Mellow wound up on the sofa, Powell facing them in one of the armchairs. "So," he said. "You found poor old Harry."

Searching in her knapsack, Mellow said, "Why 'poor old' Harry?"

"Well, you said he was dead."

"Hm." Mellow took her hand out of her knapsack holding a city identity card. She handed it over and Powell opened it.

"Yes, that's Harry, I'm afraid. Do you have a positive identification of the body?"

"Apart from him being in his own bed, no," Mellow told him. "I'm afraid Mr Kay's head is still missing."

Powell looked at her. "Yes," he said. "Yes, I can see that would..." He looked at the card again, closed it. "Do you have any suspects?"

"Our inquiries are still continuing," Mellow said. "Which is why we're here. Did you know Mr Kay?"

Powell nodded. "Not well, he's with Professor Halloran's

department, but he volunteered for security duty, did shifts patrolling the wall, so I have met him."

"It seems Mr Kay may have been dead for some time before he was found," said Mellow. "When did you notice he was missing?"

"Last Thursday," said Powell. "Professor Halloran let it go for a couple of days; he assumed Harry was just ill. Then he reported it to me, and I passed it on to the police. I assume one of your officers found him?"

Mellow nodded. "Were any other problems brought to the attention of your office? Official complaints, stuff like that?"

Powell shook his head. "As far as this office is concerned, Harry was spotless. The only contact we ever had with him was when he did his shifts; none of my people had a bad word to say about him."

"I notice he didn't live in College."

"That's not unusual, as you know, inspector. Rooms in College are limited to students and academic staff, not research assistants." Powell looked at Adam. "I see you're a connoisseur of maps, Mr Hardy."

Adam had been looking at a big, framed map mounted on the wall above the filing cabinets. "I wouldn't say that," he said, and he felt Mellow stiffen beside him. "May I?"

"Please do," said Powell.

Adam got up and went over to the filing cabinets and looked more closely at the map. Well, there it was, England as it was currently known, from The Lizard to Thanet and from the Isle of Wight to not very far north of Oxford, a truncated country. A scatter of Sisters had struck the Midlands, some of them large enough to actually rearrange the landscape. They had obliterated Birmingham and Leicester and Nottingham and Derby, and the resulting devastation had flooded and drained and flooded and drained and flooded again and become choked with dense overgrowth and woodland, a belt of almost impenetrable bogland and forest and broken landscape that more or less divided the country in half. The Badlands had become a haven for wild animals and outcasts and all sorts of myths and legends. Nobody knew how far north they extended, or what lay beyond them. Stuck on the wall like this, England seemed very small, and his wanderings in it very insignificant. Sometimes it was a struggle just to keep going on.

"I'd like a couple of my detectives to interview Mr Kay's colleagues," Mellow was saying behind him.

"They'd have to come here and do it," Powell replied after a moment, "but apart from that I don't see any problem."

"And while I'm here, would it be possible to speak with Professor Halloran?"

"I'm afraid not," Powell said. "Professor Halloran is unavailable at the moment."

"Oh?" Mellow said in a carefully neutral tone of voice. "Unavailable how?"

Trinity's head of security wasn't going to keep a tactical map on the wall of his office for anyone to see; it was a nice map, but there was no useful information here. Adam turned away and looked at Mellow and Powell.

"He's on sabbatical," Powell said. "Carrying out research. Not to be disturbed."

Mellow digested this. "So when would I be able to speak to him?"

"Not for another two weeks," Powell told her.

Mellow kept her eyes on him. "Well, that's no good, commander," she said. "A member of his staff has been murdered and the killer is most likely still in the city somewhere."

"To be honest, inspector," Powell said reasonably, "I'm not sure the professor could tell you anything that Harry's co-workers wouldn't. Harry's one of a number of research assistants; he and the professor weren't in each other's pockets."

Mellow shook her head. "You see, commander, this is how

police work works. We ask questions, and those questions lead to other questions, and those lead to other questions, and then, oh my word, all of a sudden the bad person's in custody."

"And what a wonderful world it would be if that were true," Powell said. "Look, perhaps if you were to leave a list of questions, I could pass them on to the professor and let you know his answers."

"That's not remotely ideal," said Mellow.

"It's the best solution I can think of. Or you could wait a fortnight and speak to the professor face to face." Mellow was obviously not happy. "If it were up to me, I'd get him in here right now," Powell told her. "But I'm not allowed to interfere in academic matters."

Mellow glanced at Adam, who shrugged. "Well," she said, "this is disappointing, commander. I thought we had a better working relationship than that."

"And we do," Powell said smoothly. "This is just an... unfortunate coincidence. If Harry hadn't died, none of this would matter."

"It's more than *unfortunate*," Mellow told him. "Harry didn't just die. He was beheaded and disembowelled and generally butchered, and whoever did that may do it again, and the professor might have information which could stop them."

"Well, quite," Powell said. "But in all honesty, how likely is that?"

"That really is the point, commander," Mellow said in a crisp tone of voice Adam was starting to recognise. "I won't know until I talk to him." She shook her head. "Very well. I'll have a list of questions biked over to you later today." She stood up. "But I'd appreciate the answers as soon as possible."

"Of course," Powell said. He stood up, too, and looked at Adam. "What do you think of my map, Mr Hardy?"

"It's very pretty," Adam deadpanned.

"You'll have seen better, I expect."

"Not at all." The Bureau tended to work from old Ordnance Survey sheets and road atlases, on the grounds that roads and towns were generally in the same places now as they had been before The Sisters. They made their own, more up-to-date, maps, too, but it was a slow, painstaking process, and they didn't wind up on office walls. This map was just a decoration. "But it is very pretty."

Powell narrowed his eyes slightly, and Adam had a sense that he was being weighed up. Was he as stupid as he looked? Might he be dangerous? It seemed Powell couldn't make up his mind.

"Well, I've taken up enough of your time," Mellow said. She slung her knapsack over her shoulder. "If you let me know when my officers can speak with Mr Kay's colleagues, I'll get that organised."

Powell looked at Adam a moment longer, then smiled and turned back to Mellow. "Of course. And I'm sorry I couldn't help you with Professor Halloran, but you understand how it is."

"Actually, I don't," she told him. She nodded at Adam. "Let's go."

Adam noted that nobody offered to shake hands as they left.

"What was all that about?" Mellow asked as she stomped along the path towards the gate through the rain.

"Which 'all that' are you talking about?" Adam said.

"That stare-off you and Powell were having at the end."

Adam shook his head. "He was lying," he said. "About the professor."

"Maybe not," she told him. "Academics are weird. But he was definitely not as helpful as he might have been."

He looked at the radio mast. "What kind of research do they do here?"

"Technical stuff, mostly. They designed the radios we use, and more efficient wind generators. That's why they're so pissed off about the burglaries; somebody's been nicking electrical parts, and that stuff doesn't grow on trees."

Adam stopped and looked about him, hands in pockets.

"What?" said Mellow.

"You know," he said, "just a few days' walk from here there are people who have almost nothing. No running water, no electricity, hardly any food, constantly on the edge of going under without a trace. And there are places that are even worse than that." He waved at the vegetable patches, the radio mast, the buildings they'd just come from. "And you have all *this*."

"So?" she asked. "What do you want us to do? Ride out and bring electricity to everybody? Is that what you do in 'Southampton'?"

"I keep having to remind myself that most of the country isn't like this."

"I can take you out to Blackbird Leys, if you want to see a place where people don't have anything," she said. She took a step towards him. "We've done what we have to in order to survive," she said, "and don't you *dare* criticise us for that. We've done our bit supporting communities outside the city, and we did it when we didn't have a lot to spare for ourselves." She poked him in the chest. "Don't tell us how to run our affairs."

"And now you're nice and comfortable you've closed the city off from the outside."

"That's a policy decision, not mine," she told him. "If it was up to me, we'd be out there right now planting windmills in every farm and handing out antibiotics like sweeties, but we don't have the resources."

"It looks to me like you have plenty of resources."

"There's over twenty thousand people living in Oxford now," she said. "Our duty's to them, not to the people living outside. We help our own first, because Christ knows we have our own problems."

"I'm disappointed with you, inspector."

"Yeah? Well, you're not the first, and I doubt you'll be the last. Come on." She turned away and started to walk towards the gate again, and after a few moments Adam followed, making an effort not to check whether Powell had been standing at his window watching them argue. It occurred to him that, while the map in Powell's office hadn't contained any useful intelligence, it was interesting that the head of Trinity's security would have a map of southern England on his wall, rather than a map of the city.

He was still putting the geography of the city together in his head, so it took him several minutes to realise that they weren't heading back towards police headquarters.

"Where are we going?" he asked.

"Something I want to look at," she told him.

Fine. He needed to stretch his legs after spending so long cooped up in the cell, anyway. They cycled further up the street beside Trinity for a while, past a big area of farmland, then through a junction onto a main road. A sign fixed to a wall said *BANBURY ROAD*. Here, there were more of what he was starting to recognise as university buildings, some of them still in use and others abandoned and lost behind overgrowth. The road itself was clear of old vehicles and obviously well-maintained, although they still had to steer around occasional potholes. There were fewer people here, but he noticed a steady stream of carts coming down the road past them, their loadbeds covered with tarps.

Gradually, the university buildings petered out, replaced by big old houses and more recent blocks of flats, all of them apparently occupied, although as they cycled further up the road more and more of them seemed to have been abandoned. They passed through what seemed to be a little town centre, both sides of the road lined with old shops, some open, most boarded up. Adam had a sense that this part of Oxford had been mothballed, preserved and set aside for future use, in much the same way as Guz had preserved parts of Plymouth against future increases in population. That kind of forward planning was a luxury most communities just didn't have. Further on, there were more houses, all of them occupied. They passed a collection of one-storey brick buildings with a big sign outside that said *THAMES VALLEY POLICE SUNNYMEAD POLICE STATION.*

"Gateway to the North," Mellow said.

"What?"

She shook her head. "Something somebody said to me the other day."

"I don't see any police officers about," he said.

"No," she said. "No, neither do I."

Beyond the police station were more little blocks of flats, and then Adam could see something in the distance blocking the road. Mellow stopped, and Adam stopped beside her, and they sat on their bicycles looking up the road at what seemed to be a solid wall of old vehicles, buses and cars.

"End of the road," Mellow said. Then, "Actually, that's not true. The road carries on beyond the barricade, all the way to Banbury, oddly enough, and there's some big farms just the other side. But this is the northern edge of the city. The barricade looks solid, but there's a path through it wide enough for a wagon. This is where the Banbury Road crosses the Bypass. The Bypass goes all the way around the city, so I suppose it seemed like the natural place to put up roadblocks, back in the day."

Adam looked about him. Well, it was useful intelligence, but he couldn't see why Mellow had come all this way out of the centre of town.

Two figures were walking down the road towards them from the barricade. As they got closer, Adam saw that they were wearing combat fatigues and carrying assault rifles.

"Hello," said one of them, a woman with her hair tied back in a ponytail. "Lost, are we?"

Mellow showed her badge. "Inspector Mellow, Thames Valley CID," she said.

The woman looked at the badge, said, "And your ID?"

Mellow dug her identity card out and held it up. "Is there some kind of alert on?"

"Just doing our job, inspector." She looked at Adam. "What about you?"

"He's with me," Mellow said.

"I can see that," the woman said. She snapped her fingers at Adam. "ID." Adam took his identity card out of his pocket and handed it over. "This hasn't been filled in properly," she said. "There's no address or anything."

"That's because he's a guest in the city," Mellow said. "A guest of Chancellery."

The woman looked at Adam, looked at the card, looked at Adam again. "Where are you from?"

"Southampton," said Adam.

"What's that like, then?"

"It's lovely."

The woman gave Adam a long, level look, then she handed the card back. "Next time you feel the urge to go sightseeing, you'll need a pass from the Transport Unit," she told Mellow. "We had some people killed the other day."

"Yes," Mellow said. "I know. I didn't get the memo about the Transport Unit taking over checkpoint security, though."

"That's bureaucracy for you," the woman said with a smile. "Is there anything we can show you, now you're here?"

"No," said Mellow. "No, I don't think so."

"Well, you have a safe trip back into town, then."

"We'll do our best," Mellow told her, turning her bicycle round. "Thank you."

When they'd cycled out of earshot of the guards, Adam said, "What was all that about?"

"I don't know," said Mellow. "But I don't like it."

As they passed Sunnymead police station again, Adam noticed a solitary police officer standing on the pavement outside, watching them go by.

WHEN ADAM AND Mellow got back to police headquarters, they found half a dozen heavily armed men wearing black uniforms waiting in the foyer being watched cautiously by the front desk sergeant. Adam sensed Mellow missing half a step when she saw them, and she came to a stop just inside the doors.

One of the uniformed men came over. "Inspector Mellow?" he asked. "Superintendent Price. We're here for your prisoner."

"He's not a prisoner," Mellow said tightly. "He's under my supervision."

Price was a tall, lean man, the kind who looks skinny but is actually all muscle. He had a bland, inoffensive face that was spoiled by a cruel little mouth. He said, "I'm here on the Chancellor's authority. He's wanted at Chancellery."

"Then you'll have some kind of authorisation to show me," Mellow told him. Adam had no idea what was happening, but he had a sudden sense that Mellow was doing something quite brave.

Price smiled thinly, unclipped a breast pocket of his uniform, and took out a folded sheet of paper. He held it out to Mellow. "You'll want to see this, too, I suppose," he said, showing her his badge.

"I'll want to see more than that, superintendent," Mellow told him as she unfolded the sheet of paper. "There's a gang of lads over in Cowley knocking those out for a hundred quid apiece."

Price's face hardened. "I'd have thought you'd want to do something about that." But he held out an identity card for Mellow to see.

"Yes, well," she said, plucking the card from his fingers, "we keep asking for more manpower."

Price narrowed his eyes at her. "Give that back," he said.

"I'm reading," Mellow told him, looking at the sheet of paper. "Sir."

Adam glanced over at Price's colleagues. Automatic rifles, sidearms, knives. A couple of them had what looked like grenades clipped to the front of their uniforms. They all looked fit and capable, and not one of them seemed to have anything that could be called a sense of humour.

"Well," Mellow said eventually, "this all seems in order. Although these days, who knows?" She folded the sheet of paper. "I'll keep this."

"You will not," Price said, taking it from her. "And my card."

Mellow handed it over. "You'll have to sign for him."

Price gave her a look calculated to make her take a step back. "What?"

Mellow stood her ground. "You'll have to sign for him," she said again.

"No, I won't."

"I'm afraid you will," she told him. "We do things properly here. There has to be a chain of custody." She smiled brightly. "Otherwise, things have a habit of going missing."

"No," Price snapped. He glanced at Adam. "You. Come with me."

"No," Mellow said without taking her eyes off Price. "Stay where you are. Carol?"The front desk sergeant, who had been watching the whole exchange with an expression of horrified fascination, seemed to snap awake. "Yes, inspector?"

"Do you have any custody sheets handy?"

The sergeant checked in a drawer of her desk. "Yes," she said. "Lots."

Still smiling at Price, Mellow said, "Fill one out for Mr Adam Hardy, would you? Date it today, put this as his address, and write me in as custody officer. In triplicate." She added to Price, "One copy for us, one for you, one for Registry. All proper and above board." He stared at her as if unable to believe what was happening to him.

Carol took some sheets of paper from the drawer, poised a pen over them. "What offence should I put?" she asked, tentatively getting into the swing of things.

Mellow looked at Adam, thinking. "Vagrancy?" Adam shrugged. "Yes, vagrancy. Congratulations," she added. "You've just been officially arrested."

He looked at Price, who appeared to be struggling with an urge to unholster his pistol and start shooting. "Is there always this much paperwork?"

"It is the bane of my life," she assured him. "Can you write your name?"

"Yes."

"Come on, then," she said, and she set off towards the desk, leaving Price where he was. Adam gave him an apologetic shrug and followed.

At the desk, Mellow bent over the documents and pointed. "Sign here and here," she said. "All three sheets, please." As Adam leant down to take the pen, she said in a barely audible voice, "Transport Unit. Don't annoy them." Which seemed a bold thing to say, considering she seemed to be going out of her way to annoy them.

"What?" Price snapped, coming up behind them.

"Just showing Mr Hardy where to sign," Mellow told him. "He hasn't seen anything like this before, have you?"

"No," Adam said, signing his name. "I really haven't."

"Give me that," Price said. He snatched the pen from Adam's fingers, scrawled a signature on each of the sheets without bothering to read them, grabbed one of them, crumpled it up, and stuffed it in his pocket. "We're going now." He waved at his men without looking at them. "Bring him."

"Wait," Mellow said calmly, picking up one of the other documents and looking at it.

Price took a single pace back, and Adam had that sick anticipation one gets when one realises that a fight is inevitable. He balanced his weight on the balls of his feet in case he had to move in a hurry.

"You missed one," Mellow said, holding the sheet out and pointing. "Here."

Price looked at the sheet, then he very slowly and delicately took it from her, put it on the table, and signed in the empty space. Then he signed the other copy. Then he took the crumpled sheet from his pocket, carefully smoothed it out, signed it, folded it, and put it back in his pocket. Then he held the pen out to Mellow.

"I think you'll find everything is in order now, inspector," he said in a very calm, quiet voice.

Mellow checked the custody documents. "All spick and span," she agreed. "Thank you. Sir."

Over on the other side of the lobby, a little group of policemen came down the stairs and stopped a few steps from the bottom. They all had wooden batons hanging from loops on their belts, and if they weren't quite as dangerous looking as Price's men, they at least looked serious. The two groups regarded each other casually.

"Right," Price snapped, and two of his men came up and grasped Adam by the elbows. "Inspector," he added.

"Superintendent," said Mellow. She looked at Adam, and he found her expression impossible to read. "I want him brought back here when you're done," she told Price.

"He'll be brought back when we're ready," Price told her, and he set off for the doors, the two men on either side of Adam marching him along behind.

There was a cart waiting outside in the rain with a big solidly built box on the back. It had a door secured by a hasp and padlock, and one of the Transport Unit men unlocked and opened it while the others held Adam a few paces back. He turned his head and saw Mellow standing in the doorway, hands in her pockets, all the police officers from the lobby trying to peek past her to see what was going on.

The Transport Unit man pulled down a hinged set of steps from the back of the cart, and the others urged Adam none too gently up them and shoved him into the box. The door slammed behind him, and he lay where he was on the floor of the box while he listened to the padlock being locked again.

"Hello, mate," said an amiable voice from the darkness near the front of the box. "What're you in for, then?"

"No talking!" someone shouted outside, giving the side of the box a whack. A few moments later, there was a lurch as they set off.

The box had seemed strong and well-made from the outside, but there were enough little gaps between the planks for some light to get through. Adam got into a sitting position, and as his eyes adjusted to the dimness, he saw that there were two other people in the box with him. One was a big man with straggly hair and an untidy beard; the other, curled up in a corner, was a young woman with a bruise on the side of her face.

"I'm Jim," said the man more quietly. He looked at the woman. "Don't know her name. She doesn't talk much."

Adam tried to get himself comfortable against the wall of the box. He gave the door a push with his foot, but it didn't budge.

"Tried that," Jim said. "What's the point, anyway? What are you going to do, run off down the street with them shooting at you?"

It had crossed Adam's mind. "Who are they?"

Jim tipped his head over to one side. "Not from round here, then, son?"

"No."

Jim waited to see if any more information was forthcoming. When it wasn't, he said, "Transport Unit. Special Police."

"What's so special about them?"

"Well, the police have *rules*, you see," Jim said. "And the Transport Unit don't. They make people disappear." He added glumly, "Like us."

"What did you do?"

"Me? *I* don't know."

Adam suspected this was not remotely true. "Didn't they tell you?"

Jim snorted. "Transport Unit don't have to tell you. What about you?"

"All I did was come looking for work."

Jim shook his head. "Chancellery don't like outsiders. We used to, once upon a time, but not anymore. The Chancellor says they're a *burden on our resources*."

"It looks to me like you have plenty of resources. More than people out in the country, anyway."

"Yeah," said Jim. "Maybe so. But we can't have all those people coming here and taking the stuff we worked hard for, can we? You work all your life to make a place nice, and then somebody just wanders in out of nowhere and takes it, that isn't right, is it?"

Adam squinted through a gap in the boards. "I didn't want to take anyone's stuff," he said. "I just wanted an honest day's work."

But Jim was just getting into his stride. "But where would you live? You can't just expect to be given a house, you know. Someone worked for months to fix that house up, and you just wander in here and take it."

"I hadn't really thought that far ahead," Adam told him.

"I've got nothing against them outside the city," Jim said, "but we can't just give them stuff. It's not fair."

In Guz, the policy was to assign newcomers to the farms outside the city. Not because there wasn't room for them – Plymouth's population was still a fraction of what it had been before The Sisters – but because the country needed to be settled and reclaimed, otherwise there was no point in carrying on. And also, Adam had to admit, because every new farm, every resettled village, extended Guz's influence a little further.

He said, "If someone comes here and works, that's not giving them stuff."

"But they're taking *our* jobs," Jim pointed out.

It seemed to Adam that there was more than enough work to do in Oxford to employ everyone in the area, but he thought Jim didn't want to hear that. "Anyway," he said, "I just wanted to work and I wound up getting arrested."

"Father John says we're building a better England," said the girl.

Adam froze.

"Ah, bollocks to that," Jim said. "I just want a hot meal and my own bed."

"I saw him once, in Compton Vale," she told him listlessly. "He said it'll stop raining soon and we have to be ready, otherwise the outsiders will come and take everything."

"Yeah, right," Jim said, looking at the water dripping into the box. "It'll stop raining soon."

The girl didn't reply, just curled up on herself and closed her eyes. Adam looked at her, then at Jim, who shrugged. "Weak in the head, if you ask me," he said.

The cart suddenly came to a halt. There were sounds of people dismounting from the cart, then the door was unlocked and pulled open. Adam saw Price and two Transport Unit officers standing in the road.

"You," Price said. "Out."

"No," said Adam.

"Best go with them, son," Jim told him.

Now he was in the box, it was going to be hard for them to get him out. There was only room for one of them to actually climb in, and one wasn't going to be enough to drag him out. If they were stupid enough to send someone in armed, he was going to wind up in possession of whatever weapons they were carrying. On the other hand, they didn't seem stupid, and the chances were that everyone was just going to stay here all day in the rain shouting at each other. He wondered, in passing, which of them would crack first.

He shuffled along the box until he could get through the door and climbed down into the street. The two officers grabbed him by the elbows again. Looking about, he saw that they were parked outside Chancellery, the big round building. People passing by were carefully ignoring what was going on.

"What about me?" Jim called from inside the box.

"You've still got a way to go," Price told him, slamming the door and locking it. He waved to the driver and the cart moved off again. Adam could hear Jim shouting inside the box, but his voice was soon lost in the sound of the rain and other passing traffic.

Price said, "Bring him," and he set off up the path towards the Chancellery building, the Transport Unit officers marching Adam along behind him. They went up a flight of steps to a wooden door, which Price opened, and passed inside.

The interior of Chancellery, Adam realised, was hollow, a single space with the building's dome high above. Almost the whole floor was occupied by a huge circular table with twenty or thirty chairs arranged around it, although only five of them were occupied. On the far side, opposite the entrance, an older man sat in a chair with a high back, flanked by another two men in suits. To one side, he recognised Hob and John, sitting side by side. The table in front of John was littered with sheets of paper.

Price went over to the men and there was a brief, quiet conversation. Then he took a piece of paper from his pocket and gave it to the man in the high-backed chair, and all of a sudden, the men at the table were all guffawing with laughter, somewhat to Price's discomfort. Their voices echoed around the big room.

Finally, John stood up and beckoned broadly. "Adam!" he called. "Come on in and take the weight off your feet, my friend!"

The officers on either side of Adam released his arms. He stood where he was for a moment, then walked around the table to where John had started scribbling on a fresh sheet of paper. "Chain of custody," he chortled as Adam reached him. "Inspector Mellow really is magnificent. Now we have to sign for you, too." He finished writing, scrawled a signature, and handed it to Price. "There you go, superintendent. Goods gratefully received." He looked at Adam. "Sit, sit. You're making the place look untidy."

Adam pulled out the chair beside him and sat down. Price stood where he was, holding the sheet of paper, until he realised he wasn't wanted anymore. He gave Adam a last baleful look and left, taking his men with him.

"Well," John said, beaming at Adam. "Welcome to Chancellery, young Adam. Although it's not really Chancellery; this is just where it meets. All the offices and bureaucracy are across the road in the Bodleian." He looked at the others. "I should make some introductions. Mr Hob you've already met, and this splendid chap in the big chair is Chancellor Cole. The gentlemen on either side are the Masters of Trinity and Christ Church."

Adam looked at the men, but they were regarding him as if he was a lower form of life.

"And I'm just here to take notes," John finished, indicating the mess on the table. "Full meetings of Chancellery only take place a couple of times a year. It's quite a sight, seeing this place full."

Adam looked up towards the ceiling. He saw a gallery running around the room, about halfway up, with arches looking down on the table. "I gather I'm not a murder suspect anymore," he said.

John raised his eyebrows. "A *murder suspect*?" he looked at Hob.

"There's still room for some doubt," Hob said, a sour expression on his face.

"Well, *that's* no good," John said. "A man's either a murder suspect or he isn't; he can't be both." He gestured at the papers scattered in front of him. "What am I supposed to write?"

"Nothing," Hob said with an edge of irritation in his voice. He looked at Adam. "For now."

John shook his head in exasperation and made a note.

"What *I* want to know," said the Master of Trinity, "is what the hell you were doing at my College earlier."

Adam looked at him. The Master of Trinity was a small, sharp-faced man with a neat goatee beard and a nice suit. He said, "I went there with Inspector Mellow. She's investigating a murder."

"*Investigating*," Hob said scornfully. He opened an envelope and tossed a wad of photographs onto the table. Adam saw images of the bedroom in Botley, weirdly lit, the butchered remains of Harry Kay, the word *Wayland* daubed on the wall. "She's just wandering about with her head in the air."

"I understand she was asking after the victim's colleagues," the Master of Christ Church said. "Sounds reasonable to me."

Adam looked at John, who was scribbling away industriously, hunched over the paper with the tip of his tongue poking out between his lips in concentration.

Chancellor Cole held up his hands for calm. "An attack on one of us is an attack on all of us," he said.

"Is that what it was?" Adam asked. "An attack on you?"

"Where are you from?" asked the Master of Trinity.

"Southampton." And to be honest, he was tired of telling people that. Maybe the next time he was asked he'd say 'Margate' and see what happened.

"You're no more from Southampton than I am," Trinity told him.

Adam sighed and folded his hands in his lap.

"Mr Hardy's a guest here," Hob told them. "And he's given us some good intelligence about the routes between here and the coast."

"Why would you come all this way?" asked Christ Church.

"I hadn't planned to, when I set out. I just kept moving from job to job."

"It's unusual for people to travel that far."

Adam shrugged. "We trade with Brighton, now and then."

"I don't care," Trinity said. "You shouldn't have been allowed into College." He looked at the others. "What are we coming to? Really?"

There was no way for Adam to work out what this was all about. Hob was staring at him, John was scribbling away, the two Masters were arguing, and the Chancellor was just sitting there stiffly, looking across the room. In the light from the big windows around the base of the dome, Adam thought he saw a sheen of sweat on Cole's upper lip, although it wasn't warm in here.

He said, "If you don't want me here – and I haven't spoken to a single person since I arrived who does – why don't you just let me leave?"

"The circumstances," Cole said to the other side of the table.

"We still don't know who faked the order allowing you into the city," Hob said.

"Faked from *my* office," Cole said.

"I keep telling everybody, I don't know anything about that," Adam said. "It's nothing to do with me."

"Did anyone know you were coming here?" Trinity asked.

"Did you perhaps mention to someone in the last place you worked that you intended to visit Oxford?" said Christ Church.

"I don't remember."

"So someone in Abingdon might have known you were on your way," said Trinity, who had obviously read all of Adam's debriefs.

"I've had enough of this," he said, and stood up.

"Sit down," Hob said. "Superintendent Price and his men are outside. You wouldn't get ten feet."

"Is everyone in this place crazy?" he asked. But he sat down.

"This," said Trinity, taking the photograph of *Wayland* from the others on the table and sliding it across to him. "What do you know about this?"

"I don't know anything."

"You can read it, though," said Christ Church.

"I can read," Adam said. "I don't know what it means."

"There's a neolithic chambered long barrow near Uffington," Christ Church said, waving vaguely towards the outside. "The locals call it Wayland's Smithy. Did you hear of that, on your travels?"

Adam had actually lived rough there, for a little while. He shook his head. "No."

There was a silence at the table. Hob and the Masters and the Chancellor looked at him. John carried on writing until he'd caught up, then he looked up and grinned happily. Adam noticed there were crumbs of food on the lapels of his jacket.

"You see our problem," Christ Church said. "You may be just what you say you are, an innocent stranger come to the city looking for work. But all these troubles mysteriously began when you arrived. It does stretch the boundaries of coincidence somewhat."

"Personally, I still favour taking you to the edge of the city and throwing you out," Trinity said. "But my colleagues have convinced themselves that you deserve the benefit of the doubt."

"For now," Hob said.

"And we're prepared to accept that the memo authorising *someone* to enter the city was unconnected to you," Christ Church said. On the other side of him, Hob was nodding. "Frankly, if one *were* going to infiltrate Oxford, there are easier ways to do it without attracting everyone's attention, and to be honest, you appear to be entirely clueless."

"I'm still not entirely convinced on that point," Trinity put in.

"Duly noted," Hob said.

"So we're left with the question of what to do with you," Christ Church said. "We can expel you, as my colleague suggests."

"Or we could just kill him," Trinity added.

"Well, yes," Christ Church said to Adam with a wry smile. "We could just kill you."

"But instead of doing that, we've got a proposition for you," Hob said. "You say you came here looking for work, so we want to offer you a job."

It seemed unlikely that this was a joke, but Adam still waited to see if everyone would start laughing. When they didn't, he said, "What kind of job?"

"It seems to us," Christ Church said, "that there have been certain events in Oxford recently which might benefit from a fresh eye, an outsider's perspective."

Hob picked up the *Wayland* photograph. "We want you to find out about this for us."

Adam looked at them. "You're not serious." It was the most ridiculous thing he'd ever heard.

"It's two quid a day," John piped up. "Come on; Inspector Mellow doesn't earn that."

"I don't know anything about the city," Adam said. "The only people I know here keep arresting me. And you want me to work as some kind of detective? You have a police force for that."

"Oh, go on," John said. "You'll be great."

"It's absurd."

"You'll be working alongside Inspector Mellow," Hob said. "But you'll be reporting directly to us. You're not to share anything with Chief Superintendent Maxwell."

"Why not?"

"Because the man's an arse," Trinity said. "He needs to be taught a lesson."

"The chief superintendent's position is currently under review," Hob told him. "Unfortunately, there's no one to replace him at the moment because his superintendent is also an arse."

And having Chancellery stick him into CID with no explanation would put Maxwell on notice. "I'm not sure I like being used for your little games," he said. John, apparently pleased that he got it, beamed at him.

"Well," Hob said, "you can either do this or you can spend the rest of your time in Oxford sitting on the sixth floor of police headquarters."

And that was it, really, wasn't it? That little pantomime with Price and the Transport Unit was meant to show him the stick, and now they were showing him the carrot. And it wasn't as if he could do his job if he was in a cell.

"Inspector Mellow won't be happy," he told them.

"Inspector Mellow," said Hob, "will learn to adapt."

LEVIATHAN

SEVENTEEN

MELLOW ARRIVED AT work the next morning to a pile of files and memos on her desk and Adam sitting in her chair. They looked at each other for a little while.

"You're in my chair," she said finally.

Adam got up, went round the desk, and sat on her visitor chair. She hung her coat on the hook on the back of the door. "I didn't expect to see you again," she said.

"There have been developments," he told her.

Mellow sat down and rubbed her eyes. "Am I going to like them?"

"I doubt it," he said.

It took him about twenty minutes to fill her in on everything that had happened since he was taken away by the Transport Unit the day before, and at some point she put her head in her hands.

When he'd finished, she took her hands away and sat up and blinked at him. "You're right," she said. "I don't like them. What the *fuck* are they playing at?"

"I don't know," he said. "But they gave me this to give to you." He handed a folded sheet of paper to her, and when she unfolded it, she saw it was a chain of custody protocol. She sighed. "They thought it was very funny, what you did yesterday," he told her.

"Hm." She'd spent the rest of the previous day running around trying to find out what was going on, but Maxwell, no doubt sensing something it was better to be far away from, had made himself scarce, and nobody had seen Todd since the previous afternoon. She signed the protocol, then she folded it up, tore it in half, and put the pieces on her desk.

"They gave me this, too," he said, and he took out a little leather wallet and showed her a police disc.

"You know," she said, "I'm not even surprised anymore. So, how do you propose conducting your *investigation*?"

"I was planning to tag along with you and steal all your best ideas."

Despite everything, that made her smile. She sorted through the pile of memos until she found one with the Chancellery stamp. "Yes," she said, holding it up and reading it. "Here it is. Adam Hardy, inducted into the Thames Valley Police Force. Doesn't say what rank you are, though."

"They said your chief superintendent's position might be vacant soon."

Mellow glanced at the door, then back at Adam. Then she grabbed her bag off the floor and got up. "I think I need some fresh air," she said. "Come on."

SHE DIDN'T HAVE a destination in mind, just getting out of the building and out of reach of inquisitive ears, so once they were out in the rain, they just wandered through the city centre.

"Did they really say that about Maxwell?" she asked when they were out of sight of headquarters.

"Hob said his job was under review," said Adam. "Now I'm a detective, can I have a gun?"

"No, you can't." She stopped and looked in the window of

a shop selling knitwear, neatly stacked piles of sweaters and scarves. She could see his reflection in the glass, standing beside hers. "There was a time when the Thames Valley Force was the only thing standing between this place and total chaos," she said. "More than once, actually. Now it's a joke. Chancellery and the Colleges both want to control us."

"I thought they were the same thing," he said.

She shook her head. "The way it's supposed to be set up, the Chancellor represents the city and the Colleges represent themselves and everything is supposed to run smoothly and everyone's happy, but it's not worked like that for years. The Chancellor's just a decoration run by Hob's office, and the Colleges all hate each other. Everyone's constantly sniping at each other, and we're stuck in the middle trying to do our job." She turned from the window and started to walk along the line of shops. "Maxwell and Todd are both political appointments. The best thing you can say about Todd is that he's harmless, but Maxwell is properly dangerous. He's a *terrible* policeman. What the fuck's going on here?"

A little further along the row of shops, a small crowd had gathered in the rain outside a butcher's. It wasn't unusual to see queues, but these people were just standing in a group peering in through the window. Mellow took out her badge and flashed it around and some of them drifted away.

"What's all this about?" she asked one woman.

"He won't open up," the woman told her. "He's just standing there."

Mellow pushed her way to the window and looked into the shop. Inside, she could make out a man in a butcher's apron standing motionless in front of the counter, staring at the wall. She turned to the little group of people. "All right, everybody, there's nothing exciting here. Get on your way, please." Nobody moved, which she thought pretty much summed up her life right now.

She banged on the window and shouted, "Hey! You in there!"

She had to do it a couple of times before the butcher turned his head and looked at her. She held her badge against the glass. "Thames Valley Police," she said loudly. "Are you all right in there?"

He looked at her a moment longer, looked at the wall. Mellow pressed her face to the window, but she couldn't see what he was looking at. She banged on the glass again. "Open up!" she shouted. "Or I'll get my constable here to break your door down!" Beside her, she heard Adam sigh.

That seemed to break the spell. The butcher came over and unlocked the door, and when Mellow and Adam had stepped inside, he locked it again. "It was just here when I arrived," he said. "I don't know what it is."

Mellow looked at the wall. On the tiles, someone had written *Wayland* in big greasy red letters. She was aware of Adam suddenly moving very quickly, opening the door and stepping out onto the pavement and looking up and down the street. The crowd outside scattered.

"I got here twenty minutes ago and somebody had forced the back door," the butcher was saying. "I got a delivery of lamb yesterday and I thought someone had broken in and nicked it. But the cold room was still locked, and when I came in here I saw…" He gestured at the wall.

"Have you touched anything?" she asked.

"I opened the cold room and had a look inside."

"But apart from that?"

The man shook his head. Mellow looked at the door; Adam was still standing outside, hands by his sides. People passing by were giving him strange looks.

"Did you alert the police?" said Mellow.

The butcher looked at her. "Isn't that why you're here?"

She shook her head. "We were just passing."

"I sent the lad when I realised the door was open," he said, starting to grow annoyed. "And you're the only ones to turn up. I mean, the nick's only up the road. Bloody plod."

Adam came back into the shop looking grim. He glanced at the writing on the wall. A moment later, a uniformed constable appeared in the doorway, the butcher's apprentice behind him.

"You," Mellow said to the constable. "Go back to the nick and tell Sergeant Fleet to come here. Tell him I need four officers and the crime scene technicians." The constable took a step into the shop. "No," Mellow told him. "Don't come in. Do as you're told. Take the boy with you and give him a cuppa and a sandwich or something. Tell him to wait until I get back." She looked at Adam. "Are you okay?"

"Yes," he said, but he obviously wasn't.

"Make yourself useful and go out the back and make sure nobody comes in. Don't touch anything."

The butcher was starting to look alarmed. "What do you need all that for?" he asked. "It's just vandalism, isn't it? I can't afford to keep the shop shut up."

"I'm sorry," she said. "I don't think you'll be able to open today."

"Well, that's no bloody good. I've got two hundredweight of meat in the back and it'll start going off soon."

"I'll see you're compensated," she told him. She thought that once word started to get around, he was going to find that his customers went somewhere else. She looked around the shop and mentally said goodbye to whatever else she had planned to do that day.

"WELL, THE GOOD news is that it's not human blood," said Professor Solomons. "We'll probably be able to tell you in a couple of days, but judging by the amount I'd say it's probably from a chicken. Finger-painted, like the other one." He sat back and smiled. "So, all you have to do is find someone with chicken blood all over their hands."

"And here was I thinking police work was difficult," Mellow said. They were sitting in Solomons's study, fresh prints of the photographs from the butcher's shop scattered across his desk. "Do you think it's the same person?"

"Oh, that's for you to judge," he told her. "I'm not a handwriting expert, but even if I was, I'd be cautious of making comparisons. I say, would you mind very much putting that back, please?"

Mellow looked over her shoulder. Adam had been wandering along Solomons's bookcases. He'd opened one and taken out a little hardbacked volume in green covers. "This is a first edition," he said. "It's over three hundred years old."

"Yes," Solomons said. "It may be the only surviving copy in the world and it's very delicate, and I'd prefer it if you didn't handle it."

"Come back here and stop embarrassing me," Mellow said, but she didn't put any force behind it.

Adam put the book back into the bookcase and closed the glass door. He returned to the desk and sat down beside her. They'd spent all morning at the butcher's shop, then Mellow had walked the butcher back to headquarters and interviewed him and his apprentice while Adam sat in and said nothing.

"Why did you run off like that back there?" she asked when they'd done with the interviews and the butcher, still complaining loudly, had been sent home with a hurriedly written form to apply for compensation.

"I thought whoever did it might still have been there," he said. "Why?"

He shrugged. "If you did something like that, wouldn't you want to watch what happened?"

She thought about it. "Okay. Did you see anyone who looked suspicious?"

"No," he said, but she thought he didn't sound certain.

Solomons regarded them both. "Please don't take this the wrong way, but is everything all right?"

"Well, I have two apparently connected murders fifteen years apart, and a man cut to bits in his own bed," Mellow said. "So, no. I can't speak for Constable Hardy, though."

"Sergeant," he said. "I want to be a sergeant."

"You only became a copper yesterday," she told him. "We don't promote people that quickly." And then she remembered Wallop and realised that, apparently, they did.

"Quite," said Solomons. He opened a file. "The other good news, of course, is the fingerprint." He held up a photograph of a single bloody fingerprint on the wall of the butcher's shop. "You'll want your own people to make the comparison, of course, but it's a good match for this one." He held up another photograph, a fingerprint rendered ghostly by powder on the side of the cooking pot on Harry Kay's stove.

Mellow looked from one to the other. "How good?"

"I'm not a fingerprint expert, but I'd say eighty percent." Mellow looked suitably impressed. Solomons took another fingerprint photo from the file. "The crime scene technicians found this one on the butt of one of the rifles at the scene of the Cumnor murders."

Mellow leaned forward and looked. "Why haven't I seen this?"

"Because Mr Hob's office requested that all the files be sent to them." He coughed apologetically. "I kept copies."

"Do they know you've got copies?" she asked, looking at the photographs.

"No."

She smiled. "Naughty, Michael. Very naughty. Is it the same person?"

"I'd say so, yes." Solomons collected the photographs and put them back in their respective folders. "Which doesn't mean that this person is your killer. It just means the same person was at each scene."

"At the moment, that is a significant step forward," she told him. The Thames Valley force's fingerprint index was seventy years old and ran to at least six thousand cards; it was going to take their two fingerprint technicians months to check for comparisons, and even then there was no guarantee they'd find a match, but if they ever had a suspect it would help place them at the scenes. "What about Mr Kay?"

"Oh, that's easy," Solomons said. "He was hacked to pieces. Reg and Liz found a hatchet under the bed, probably used to chop wood for the stove. He died of catastrophic blood loss, almost certainly before any of the major dismemberments. Stab wounds all over his abdomen and thorax, at least thirty of them." He paused, thinking. "I gather Professor Halloran is unavailable?"

Mellow looked at him. "How did you hear about that? *I* didn't hear about it until yesterday."

Solomons shrugged. "Word gets around."

"I'll bet." The Colleges were constantly spying on each other, looking for advantages in resources and status. It was interesting that Solomons had access to that kind of information, though. "Do you know him?"

"Not well, but we have met, from time to time." Solomons got up from behind his desk and went over to one of the bookcases. Opening the door, he took a little framed photograph from a shelf and brought it back to Mellow. "This was taken at a dinner four years ago. Halloran is second from the left."

In the photograph, seven unsmiling men in formal clothes were standing, drinks in hands, in front of an elaborate stone fireplace. Commander Powell was at the end of the row. "I didn't think you mixed that much," she said.

"We're scientists," Solomons told her. "We consult, swap ideas. However much our superiors would rather we didn't."

Halloran was a stern-looking man in his mid-forties with a prominent chin. "I wouldn't have thought there was much overlap between you and Halloran."

"The professor is an epidemiologist," Solomon said.

Mellow looked up from the photograph. "I assumed–"

"You assumed because he's at Trinity he must work in some technical discipline." Solomons shook his head. "Really, inspector."

"So Harry Kay worked with infectious diseases?"

"Not directly, no. Epidemiology concerns itself with the study and control of the spread of infectious disease. It's an important discipline; disease and starvation killed many more people than The Sisters."

"There was a flu outbreak in Northampton a few years ago," Adam said. "Everybody died." Mellow looked at him, thinking that had been addressed directly at her. *I'll tell you a secret if you tell me one.*

"Just so," said Solomons, who apparently didn't find it unusual that someone knew what was going on in Northampton. "Something like that here would be devastating. Professor Halloran and I are members of a committee which advises the city on public health matters, which is how I know him."

"Is a sabbatical a common sort of thing?" Mellow asked.

"It's not uncommon. I would add, though, that if *I* were on sabbatical and one of my researchers had been murdered, I would make myself available to any investigators. But that's Trinity for you."

"What was Powell doing at this dinner?" she asked.

Solomons settled back into his chair. "I'd have thought that was obvious."

"They don't let you people mix without a chaperone?"

He smiled. "Couldn't comment. Sorry."

Adam reached over and took the photo from her and looked at it. "So, which one's your chaperone?" he asked.

"Well, I'm in an unusual position in that I'm in constant contact with outside agencies such as the police." Solomons nodded at Mellow. "I'm rather afraid my College have given me up as a lost cause where security is concerned."

"Or they limit what you know," Adam said.

Solomons nodded slowly. "That has occurred to me, numerous times," he said. "I'm sorry, who did you say you were again?"

"Constable Hardy is not from Southampton," Mellow told him, and this time Adam didn't try to correct her.

"Oh," Solomons said, clearly baffled. "Excellent."

Mellow gathered the photographs together and put them into an envelope. "If someone was on sabbatical, where would they be?"

"Well, that would rather depend on their area of study," Solomons said.

"An epidemiologist, say. Hypothetically."

"Hard to say. It could conceivably involve fieldwork, it could involve sitting in your rooms and writing a paper." Solomons sat back and clasped his hands across his stomach. "It might be worth mentioning, though, that the Colleges tend to guard their resources very jealously. They don't like us wandering around the city."

"They don't seem to mind their research assistants living outside College," Adam pointed out.

"Yes," Solomons admitted. "Mr Kay lived in Botley." He shrugged. "It's a matter of space; we can't accommodate everyone. The most valuable resources remain in College." He looked at Mellow. "If you were thinking Professor Halloran is out in the field somewhere and you'll somehow be able to engineer a meeting with him, I'd advise you to forget it. There *will* be someone keeping an eye on him."

"I'm struggling to see how I can do my job properly, Michael," she said, popping the envelope into her bag.

He looked at her for a few moments. "You know there's some friction between the Colleges and the city?"

She snorted. "When is there not?"

"Even more so, at the moment. One only hears rumours, of course, but it's a bad time to be expecting full cooperation from the Colleges. I'm sorry."

Mellow stood up. "Well, somebody needs to grab the Colleges by the ears and give them a fucking good shake, then," she said. "Before somebody else gets cut to bits."

EIGHTEEN

As FAR AS Morty was concerned, his stay in the city was going splendidly. He had fresh clothes, he'd found himself a more permanent hiding place in an abandoned house on the other side of the river from the place he'd hidden when he first arrived, and he'd discovered that he could summon Wayland just by writing his name. He'd found he could move among the locals without too much trouble, although he'd almost had a nasty moment in a shop where he was queuing up to offer to do some work in return for a chicken or something. When the woman in front of him got to the counter and asked for some sausages, she handed over a handful of little metal discs instead, and Morty, sensing danger, had turned and left the shop empty-handed.

Money was meaningless to him. He didn't know what it was or how it worked, but cautious observation in other shops suggested that it was important. If you wanted something, you had to give some of the little metal discs in return. This wasn't a problem, particularly; if he wanted food, he could steal vegetables from back gardens and chickens from henhouses, which had its own hazards, although the locals didn't seem to have guns. Still, he was intrigued by the idea of money and he made a mental note to see if he could find some in the next house he broke into. He was starting to think he would need some if he was ever going to leave the city; he'd crossed the river on the ferry one morning when it was busy, and he'd simply walked on board in the middle of a crowd of other people and nobody had noticed. It was only later that he saw people at other ferries paying for their passage and realised how lucky he'd been not to be stopped.

It was a lesson to pay attention and not make assumptions. This was a strange place, and not all its dangers were immediately obvious, so he made cautious forays out into the city, in the early evening or the morning at first, when darkness gave him some cover, but in daylight later as his confidence grew. He covered a lot of ground, getting to know the streets and roads, noting places where he could hide if he needed to. He didn't take the heads with him, for fear that he might be stopped. And besides, they talked all the time, either to him or to each other, and it was distracting. So he left them in his hiding place, propped up facing each other so they could gab as much as they wanted.

He found it was relatively easy to move around unseen in the residential areas of the city; whole neighbourhoods had been abandoned, and even in the ones that were not he could cross quite large distances by keeping to people's back gardens so long as he was careful. It was less easy to remain hidden in the city centre, although even here there was a network of little streets and alleyways that nobody seemed to use, and anyway, there were plenty of people about and he found he could lose himself in crowds. He became, if not a familiar figure, at least one that didn't attract attention, loping along through the rain and sleet, Morty Face turned to the world.

And the sheer number of people was dizzying, intoxicating. There were only a few hundred people in the Parish; here, there were too many to count, even if Morty had ever been taught to count to more than ten. All his life, Morty had been invisible, ignored by his parents unless they needed him for some job or other, so insignificant to his neighbours that they couldn't even be bothered to remember his name. Now he was properly invisible, indistinguishable from all the other raincoated people on the streets, and it made him feel powerful. They had no idea what walked among them and they had no defence against it.

At night, and when the weather was particularly bad, he retreated to his bolthole, where he listened to the heads alternately berating him and each other. Albie Dodd's head had definitely seen better days – it was covered in mould now, and stuff was leaking out of its ears, and even Morty was starting to notice the smell – but the other one, the new head, was in better shape, even if he had taken a big chunk out of its lower jaw when he was cutting it off. Life, by Morty's standards, was pretty good here. He was dry and he was safe and there was easy access to food. There was even, when he finally managed to get it going, a stove in the kitchen so he could cook and heat water.

Life was so good that Morty grew bold. One night he broke into a shop in the centre of the city and, using the blood of a chicken he'd taken from a coop out in the suburbs, he carefully wrote Wayland's name on the wall. He wasn't entirely clear why he did this, except that it seemed like a good idea at the time. Sometimes, you had to trust your instincts.

And it worked. Keeping an eye on the shop, he saw Wayland appear and go inside, and his heart soared. He moved closer, to the edge of the little crowd which had gathered outside the shop, and all of a sudden Wayland burst through the doorway, scattering the crowd, and stood on the pavement looking around. Morty and some of the others moved away, but for just a moment he could have reached out and put his hand on Wayland's shoulder, and it made him feel giddy.

Out walking one morning, he found a little network of backstreets he'd never encountered before, and he decided to explore. It was on the very edge of the city centre, where it gave way to the big old buildings with all the guards. He liked the look of those buildings, and he wanted to see what was behind their walls, but he thought he ought to wait until he'd taken a good look at them on the outside and worked out any possible entry and exit routes.

The backstreets ran behind several rows of shops and office buildings with fronts on the main street, and he'd been wandering along for about five minutes when a patch of white on the generally grey, dingy background caught his eye. When he went over, he found it was a deeply recessed metal door, protected from most of the rain by the surrounding buildings and a brittle plastic canopy. On the door, someone had written *Wayland* in white paint.

Morty stood staring at the word, completely frozen. If anyone had come along right then, he would probably have wound up being arrested and taken away. How could it be here? He hadn't done it, had he? He looked at his hands, but there was no white paint on his fingers, and there were no suspicious blank spots in his memory, and anyway, where would he have got white paint from? The paint looked fresh; it had run a little on the metal of the door. He reached out a trembling hand and touched the top of the *l* with a finger, rewarded with a little sticky white spot on his fingertip.

There could only be one explanation. It was a reply. Wayland himself had written this, in response to Morty writing his name on the wall of the butcher's shop. He was acknowledging Morty's presence. The sudden realisation gave Morty that giddy feeling again. This was an extraordinary advance; the only time they had ever spoken, Wayland had threatened to shoot him, and now here he was, basically welcoming Morty to the city.

He stood there for quite a while in the rain, unwilling to let the moment pass. He wondered if there was any way that he could remove the door and take it with him, because this was a souvenir beyond price. He'd need tools, and a lot of quiet, undisturbed time.

He was also, he thought, going to need some paint.

NINETEEN

"You know," said Mellow, "it's just possible that this is starting to get out of hand."

"On the bright side," Fleet said, "at least they're not written in blood."

Poking around in some rubbish piled up against the back wall of the living room, Adam barely heard them. The house was damp and cold, and it smelled of mould and animals, and all he wanted was to get out into the fresh air again.

They were in a part of the city that Mellow called 'Blackbird Leys', and, as she had once promised, it was not a particularly prosperous place. Nobody here had bothered to remove abandoned cars, and the streets were choked with weeds and lined with rusting wrecks. Even the houses which appeared to be occupied looked run-down and neglected, and he hadn't seen a single wind generator anywhere.

"The city gave up down here," she told him when they arrived. "No Colleges in the Leys, you see."

He turned. Mellow and Fleet were standing looking at the wall over the long-dead fireplace, where *Wayland* had been daubed in white paint, and the word gave him a shiver. It was as if his past, like an avenging angel, had followed him here from the Parish to punish him.

"How did we hear about it?" Mellow asked.

"One of the local plods heard someone talking about it," Fleet said. "He mentioned it to his inspector. Don't know how long all that took, though; this could have been here a while."

She looked at Adam. "What do you think?" All he could do was shrug, and she gave him a sour look. "How many's that now?" she said to Fleet. "I've lost count."

"Me too, boss. Ten? Twelve?"

Mellow shook her head and looked at the wall again. "Jesus Christ," she said.

It must have been frustrating for her, Adam thought. All her investigations had ground to a halt. She'd finally let him read the file on the body found with a spike through its chest and its face burned off, and the sense of relief he'd felt had been almost dizzying. There was no way he could have sneaked into Oxford, got across the Thames, made his way to the north of the city, carried out the murder, and left again, all unnoticed and without remembering he'd done it. It wasn't physically impossible, but it would have taken days to plan and prepare and carry out; it wasn't something he could have done on the spur of the moment during a few hours of blackout.

None of that, of course, helped Mellow, who was no closer to solving that murder than she had been on the first day of her investigation; the body remained unidentified, and a search through missing persons reports had proved fruitless. It seemed to be connected somehow to the death of a criminal called Courtenay Fox, who had disappeared fifteen years earlier and whose body had been recently found by accident, but there seemed no way to work out what the connection was.

The murders in Cumnor had been taken away from her, but the fingerprints connected them to the murder of Harry Kay, the investigation of which had also ground to a halt. No one in the area had seen anything out of the ordinary in the days around his death, and Adam had started to read through the transcripts of the interviews with his colleagues at Trinity and given up halfway through because they were all the same. Harry Kay had been a pleasant, unassuming man who kept himself to himself, did his work and his volunteering for Security and then went home to his little house, where he lived alone. Nobody knew what his home life had been like, or what his interests had been, and he didn't mix much outside work. If he hadn't been hacked to pieces, Adam doubted anyone would have noticed he was missing.

Professor Solomons had been unable to give a definite date of death, but Harry Kay had last been seen at Trinity while Adam was still in a cell at police headquarters, so nobody was accusing him of *that* murder. On the other hand, it didn't explain the name written on the bedroom wall, and he didn't think it was just a coincidence. Someone in Oxford knew what had happened in the Parish; did that mean they knew who he was?

And now the name was all over the city – it had even, to Mellow's annoyance, turned up in Headington – but mostly in poorer areas like this. Mellow was of the opinion that most, if not all, of it was the work of copycats. Either that or Harry Kay's murderer had an accomplice; it seemed like too much work for one person tramping around Oxford with a tin of paint.

Meanwhile, Adam kept to his side of the bargain with Chancellery. Every afternoon, he wrote a report about the progress of the investigation into Harry Kay's death and the proliferation of *Wayland* across the city. Then he went down to the front desk and made small talk with the duty sergeant for a while until someone came to take his report away. The first couple of times, Maxwell had come down to the ground floor, no doubt expecting Adam to have left his report at the desk and clearly annoyed that he couldn't take it away and read it. The chief superintendent was in a bit of a quandary. On the one hand, Adam was theoretically a police officer and could therefore be ordered to hand over his report. On the other, he seemed to have been taken under the wing of Chancellery and Maxwell had to walk very carefully. In the end, he'd given up coming down to the desk, but Adam still waited until he could hand the report over to the courier, just in case.

He still couldn't work out where Maxwell stood in the dynamics of the two groups which controlled the city. Mellow had said he was a political appointee, but not whose appointee he was, and it was impossible to tell. It might have been that he was just angling to position himself to be on the right side when power shifted in Oxford – and it seemed obvious to Adam that power *was* shifting; Mellow seemed to believe that the Colleges were becoming increasingly secretive and defensive. Adam had seen something like it before, in Guz. The commodore usually used a heavy hand to put a stop to it, but there had been a brief period when political assassinations had been in fashion. It would be interesting to see what happened here.

"All right," Mellow said. "Usual routine. Make sure nobody else gets in here before the crime scene technicians. I want photographs and fingerprints, anything that looks as if it was left here recently."

"Boss," said Fleet.

They went outside into the rain. The front door had been broken open some considerable time ago and bits of it lay in the hallway and half-buried under overgrowth on the path. A uniformed constable from the local police station was standing on the pavement. Mellow had a brief word with him, then they collected their bicycles and rode back into the centre of town.

THERE WAS A map of the city on the wall of Mellow's office, and when they got back, she put a little pin in it to mark where the latest *Wayland* had been found.

"It's fifteen," Adam said, counting all the other pins.

"It's not all the same person," she said.

He shook his head. "The handwriting's different. The last one was all in capitals."

She sat down behind her desk and stared at the map. "Have your friends in Chancellery told you why they want to know about this?"

"They're not my friends," he said. "And no." He hadn't heard a word from Chancellery since he'd been released and recruited into the Thames Valley force.

She shook her head. "Well, it's becoming a thing, whatever it is."

He put his hands in his pockets and looked at the map. It was far from being as detailed as pre-Sisters maps he'd seen, but it showed main roads and side streets, and it showed how central Oxford was a long, narrow peninsula trapped between the Thames and the Cherwell. Beyond that, an x marked where every checkpoint and roadblock cut the suburbs off from the outside world.

"How long is it since you closed the roads?" he asked.

Mellow was sorting through a pile of folders which had been left on her desk while they were out. "Eighteen months, two years," she said. "Why?"

He nodded. "The marks for a lot of the roadblocks look recent. The one at the top of the Banbury Road's old, though."

"We didn't have a tea party in the early days after The Sisters," she said. "A lot of people came along wanting to take what we had. They couldn't get across the rivers; the only way into the town centre was down from the north, so we blocked the roads up near the bypass."

"What happened to them?" he asked. "The people who came along?"

"Most of them buggered off to look for somewhere easier to rob. Some of them settled out in the suburbs. We buried the rest on the other side of the bypass."

"How long is it since you had any trouble from outside?"

She thought about it. "Can't remember. Years. Not since I was little, anyway. Oxford's too big and there's too many of us; the best any bunch of bandits could do these days is rob a bunch of houses on the outskirts, and then we'd send the militia out and kill them."

"That's a long time to be secure," he said. "It's not like that everywhere."

"I don't doubt. Is that why you're here? Checking out our defences?"

He turned and looked at her, but she was sorting through the contents of one of the folders. *One of the reasons, yes.* "No." They'd long since given up any pretence, just between the two of them, about him being from Southampton and coming to Oxford looking for work. "It's odd though, don't you think? Going that long without anyone trying to steal what you have?"

She looked up from what she was reading. "We're not a pushover," she said. "Word gets around."

Adam wasn't so sure about that. Guz wasn't a pushover either, and they still had bandits – mostly from Cornwall and the Somerset coast – occasionally preying on their outlying communities.

There was a knock at the door, and one of Mellow's detective constables looked in. "Message from Professor Solomons, boss," she said. "Sends his regards and says the files you asked for are ready for you to pick up."

Mellow seemed to take a fraction of a second longer than necessary to process this. Then she nodded. "Okay, Polly, we'd better go over to Christ Church and collect them, then." When the constable had gone, she thought a moment longer, then looked at Adam. "Put your coat on."

Solomons was in one of the College's lecture rooms when they arrived. "Thank you for coming," he said, shaking hands.

"I'm afraid you catch me at a rather busy time; I have a lunch appointment with one of my colleagues."

"It's good of you to see us, Michael," Mellow said in a careful tone of voice.

"Nonsense, it's my pleasure." Solomons opened a battered old leather briefcase and took out two slim cardboard folders. "My notes on the toxicology report on Harry Kay."

Adam looked around the room. It wasn't very large, just big enough for a table at the front and two rows of tables with a pair of chairs at each. The front wall was mostly blackboard, smudged with ghostly old chalk marks. Adam made out the words *pancreas* and *necrosis*.

"I've been looking forward to seeing this," Mellow said, taking the folders.

"Just so," said Solomons. He closed his briefcase. "And now, lunch awaits. I'll walk you back to the gate."

"There's no need," Mellow said.

"Not at all," Solomons told her. "It's on my way."

They left the lecture room and went down the corridor to the stairs at the end. They walked down to the ground floor and along another corridor, and Solomons pushed open a door and led them outside.

"I'm sorry for the cloak and dagger stuff," he said when they were out of earshot of the building, "but I'm afraid I think there may be listening devices in my rooms."

"You have surveillance technology here?" said Adam.

Solomons smiled sadly. "We're technical people, Mr Hardy. We've managed to recreate quite a lot of pre-Sisters technology, to some degree or another, not all of it beneficial. But please, we don't have long. You'll recall that the last time we met I showed you a photograph of Professor Halloran."

"Yes," Mellow said.

"And you'll recall, because you're attentive, that he has quite a memorable face."

"He's got a big chin."

Solomons nodded. "Quite. It's actually a congenital deformity. It's caused him some discomfort all of his life, and when he was younger, he had extensive dental work."

Mellow thought about that for a few steps. "Recognisable dental work?" she asked.

"Oh yes. This is work you'd only find being carried out in hospital. I doubt whether more than two or three people in Oxford would have had work like that carried out, and there would be records." Solomons looked into the distance. "You know I don't like to speculate, but it suddenly occurred to me that if Professor Halloran were to die, for some reason or another, his teeth could be used to identify him."

Mellow thought about that, too. "Unless his teeth and lower jaw were damaged or destroyed somehow," she said.

Solomons nodded. "That would muddy the waters considerably," he agreed. "Particularly if the examining pathologist concluded that the damage was due to a beating rather than a deliberate attempt to conceal his identity."

"Everyone makes mistakes, Michael," she told him.

Adam could see the front gate of the College ahead now, guarded by two armed Security men. Solomons said, "Of course, if someone *were* to inflict injuries like that, it would suggest they knew about the work he'd had done."

"Yes," said Mellow. "Yes, I see that."

"Well," Solomons said, "I'm afraid this is where we part company." He stopped and they shook hands. "I hope the information will be useful to you."

"Yes." Mellow held on to his hand a little too long. "I'm sure it will. Thank you, Michael. Take care. Please."

He nodded. Then he gave Adam a long look and smiled and turned and walked away towards a nearby building.

Mellow and Adam collected their bicycles and one of the guards let them out of the College and onto the busy street which ran alongside. Mellow was silent for quite a while as they cycled back towards police headquarters, and Adam let her think. They passed a building where two men with stiff brushes were trying to scrub the word *Wayland* off the door. He couldn't remember if that one was new or not. It was starting to feel as if the whole city was accusing him. *We know what you did.*

"Even if Michael's right, I can't do anything with this," Mellow said finally.

"Why not?"

"You heard what he said. If the Morton Street victim *is* Halloran, and if his teeth and jaw *were* smashed to hide his identity, it had to be done by someone who knew about his dental surgery."

"It could have been a family member," Adam pointed out.

Mellow shook her head. "This isn't a domestic. Your average domestic is a spur of the moment thing; it doesn't involve crucifying somebody, then hammering a spike through their chest, then smashing their jaw with a hammer and burning their face and hands off."

"But it suggests someone who knew him well or worked closely with him."

"It does," she said grimly.

"*If* it's him."

"Solomons thinks it might be," she pointed out. "He's sure enough not to want to talk about it in his office where someone else might be listening to the conversation."

"He was protecting you, not himself," Adam said.

Mellow nodded. "Yes. Yes, I know. He thinks this is a political thing. And that's why I can't do anything about it. If Michael's right and it *is* Halloran, and this *is* a political killing, and I go stomping around in the middle of it, we'll all wind up disappearing."

"It suggests whoever did it also killed Courtenay Fox, or

at least knows how he was killed," he said. "Does that mean Courtenay was a political killing, too?"

She didn't answer immediately, and when he glanced across, he saw that she was scowling. "Halloran links to Courtenay, and Courtenay links to Leviathan," she said.

"Excuse me?"

She told him about the riots fifteen years earlier, and about Leviathan, which sounded less like a gang or a single killer than some kind of death squad, something designed to spread terror among a population. It sounded, he thought, uncomfortably like what he had done in the Parish.

"It also means that Trinity probably know Halloran is dead, or at least that he's missing," she added. "All that stuff about a sabbatical is bullshit to make us go away. Maybe they killed him themselves, or maybe they're just trying to figure it out without involving us, but they know he's not where he's supposed to be."

"So does that link him to Harry Kay?"

She laughed bitterly. "That would be convenient, wouldn't it? Instead of three murderers we've just got one." She thought about it. "You know, I don't know anymore. I really don't. And you know what the funniest thing is? You're the only person I can talk to about this stuff."

He didn't think she meant it as a compliment. They turned a corner into the back street that led to the yard behind police headquarters. "Don't talk to anybody about this," she told him. "Not a soul."

"All right."

"For one thing, we've got no evidence."

"And if we tell anyone, we'll probably wind up dead, too."

"There is also that, yes." Mellow got off her bike and banged on the gate. A little spyhole opened at head-height. "It's me, Terry," she said, holding her badge up where the officer inside could see it. "And Detective Constable Hardy."

There was a moment's quiet sniggering at that, then the gate was cranked open far enough to let them wheel their bicycles through. As they were returning the bikes to the shed, Mellow said, "Come and have dinner tonight. I'll pick up a chicken or some chops on the way home."

He thought about it. "Yes," he said. "All right."

"And put some clean clothes on," she told him. "You're starting to get stinky again."

"That's hardly a surprise," he said, following her towards the back door of the building. "I live in a police cell."

THAT EVENING, THEY cycled through the wet streets to the Cherwell ferry and crossed over into Headington. Cycling through the wet streets, they didn't talk much, and for the first time in a very long time it seemed like an effort to Mellow. She felt exhausted. Solomons was right; she needed a break, or at least a period when her life wasn't surrounded by madness. That wasn't going to happen, though.

At the house, they wheeled their bicycles down the side path and out of sight and came back to the front door. As Mellow was digging in her pocket for her keys there was a scuffling sound behind her, and when she turned to look Adam was holding a young man in a chokehold that looked simultaneously fiendishly complicated and ridiculously simple. The young man was gurgling and trying to break the hold, but Adam didn't seem to be making any effort at all to hold on to him.

"Friend of yours?" he asked.

She peered at the young man's face in the light coming from the living room window. "Never saw him before in my life." A movement across the road caught her eye, and she looked just in time to see a long-armed shadow moving away up the street.

Adam loosened the hold a fraction. "Who are you and why are you hiding in the inspector's garden?"

The boy managed to take a breath. "My name's Rocco Barnes," he gasped. "I'm a friend of Ruth Sharpe."

Mellow's mind briefly went blank. There was just too much going on, too much to try and keep in her head. How the fuck was she supposed to keep up?

She saw Adam looking at her, his head tipped to one side. "Bring him in," she said, finding her keys and unlocking the door.

In the hall, Adam refused to let the boy go. Her father came out of his room and looked at them all. "You're back, then," he said.

"Hello, Jack," Adam said, as if he wasn't one sharp move away from breaking the boy's neck. "Good to see you, too."

"Who's your friend, then?"

"Go and put the kettle on, Dad," Mellow told him. "Let's all have a cuppa and calm down." To Adam, she said, "Let him go."

Adam clearly didn't think this was a bright idea, but he released the boy, although he stayed close to him, ready to choke him again if necessary.

"Did Ruth send you?" Mellow asked.

"No," said the boy, rubbing his neck. "I don't know where she is. She's gone, her mother's gone, the house is empty. Do you know where she is?"

"No," Mellow said. "No, I don't." She thought for a moment. "Come on through."

They sat at the table in the dining room. Adam made Rocco take his coat off, and he patted him down for weapons, although the most dangerous object he came up with was a fountain pen. Mellow gave herself a couple of seconds to catch her breath and try to regain control of the situation.

"How do you know Ruth?" she asked.

"I'm a student at Trinity," Rocco said. In the light, without his coat, he looked no more than twenty. "There was a problem with the radio setup at police headquarters last year and I got sent to sort it out and we got talking. After that we chatted sometimes over the radio." He looked awkward. "And then we sort of started seeing each other."

"I thought that kind of thing was frowned on."

"We're not supposed to mix with townies," he said. "But it's a stupid rule. Everyone sneaks out of College now and then to see somebody."

"What do Security say about that?"

"They can't stop us. There's lots of ways to get out; they can't keep us prisoner."

Well, there was no law against it, not city law anyway. And using the radio at headquarters to chat to your boyfriend in off moments was barely even a disciplinary matter; the worst that could have happened to Ruth because of that was a quiet chat with her superior, and as her superior was Superintendent Todd, she could reasonably have expected to get away with it forever. It certainly wasn't something someone would be disappeared for.

She said, "Officially, Ruth has been transferred to one of the suburban stations, but I can't find out which one."

"Well, fine," said Rocco, "but she wouldn't have moved to another part of the city as well, and there's nobody at the house. Her mother couldn't get about very well."

"Did you ask any of the neighbours about it?"

He shook his head. "I didn't dare."

"Why did you come here?" Adam asked.

"Ruth said I could trust the inspector," Rocco told him. He looked at her. "I mean, I *can* trust you, can't I?"

"Yes," she said. For all the good it would do. "Does anyone know about you and Ruth?"

Rocco shook his head. "I mean, they know I was seeing *somebody*, but everyone's doing it."

"Do they know you're here?"

"No."

"You didn't say to your best pal 'I think I'll just pop over to this address in Headington and have a chat with Inspector Mellow'?"

"I'm not stupid, you know."

"Hiding in people's gardens isn't that bright," Adam told him.

"Well, what was I supposed to do? Walk into police headquarters and report Ruth missing? It's them that made her missing."

Mellow raised an eyebrow, but it wasn't really a surprise. "Did Ruth say something about the force?"

"She said I wasn't to trust anybody but you," Rocco told her. "She said something had happened to the police. There were a lot of new faces on the force, and fewer people she knew. She didn't trust her bosses."

Mellow's father wheeled himself into the dining room. He had a plank set across the armrests of his chair, and on that he'd balanced a tray with a teapot and four mugs and sugar and milk. Adam got up and took the tray from him, put it on the table, and her father moved down to the end of the table and looked at them all.

"So," he said, "anyone want to tell me what the fuck's going on?"

"Later, Dad." She looked at Rocco. "So, you think Ruth's gone missing, and you think the police had something to do with it?"

He nodded.

"That's quite an accusation, you know," she went on. "Why would the police do something like that?"

He didn't answer immediately. He looked around the table. "Because of the radio."

"Which radio?"

The boy seemed to be sinking into a pit of misery. "We built a radio. Ruth and I." He paused. "I stole the components from College."

Mellow stared at him. "That was you?"

He nodded.

"I've been investigating those thefts for weeks," she told him. "Trinity's security were convinced someone was breaking in and taking that stuff."

He nodded again. "I made it look that way."

She sat back rubbed her eyes. "Well," she said. "I don't know what to say. Congratulations. You obviously have a bright future in crime ahead of you if things go wrong with academia. What did you want a radio for?"

He shrugged. "At first it was just something we could do together. It was fun. We weren't hurting anybody." He paused. "Then Ruth said we could use it to try and locate Red Three."

Mellow felt her heart sink. "She said she thought it was in France."

"It's not, though," he said. "We finally got a good fix on it the night before she disappeared. It's north of here. A long way north, up around York."

Mellow glanced at Adam, who had suddenly become very still and seemed to be pretending not to listen. "Is that where you're from?" she asked.

"No," he said. He seemed to think about it, then he said, "I'm Red Two."

Rocco actually gawped at him. "You're from *Plymouth*?"

Adam looked at Mellow and sighed. "Yes."

"What's it like?" the boy asked.

"It's not like here."

"And we'll have a little chat about that later," Mellow said. She looked at Rocco. "So, you and Ruth were wandering about Oxford with a radio set?"

"Oh yes," he said enthusiastically. "It's only about this big" – he sketched something about the size of a large suitcase – "with a directional antenna. We'd go out at night and try to pick up Red Three, then find the strongest signal. Then we'd move and do it again."

"Where did you go?"

He shrugged. "Out to the edge of Cowley, over to Cumnor. We used to set up in abandoned houses. It would have been better if we could have gone out of the city, for a wide baseline, but we did the best we could."

Again, none of this was illegal, particularly, apart from using a radio made of stolen components. Then again, the Colleges were very careful who they shared their secrets with, to maintain the city's dependence on them. She asked, "Where's the radio now?"

Rocco looked down at the tabletop. "At Ruth's house."

Not anymore, probably. Mellow got up and started to pour the tea, to give herself some time to think. She took a mug down the table and put it down in front of her father, who gave her a sour look, although she could tell he was fascinated.

"All right," she said, coming back to her chair. "How long until you're missed?"

"Not till morning," Rocco said. "Maybe not till the afternoon; I don't have any classes in the morning."

Mellow nodded. "Okay, so, you stay here tonight. The ferry will have stopped running by now, so you can't go back into town until first thing tomorrow anyway. We'll decide what to do after breakfast." She looked at her father. "I got a chicken on the way home."

Jack gave them all a long, level look. "Well, I hope it's a bit bigger than that last one you bought," he said. "Otherwise, one of us is going to be making do with veg."

AFTER DINNER, MELLOW took Rocco upstairs and showed him the little room at the back of the house where he would be sleeping. It wasn't much more than a boxroom, and the bed was so short that you had to sleep curled up, but it was cosy, and Rocco was pretty much out on his feet. She took some bedding out of the airing cupboard on the landing and left him to it.

Back downstairs, Adam and her father were sitting at the kitchen table with a bottle of potato vodka and two glasses. She got herself a tumbler from the cupboard, sat down with them, and poured herself a drink.

"He won't be able to go back," Adam said. "It's a miracle he's lasted this long."

Mellow mentally toasted Ruth and her mother and took a big swallow of vodka. "We can face that one tomorrow," she said. She looked at him. "Plymouth."

He looked suitably abashed. "We call it 'Guz', these days," he said. "Don't ask me why, I don't know."

"What's it like?" Jack asked.

Adam thought about it. "Actually, it *is* like here, in a lot of ways. We survived The Sisters for much the same reasons you did; we had a lot of very smart, capable people all in one place. The difference with us was that it was the Royal Navy base at Devonport, and they took charge from day one. There's about thirty thousand people in the city itself, maybe another twenty thousand in local communities and farmsteads. We trade along the south coast with places like Southampton and Brighton."

"So you're telling us you're a sailor?"

"I have bad news for you," Mellow said. "You're a long way from the sea."

Adam grunted. "The organisation I work for handles intelligence and security," he said. "Since the weather began to ease off a bit, we've been sending people out in ones and twos to see what state the country's in." He shrugged. "That's what I do."

"So what state *is* it in?" said Jack.

"Some places are doing better than others, but on the whole

it's not in great shape. I was in Wales last year and there are people there who hadn't seen an outsider since The Sisters came down. They thought everyone else in the world was dead."

There was a silence at the table, while they all thought about that. "So you're a spy," Mellow said.

Adam shook his head. "It's a lot more complicated than that."

"What are you doing here? Checking us out?"

He looked at them. "Have you ever heard of Father John?"

They shook their heads.

He sat back and took a drink, put his glass back on the table, and told them a potted version of Guz's encounter with Father John. Jack seemed fascinated by the story of faraway places, but Mellow's expression suggested someone who was witnessing her life, which had already been complicated enough, becoming even more complicated before her eyes. By the time Adam had finished, she was sitting with her head in her hands.

"So you've come all that way just to see if this bloke's here?" Jack asked him.

"In a roundabout sort of way, yes."

"Well, I've never heard of him. How about you, Leonie?"

"I should arrest you," she said without raising her head. "I mean, seriously, no ifs or buts. I should arrest you."

"He's here. Or he was, anyway." He told them about the woman in the Transport Unit wagon. "Thing is," he said, "I think that was a setup. It's too much of a coincidence, me and her winding up in the same wagon and her just dropping Father John's name. Which suggests someone in authority knows who I am and what I'm doing here."

Jack looked thoughtful. "You think he's been doing what he did in Guz? Taking over?"

Mellow sat up and drained her glass. "Fuck," she said. "Fuck, fuck, fuck, fuck." She looked at Adam. "Fuck."

He shrugged.

"Well, Compton Vale's real enough," Jack said. "It's north of here, other side of Woodstock."

Mellow got up and walked over to the sink and stood with her hands in her pockets looking out of the window. It was pouring with rain, and gusts of wind were lashing the trees in the garden. Rocco must still be awake, because she could see the wind generator in the light from the back bedroom, its blades turning so quickly they were almost invisible.

She said, "So the authorisation to let you into Oxford might not have been a coincidence after all. It might really have been meant for you."

She heard him sigh. "I don't know anymore," he said.

She turned from the window and looked at them. Her father was pouring himself another drink; Adam was sitting looking miserable. She didn't know what to make of what he'd told them; the only thing she knew was that there was nobody she trusted enough to share it with.

She went back over to the table and sat down and poured herself another drink, because why not? "Well," she said. "This has been an eventful evening." She rubbed her face. "I have absolutely no idea what to do about any of this."

"You should go, son," her father told Adam. "Sneak out of the city and go back to Plymouth or *Guz*, or whatever you call it."

"I think if I left now, it'd cause trouble for both of you."

"We would *cope*," Mellow told him. She drained her glass. "It's what we do."

"So," said Adam, "are you going to turn me over to the Transport Unit?"

"Oh, don't be ridiculous," she told him, pouring herself another drink. She'd pay for it in the morning, but right now it seemed the only rational response to whatever was going on. "You know very well I'm not going to; you wouldn't have told us any of that if you thought I would." She took a sip. "You know, two weeks ago the only things I had to worry about was investigating burglaries at Trinity and trying to find out who was making illegal vodka."

"At least you solved the burglaries."

She chuckled ruefully. "And I can't even tell anybody because Rocco will just go missing." She looked at him. "You think Red Three's important?"

"*I'll* certainly be telling my boss about it the first chance I get. It's the first evidence we've had that there's anyone at all on the other side of the Badlands."

"Important enough to kill people to keep it secret?"

"It seems that way."

She drank some more vodka. "I liked Ruth," she said. "And I liked her mum. They didn't deserve this."

"Leonie," warned her father, who recognised her tone of voice.

"No, Dad," she told him. "We're supposed to be police officers. We're not supposed to let this kind of thing happen." She finished her drink, put the tumbler back on the table with more force than was necessary. "We're supposed to stop it."

TWENTY

SHE COULDN'T FACE breakfast the next morning, so while Rocco and Adam and her father tucked into sausage and egg, she nursed a slice of toast and a mug of strong tea and tried to explain to Rocco why he couldn't go back to Trinity.

"I'm not sure about that," he said. "I've got work to do."

"If you go back, they'll eventually connect you to the burglaries," she said through her headache. "And that will connect you to the radio, and then they'll make you vanish."

"You also know where I'm from," Adam added without looking up from his breakfast. "And I wouldn't like that to be common knowledge."

"I wouldn't tell anybody," Rocco said.

"You would," said Adam. "Eventually."

Rocco turned back to Mellow. "But surely if I go missing, they'll know for sure that I had something to do with the radio."

"They're going to know soon anyway," she told him wearily. "Nobody knows you're here, so you should be safe enough so long as you don't go out. I'll work out what to do with you later. Maybe we can sneak you out of the city."

"What the fuck am I supposed to do outside the city?" he asked. "I'm an electrical engineer."

"You can come with me," Adam said.

Rocco gawped at him. "To *Plymouth*?"

"Seriously?" said Mellow. It had somehow slipped her mind that Adam would be leaving Oxford at some point.

"Sure." He put his knife and fork neatly on his plate and sat back. "We can always use skilled people."

Rocco thought hard about that. "All my stuff's in College, though."

"We can get it sent on to you," said Mellow. Adam raised his eyebrows. "I don't know," she said. "We'll think of something. The point is," she went on, "if you go back to Trinity, you're going to die. You're going to die and when somebody asks what happened to you, they're going to say you had an accident or you've run off."

"Or you're on sabbatical," said Adam.

That didn't get a reaction from Rocco. He said, "My clothes and my books and stuff."

"Rocco," she said gently. "Those things are no good to you if you're dead."

He shook his head slowly. "I don't know," he said.

"Look," Adam told him, "stay here today and have a think about it. We'll have a chat about it tonight."

"I don't know," Rocco said again. "If I don't go back today, I'll be in trouble."

"You're *already* in trouble, son," Mellow's father told him. "You were in trouble when you started stealing stuff from your College. It just hasn't caught up with you yet. By rights, Leonie should be arresting you and marching you down to the nick. If she doesn't, that means *she's* in trouble. If I don't go up to Headington police station and report you, *I'm* in trouble." He waved a hand in Adam's direction. "If he–" He stopped.

"I'm in trouble all the time," Adam said.

Mellow shook her head. "Stop being such a little fucking ray of sunshine, Dad." She said to Rocco, "He's right, though. This is going to catch up with you sooner or later. You might get back there today and find them waiting and that'll be the last anyone ever sees of you. You do understand that, don't you?"

He swallowed hard. "Ruth," he said.

"Ruth's gone," she told him as gently as she could. "And the fact that you're still here means she didn't give you up. That means she was really, really brave. And you're going to have to be really brave, too."

"I want to know who did it," he said. "I want to know who took her."

"And so do I. And I'm better fixed to find out than you are, because I'm a police officer." She hoped she sounded more confident than she felt.

"WERE YOU SERIOUS about taking him with you?" she asked later, as she and Adam cycled towards the ferry.

"It's a long way, and it's not exactly a fun journey, but at least he'd be safe in Guz," he said. He added, "Maybe you should start thinking about it, too."

She glanced at him in surprise. "Me? Not a chance."

"Something's happening here," he said calmly. "The Colleges and the city are fighting over who runs the place, police officers are disappearing and being replaced by people you've never seen before. Now you're harbouring a fugitive."

"He's not a fugitive yet," she told him. "He's not even a suspect, as far as I know." But he was right; Rocco had confessed to theft, and it was her duty to arrest him. It was up to her discretion *when* she arrested him, but at the very best she was poking around the edges of a disciplinary offence. Which was really the least of her problems; whoever was behind all this would assume, would *have* to assume, that Rocco had told everyone in her house about Ruth and Red Three. She said, "I'm not going anywhere."

"Once they notice he's missing it won't take them very long to connect him to Ruth," he said. "And not long after that they're going to connect Ruth to you, and they're going to do the sums."

"Ruth and I were friends," she said. "We went through training together. It's not evidence of a conspiracy."

"I'm not sure your standards of evidence really apply here."

She shook her head. "I've got a job to do; I'm not going to run away."

"What about your father?"

"There's been Mellows in Oxford since before The Sisters; he won't leave. And don't try to use him as a lever again, please."

"I won't if you don't use him as an excuse to stay."

They glanced at each other.

"So," she said finally. "Any ideas about what to do next?"

"I think the important thing to do at the moment is carry on as if nothing's happening. Don't do anything suspicious."

"And how are *you* going to manage that?"

"My advantage," he said, "is that everyone *already* thinks I'm doing something suspicious."

AT HEADQUARTERS, THERE were more files and memos waiting on Mellow's desk, and a uniformed constable sitting on her visitor chair.

"Having a bit of a rest are we, constable?" she asked, taking off her coat.

"Message for Detective Constable Hardy," the constable said, standing and looking at Adam. "The chief super says he's wanted at Chancellery."

Mellow looked at Adam, who shrugged. "All right, constable," she said. "Message received. Now, if you don't have anything to do, I'm sure I can find something."

The constable smirked and left.

"Discipline seems to be slipping," Adam said.

"No kidding. Do you want me to come with you?"

He shook his head. "I know the way."

"Come straight back here when you're done," she told him. "Don't wander off."

"Will do," he said with a smile.

When he'd gone, Mellow sat down at her desk and regarded the pile of paperwork, the bottom strata of which had been sitting here for several days. She took the memos off the top and leafed through them. About halfway through, she stopped and read one again, and one more time, while her heart sank.

She got up and took the memo down the corridor to Todd's office, knocked on the door, and opened it, and was brought up short by the sight of a tall woman sitting behind Todd's desk. She was wearing civilian clothes, and it took Mellow a moment to recognise Inspector Kelly, latterly the station inspector at Sunnymead. Mellow felt her mind derail, just for a moment.

"You look surprised to see me, detective inspector," Kelly said.

"Um, well, yes, ma'am."

"You've obviously not been keeping up with your advisories," Kelly told her. "Superintendent Todd has retired due to illness and I've been asked to keep his seat warm."

"Oh," was all Mellow could manage to say. Todd had been absent for several days, but nobody had mentioned an illness.

"Not a popular decision, inspector?" Kelly asked.

"Not for me to say, ma'am," Mellow said, recovering herself. "Welcome to CID."

"Thank you. I'm still finding my feet. I'd like you to get the detectives together in the squad room this afternoon so I can have a little chat and introduce myself. Sometime after lunch, I'll leave the time to your discretion, workload allowing."

"Yes, ma'am."

Kelly looked at the memo crumpled in Mellow's hand. "Was there something in particular you wanted?"

Carry on as if there's nothing happening. "I… just wondered why this was on my desk, ma'am."

"Let me see." Mellow handed the memo over. "It's a missing persons report for someone called Rocco Barnes." Kelly looked at her and raised an eyebrow.

"Yes, ma'am, but missing persons are the responsibility of uniform branch, in the first instance, unless there's suspicion of foul play, which there doesn't seem to be here. Are CID supposed to be doing missing persons as well now?"

"As well as…?"

Mellow took a breath. "Ma'am, I'm running two full-scale murder investigations and a cold case at the moment. Not to mention the burglaries at Trinity, and although we've recovered parts of that still, we still don't know who's responsible. I don't have the manpower to go out looking for some student."

Kelly regarded her calmly. "Well," she said, "we'll have to see about getting you some more manpower then, won't we?"

Mellow blinked. "Ma'am."

Kelly shook her head and looked at the memo again. "Leave it to the plods for the moment. He was only reported missing this morning; he's probably sleeping off a hangover somewhere." She handed the memo back.

"Ma'am."

"Anything else?"

"No, ma'am."

"I'm sure you have a lot to do, then. I'll see you after lunch."

"Yes, ma'am." Mellow turned to go.

"Oh," Kelly said, "and you won't be seeing Chief Superintendent Maxwell for the next few days. He's feeling a bit under the weather."

Not that Maxwell had ever exactly made himself conspicuous. "So you'll be in overall charge, ma'am?"

"Just until the chief superintendent gets back. Is there a problem with that?"

"No, ma'am. Just so long as I know who's running things."

Kelly nodded. "This afternoon, inspector."

"Ma'am."

Mellow went back to her office, closed the door, and sat behind her desk while she waited for her heartbeat to return to normal. Not that she would miss him, particularly, but she wondered whether she would ever see Maxwell again.

DESPITE HIS PROMISE to Mellow, Adam didn't go straight to Chancellery. He took his favourite bicycle from the shed and went for a wander.

He found that he liked Oxford; the people here had done an extraordinary thing in the years of the Long Autumn, and they'd done it without a lot of what Guz would have regarded as advantages. Both cities had established order, but they had done it in different ways. In Guz, there had never been any question that the Navy was in charge, but here the city and the Colleges had somehow managed to govern together and to thrive, and now that relationship seemed to be fraying. He'd been accused in the past, not without justification, of going native, of identifying with the community he was visiting over the needs of his mission, and he thought he was probably doing that now. He should, by rights, sneak out of the city at the first opportunity. He'd learned an enormous amount about Oxford and how it worked; it was going to take weeks to debrief him. But he was caught up in whatever was going on here and he wanted to find out what it was. And he wanted to know if Father John was here.

He passed two new *Wayland*s; one, on a shop window, had run so much in the rain that it was almost unrecognisable. The map in Mellow's office was starting to look bristly with little pins, and nobody had yet been caught in the act of painting.

Past the Chancellery building, he turned up the road alongside Trinity and rode up to the junction with the Banbury Road. Just before Summertown, the little town centre he'd noticed the first time he and Mellow had cycled up here, he turned off the Banbury Road and followed a couple of side streets until they emerged onto a main road paralleling the Banbury Road. A short distance further north, this road was blocked off with a huge rusting traffic jam of old lorries and vans and buses. It must have taken weeks to get all those old vehicles up here and dragged into place, and there was no way to get a cart or a horse through or around it. The side streets around it were all blocked, too, but he thought a person on foot might be able to pick their way through here. It didn't seem to be guarded. He stood for a while, thinking.

He turned south and rode unhurriedly back into the city centre, left his bicycle against the railings outside the Chancellery building, and went up the steps. A Transport Unit officer was guarding the door and let Adam through when he showed his police badge.

Inside, Hob and the Master of Trinity were seated at the table. There was an untidy scatter of papers and pens and pencils on the table beside Hob, which seemed to indicate the presence of John, although he was nowhere to be seen. The Master of Christ Church and the Chancellor also seemed to be absent.

"You took your time," Hob said. "We've been waiting half the morning for you."

"It's a busy job, being a policeman," Adam said. "Where are your friends?"

"Adam!" John's voice boomed out from above them. "Hello!" Adam looked up and saw the plump clerk hanging over the balcony of the gallery. "Be down in half a mo!" His grinning face disappeared.

"The Chancellor and the Master of Christ Church have other duties," Trinity said. "Sit down."

Adam picked a chair at random and sat. "Just out of interest," he said, "who actually runs this place?"

"Between you and me, we do," Hob said, indicating himself and Trinity. "I run the city, and the Master here speaks for the Colleges. Everything else is just for show, and frankly it's childish and boring."

"What's childish and boring?" John asked, emerging red-faced with effort from a stairwell.

"Mr Hardy was asking who runs Oxford," Trinity said.

"Oh, these two gentlemen," John said, coming to the table and sitting down. "And a *bloody* good job they do of it, too. Top men." He proceeded to search through the papers on the table, looking for a blank piece.

"We don't need this," Hob said, waving his hand to indicate the huge room. "We could do everything just as well in an office somewhere."

"Oh, come on," said John. "This is *splendid*. Where's your sense of history? This building's about five hundred years old. Imagine that." He pointed his pencil at Trinity. "How old's your College?"

"It was founded in 1555," Trinity said.

"There you go!" John said. "History! This is what we're fighting to preserve. And you want to hide in an office."

"It's poncey and it's unnecessary," Hob said.

"Nonsense," John said, shaking his head. "The people love this. Everyone in their robes sitting around the table twice a year. It connects us to the world we lost, gives us something to work towards regaining."

"There's a lot of it that we shouldn't bother trying to regain."

"Exactly!" John cried happily. "A lot of people thought The Sisters was a disaster."

"It *was* a disaster," Adam said.

"But it was *also* a chance to start again," John said. "A chance to make things better." He suddenly seemed to become aware that everyone was staring at him. "I feel very strongly about this," he said more quietly. "I'm not going to make an apology for it. The people love pageantry; we should have more of it, not less."

There was a silence around the table. When everyone was reasonably certain that John wasn't going to speak again, Hob said, "We're no closer to finding out who this *Wayland* is."

"No," Adam said. "We're not."

"Because he seems to be every-fucking-where now," Hob told him, taking a thick wad of photos from his briefcase and tossing them down on the table. Adam saw the word *Wayland* repeated over and over again, in larger and smaller letters and in a variety of paint colours.

"The consensus of opinion among the police is that they're not all being painted by the same person," Adam said,

"Well, *that's* a staggering insight," Hob said in a loud voice. "Well done, Thames Valley Police. Take a well-deserved holiday."

"Problem is, Wayland's starting to be a bit of a folk hero to the great unwashed," John put in. "There was a bit of trouble down in the crappy bit of town last night."

"Blackbird Leys," Hob supplied with great restraint.

"Yes. There. Police patrol had some stuff thrown at them by some yobbos. Bricks and bottles and stuff. Yobbos were shouting 'Wayland'. What do you think about that?"

Adam had no idea.

"And College staff have been attacked in the city," Trinity said. "One of Christ Church's librarians was badly beaten. Whoever did it hung a sign with *Wayland* written on it round his neck."

"His name's everywhere," Hob said. "It's a call to arms."

"Wouldn't surprise me if someone was paying people to paint it on walls," Trinity mused, and Hob gave him a sour look.

"And not a word of this in your reports," Hob said to Adam. Adam had spoken to some locals living near some of the graffiti, and they had seemed as mystified as anyone else about it. "You probably have access to sources of information I don't," he said.

"We gave you a badge so you could go out and ask questions," Hob told him. "If you can't be bothered to use it, we might as well take it away and put you back in that cell."

"Speaking of which," Adam said, "I still haven't been paid."

There was a moment's silence. Hob and Trinity looked at John. "I'll chase that up," he muttered, making a note. "Not my responsibility, though, to be fair."

Trinity said, "If this 'Wayland' does become a rallying figure for the lower classes, it will be all but impossible to break. Even if we do find out who's responsible, any punishment risks creating martyrs."

"So it's already too late," Hob said.

"If the city can't protect us, the Colleges will take matters into their own hands," Trinity told them. "That's not an empty threat. You know that."

John looked up from his scribbling. "Steady on," he said. "Let's not lose our minds."

Adam said, "I think, unless you really do know something I don't, that you're blowing this up out of all proportion."

"It's an insurrection technique," Hob said, with such a direct look that for a moment Adam thought he knew everything that had happened in the Parish. "Spread fear and division. Get everyone running around like headless chickens."

Another silence. Trinity said, "Are the police any closer to arresting Harry Kay's murderer?"

"I was starting to think you'd all forgotten about him," Adam said.

"Don't be insulting," Trinity snapped. "The man was a member of my College."

Adam wondered how safe it was to bring up the subject of Professor Halloran, decided against it. "There is fingerprint evidence which seems to indicate someone who had been in Harry Kay's house was also present when the first graffiti was painted."

"First one you know about," John put in without looking up.

"Yes, fair enough, the first one I know about. But the same person was in both places."

"And the fingerprint isn't on file?" Hob said.

"The police are checking, but it's a slow business. They haven't found a match yet."

"Put more people on the job," Trinity said. "Speed it up."

"I'm not sure that would help," Adam said. "From what I'm told it's quite a particular discipline."

"Nonsense," John said, making a note. "Many hands make light work. They'll learn on the job."

Adam could guess how Mellow would react to that, but he didn't say anything. He had a momentary sense that the purpose of him being here wasn't to say anything, but to watch these men arguing. Which was patently absurd.

Hob looked at him. "Buck your ideas up," he said. "Find out who's doing this."

"I told you, lots of people are doing this."

"Then find out who they all are."

"That could be a lot of people."

"Then we'll deal with all of them. Get us a name."

"What did they want?" Mellow asked when he got back to her office.

"Your city is being run by crazy people," he told her, starting to take off his coat.

"No," she said, getting up from behind her desk. "Leave it on. We're going for a ride."

"Where?"

"I want to have another look at Harry Kay's house."

They went down to the yard and got their bikes and cycled off towards the Botley ferry. The rain had eased off to a light drizzle, and the streets were full of people and traffic.

"There have been some changes to the command structure of the Thames Valley force," Mellow said when they were out of sight of police headquarters. "Superintendent Todd, my superior, has apparently retired and been replaced by someone who until a short while ago was the uniformed inspector at Sunnymead police station."

"That name seems to pop up quite a lot, doesn't it?" Adam said.

"It does. Also, Chief Superintendent Maxwell is off sick, so Todd's replacement is now running the Thames Valley Police Force."

Adam thought about that. "Well, Hob did say his position was under review."

"It's not funny," she told him.

"No," he said. "I suppose not."

"I didn't like either of them, particularly, but I didn't want them to disappear." She thought about it. "Well, Maxwell maybe. What *did* they want at Chancellery?"

"They're obsessed with Wayland; they think he's becoming a folk hero."

They cycled on a little way. "You know, all this stuff started happening when you arrived," Mellow said.

"There was something wrong with Oxford long before I got here, inspector," he said. "You just got used to it."

"So what are we going to do?"

"There is no *we*, inspector. There's me, and there's the Thames Valley Police Force."

"You're just a laugh a minute this morning," she grumped.

"I don't know," he said. "I think the Colleges and the city have both decided they've had enough of sharing power. What that's got to do with Harry Kay and Wayland, I have no idea.

I *have* noticed that they've never said anything about the body you found in Sunnymead, the one that might be Professor Halloran."

"Maybe it's not him after all."

"Or it is and they know everything about it."

THE BOTLEY FERRY was on the city side of the Thames. Mellow bought two tickets and they wheeled their bicycles on board and stood for ten minutes while the ferrymaster waited to see if any other passengers were going to turn up, but it seemed nobody else wanted to cross the river at the moment, and in the end the engine houses on both banks sent up great clouds of steam and the ferry started to inch slowly towards the other side.

"How many ferries are there?" Adam asked, looking at the powerful swirling of the river beneath them.

"Two each on the Thames and the Cherwell," Mellow said.

"And there's no other way across?"

She shook her head. "It's more or less impossible to approach the city from the south; the land between here and Abingdon's almost completely flooded. West and east is very rough ground, but I suppose you know that."

He nodded.

"There's only a couple of roads that aren't underwater," she went on, "and they flood during monsoon anyway."

Adam thought again of Hob describing Oxford as an island. He said, "People in the Chilterns talk about coming here for work, but none of them mention the Colleges or a police force or anything like that."

"That's because most of them didn't actually come to Oxford," she said. "They stopped short, at farms outside Abingdon. Or they got as far as Blackbird Leys and gave up." She looked towards the front of the ferry. "Places like Cowley and the Leys, they're not bad places. The people who live there aren't bad people, they're just like anyone else. The city just abandoned them. The Leys in particular; it's over the other side of the Bypass. To a lot of people, it's not in Oxford at all."

"I was just trying to work out how Oxford can have all this... stuff, and nobody seems to have heard about it." He nodded at the engine house on the other side of the river.

"If you'd come in from the north, you'd probably have met a lot of people who'd have told you about how things are here," she told him. "We always did most of our trading to the north, because it was just easier. And let's face it, who travels very far these days anyway? Apart from you, of course. I've never been out of the city."

He looked at her. "Really?"

"And that's not unusual."

He supposed most people didn't go very far from Guz, either, but you could travel quite a long way out into the West Country and still hear stories about the Navy and their city. "Is there a lot of resentment towards Chancellery in places like Cowley?" he asked.

She looked at him. "What do you think?"

He thought that there were parts of the city where the idea of a vague, ill-defined folk hero might take root, a figure around whom old resentments could gather. He thought he could understand why Hob and the Colleges were so worried.

The ferry reached the Botley side of the river, and they cycled off down the road towards Harry Kay's house. His street was deserted, the police and forensic technicians long gone, and when they parked their bikes outside number 32, Adam saw that the front door had been left ajar.

Mellow tutted. "That shouldn't have been left like that," she said. They stood at the front gate and looked at each other.

"Why did you want to come here today, by the way?" Adam asked.

"I didn't. I just wanted to get out of the building so we could talk about what's been going on this morning."

"So what are we doing here?"

She looked up the street. "We had to go *somewhere*."

"I think you should let me go first," he told her.

"I've got the gun," she told him, unholstering her sidearm and setting off up the path towards the door.

"We've really got to talk about that," he said, following her.

At the front step, Mellow put her fingertips on the door and pushed. It didn't open easily; the hall carpet had swollen with damp. "Thames Valley Police!" Mellow shouted into the hallway. "Come out and make yourself known!"

No sound from inside the house.

"Armed police!" Mellow shouted. "Come out!"

Nothing.

Pistol raised, she stepped forward into the hall, took a couple of steps, and looked into the living room. "Well," she said.

He looked past her shoulder. The living room looked at if it had been hit by a tornado. The furniture had been overturned and the upholstery slashed, books had been spilled from the shelves and scattered across the floor.

"Bollocks," Mellow said.

It was the same story in the back room. In the kitchen, drawers had been pulled out and emptied all over the floor. The back door was wide open. One of the kitchen chairs had been pulled across against the cupboards on the other side. There was a single size twelve bootprint on the seat.

Upstairs, the damage wasn't so extensive. Maybe the smell, which was still considerable, had put off whoever had been here. In the front bedroom, the wardrobe had been shifted out from the wall, and in the back an attempt had been made to rip the carpet up.

Adam and Mellow went back downstairs and stood in the kitchen. Mellow put her gun away. Adam went over to the chair and looked at the bootprint, then he looked at the row of cupboards on the wall. "I don't think your officers left the house unsecured," he said.

"The front door hasn't been forced, though," said Mellow.

"No, it hasn't." Adam climbed up on the chair and looked into the open cupboards. "Who would have had keys?"

"Trinity security had a spare set," she said, looking around the kitchen. On the stove, the pan of stew had grown a cap of mould. "That's how the constable who found him got in."

"They couldn't have sent someone over themselves?"

Mellow shook her head. "Jurisdiction."

Adam reached up and felt along the top of the cupboards. "The back door's still broken; they could have entered and left that way," he said. "But they used the front door and they left it open. Why do that?"

"To make us think it was just someone looking for something to nick," she said, "but any half-competent crook would have come in the back."

He got down off the chair and went back into the living room and looked at the overturned furniture. He squatted down to look at one of the armchairs. The fabric on the bottom had been torn off, exposing the springs and padding underneath. "You think Trinity did this?" he asked.

"I think whoever it was had a spare set of keys, and that narrows it down. Whoever it was, they didn't make a very good job of it." She stirred her toe among the books scattered on the floor. "By the way, there was a missing person report for Rocco waiting on my desk when we arrived."

Adam reached into the space under the chair and poked a finger around in the padding. "Well, we expected that. Not so soon, maybe." He pushed his arm deeper in the chair and felt about, then sat back on his heels and looked around the room. "What do you think they were looking for?"

"Don't know. Maybe Harry was bringing his work home with him."

"His work which involved researching the spread of diseases."

"Hm. Anyway, if it *was* Trinity, it's a breach of protocol.

So I can march into Powell's office and give him a talking-to about it, or I can pretend to be a dumb plod and assume this is just some little toerag breaking in to look for something to sell down in the Leys."

"Dumb plod is probably safer," he told her, standing up.

She shook her head. "This is such a fucking *mess*." She saw him looking at her. "And don't tell me to leave again. I'm still a police officer and I still have a job to do." Although the chances of making any meaningful arrests were rapidly dwindling away. "Come on," she said. "I've got to organise a meeting; the new super wants to make a speech."

IN THE END, Mellow managed to get half the CID squad together; a dozen more were out on various inquiries. If newly elevated Superintendent Kelly realised this, she didn't make any sign. She looked around at the detectives sitting in the squad room and her gaze alighted momentarily on Adam, who had tucked himself away in a corner, before moving on.

"Good afternoon, ladies and gentlemen," she said finally. "For those of you who haven't heard the station gossip yet, I'm Superintendent Andrea Kelly. Superintendent Todd has retired on the grounds of ill-health, and I'll be taking over the running of CID from him." She paused for a reaction, but there was none, and she looked a little disappointed. "Superintendent Todd was an outstanding officer, and I'm sure we're all grateful to him for his contribution to the department. I hope I can live up to his example." She looked around the room again, daring anyone to smirk at this, but Oxford's detectives had good poker faces.

"Unfortunately," she went on, "this department has been falling short for some years now, and Chancellery has noticed a fall in the number of convictions originating from CID, while recorded crime figures have been rising." This finally got the reaction Kelly was clearly looking for, a general fidgeting among the detectives in the room. She clasped her hands behind her back. "This is obviously not an ideal situation, and it's going to change," she told them. "There is going to be a reorganisation of the department. From tomorrow, twenty new officers are going to be joining us, including two detective inspectors. The department will be organised into three squads; one will deal solely with murder, another will deal with organised crime, and the third will deal with robbery. I'll be posting your assignments on the noticeboard tomorrow morning, so make sure you check to find out which squad you'll be working in. As befits an expanded department, Chancellery will be granting us increased resources, but it's not enough to just throw money at the problem. We all have to work harder, otherwise there *will* be some redundancies." This produced a level of muttering she seemed to feel gratifying. She raised a hand for silence. "With the help of Inspector Mellow, I'll be carrying out performance reviews, and we'll be identifying where improvements can be made." Everyone looked at Mellow, who was carefully staring off into an imaginary distance. "From tomorrow, it will be a brave new world. This will be a better, more efficient, and more effective department. Thank you." And she turned and left the room, ignoring the raised hands among her audience.

There was a sudden hubbub in the squad room, most of it aimed at Mellow, who raised her hands in surrender and went to take refuge in her office.

She'd barely sat down when there was a knock on the door and Fleet looked in. "Boss?"

"I don't know, Peter," she said. "This is all news to me. I only found out she was here this morning. Let's wait and see what happens tomorrow. She's a new broom and she wants to make an impression; maybe all this will blow over eventually."

Fleet didn't look convinced.

"While you're here, was Harry Kay's house secured when the forensic technicians were finished with it?"

"Yes, boss. Did it myself. I had to wedge the back door shut because the lock was buggered, but it was secure."

"What about the keys?"

"Logged them in with the rest of the evidence. What's up?"

"I was out there earlier; it looks like someone broke in looking for something to rob. Could you get the doors and the windows boarded up, please?"

Fleet looked nonplussed. "Will do. But I was the last one out of there and it was secure when I left."

"I know it was, Peter. And don't worry about all this other stuff. Everything will settle down soon."

"Not convinced, boss."

She sighed. "I don't blame you. Let's just try and do our jobs, eh?"

As Fleet left, Adam looked round the door. "You have a roomful of disgruntled detectives down the corridor," he said.

"I have one right here, too," she said. "You might put a word in for me with your friend Mr Hob, the next time you see him."

"The last thing you need right now is Hob paying attention to you," he told her.

"No." She sighed. "No, I know. Where were you planning to spend tonight?"

He shrugged. "I was going to go upstairs."

She shook her head. "Come and have dinner again. I don't want to come in tomorrow and find out you've been transferred."

"WELL," HER FATHER said later, when dinner was over and they were sitting at the dining table with a bottle of vodka, "that's how things used to be organised, back in the day. Robbery Squad, Murder Squad, Criminal Intelligence, Major Crime."

"I know, Dad, but that's ancient history. Things have changed."

"It used to be a *lot* more complicated, according to my dad."

"The Force is different now, Dad," she told him. "As you very well know. There hasn't been the need for any of that stuff, and there isn't any need for it now. We're policing twenty or thirty thousand people, not the whole of the Thames Valley. How many murders have we had this year?" She glanced at Adam. "Until now."

"Maybe they're expecting a massive rise in crime," Adam said.

"Well, they're a little late there, aren't they?"

Adam looked at them. Rocco, discovering that he had been reported missing and was now basically on the run, hadn't been particularly hungry. He'd picked at his dinner for a while, then excused himself and gone upstairs. It was only a matter of time before someone drew a line connecting him to Ruth Sharpe and from there to Mellow, and Adam didn't know what would happen then. He had a sense that time was getting short, though.

"I've been thinking about what you told us last night," Jack said. "About how this Father John takes a place over. Bit by bit, from the inside."

"Well, he's only tried it once, that I know of," Adam said. "And it didn't work."

"It almost did though, didn't it?"

"Yes," he admitted. "Almost."

Jack looked at them for a few seconds, as if trying to decide whether or not to go on. "There's a police station called Sunnymead in north Oxford," he said finally.

"Yes, I've seen it," Adam said.

Jack nodded. "And you've heard about the riots."

Adam glanced at Mellow, who was frowning at her father. "Yes."

"Well," Jack said, "the first night of the riots, a mob attacked Sunnymead nick. They dragged everyone outside and killed them in the street. That's the story, anyway."

Mellow's frown deepened. "Dad?" she said.

"I used to have a pal," Jack said. "We'll call him Jimmy. Jimmy and I went through training together, but afterwards we were assigned to different stations and we didn't see that much of each other anymore. During the riots, though, we were all lumped together and sent wherever there was trouble, and I bumped into him again one night in Cowley.

"That was a bad night. I don't know if it was worse anywhere else, but it was the worst night we had. People were setting fire to houses, throwing bricks at us, shooting at us. I heard later that our superintendent was thinking about pulling us out, abandoning the place, maybe cordoning it off, but we held on somehow, and sometime early in the morning the trouble started to die down and those of us who'd been there all night were pulled back for a break.

"So we were all in this old church. There was tea and sandwiches, but most of us were too tired to do much more than sit on the floor. We all smelled of smoke, from the fires. I didn't get the smell off my skin for days. Down the front we'd set up a treatment station for the injured, and I remember there was a lot of screaming." He looked at them, looked at the window. "We didn't have painkillers or anything much to treat people with. We'd asked the Colleges to send out some doctors, but they didn't want their people on the streets that night, so the police doctors had to do their best." He shook his head.

"Anyway, I can't remember how we got onto the subject, but me and Jimmy were sitting there on the floor near the back of the church and he started telling me about this constable from his police station, he called her Lucy. Lucy used to patrol up on the Banbury Road, and the top end of her patrol area was near Sunnymead nick, and some nights if the weather was really bad she'd pop in and they'd give her a cuppa before she carried on.

"So she'd told Jimmy that she'd been on patrol the night the rioting started, and as she got near Sunnymead nick she saw that the whole place was lit up, inside and out, and all these wagons were parked outside, half a dozen of them, which was unusual. She was going to go in and see what it was all about, but she said she had a bad feeling about it and she decided to hide in a garden and watch for a while before she decided what to do next.

"She waited there, out of sight, for about half an hour, then people started coming out of the building. She said there were people with guns and they were leading a line of other people out, people with their hands bound behind their backs and bags over their heads.

"Lucy didn't know what to make of all this. She told Jimmy it looked like the nick were moving a lot of prisoners, thirty or more of them, she lost count. They got the prisoners on the wagons and they drove off up the road towards the barricades. A few minutes later, some carts came down the other way, full of people. They stopped outside the station and everybody got off and went inside, and about quarter of an hour after that the drivers came out and the carts drove off the way they'd come and a minute or so after that the outside lights went out.

"And that was that. Lucy stayed hidden for a while, trying to work out what to do, then she decided it was better to leave it alone and she cycled off on her patrol." Jack took a mouthful of vodka.

"And why have I never heard about this before?" Mellow said.

"Because Lucy and Jimmy disappeared," Adam said.

Jack nodded. "At some point, Lucy and Jimmy must have been chatting, and she told him what happened that night. By then, everybody knew the story of the massacre at Sunnymead and we thought we were literally fighting for our lives. Lucy had gone and told her inspector about what she'd seen and he was as baffled as she was. And the day after Lucy told Jimmy all this, she didn't turn up for her shift, and neither did her inspector. Nobody knew where they'd gone, but everything was in chaos so somebody got promoted to replace the inspector and we just carried on."

They sat there in silence for a while, the rain pounding down outside. "I didn't see him again after that night," said Jack. "I went over to his nick one day, just to see how he was, and they told me he'd been transferred, nobody knew where. So I went to where he lived and his house was empty. He had a wife and a little boy and they were gone, too. I'm not stupid, I knew something was going on, but I knew that if people found out I knew about it I'd wind up being 'transferred' as well. So I kept my mouth shut, didn't tell anyone, not even your mum."

Mellow reached out and put her hand over his.

"So what do you think happened that night at Sunnymead?" Adam asked.

Jack shrugged. "I didn't know what to think, until you told us that story yesterday. Now I wonder if the people Lucy saw being loaded onto the wagons were the coppers from the nick, and they were replaced by people from outside the city."

"You can't just *steal* an entire police station, Dad," Mellow said. "People would– oh."

"Sunnymead nick was attacked sometime early in the morning," Jack told Adam. "Fighting was breaking out all over the city by then, so there was nobody available to go and help. By the time things started to calm down, the bodies had all been taken away and cremated and officers had been redeployed to staff the station. That's the story, anyway."

"But the station *was* attacked?" Adam asked.

Jack shrugged. "I went up there not long after the riots ended; a lot of us did, just to pay our respects. There were some scorch marks on the walls, some of the windows were boarded up. The locals say there was a mob there that night, but who's to say what it was they saw?" He leaned forward a little in his chair. "But here's the thing. When I went up there, I didn't recognise a single copper in that nick. They were supposed to have been brought in from all over Oxford, but you'd think I would have known one or two of them."

Mellow stared into space, thinking. "That's *insane*, Dad," she said. "You're saying someone kidnapped everybody at Sunnymead and then faked a *massacre*? *Why*?"

"It's one way of getting a lot of people into the city all at once, without anyone realising," Adam mused.

"No," said Mellow. "No. This bloke Jimmy was having you on, Dad. Or this Lucy was having *him* on. It's an insane story."

"Jimmy really did vanish, Leonie," Jack told her. "And his wife and little boy. That was real enough."

"They didn't have to go to all that trouble," she said. "They could have come in quietly in ones and twos, it's not that hard."

"But would they have wound up in control of the police station on the only main road out of the city?"

"So you're saying we were *invaded* fifteen years ago and we didn't notice?"

Adam shrugged. "It's a bit *extravagant*," he said. "But it would work, if you wanted to take control of a police station. That would be a good foothold to have in a place like this."

"And those people went on to have careers in the force," Jack reminded her. "Some of them are in Chancellery now."

Mellow shook her head. "Someone senior would have to be in on it," she said. "The super or the chief super or Chancellery. You can't just stick a bunch of strangers into the police force without someone noticing, there'd have to be paperwork, records. All of that would have needed faking." She looked at her father. "Susan Bates had to have known about this. Any redeployment to Sunnymead would have gone across her desk; she'd have noticed that she didn't recognise any of the names."

"Maybe not," Jack said. "The chief super can't know *everybody* in the force by name. And don't forget, we were in complete chaos for at least a year after the riots. By that time, those people were already bedded in." He nodded at the notebook. "I don't like to think badly of Susan, she was an outstanding copper. At worst, I think she didn't pay attention, and I can't blame her for that after what we went through."

"It does suggest, though, that there was already someone here," Adam pointed out. "Someone in a position to know how things work and produce fake paperwork and put it in the right place."

Mellow sat back and folded her arms. "We still haven't even come close to *why*. What difference has it made?"

Adam thought of a short training course he'd had, years ago. Not with a military trainer, this one, but with a civilian named Gaunt who had the dry, plodding air of an academic. Like a lot of his training courses, at the time he hadn't been able to see what possible use it was. *There are two ways you can take over a community,* Gaunt had said. *You can ride in with all guns blazing, kill a lot of people, and impose yourself on them by force. And that undoubtedly works, although it's expensive in terms of men and materiel and effort and you wind up in control of a community in which resentment isn't far below the surface, so you spend a lot of time having to manage that and watching out for rebellion. Or you can do it gradually, perhaps over a period of years. You infiltrate the community without anyone noticing, you whisper lies in people's ears – or better still, half-truths, because they're harder to disprove. You amplify divisions and exploit them, manoeuvre people you trust into important positions. I think we know who we're talking about.*

Indeed. With thirty followers, Father John had managed to deal a grievous blow to Guz, one it had taken years for the city to recover from. If they hadn't been so impatient, they might have succeeded. That was a lesson a man might take to heart, if he was going to try again somewhere else.

"We don't have any proof of this," Mellow told them. "Not a scrap. And even if we did, it doesn't prove this 'Father John' was involved."

"We could just ask one of these fake policemen," Adam said carelessly.

Mellow stared at him.

"They wouldn't tell you the truth," Jack said.

"Oh, they would," Adam told him.

"No," Mellow said, feeling a rising anger. "No, we are *not* going to kidnap somebody and beat a confession out of them. I'm still a fucking police officer, I'm not doing that."

"So what do you suggest?" he asked. "The moment you go to your superiors with this story we'll all quietly disappear."

"I don't know." Mellow looked at her glass, pushed it away from her, suddenly realising there was literally nobody she trusted. "I don't know."

They sat there in silence for a while. Finally, Adam said, "How far away's Compton Vale?"

Jack, who had been sunk in thought, looked up and blinked. "Depends what you mean by 'far'," he said. "You could probably walk there and back in a day, if the road's in a good state. We used to do a lot of trading with the farmers up there when I was little, but they started to get standoffish and decided they wanted to keep all their produce to themselves. Eventually we stopped bothering them. Just a sec." He wheeled himself away from the table and out into the hall.

"Do you think you could cover for me for a day?" Adam asked Mellow.

"You want to go up there?"

"I think somebody wants me to. It might be worth a look."

"I'll go with you," she said.

He shook his head. "You'd be missed, but Hob and the Colleges want me to be out and about investigating this Wayland thing; at a pinch, if anyone asks, you can tell them that's what I'm doing." They looked at each other. "I'll be back in a day."

"And if you're not?"

"If I'm not, put your father and Rocco on a cart and get out of here. Go east so you don't have to use the ferries, then south to Goring. When you get there, ask for directions for Blandings. There's someone there called Betty Coghlan; she'll look after you." Betty would immediately hand them over to Chrissie, but it was better than staying here to disappear, and at least some intelligence would reach the Bureau.

"None of that is going to happen," she told him.

"None of what's going to happen?" asked Jack, coming back into the kitchen with a big wad of papers in his lap.

"Doesn't matter, Dad," Mellow said, giving Adam an angry look. "What's that you've got?"

It was the remains of an old AA road atlas, the creased and worn and curled pages torn from their original spiral binding. "Here you go," Jack said, going through the pages until he found the one he wanted.

Adam got up and leaned over the page. Here was Oxford as it had been in a misty, distant, legendary past, when the rivers had been gentle watercourses rather than swollen impassable obstacles. None of the bridges had been washed away yet, the Vale of the White Horse was farmland dotted with villages that had still been thriving communities, and you could drive from where the Parish was now to Oxford in less than an hour instead of slogging for days across a flooded, boggy nightmare.

Jack pointed at the word *Woodstock*, about ten miles northwest of the city, then another couple of miles northwest of that. "You're on the edge of the Cotswolds here," he said, putting the tip of his finger on a little dot marked *Compton Vale*. "You're thinking of going there?"

Adam nodded. Although looking at it on the map, he was going to need a bike if he meant to get there and back in a day. "You said they stopped wanting to trade with you," he said. "How long ago was that?"

"Oh, Christ, I can't remember. It was years and years ago,

and it didn't happen all at once anyway." He thought about it. "Twenty years? Maybe longer than that?"

Did that work? Adam couldn't decide; it was hundreds of miles from Guz over difficult terrain, a journey even he wouldn't have undertaken without a lot of forward planning. Father John and his people had fled with nothing much more than the clothes they stood up in. Could they have made it that far?

"You need the old A44," Jack said, tracing the road. "It used to be in pretty good nick, once upon a time, but I don't know what it's like now. You think the people who took over Sunnymead nick came from Compton Vale?"

Adam traced the old road back to a complicated-looking junction beyond the Bypass. All he had to do was get past that without being seen. "I won't know until I go there," he said.

TWENTY-ONE

THE FERRY ACROSS the Cherwell started running at seven in the morning. Adam and Mellow didn't talk much as they were winched across the river in the rainy pre-dawn darkness and cycled into the centre of town, and not far from police headquarters Adam turned north and shortly reached a fork in the road. The right-hand fork was the Banbury Road; he took the left-hand one, just another early-morning worker in a hooded coat on his way to his job.

Just before the big barricade, he turned off the main road, dismounted, and carried his bicycle around a smaller roadblock on a side street and wheeled it up a cul-de-sac of abandoned houses. At the end was the remains of a wooden fence, long ago rotted and broken down by overgrowth. He struggled the bike through this barrier and found himself in the car park of an old hotel, north of the barricade.

It looked as if the hotel had been left derelict ever since The Sisters, and he didn't see anyone as he pushed the bicycle past the main buildings and up to a huge overgrown hedge that seemed to stretch all the way around the site. There were gaps in the hedge where animals had forced their way through, and he managed to get the bike cautiously through one of them and out onto the Bypass, where he paused against the hedge, waiting and watching.

According to the map, he was now several hundred yards west of the manned barricade at the top of the Banbury Road. In both directions, abandoned cars had been dragged onto the verge and left to rust. Directly ahead, across the road, was an old garage. He took a breath and wheeled the bike – unhurriedly, because nothing looks more suspicious than someone moving at speed – across the road and in among the rows of ancient petrol pumps, and paused again, listening.

When he was sure he couldn't see or hear any pursuit, he found the garage's exit onto the A44, and cycled away into the growing daylight.

WELL, THAT WAS fairly straightforward. So straightforward that for the first couple of miles he expected armed people to burst from the overgrown trees and bushes lining the road, but it seemed to be deserted. As Jack had said, the road was in fairly good shape, at least this close to Oxford, and when he reached the big junction and stopped for a while to observe, he found it was completely unguarded, and he wasn't sure what to think about that.

It was good to be out of the city, though. The awkward truth was that he didn't feel comfortable among lots of people. He spent so much of his time alone out in the countryside that even when he returned to Guz he started to feel fidgety after a few days; the flat he kept there was less a home than a place to spend a few nights when he was in town. He felt better just to be cycling out into the countryside in the rain.

He was a couple of miles from Woodstock before he saw anyone, a figure standing by the side of the road with the hood of its coat pulled up against the rain and a shotgun slung over its shoulder. As he passed, the figure raised a hand in greeting, and he waved back and cycled on. Well, if there was anything up the road they knew he was coming now.

He'd been cycling alongside a high wall for some time now, and ahead of him he saw a group of people standing at a big gateway. The gate looked solid, made of interlocking railway sleepers or something, and outside on the pavement there were four more people with guns. Adam waved to them as he went by, and after a few moments a couple of them waved back, but they all paid attention as he passed. He wondered what was on the other side of the wall.

And then he came round a bend in the road and he was in Woodstock, and it was... *pretty*, even in the pouring rain. A lot of people had worked very hard, down the years, to keep the little town in good repair. All the buildings were solid and clean, their roofs secure, windows unbroken. Neatly maintained trees lined the streets. He passed a pub, and a row of shops, and if all the shops weren't selling what they had originally – he saw old signs for a café and a mobile phone shop and a computer repair business – they were all selling *something*. Shoes, clothes, vegetables, meat, guns. He passed an ironmonger's and a bicycle repair shop, and a tailor's whose sign announced that it had been established more than a century and a half ago. In Oxford, you were always aware that people were doing their best to get by, adapting to the world after The Sisters. Here, it was almost as if The Sisters had never happened. People with skills had been busy here, carpenters and stonemasons and glaziers and bricklayers, and someone had been directing them.

The main street was busy with horses and bicycles and carts and people shopping, and the people looked content and healthy and well-fed and well-dressed, even by the standards he'd seen in Oxford. They made the people of the Parish look like mediaeval peasants.

He was through the centre of the town and out the other side in a few minutes, and the houses on the outskirts were just as neat and well cared-for as all the others. The road started to climb up a long hill, and then he was out in the countryside again. A few minutes later, he came to an old road sign, rusted and almost illegible, on which it was still possible to make out the words *Compton Vale* and an arrow pointing off to the left. A hundred yards or so further on, the road forked, and Adam bore off to the left.

The road here was narrower and rose in a series of shallow curves up another hillside, but it was well-maintained, and the vegetation on either side had been cut back and managed. About twenty minutes later, he stopped pedalling at the brow of the hill. From here, the road dropped down into a little village and then out again along the floor of a broad, steep-sided valley.

For a moment, he couldn't quite make sense of what he was seeing. The valley had been stripped of trees, and hundreds of huts and brick buildings had been erected for as far as he could see. Many of the brick buildings had tall chimneys, from which so much smoke was emerging that it drifted across the valley in horizontal panes. Even from up here, he could smell burning wood and coal and metal.

As he stood there, he heard the sound of horses' hooves on the road behind him, and when he turned to look he saw a big wagon drawn by four horses patiently coming up the hill. As it reached him, he moved over to the side of the road.

"Oi," said the driver as the wagon went past. "What're you doing?"

"Just taking a rest," Adam said.

"Well, you're in the fucking way," the driver told him. "There's two more loads behind me."

"Sorry," Adam called. "I'll be on my way again in a second." The driver waved a hand dismissively and then the wagon was past him, and he saw that its load bed was covered with a couple of big tarps, from which various bits of scrap metal protruded, and all of a sudden the valley made sense. It was a manufactory, a valley full of smelters and forges and workshops. Guz had places like this, on a smaller scale, scattered about the countryside just outside the city, recycling reclaimed scrap for more useful purposes. This was huge, though. If there had ever been farms here trading with Oxford, as Jack had said, they were long gone.

It seemed, at any rate, that on his bicycle and in his raincoat he fitted in here, which was promising, because he was going to have to go into Compton Vale and it was better to go into a place openly than to skulk about. He followed the wagon down the road, close enough that anyone who saw him would think they were together, but not so close that it would annoy the driver, and like this he made his way slowly down the hill and into the valley.

Compton Vale was smaller than Woodstock, but it had the same Cotswold stone buildings, the same busy main street, the same sense that someone had worked hard to retrieve it from the chaos of The Sisters and the century-long collapse of the Long Autumn. Still, it was not like Woodstock. Woodstock was a pretty picture; Compton Vale felt more like a workplace – it was sooty, a little rougher around the edges, a place with a purpose.

At the far end of the main street, the road ended in a junction. The cart turned left, and Adam saw, a quarter of a mile or so away, that a wire fence had been strung for hundreds of yards across the mouth of the valley. A line of wagons was waiting to pass through a big set of gates guarded by armed people wearing military fatigues and rain ponchos. Adam turned right, and right again down a quiet side street. He left the bike leant up against a hedge between two houses and walked back onto the main street.

The trick was to look as if you belonged, to walk as if you knew where you were going and had a purpose for going there. It was harder than it looked. *The natural inclination is to gawp, sir*, a trainer had once told him. *We don't want to gawp. We don't gawp when we're walking up our own street, do we?*

So, no gawping. He walked along, not too fast, not too slow, and with his hands in his pockets and the hood of his coat pulled up he didn't look much different to anyone else on the street. He walked past food shops and clothes shops. He walked past a bank, and judging by the number of people going in and out there was money here, too. Veils of rain and sleet blew across the village, but the street wasn't flooding, which suggested the drains were being maintained. It took a lot of work and attention to keep even a village like Compton Vale functioning, which was one reason why so much of the country was in such a mess. Infrastructure didn't run itself, and it needed people who knew what they were doing, and a lot of that knowledge had just been lost in the early years of the Long Autumn, when people had been too occupied with trying not to die to worry about the sewers.

Which made Compton Vale, this place which had once been just a bunch of farms trading with Oxford, easily as well-organised as Guz, even before you took into account the industry which filled the valley. And he was going to have to come back another day and check that out.

Halfway along the main street, there was a larger, somewhat more imposing building, three-storied and flat-roofed, and there was a small crowd outside waiting to go in. Adam crossed the road and joined them, which gave him the opportunity to stand still and look around without looking suspicious. A couple of people gave him looks when he joined the crowd, but he nodded hello and received nods in return and all of a sudden he wasn't a stranger, he was just another bloke standing around in the rain like everyone else.

He had no intention of actually going into the building, even as part of a group. *We never enter an unfamiliar structure unless we know where all the exits are, sir,* another trainer had told him. Well, like quite a lot of those rules, he'd broken that one from time to time. It was one thing handing out little catchphrases in a nice dry classroom, it was another trying to make them work out in the field. But this was one time where it was wise advice.

More people were joining the crowd around him, as the ones at the front shuffled bit by bit towards the doors. He half-turned to slip away, and a voice behind him said, "No, don't go."

Adam looked over his shoulder, and there was Hob, standing behind him wearing a rain poncho with its hood pulled up. He didn't seem to be armed, but the two men on either side of him in camouflage fatigues certainly were. Assault rifles, shotguns slung over their shoulders, knives, sidearms, grenades. An absurd amount of weaponry. Adam felt the people around him trying to put some distance between him and them without appearing to look suspicious.

"Go on in," Hob told him. "You never know, it might be interesting."

For a terrifying fraction of a second, he considered trying to fight his way out, but he wouldn't have got far. He took out his police badge and held it up. "You're under arrest," he said.

Hob smiled and shook his head. "In," he said, nodding at the building.

Adam turned and stepped forward, and the crowd parted to let him walk through the door into a marble-floored vestibule. He pulled back the hood of his coat and looked about him. Directly in front of him was another set of doors, one of them open, and through that he could see a big room with a lot of people sitting on chairs. On either side, staircases rose to the first floor.

"Up," Hob said behind him. "It'll be more private up there."

Adam went up the left-hand staircase and stopped at the top. He looked round and saw Hob and the two soldiers coming up behind him. For a few moments, he could have made a run for it, but he didn't know the layout of the building, and for all he knew, the first floor was full of armed people. Then Hob and the soldiers were on the landing with him and Hob was pointing to a door on the left.

He went over to the door and opened it, finding himself in an open gallery that ran around three sides of the building, looking down on the big room he'd glimpsed. Down below, perhaps three or four hundred people were sitting on rows of chairs talking loudly. At the front of the room was a stage with a lectern on it.

"Wait here," Hob told the soldiers, and he let the door close behind him. "Have a seat," he told Adam, gesturing at a row of chairs arranged along the gallery.

They sat, and Adam craned his neck to see over the balcony. The people sitting down in the hall were just ordinary villagers, men and women of all ages, even a lot of kids. They looked like the audience for a play, or a town meeting.

"So," Hob said. "What do you think of Compton Vale?"

"I'm here looking for Wayland," Adam tried.

Hob looked disappointed. "No, you're not," he said. "I know all about Wayland. I know all about those stupid farmers in the Parish and their stupid little war. I could have taken the Transport Unit up into the hills and cleared them out months ago."

It was no great surprise that Hob had sources in the Parish. "Why didn't you?"

Hob snorted. "*He* wouldn't let me. He said we have greater priorities, a higher purpose, we couldn't allow ourselves to be distracted."

"*He* being Father John?"

"Father John," Hob said sourly. "Yes." He sniffed. "Anyway,

too late for that. The Navy's there now, isn't it?"

There seemed no point denying it. Adam didn't say anything.

"And soon there'll be more of them, won't there?" Hob went on. "And then we'll be staring at each other across the Vale of the White Horse, both of us waiting for the other one to make a move. If there's a war, nobody wins and lots of people get hurt."

Adam looked at him. "War?"

"That's what you want, isn't it?"

"*I* don't." Adam looked down into the hall again. The crowd seemed to be getting a little restless now, the chatter getting louder.

"You don't know what your superiors want, though."

"I don't know what you want, either." Down below, a tall young man walked out onto the stage. "Who's this?"

Hob looked over the balcony. "Glebe," he said with a sour edge to his voice. "One of his bright young things."

"Do you know what killed the most people?" Hob asked. "It wasn't The Sisters; it was disease and starvation. That's the balance of power in Oxford; the Colleges control all the medical care, provide all the doctors. Have you seen the John Radcliffe? The hospital?"

Adam shook his head.

"It's a fortress. They don't want anything or anyone to get in or out unless they allow it. No one gets antibiotics or vaccines or surgery unless they say so; Inspector Mellow's father would have died without them. There's an outbreak of measles in Cheltenham and the Colleges won't lift a finger to help. They say they don't have the resources, which is bollocks. The thing is" – he turned and smiled thinly at Adam – "the Colleges don't actually have a lot of land. The city controls all the farms, and without *them*, the Colleges would starve." He looked down into the body of the hall again. "I mean, it's more complicated than that, of course, a lot messier. Chancellery isn't there to run Oxford, really, it's there to keep the peace between the city and the Colleges so everyone doesn't die of starvation or blood poisoning."

"It seems to work."

Hob made a rude noise. "It's a farce. The city hates the Colleges, the Colleges hate the city, the Colleges hate each *other*, and everyone hates Trinity. It's a miracle anything gets done at all, and it's long overdue for a shakeup."

Glebe reached the lectern and stood for a few moments looking out over the audience. The hall was packed now; Adam could see people standing three-deep around the edge of the room. Glebe said a few words, but the acoustics in the hall weren't very good and Adam couldn't make out what they were. The audience heard them, though, because there was a swell of cheering and clapping and stamping feet, and Glebe, smiling broadly, stepped away from the lectern and gestured to the side of the stage, and as if in response, John the plump clerk stepped out from behind the side curtains and shambled towards the lectern, one hand in his jacket pocket and the other waving enthusiastically. The crowd surged to their feet, clapping and shouting, and in return John punched the air in a pantomime of victory. Adam felt his mouth drop open.

Hob leaned close to him and spoke over the racket in the hall. "There," he said. "I said you'd learn something interesting."

THEY BOUND HIS elbows behind him and put him into a cart and drove him out of Compton Vale with an armed soldier on either side of him and more soldiers on horseback riding ahead of and behind them. Escape never crossed his mind, though. He was too busy considering how stupid he'd been.

For almost the whole of his life, whenever he'd heard the name *Father John*, he'd imagined some kind of Old Testament religious fanatic, a tall, thin old man in long robes, with a long white beard and hair and a ranting, messianic gleam in his eyes. He had never once pictured a pudgy bureaucrat in his fifties. But John had still been a young man when he fled Guz, still in his twenties, and he'd obviously prospered since then. *I was alone in a room with him for twenty minutes…*

They went back up the hill, past more wagons laden with scrap coming the other way, and down to the main road and through Woodstock. The driver didn't seem in any particular hurry and the locals had plenty of chance to look as they went by, but nobody did. Adam noticed brief glances, then people looked away, became more interested in the shops or a conversation with a friend or just getting to wherever they were going. Obviously it didn't do, around here, to pay too much attention to some things.

On the other side of Woodstock, they were back on the road to Oxford. They passed a line of people trudging through the rain at the side of the road carrying various pieces of agricultural equipment – spades and scythes and rakes – obviously a work crew on the way home. At the very end of the line – some yards back from the end of the line, actually – one figure caught Adam's eye. It was tall, and under its rain poncho it seemed stick-thin, and there was something about its body language, a kind of stalking lope in the way it walked, that reminded him of someone. As the cart passed by, the figure turned its head and watched, but with the hood of its poncho pulled up all Adam could see was a scrubby, untidy beard. It had a sack slung over one shoulder, and in its other hand it was carrying what looked like a tin of paint.

Then they were past, and turning in to the big gate in the wall which Adam had passed earlier. Someone inside cranked the gate open, and they passed through.

Beyond the gate, a long, gravelled driveway ran off uphill into the far distance towards what seemed to be an enormous building. On one side was farmland for as far as Adam could see, and people moving in the fields. On the other side were rows and rows of long wooden huts, solidly built, each one with its own wind generator and a couple of chimneys pluming smoke. A big parade ground had been laid out in a gap between the rows of huts, and Adam saw ranks of soldiers drilling in the pouring rain. If they weren't drilling with quite the same single-minded determination of Marines, they still looked disciplined and capable, and they all had automatic rifles.

As they drew closer, Adam saw that the building at the top of the hill was a colossal house, almost a palace, covered in spires and pillars. It wasn't as tall, say, as police headquarters in Oxford, but it seemed to go on and on and on. They passed through an archway into a big courtyard lined with stables, then into another courtyard, and finally through a third archway and out into a huge gravelled open space that looked out over a great misty rainy vista of farmland to the wildly overgrown landscape beyond. At the edge of the open space, overlooking the view, a wooden cross about the height of a man had been set up.

The cart pulled to a stop and the soldiers hauled Adam to his feet and more or less threw him onto the ground and then marched him through a doorway and into the house.

Inside was like nothing Adam had ever seen before, huge marble-floored halls and corridors lined with pillars, statues and busts of figures from antiquity everywhere, enormous paintings on the walls of men and women and children in frankly impractical and ridiculous clothes.

The soldiers forced him up two long staircases to the first floor, and here it was more of the same. They walked for what felt like miles along corridors lined with closed doors. Finally, they stopped at one door and opened it, and Adam saw inside what looked like a cupboard. The soldiers pushed him inside and he heard a key turn in the lock, and then he was standing there in darkness.

TWENTY-TWO

WHEN MELLOW GOT to police headquarters, she found the squad room packed with officers, many of whom she had never seen before. A lot of them were gathered around the noticeboard, to which three big sheets of paper had been pinned.

She shouldered her way through the crush to stand beside Fleet, who was reading the notices. The three sheets of paper were headed *Robbery*, *Murder*, and *Organised Crime*. Beneath the headings were lists of names. She found her own at the top of the *Robbery* sheet, and the rest of her team scattered across all three squads.

"Looks like they split us up," said Fleet, whose name was on the Organised Crime list.

Mellow shook her head. "No," she said. "No, I'm not standing for this." She turned and stomped out of the room.

Kelly wasn't in her office, so on a hunch Mellow went up to the fifth floor. In what had been Maxwell's outer office, Lucy the secretary had been replaced by an unsmiling uniformed sergeant in his late thirties who started to stand and protest behind his desk as Mellow burst through the door.

"No," Mellow said, pointing at him as she went past. "You stay where you are, sergeant. Don't you *dare* move." She marched across the office, grabbed the handle of the inner office door, and opened it with a great deal more force than was necessary.

Inside, Kelly was sitting at Maxwell's desk, looking up from some documents with an expression of annoyance. "Inspector," she said.

"Ma'am, I have to protest," Mellow told her.

Kelly sat back. "You'll have seen the new table of command, then."

"Yes, ma'am, and it's unacceptable."

Kelly gave her a hard stare. "It's *what*, inspector?"

"You've split my squad up."

"Yes, I did," Kelly told her. "Mixing old hands with the new faces. It's more efficient. And it's not *your* squad."

Mellow felt the anger within her start to stumble. "I've been put in charge of the Robbery Squad."

"Indeed you have." Kelly smiled. "And I'm sure you'll do a splendid job."

"But I still have two murder cases ongoing."

Kelly nodded. "Yes, you have." She consulted the documents on her desk. "You'll hand those over to Inspector Delany by the end of tomorrow."

"Ma'am—"

Kelly raised a hand. "I'd advise you to think carefully, before you say something you'll regret. You'll brief Inspector Delany on your ongoing investigations and hand over all the paperwork, and you'll do it before the end of tomorrow, and you'll do it with good grace."

"With respect, ma'am, this isn't *remotely* efficient."

"Are you about to make a breakthrough on either of the cases?"

"Well, no, but—"

Kelly lifted her hand again. "Then this would be an ideal time to make the handover. Delany's a good officer and there are enough original detectives on the new squad to carry through the transition. It was never going to be completely effortless, but we've tried to make it as smooth as possible."

Mellow wondered who *we* was. She said, "Ma'am—"

Kelly raised her hand, and Mellow was entirely tired of her doing *that*. "If you don't like the new structure, you're more than welcome to hand in your badge. You'll have to brief Delany either way."

Mellow blinked at her.

"We anticipated a certain amount of friction," Kelly told her. "There are always people who can't let go of the old ways of doing things, that's inevitable. But this change *is* happening, inspector, and I won't have dead weights holding it back."

Mellow blinked again.

Kelly regarded her a few moments longer, then she looked at the paperwork on her desk. "So, if there's nothing else, I do have a lot of work to get through today."

She didn't move. She stood there as if she was counting to ten, the way Maxwell used to, but really she was trying to decide. All her life, the Thames Valley Police had been a comforting presence, something which kept her and everyone else in Oxford safe, and if after joining them she had discovered that life was often more complicated than that, she had still believed it was a force for good. Now she didn't know anymore. The force felt toxic, dangerous, compromised, and there was nothing she could do to change it. The smart thing to do would have been to put her badge on Kelly's desk and go downstairs and draft her resignation. But she didn't. She just stood there.

Kelly looked up from the documents and raised an eyebrow, and that broke the spell. Mellow turned away.

"And the next time you decide to march into my office," Kelly told her, returning to the documents, "knock first."

✳   ✳   ✳

BACK IN HER office, she sat looking miserably at the pile of files and folders and envelopes which had been accumulating ever since the presumed body of Professor Halloran had been found at Morton Street, and she silently cursed pretty much everything. She cursed the Colleges and the city authorities, who seemed to be locked in a battle for control of Chancellery. She cursed the unlamented Chief Superintendent Maxwell, and his ham-fisted attempts at playing politics. She cursed the possibly mythical Father John and his hypothetical undercover takeover of Oxford. She cursed Guz. She cursed Adam, on whose coattails all manner of ill-luck and catastrophe seemed to have ridden into her city. She cursed herself, over and over again.

She sat back in her chair and closed her eyes and tried to make sense of it all. Halloran seemed to have been killed either by the same person who had killed Courtenay Fox, or by someone who knew the circumstances of Courtenay's death. Courtenay had disappeared not long after the Sunnymead massacre, which apparently might not have been a massacre at all. Halloran's body had been found in Sunnymead.

She opened her eyes and sorted through the files until she found the photographs of the fingerprints found at the Cumnor murder scene and Harry Kay's house and the first of the *Wayland* graffiti incidents. She looked from one to another of them for a while, then she went down to the first floor, where the force's fingerprint archive was kept in a cramped room at the back of the building.

There was a table in the middle of the room, at which sat two fingerprint technicians with jewellers' loupes and magnifying glasses and little piles of fingerprint cards. They looked up as she came in, and she was relieved to see that she at least recognised them.

"I'm looking for a card," she told them. "Name of Hardy, initial A. It'll be a recent one."

"You could have just sent a message down, inspector," said one of the technicians. "You didn't have to come down yourself."

"I'm not that busy at the moment, Sarah," she said nonchalantly.

"That's not what we hear," said the other technician, an older woman named Nancy. "All kinds of ructions upstairs."

"We'll all be more efficient when it's done," Mellow told them, forcing a smile.

Sarah was sorting through the cards on the table. She plucked one from the pile and held it out. "There you go. Hardy, initial A."

Mellow frowned and stepped forward and took the card. "That was suspiciously handy," she said.

"We've had so many requests for that card, we stopped putting it back in the drawer," Nancy told her.

Mellow raised her eyebrows.

"He's a popular boy, Hardy, initial A," said Sarah. "That card's been backwards and forwards to Chancellery half a dozen times."

Mellow looked at the smudges of Adam's fingerprints on the card. "I didn't know they had their own fingerprint people."

"Who knows what the Colleges have got?" Nancy said.

"Did they say why they wanted it?"

Nancy shrugged. "All we ever get is a courier coming in with a chit. They take the card away and they bring it back a bit later."

Hob's department, double-checking the police's work. Mellow didn't know why she was even sparing the energy to be annoyed. She held out the photographs. "Could you do me a quick comparison on these?"

Sarah took the photographs. "No need," she said, looking at the first one. "This one isn't him, it's Wayland. From that poor man's house in Botley." She showed it to Nancy, who nodded.

"We've been looking at these a *lot* lately."

"There *was* a Hardy one from that crime scene," Nancy put in.

Mellow nodded, remembering Adam touching the cooking pot in Harry Kay's kitchen.

Sarah looked at the next photograph. "And this is from Ernie Kyle's butcher's shop. Wayland again." She looked at the final one. "Ooh. Haven't seen *this* one before. Where's it from?"

"Never you mind. Is it Wayland?"

"Oh yes." Nancy leaned over to look and nodded.

Mellow stared at them. "You've hardly looked at it; you can't possibly tell."

"They've got us going through the entire archive looking for a match," Nancy told her, indicating the stacks of cards. She nodded at the photographs in Sarah's hands. "I'd know this print anywhere; I've started seeing it in my sleep."

"So none of these is a match for this," Mellow said, holding up Adam's card.

"Nah," said Sarah. "Not even close." She handed the photographs back. "What's he supposed to have done?"

"You probably wouldn't believe me. Did you check for matches with the prints from the Morton Street crime scene yet?"

"We didn't have to," said Nancy. "Every print from that scene came from a copper."

Mellow sighed.

"We keep prints of every police officer," Sarah explained. "For elimination purposes. We found pretty much the entire elimination set from Sunnymead nick at Morton Street."

"We always check the elimination cards for the nearest nick first," Nancy said. "Because the bloody plod can't resist wandering about touching everything. Can't you do anything about that?"

"I've tried. You can't tell plod anything." Mellow remembered having her fingerprints taken when she joined the force. "It must be a bit of a faff," she said casually. "Moving cards around when people get transferred."

"It's less bother to just leave the cards where they are and get new ones made," Nancy told her. "And it happens less often than you'd think, anyway; some people spend their whole career at the same nick. Look." She got up and went over to one side of the room, where the wall was seemingly composed entirely of little drawers about six inches wide. She went along the wall, selected a drawer, and pulled it out. "Here's Sunnymead."

Mellow stepped up behind her. The drawer was about a yard deep, packed with fingerprint cards separated into blocks by little tabs, each with a year written on it. "That's a lot of coppers," she said. "What happens when somebody dies? Do you leave those in here, too?"

"Nah, we weed those out and put them over there." Nancy waved at the far end of the wall of drawers.

"We didn't do that with Sunnymead, though," Sarah said from the table. "Didn't seem respectful, somehow."

"Yeah, we left them there," Nancy said, pointing to a little block of cards at the back of the drawer. "They all died in the massacre."

"That's kind of sad," Mellow said. She reached out and plucked one of the cards from the little block and held it up. Yarrow, J. Constable. She turned it over, saw neatly written dates and file references to the Personnel archive upstairs. DECEASED had been stamped across the back. She picked another one. Smith, W. Sergeant. Deceased. She put the cards back, counted about a dozen towards the front of the drawer, and took another one. Dyson, M. Constable. Constable Dyson was not deceased. Nor was the next one along, Constable Noakes. Nor Constable Howard. "Well," she said, putting the cards back. "I don't envy you all the paperwork. I've got enough of my own."

"We manage," Nancy said with a smile, closing the drawer.

"We could maybe use a helping hand or two, though," Sarah told her. "That never hurts."

"I'll put in a word," Mellow told them. "And thanks for the help with this." She held up the photographs.

"Any time," Nancy said. "Always good to see a friendly face."

Back upstairs, Mellow closed her office door and sat at her desk and wrote down the names of constables Dyson, Noakes, and Howard. She added the Personnel file references she'd memorised, the dates their fingerprints had been taken when they joined the force, and the dates their fingerprints had been taken again when they were transferred to Sunnymead. Then she sat looking at what she'd written.

If Adam and her father were right, these three men were among the people who had been brought into Oxford to replace the abducted officers of Sunnymead police station. According to the dates on the cards they had all joined the force at the same time, which wasn't itself suspicious. And their new post-transfer fingerprints had all been taken on the same date, which again wasn't suspicious, because they'd all supposedly been transferred at once. What *was* suspicious was that it was a date six days *before* the massacre at Sunnymead.

She sat back and thought about that. It was such a small mistake, such a tiny thing. She could imagine some overworked clerk, in the immediate aftermath of the riots, scribbling the wrong date on one of the cards, maybe even two. But three? She didn't buy that, and she wondered what had happened. Had the cards been prepared in advance, ready to be quietly inserted into the records, when there had been some delay in the plan? Had they forgotten about dates on the cards? Or had they just decided to slip them into the drawer anyway and trust that nobody would ever notice?

It wasn't proof. And even if it had been, there was nobody in authority she could take it to. And even if there was, they wouldn't believe her. She still wasn't certain she believed it herself. Someone staged a massacre and used the cover of that to insert thirty people and all their paperwork into the Thames Valley Force? Ridiculous.

Except there were more and more unfamiliar faces on the force, and officers were quietly going missing, and she couldn't shake the feeling that the takeover that had supposedly begun fifteen years ago was accelerating all of a sudden.

She rubbed her eyes. Maybe Adam and her father would turn out to be wrong. Maybe she was jumping at shadows. Maybe Ruth Sharpe would walk through the door in a minute and tell her it was all a big misunderstanding. She looked at the door, but it didn't open.

"THIS IS BEING handled really badly," said newly minted Detective Inspector Delany. "It's an embarrassment."

"Mm," Mellow said. The morning had passed in a blur of new faces, people not knowing which office they were supposed to be using, complaints, and resentment.

"What's got into their heads?"

Mellow had spent some time toying with the idea that Kelly's reorganisation of CID was all a stratagem to take the murder investigations away from her, and while that had served to make her feel rather important for a while, she couldn't really take it seriously. "I don't know, Carrie," she said. "I suppose we'll just have to make the best of it somehow."

Delany looked around the office – her office, as of the end of tomorrow, in a move Mellow could only ascribe to spite on Kelly's part. "At least you get an office on the fifth floor."

"That's not really the big thing it used to be," Mellow told her.

Delany looked thoughtful. "What happened to Ruth Sharpe?" she asked. "I was asking around and nobody's seen her."

"Ruth's been transferred," she said.

"That's a shame. I was looking forward to catching up with her."

"She'll pop in from time to time, I'm sure." Mellow and Ruth and Delany had been cadets together, and it was a relief to see a familiar face, even if the familiar face was about to take her job away from her.

Delany frowned at her. "Are you okay?" she asked.

"Just a bit tired," Mellow said. "I've still got to sort out all my paperwork, but I should have it ready for you by tomorrow afternoon. Say four o'clock?"

Delany looked at her a moment longer. "That sounds good to me," she said. "I still have to meet my squad properly, anyway." She stood up and started to move towards the door. "We should meet up after work one day. Maybe pop over and have dinner or something. We haven't had a chat in ages."

Mellow wondered if either of them would survive long enough to do that, but she nodded. "That would be nice," she said.

When Delany had gone, Mellow sat back and stared at the wall for a while. She supposed she ought to have a briefing with the robbery squad, but she didn't feel any great urgency. If she assumed the business of the still and the poisonous vodka fell under the jurisdiction of organised crime, she only had one big robbery case going on, the burglaries at Trinity. It wasn't a particularly big case, if you ignored the politics involved, and Rocco's confession about the radio parts had wrapped it up, but she couldn't tell anyone about that, so what was the point?

There was a knock at the door and Fleet looked in. "Message from Commander Powell, boss," he said. "He sends his compliments and says could you go over to Trinity."

Mellow looked at the window. It was pouring with rain and intermittent sleet outside. "Is there any particular reason why he can't come *here*?" she asked. Then she sighed. "Doesn't matter. Forget I asked." She got to her feet and picked up her bag. "Come on then, Peter," she told him. "You're still a member of my team till tomorrow so you might as well come, too."

THIS TIME, THERE was no genial welcome at Trinity, no jolly banter with the guards. They weren't even allowed into the buildings. Powell, wearing a waterproof poncho, was waiting for them in the courtyard outside. He didn't offer to shake hands.

"Not a very warm welcome, commander," Mellow said.

"Have you found our student yet?" Powell asked.

"That's being handled by the uniform branch, so I don't know," Mellow told him. "And you only told us he was missing yesterday. I saw the report."

Powell looked stonily at her. "We searched his rooms this morning and we found this, among other things." He took his hand from the pocket of his poncho and held up a little glass tube with a metal wire sticking out of either end.

You stupid sod, Rocco. Mellow fought for calm and leaned forward to look at the object. "What is it?"

"It's a radio diode." Powell folded his fist around the object and returned it to his pocket. "It's one of the stolen components."

"Are you sure?"

"It has a serial number on it."

Mellow nodded. "And you say you found other things?"

"Other radio components. Hidden at the back of a drawer."

Mellow felt events suddenly accelerating to overtake her. If they'd been standing in Powell's office, she was sure her body language would have given her away, but standing outside with rain dripping from her hood and running down her face she just looked cold and wet and miserable. "Right," she said. "Well, you'd better let me have them, then."

"What?" Powell snapped.

"If this boy… um…"

"Barnes," Powell said.

"If this boy Barnes is responsible for your robberies, it's evidence."

"No," said Powell.

Mellow blinked water out of her eyes. "I'm the investigating officer, commander. It's my evidence."

"No," said Powell.

"And I'll need to see his rooms."

"No," said Powell.

"With all due respect, you're not being very helpful here, commander," she told him. "For weeks you've been sending me memos asking how the investigation was progressing; now we finally seem to have a breakthrough, you don't want to cooperate."

Powell seemed to have entirely forgotten that Fleet was standing there, too. He stepped forward until he and Mellow were almost toe-to-toe. "I want him found, inspector," he said. "If you can't find him, we'll find him ourselves."

Powell was almost a head taller than her, but Mellow didn't back down. "If he's not in College, that's going to raise some jurisdictional issues, commander," she said.

"I don't care about that," he told her. "I just want him found. If you can't do that, I'll have to speak with your superiors."

They stared at each other for what seemed to Mellow to be quite a long time, until Fleet noisily cleared his throat and Powell glanced at him, then back at her. He took a step back. "Just find him, inspector," he said, and he turned to go back inside.

Mellow started back towards the gate, Fleet walking beside her. After a few moments, he said, "I'm almost glad I'm going over to organised crime."

"I'm sure it'll have its moments," she said.

He grunted. "At least I won't have to see *that* twat again."

*   *   *

DINNER THAT EVENING was subdued. Rocco was still miserable about being declared missing, and Mellow decided not to tell him that he was now wanted for theft as well, even though she wanted to box his ears for hiding the radio components in his room. At least Powell hadn't mentioned Ruth; that would have been a tricky subject to try and navigate. Did that mean Trinity still didn't know about her?

She didn't feel much like talking, anyway. She didn't want to talk about what she'd found in the fingerprint archive, or the CID reorganisation, or anything really. The whole day felt like a long, slow, bad dream and all she wanted to do was have her dinner and a shower and go to bed and pull the covers over her head. Her father obviously wanted to continue last night's conversation about whatever had happened at Sunnymead fifteen years ago, but he was smart enough to realise no one else was interested, so he kept things going with occasional harmless anecdotes about his time on the force.

Still, it was an effort, and Mellow was relieved when they'd finished and Rocco went back upstairs to read. She collected the plates and took them over to the sink and stood looking out into the rain-lashed darkness beyond her reflection in the window. As she'd been leaving work, word had gone round that one of the city representatives in Chancellery had stood up in the middle of a meeting, held up a little banner with *WAYLAND* painted on it, and launched into a speech about the city's neglect of the people in the southern suburbs. There had been a scuffle, and he'd briefly been arrested. It felt to Mellow as if the city was slowly coming unglued, and there was no way anyone could stop it.

"He'll be back," her father said from the table behind her.

And there it was, the thing she *really* hadn't wanted to talk about, or even think about. She ran water into the sink.

"What do you think we should do?" asked Jack.

"I don't know, Dad," she said, taking up one of the plates and starting to wash it. "Wait and see what happens, I suppose."

TWENTY-THREE

THEY LEFT HIM in the cupboard for a long time. It was quite a large cupboard, and it smelled of wood and old furniture polish, and he paced cautiously around it, bumping into the shelves that lined the walls. With his arms stretched awkwardly behind him, he was able to grope along some of the shelves, but he wasn't able to identify anything on them by touch. Bottles and jars, rolls of cloth, wooden boxes. Nothing immediately useful. He found his way around to the door and leaned on it experimentally, but it felt solid. It was going to be all but impossible to pick the lock with his hands behind his back, and he didn't have anything to pick it with anyway. He thought maybe lockpicks should be included in the Bureau's field equipment from now on, if he survived long enough to make the suggestion.

In the end, he retreated to the back of the cupboard, got down on his knees, and from there shuffled into a sitting position against a shelf, and after a while he managed to nod off. *We always take every chance to have a nosh and a kip when we're out in the field, sir,* a trainer had told him. *Because we never know when we'll get a chance next time.*

He was awakened some time later by the sound of the door being unlocked. He got his legs under him, but he didn't seriously think about fighting; he might, if he was lucky, be able to disable one person with his feet, but he didn't know what he would do after that. The house was enormous and he didn't have a good idea of its layout, and his hands were secured behind his back. He'd got out of a similar situation in Margate, but that had been due to luck more than anything else.

The door opened, flooding the cupboard with light from the corridor. Then there was a click and a light came on above his head and he had to close his eyes against it.

"He wants to see you," Hob's voice said. "He wants to see the look on your face when you realise who he really is."

Adam opened his eyes and squinted against the light. Hob was standing in the doorway. "I'll try to look surprised."

Hob gave him a long look, then he half-turned and looked out into the corridor. "Get him out of here," he said to someone outside, and a moment later two soldiers appeared in the doorway, one armed and one not. The unarmed one came into the cupboard and hauled Adam roughly to his feet and shoved him through the door and then marched him along the corridor, up a flight of stairs, along another corridor, and stopped beside another door. Hob knocked and opened it. "In," he said, and the guard pushed Adam through the doorway.

He found himself in a small, cosy drawing room with more paintings of long-dead rich people on the walls and a roaring fire burning in a black marble fireplace. A pair of armchairs were drawn up to the fire, a little round-topped table between them, and in one of them sat a grinning Father John, suit rumpled and tie askew.

"Adam, my friend!" he said in a jolly voice. "Come on in and sit down. It's about time we had a chat." He looked past Adam and said, "That'll be all, Dick."

"I should stay," Hob said.

John grinned. "Oh, I'll be safe enough. Adam's not going to cause any trouble. Are you, Adam?"

"No promises," Adam said.

John laughed. "That's the spirit. Game to the very last."

Hob thought about it for a few moments, obviously unhappy to be dismissed and probably not too pleased with the way John put a slight emphasis on 'Dick'. Finally, he nodded at the guard and turned and strode out of the room. The guard followed and closed the door behind him.

"So," John said. "Here we are. Alone at last."

"Well, it's not the first time," Adam reminded him.

John chuckled. "No, it's not, is it? Did you guess? Did you guess who I was?"

"No," Adam said. "I really didn't."

That made John happy. "I must say I'm *awfully* flattered that your people remember me at all."

"You did cause quite a lot of trouble."

"Trouble? Me?" John sounded affronted. "All I wanted to do was help."

"You started a coup."

John laughed. "Is that what they call it? Well, that's exactly what I'd expect from a military dictatorship. All *I* did was suggest some ways things could be done better, but the people who run Plymouth don't like the lower orders questioning the status quo. They stuck me and my friends in a cart and sent us out into the storm, left us to fend for ourselves."

"That's not what happened," Adam said.

"You weren't there. You need to wake up and see things the way they are, not the way *they* want you to see them." He indicated the empty armchair. "Sit down." He watched Adam lowering himself awkwardly into the chair. "So, young Adam, what are we going to do with you?"

"You could let me go," Adam suggested.

John thought about it. "I could," he agreed. "I could indeed.

Richard wants to have you executed for spying on us. What do you think about that?"

"I'm opposed," Adam told him. "On general principles."

"Richard likes to think he's a sophisticated thinker, but really he just sees things in black and white; he has no idea how complicated things can become. Did you know he hasn't travelled more than fifteen miles from here in his entire life?"

"You could say that about most people."

John nodded. "But you and I, we've *travelled*. We've seen how things really are, we know that things *aren't* black and white. Richard sees the world within a day's ride away from where he stands; we see the bigger picture."

That would be a remarkable thing, if it were true, Adam thought. Most of the time, he had to satisfy himself with a vague understanding that there *was* a bigger picture, without the faintest idea what it was.

"How did you know who I was?" he asked.

John gave him a sly look and tapped the side of his nose. "You're not the only people to understand the importance of Intelligence."

Adam assumed that meant Hob had sources in the Chilterns somewhere. He thought he could probably make a spirited attempt at killing John, even with his hands behind his back, but not without making a lot of noise, and he doubted he'd be able to finish the job before someone came in and shot him.

"So, what happens now?"

John looked thoughtful. "Well," he said, "I *could* let Richard have you. But I don't see any need for unpleasantness, do you?" He smiled. "Tell you what, Adam, why don't you stay here for a couple of days?"

Adam raised an eyebrow.

"As my guest," John added. "Do you know what a *diplomat* is?"

Adam nodded.

"Well, let's think of you and me as diplomats," John suggested. "Ambassadors, if you like. Me representing my people, you representing yours. Perhaps we can discuss some kind of *accommodation* between us."

Adam didn't think Guz would be remotely pleased with him acting as their ambassador, but he didn't see he had much choice but to play along. He said, "I can't sign treaties or anything."

John laughed. "All right," he said, "we can leave the *treaties* for another day. But how about it?" He spread his hands. "It's warm and dry here and the food's *excellent*."

"But I wouldn't be able to leave."

"Well, *eventually*," John mused. He smiled at Adam again. "When I'm ready."

"It's not really a choice, is it?" Adam pointed out. "Stay here or be shot."

John shrugged. "Life's like that sometimes, isn't it?" He leaned over and tapped Adam on the knee. "Come on, Adam!" he said cheerfully. "A couple of days of wining and dining and pampering. You and I can have a chat and set the world to rights."

From what Adam had seen of the world, he thought it would take a lot more than two men having a chat to set it to rights. But he nodded.

"That's the way!" John said, beaming. "You and I, we're men of vision, we want the world to be better, not like the great unwashed out there." He waved vaguely towards the curtained windows.

"I think the great unwashed want the world to be better, too," Adam said.

"Yes, but your average farmer can't see beyond the nearest hill. We don't just see beyond it, we've *been* there. We're going to get on like a house on fire." He raised his voice. "Tom! Tom, come in here!"

The door opened and Glebe, the young man from the town meeting, stepped into the room.

"Adam, meet Tom; Tom, meet Adam," John said. "Tom, Adam's going to be staying with us for a few days. Could you show him to his room, make sure he's comfortable?"

Glebe was wearing cord trousers and a jacket over a shirt and sweater. He was clean-shaven and neatly barbered, and he looked about fourteen years old. "Of course," he said genially. He looked at Adam. "If you'd like to come with me?"

Adam sat where he was for a few moments, looking from one to the other of them, then he struggled to his feet and stood in the middle of the room.

"If you go with Tom, he'll look after you," John said. "Have a good rest and I'll see you tomorrow."

Glebe stood to one side to let him pass through the door and out into the corridor, where two soldiers were waiting. He looked at them, and they looked at him, and it was obvious that, while they weren't particularly worried about him, they weren't going to put up with any nonsense.

Glebe led the way down a series of corridors and eventually stopped at a door. He opened it and stepped aside, smiling. There was, to Adam's mind, far too much smiling going on here. He looked through the doorway and saw a cosy little bedroom with a double bed and a little table and a couple of chairs. He stepped inside and one of the soldiers quickly released his arms and withdrew, and the door was closed and locked.

Well.

For decades, Father John had been a mythical monster, a nightmare from the sodden, howling, inhospitable wilderness beyond the boundaries of Guz, a practical warning about lowering your guard and letting strangers into your home. Parents still threatened their children with him if they refused to go to bed. It was an image that Adam was having some trouble reconciling with the plump, rather untidy clerk who seemed to be running things here. He wondered if Chrissie would ever believe him when he finally made his report. If he lived to actually make a report.

He went around the room. The door was solid, the lock was sturdy, and he had nothing to pick it with. Carpet underfoot, which suggested damp had never got in and someone had been looking after the place ever since The Sisters came down. No mirrors on the walls, and none of those slightly spooky old paintings either, which was a relief. A door to one side opened onto a little bathroom. He tried the shower and the water was hot and at a pretty good pressure.

In a little wardrobe, he found fresh clothes which looked as if they would fit him. Going over to the curtains and pulling them aside, he saw that bars had been fitted to the outside of the window, which somewhat spoiled John's pretension of hospitality. On the table, there was a plate of sandwiches and an open bottle of beer. Adam lifted the top of one of the sandwiches. Chicken and lettuce. It was a long time since he'd seen a lettuce; there must be greenhouses somewhere on the estate.

He took his coat off and draped it over one of the chairs and went and sat on the bed. He couldn't get out of the room, and the only things he could use as weapons were the plate, the bottle, and the furniture. And he wasn't sure about the furniture; it was on the flimsy side, the kind of furniture he suspected had once been described as 'elegant'.

And anyway, he wasn't going to get far trying to fight his way out of the house. He was going to have to think of another way to get out of here. He sighed and looked around the room again. Presently, he reached out and took one of the sandwiches.

HE WAS WOKEN the next morning by the sound of the door being unlocked. By the time he had his eyes open, an older man was coming into the room carrying a tray.

"Good morning, sir," the man said, going over to the table. "Did you sleep well?"

Adam sat up in bed. "Yes," he said. "Thank you." He glanced over at the doorway, saw a guard standing there.

The old man went over to the table and set the tray down. He took the plate and empty beer bottle, then he left again and the door was closed and locked.

Adam got out of bed and went to look at the tray. On it was a plate with two rashers of bacon, two sausages, scrambled eggs and some fried potatoes. There was a little basket of bread rolls still warm from the oven, a little saucer with a lump of butter on it, a mug of milky tea, and a bowl of sugar.

He drew the curtains and looked out onto a grey, drizzly morning. The room seemed to be at one end of the house, looking down on the end of great gravel forecourt he'd seen yesterday. Beyond that, the land fell away into a misty uncertain distance of farms and wooden buildings. He wondered if Mellow had taken his advice and left Oxford.

After breakfast, he had a shower and dressed in the fresh clothes from the wardrobe. He was just tying his boots when there was a knock on the door, the key turned in the lock, and Glebe was standing outside with a couple of guards.

"Ah, good, you're up," he said. "Father John's compliments, and would you care to join him?"

"Join him where?"

"A little excursion, I believe, a bit of fresh air. Father John likes to keep an eye on things."

I'll bet he does. "Sounds good to me," he said.

Two carts were drawn up on the gravel outside the entrance to the house. One of them contained four armed guards, the other contained John and Hob.

"Adam!" John called when he saw him. He beckoned exaggeratedly. "Come on, climb aboard! I thought you might like a bit of a tour."

"Absolutely," said Adam. He climbed up into the cart and sat next to Hob, who had a sulky look on his face. "Morning."

Hob barely grunted in reply.

"Good morning!" John said happily as the cart set off. "Did you sleep well?"

"Very well, thank you," Adam said.

"And breakfast?"

"It was very good." Adam patted his stomach.

"Excellent! I thought we'd go for a little jaunt this morning, show you about a bit."

"Okay." The cart turned off onto a sloping gravel track that led between neatly kept fields towards a group of buildings in the distance. "How many people do you have here?"

"Oh, I don't know," John answered cheerily. "We've never counted, have we, Dick?"

Hob didn't answer.

"Well, lots, anyway," John said. "And do you know what, Adam? Nobody goes hungry. In fact, we usually have a surplus. We trade with a lot of the villages west of here."

Adam could see people out in the fields, figures in ponchos and long raincoats with rakes and hoes and spades moving along the rows of potato plants. He couldn't see any enforcers standing guard to make sure they did their work, but he noted that the track wasn't taking them anywhere near the barracks closer to the main gate. He was being shown the civilian part of the estate, not the military part.

The buildings were a dozen or so single-storey wooden structures arranged on either side of the track, like a tiny village. People were already emerging as they approached, waving their hands and shouting, which baffled Adam for a few moments until he realised they weren't shouting. They were cheering.

The carts drew to a halt and were immediately surrounded by a cheering crowd at least fifty strong. Grinning hugely, John got down, and within moments he was lost in the crowd.

Adam got down, too, and found himself standing some distance off the edge of the crowd with Hob. The guards from the other cart had also dismounted, and were standing watchfully in a little group as John moved through the farmers, laughing and shaking hands and having a few words with each of them.

"Look at them," Hob said sourly. "They love him."

Adam glanced at him, then back to John working the crowd. "This isn't fooling anyone, you know."

"Oh, it's real," said Hob. "They really do think the sun shines out of his flabby arse. You saw the town meeting yesterday; do you think we laid that on just to impress you?"

"I don't know what to think."

"You know, I'm trying to decide how stupid you are," Hob told him.

"I think it's safe to assume I'm pretty stupid," Adam said.

"Oh, I don't think so. I think you just weren't properly briefed."

"It wouldn't be the first time."

"I was ten years old when he came here, him and about a dozen of his people," Hob said. "This area was all farms back then and we were getting along all right. We were even trading with Oxford."

"Yes, I know."

"He had a vision, a purpose. He said they'd united all these little towns and villages all over the Cotswolds and we could join them. He said we could have a better future." Hob shrugged. "Who wouldn't want that? He told us there was an army waiting in the West and one day it was going to come here and those of us who survived would be living under a military dictatorship, but if we all worked together, we could resist them. That was the choice he gave us. Live free with him running things or live as slaves under your control."

"We usually prefer cooperation," Adam said. "Although that doesn't always work."

"It didn't work in the Parish, did it?"

"To be fair, they'd pretty much fucked themselves up before we arrived. Someone needed to take charge."

Hob shook his head. "He told us Oxford was our enemy. We sent them sheep and pigs and vegetables, and they sent us… well, not very much, as it turns out. We wanted antibiotics and wind generators and all the stuff the Colleges were building, and they kept that for themselves. They wouldn't even let us use the hospital. They were sucking us dry."

"So you stopped trading with them."

"Of course we did – what would you have done?"

Adam shrugged, as best he could. "Not my problem."

"You should have heard him back then. He was travelling all over the Cotswolds, giving speeches, and he was *brilliant*. We were a bunch of farmers, and he turned us into a nation. He made us proud. And now we run Oxford."

"Except you don't, do you?" said Adam. "You don't control the Colleges."

Hob watched John for a few seconds longer. "Their time's coming," he said. "Their time's coming." And he turned and walked away through the rain.

TWENTY-FOUR

MELLOW ARRIVED AT the Cherwell ferry the next morning to find that it was gone. Not just stuck on the other side of the river; not there anymore. A crowd of people and carts had gathered at the landing, some of them bemused, some of them angry. Some of them were shouting across the river at a similar crowd which had gathered on the opposite bank.

Mellow wheeled her bicycle down to the water's edge and looked up and down the river, but the ferry was nowhere to be seen. She spotted a uniformed police officer on the edge of the crowd, surrounded by half a dozen people who weren't quite shouting at him, and she went over and showed everyone her badge and most of them drifted off. "What the fuck happened?" she asked.

"Someone cut the cables last night," the constable said, obviously grateful to her for rescuing him from the frustrated travellers. "Sawed clean through them." He pointed across the river, where smoke was still drifting from the doors and windows of the opposite engine house. "Then they set fire to the winch."

The cables were as thick as Mellow's wrist; it would have taken ages to saw through them. She had a sudden image of horses being dragged under the surface of the river. "Where's the ferry?"

The constable spread his hands helplessly. "Probably just going past Goring by now."

"What about the Marston ferry? I've got to get to headquarters."

"I haven't heard about any trouble up there," the constable admitted. "But I reckon it'll be busy."

It was also a long way out of her way. She had to cycle all the way upstream to the other crossing, hang around for over an hour before there was space for her on the ferry despite trying to use her badge to jump the queue, then cycle back down the Banbury Road from Summertown. By the time she reached her office there was a note on her desk summoning her to Kelly's office for an urgent meeting. On top of it was a note putting the meeting back, and on top of that was another note putting the meeting back again.

When she got up to the fifth floor, Kelly was waiting along with Delany and the newly appointed detective inspector in charge of the organised crime squad, a man whose name Mellow couldn't remember. Smith? Smythe?

"Sorry," she said, sitting down. "I had some trouble getting here."

"We know," Kelly said wryly. "What's the situation at the ferry?"

"When I left there was one uniformed constable on the Headington side and a lot of people shouting at him. Does anyone know what happened?"

Kelly glanced down at an open folder on her desk. "It seems that at some point early this morning, someone cut the ferry loose and let it drift away downriver," she said. "Then they set fire to the engine house on the city side. We don't know who yet, but they left a *Wayland* banner behind. Fortunately, the first officers on the scene had the presence of mind to take it down before too many people saw it. The ferrymen and their assistants have been arrested and they're being questioned by the Transport Unit."

"Why?" asked Mellow.

Kelly looked at her. "Inspector?"

"Why the Transport Unit?" She looked at the others. "All they'll do is beat them up until they'll confess to anything."

"It's been decided that a more direct approach is appropriate," Kelly said. "And I can't say I disagree; this force has been pussyfooting around for too long."

Doing proper policing, you mean, Mellow almost said, but she bit her tongue.

"Chancellery is of the opinion that this incident is some kind of protest over the arrest of one of the city representatives yesterday afternoon, and again I think I agree," Kelly told them. "It wasn't the only one last night. A firebomb was thrown at the Chancellery building, and another at the front gate of Trinity." She glanced down at the folder again. "Trinity's security guards opened fire in response, and one person was fatally injured."

"Oh, Christ," Mellow murmured.

Kelly raised an eyebrow. "Trinity were well within their rights to defend themselves, inspector."

"With respect, ma'am, I doubt everyone's going to see it that way."

"Which is why we're not going to let this get out of control," Kelly said. "It's Chancellery's judgement that the Old Families are behind all this." She clasped her hands on the desk in front of her. "We've been too soft on them for too long, but that's going to change. This afternoon I'll be circulating an action plan, and I want the three of you to liaise to present a list of targets and objectives." She looked at Mellow and sighed. "Inspector?"

"Sorry, ma'am," Mellow said, "but are we talking about what I think we're talking about?"

"Raids," Kelly said. "Arrests. Confiscations. The intention is to put them on notice."

"If we lean on the Families, they're just going to lean back."

"And that's how they've got away with it for so long," Kelly told them. "We've been afraid of provoking them and we've let them get fat. They've been laughing at us, and that stops now. We're going to teach them who really runs Oxford."

There was a silence in the office. It occurred to Mellow that neither Delany nor Smith/Smythe had even spoken up, let alone raised any objections.

"Ma'am," she said carefully, feeling herself walking along the edge of a cliff, "I'm sorry, but this is how the riots started fifteen years ago. We went in feet first and we almost lost control of the city."

Kelly regarded her for a few moments. "That's not going to happen this time, inspector," she said. "Now, we all have things to do. Have you handed your caseload over to Inspector Delany yet?"

"No, ma'am."

"Well, I suggest you take care of that first and then we can all concentrate on important matters."

It seemed they had been dismissed. Delany and Smith/Smythe left the office without even looking at her, as if acknowledging her presence would somehow mark them as dangerous troublemakers.

Back in her office, she sat for a while just staring into thin air until her heart rate went back to something near normal. She counted to ten very slowly, and when that didn't help she counted to ten again, and again. She looked at the piles of folders and envelopes on her desk, and experienced an almost physical urge to take them all downstairs to the boiler room and stuff them into the furnace. She swore under her breath, very quietly, over and over again.

The top folder was the Trinity burglary investigation. She supposed she ought to add a note about Powell identifying Rocco as the thief, but equally she could probably sit on that indefinitely now, considering what was going on. She laid it aside for the moment.

The next folder was the still, and she was at a bit of a loss to know whose responsibility that was. It certainly wasn't robbery or murder; did it count as organised crime? Screw it; let Smith/Smythe deal with it.

She worked her way down through the pile, conscious that very few of these cases were going to progress much while the Thames Valley Force was at war with the Old Families. She doubted whether any of the force's currently active cases stood much chance of being solved now.

About two-thirds of the way down the pile, she was momentarily puzzled to discover herself reading what seemed to be notes about property deeds. Then she realised it was the research she had ordered former Sergeant Wallop to do on the ownership of the Sunnymead murder site. It felt as if she had sent him to do that about a thousand years ago.

The first surprise was that he had done it at all, actually gone over to the Chancellery archives and sorted through the records. The second was that, out of sheer bloody-mindedness or whatever, he had done a thorough job. The third surprise was that he'd actually found out who had owned the site before The Sisters.

Mellow sat back in her chair and held the sheet of paper out in front of her. Wallop's handwriting was terrible, but there was no mistaking what he had written. The unit where they had found the body had belonged to a company calling itself *Geo. Fox & Sons (Knitwear) Ltd*.

SHE WAS ONLY halfway up the front path when Doug opened the door.

"Douglas," she said.

"Leonie. It looks like you've brought us bad news."

Was it that obvious? "You might have noticed there's a lack of good news at the moment. Is your mum in?"

Doug regarded her calmly for a few moments, then he stepped to one side. "She is. Come on in. She's in the office."

Effie was sitting at her desk when Mellow appeared in the office doorway. "Leonie," she said. She looked at Mellow's feet. "You're tramping water all over the house."

Mellow looked down and realised that she'd forgotten to pause and change into a pair of slippers in the hallway, and the embarrassment about that somehow made all her anger drain away. "Sorry," she said.

Effie shook her head. "Doesn't matter, it'll mop up. Come in and sit down." She looked past Mellow. "Make us some tea, Douglas."

"Yes, Ma," Doug said, moving past on the way to the kitchen.

"And I think a plate of biscuits would be nice, too."

"Yes, Ma."

Mellow stepped into the office and sat down on the sofa and Effie looked at her. "Have you noticed how tea's getting really expensive these days?" she asked.

"Yes," said Mellow. "I have."

"It's getting harder and harder to get hold of it, of course," Effie said. "Back in the day there was tons of it, all of it sealed and vacuum packed in old supermarkets and warehouses and waiting for someone to come along and just take it. Same with coffee, and sugar, and tobacco and lots of other stuff. Amazing it lasted this long. But now we're starting to run out; we have to go further and further out into the country to find places that haven't already been stripped."

"*We* being you and the other families."

"And Chancellery. Ever since they set themselves up, we've been competing for resources. They're the ones who set the prices for your tea and coffee, and they're the ones who're making all the money."

"Is that what you kept at Morton Street?" Mellow asked after a moment. "Tea and coffee?"

Effie gave her a long, level look.

Mellow opened her knapsack and took out a long brown envelope and held it out. "This is the original deed for the sheds at Morton Street," she said. Effie took the envelope, looked inside, and took out a folded sheet of paper. "Be careful with that," Mellow said. "I have to take it back to the archives."

Effie looked at the document, turned it over and read the other side, and she smiled. "I always wondered what it was originally used for," she said. "Turns out it was jumpers. Funny old world."

"You could have mentioned it, Effie," she said tiredly.

Effie shrugged and put the deed back in its envelope. "Would it have made any difference?"

"You told me you'd never heard of the place before."

"Oh, come on, Leonie. I'm a *criminal*."

Mellow shook her head in exasperation. "Who was he?" she asked. "Geo. Fox?"

"My great-great-grandad George," Effie said. "My dad used to say he was a big man in Oxford."

"He certainly owned a lot of property." It had only taken Mellow an hour in the archives to find all this, once she knew what she was looking for. "Including, somewhat ironically, the building we use as police headquarters now."

Effie beamed at her. "Really? I didn't know that. That's really funny."

"He wasn't an Oxford boy, though, was he?"

Effie shook her head. "His family had a big farm the other side of Woodstock somewhere, my dad said. That's where he started out."

"The company's registered office was in Compton Vale," Mellow said.

"That's it." Doug came into the office with a tray of tea things. "We're talking about your great-great-great-grandad," Effie told him. "He owned a lot of Oxford, back in the day."

Doug put the tray down on the table. "And lost it all when The Sisters hit," he said.

"Oh, he died a long time before The Sisters, dear," Effie said.

When Doug had gone again, Mellow asked, "What happened to the farm?"

"Oh, I'm sure I don't know," Effie said. "My dad could have told you; he had a lot of contacts with people out there."

"Even after they decided they wanted nothing more to do with us?"

Effie smiled at her.

"Did your dad ever mention what happened?" asked Mellow.

"He said some outcomers turned up, about twenty-five years ago," Effie said. "From Stow or Chipping Norton or somewhere like that. Cheerful people, he called them. Well-fed, well-equipped, full of big ideas about how to do things, full of optimism. People round there were short of a lot of things, back then, but the thing they were shortest of was optimism." She shrugged. "Wasn't too long before the cheerful people were running things."

"Did your dad," Mellow said, "ever mention someone called Father John?"

Effie smiled at her again. "This conversation's a long way from Morton Street, all of a sudden."

Mellow took another envelope from her knapsack and handed it over. "I found the deeds to some more of George Fox's properties," she said. "Or at least, properties Fox and Sons owned."

Effie removed another deed from the envelope and unfolded it.

"They owned stuff all over the city," Mellow went on. "Including this house. And that one." She nodded at the document Effie was holding. "The house where we found Courtenay's body."

"Well," Effie said, reading the deed. "Fancy that." But she'd stopped smiling.

"Bit of a coincidence, that, wouldn't you say?"

Effie didn't reply. She put the document down on her desk.

"I don't know what's going on here," Mellow said, "but I could charge you with impeding a police investigation, you know."

Effie wagged a finger at her. "You see, that's the problem with the police, right there. 'Impeding a police investigation'. You're policing as if The Sisters never happened, just following a bunch of old laws and regulations because you don't know any better. The world's changed and you never changed with it."

Effie hadn't the slightest idea what had been going on in her life recently. "I could still charge you."

"And what good would that do?" Effie asked. "Would it make you feel a bit better for a little while?"

"It might. And it might be worth it just for that."

Effie tipped her head to one side. "One of those days?"

"One of those days," Mellow agreed.

Effie thought about it. She got up and closed the door, then she sat down on the sofa beside Mellow. "There are parts of this story that you're not going to like," she said after a few moments. "But what you've got to remember is that a lot of them happened at a bad time, and they happened for what seemed like the best reasons. You mustn't blame anyone."

"I'm a police officer," Mellow told her. "I literally spend all day looking for people who're to blame for things."

"Well, let's just pretend you're not a police officer and I'm not a criminal, just for five minutes. It's just you and me sitting here, friends talking."

"We're not friends, Effie."

"Oh, we are." Effie took the cosy from the teapot and poured tea into their cups. "From what I hear, I might be one of the few friends you still have."

"What have you heard?"

Effie put the teapot back on the tray and replaced the cosy. "I've heard there's a big shakeup going on in the police. Lots of new faces, new bosses. I've heard you're being quietly moved to one side." She smiled gently. "You should see the look on your face. Of *course* we keep an eye on what's going on with the force. You have your grasses, and so do we. It's the natural way of things."

"It is *not* the natural way of things," Mellow told her, feeling the edges of the anger coming back.

"Well, we'll just have to agree to disagree about that, then. But it's very sweet that you think the world's black and white."

"Don't patronise me, Effie," said Mellow. "How did Courtenay's body wind up in a house you own?"

"Because I put him there."

Mellow's mouth dropped open.

In the ensuing silence, Effie added milk and sugar to her cup and stirred it. "My dad did a lot of business with the cheerful people in Compton Vale, down the years," she said. "He was a hard man to impress, but they impressed him. They were organised and they were efficient, and they pretty much owned the Cotswolds. He said there were thousands of them, they controlled Stroud and Cirencester and Cheltenham and they weren't flashy about it, and he liked that, too. They had a lot of stuff, tools, non-perishables, and they were happy to bring it into the city so long as it was done on the quiet. We did well out of them for quite a while. You're not drinking your tea, dear."

Mellow automatically reached for her cup, her mind working to catch up. "I've never heard about any of this before," she said.

Effie smiled humourlessly. "Of course you didn't," she said. "It was our secret." She shook her head. "Anyway, this went on for a few years, and then one night we had a visit from three of the cheerful people. Ma was sick by then and Dad didn't like people disturbing us at home, but he made an exception for them, tea and cake and everything. Then they shut themselves in the front room with Dad and Courtenay and they talked for hours.

"Dad never told me what happened; I had to get the story out of Courtenay later, but according to him they wanted a favour from us. They said they had some smart young people out in Compton Vale who'd benefit from a spell working in Chancellery. Problem was, Chancellery's a closed shop, the Colleges won't allow outsiders to work there. So what they needed was someone to make it look as if these people were Oxford residents and put a word in and get them jobs. Little jobs, nothing senior. Clerks, secretaries, that kind of thing."

"And your dad did that?"

"I assume so; I didn't hear anything else about it. It wasn't a big thing."

"They'd have needed ID cards and somewhere to live, Effie. Records, stuff like that."

Effie shrugged. "Dad knew someone in Chancellery who owed him favours. All they had to do was fill out some forms."

Chancellery's obsession with registering everyone in the city was strictly enforced; once upon a time it had been a hanging offence to falsify records, and it could still bring you one or two years' hard labour on one of the farms to the north of the city. It was not just a matter of filling out some forms.

"Yes, all right," Mellow said. "Let's put that on a shelf for the moment. What's it got to do with Courtenay winding up in that house in Cowley?"

But Effie wasn't going to be hurried. "That was the last we heard of it, as far as I know," she said. "Courtenay never said anything about it, anyway, and I forgot about it."

Mellow suspected this was not remotely true; Effie wasn't the forgetful type. It belatedly occurred to her that she should be making notes, but it was too late now.

"Everything was fine for a few years," Effie went on. "Then the police started to put pressure on us all of a sudden, us and the other old families. People were arrested and we never heard from them again, other people just went missing. There were a lot of raids. We used to store stuff up at the Morton Street warehouses until we could move it on – we had a bit of an agreement with Sunnymead nick, they didn't bother us and we didn't bother them. And one day they just broke in and emptied the place. We lost a ton of stock, Dad was livid."

"I'll bet," Mellow said dully. She definitely should be writing this down.

"Anyway, they kept pushing us and we started to push back. There were some fights with the police, here and there. Then there was the massacre at Sunnymead, and that was all they needed to go to war on us. We never did find out who did that; it wasn't us, even if Dad was angry enough to have done it."

Mellow thought of her father's mad story about the kidnapping of Sunnymead's police officers and the massacre staged to cover it up. It would be a lot easier to make something like that work if you already had some smart young people working in Chancellery, in places where they could falsify the records of the replacement officers.

"Were you out on the street during the riots?" Effie asked.

Mellow shook her head, although she thought Effie knew perfectly well that she wasn't. "Dad was."

"Yes," said Effie. "Yes, I know. You're still not drinking your tea."

"No offence, Effie, but I'm not really in the mood for tea."

"It's not cheap these days," Effie reminded her.

"I'll leave you a couple of quid to pay for it."

Effie looked hurt. "There's no need to be snarky, Leonie."

"You've just told me your dad was involved in plots to falsify official records and suborn police officers; I think I'm being a bit restrained, to be honest."

"Suborn?" Effie scoffed. "We didn't suborn Sunnymead nick. I told you, it was an agreement, a gentleman's agreement, for everyone's mutual benefit. That was the way we used to do things, and if you ask me it was a better world back then."

They looked at each other for a few moments. Finally, Mellow said, "Courtenay."

Effie got up and Mellow thought the conversation was over, but she walked over to the window and looked out into the gathering rainy gloom. Mellow had no idea what time it was; she still had to get back to headquarters and complete her handover with Delany, but leaving never occurred to her. She had a sense that she'd stepped entirely out of her job, and the scary thing was that it felt good.

"What do you think Leviathan was?" Effie asked.

"Dad thinks it was a gang," Mellow said. "Someone using the riots to try and take over."

Effie looked at her. "What about you? What do you think?"

Mellow shook her head. "I don't know. I used to think it was a myth, a scary story."

"And what do you think now?"

"I don't know anymore."

Effie looked out into the garden again. "My dad said it was the police," she said. "He called it a death squad. They were *assassinating* us."

Mellow was shaking her head again. "I would have heard about it," she said. "*Dad* would have known about it. There's no way anything like that could have been kept secret."

Effie shrugged. "Well, you can keep believing that, I suppose." She came back and sat down beside Mellow and spent a few moments gathering her thoughts. "Courtenay went missing two days after Dad," she said. "About a week and a half into the rioting. We didn't know what to do. I mean, it was chaos.

We were fighting you and Leviathan was hunting us. We were barely hanging on. The next day, one of the lads said he'd found a body at the warehouse."

"At the warehouse," Mellow said. "The one at Morton Street."

"Yeah. Dad and Courtenay used to deal with things like that, but they weren't there, so I went up to Morton Street myself, and there he was, just lying on the floor. They'd burned his face and hands off, but he was wearing the same clothes Courtenay had the last time I saw him, and I knew who it was."

"Oh, Effie," Mellow said quietly.

Effie looked at her. "You have to understand that, as I was looking at him, I knew I was dead, too. Dad and Courtenay ran things, and without them there was nobody in charge. Even if Leviathan didn't get me, when the riots ended somebody would come along thinking they could take everything away from me." She shook her head. "I had two kids; Douglas was sixteen, Archie was twelve, I had to protect them." She thought for a few moments. "So I decided not to tell anyone about Courtenay. If everyone thought he was still just missing there'd be a chance that he would come back one day, and that would make the scumbags think twice about coming after me for long enough for me to establish myself."

"What about the person who found him? Didn't they recognise him?"

"He wasn't recognisable, Leonie."

"So you hid his body."

"Not just me," Effie said. "Your dad helped me."

"Now just a fucking *minute!*" Mellow shouted.

Effie held up a hand. "Calm down, Leonie. Just calm down a minute and listen."

Mellow was shaking her head. "No," she said. "No, you are *not* dragging Dad into this. He'd never do something like that."

Effie looked at her calmly. "There isn't another man in

Oxford I trust as much as I trust Jack Mellow," she said. "He'd have taken a bullet for me. I got word to him and asked him to help me and he did." Mellow was still shaking her head angrily. "It's true, love. Ask him. He's a good man, your dad, and he was a bloody good copper. He tried to talk me out of it, but he understood the danger I was in. We got Courtenay out of Morton Street that night and we put him in an abandoned school down the road, and after that we moved him from place to place until we got him to Cowley."

Mellow put her head in her hands. In the silence, she heard unhurried footsteps out in the hallway. They stopped outside the door, then moved back towards the kitchen.

"Anyway," Effie said. "When I heard about you finding the body at Morton Street, it felt like it was all starting again, so I got Archie to move the still and the stock of vodka to the house in Cowley and he went to the nearest nick one night and pinned a note to the back door to tip them off. To warn you."

The fact that she'd just solved the case of the still sailed past Mellow like a ship far out at sea, almost unnoticed.

"It's the same people who killed Courtenay, Leonie," Effie said. "They could have taken that poor man outside the city and just shot him, it would have been less effort. But they killed him like they killed Courtenay, and they left him where they left Courtenay. It was a warning, to me, to *us*. They're coming for us again."

Mellow sat where she was, face in hands. She wanted to go home and curl up in bed and pull the covers over herself until all this went away, except if she did that she'd have to have a conversation with her father about it and she didn't think she could face that. "You could have just *told* me," she said. "I would have come and had a quiet chat if you'd asked, you didn't have to go through all that rigmarole."

"Well, I'm not proud of what I did, there's not been a day gone by that I haven't thought about Courtenay under the floorboards of that house. Also, your dad made a list of all the laws we were breaking. It was quite a list."

Mellow sat back on the sofa, everything that had happened today tumbling around in her head. "Why are you telling me all this now?"

"Because there isn't time to wait for you to work it out for yourself anymore," Effie told her. "It's already started; people are going missing again."

MELLOW WENT THROUGH the rest of the day in a fog. She half-expected Adam to walk into her office at some point, but he never did. She handed over her case files to Delany, but the Morton Street deeds and Wallop's notes stayed in her knapsack. She cleared her filing cabinets of folders containing resolved murder cases and co-opted two uniformed constables to take them down to Records and stand there as witnesses while she and Tommy signed them in. As she watched the old man filling in forms, she couldn't stop thinking that he'd told her he had been stationed at Sunnymead at the time of the riots. *Where are you from?* she thought. She knew that if she checked the Personnel records she'd find a file saying that Tommy was Oxford born and bred, but would it be real, or would it have been put there by one of the smart young people Frank Fox had found jobs for? Was there anyone in the Thames Valley force who was real?

Sensing her looking at him, Tommy glanced up from the paperwork. "Is something wrong, inspector?"

You have no idea. Or maybe you do. She shook her head. "Do I have to stand around for this?" she asked. "I've got a lot to do."

"Those are the regulations," Tommy told her.

"Can't I just sign all the forms and leave them for you to countersign? One of these lads can stay here and witness them." She indicated the constables, who were starting to look bored.

"It's not very regular," Tommy said uncertainly.

"Yeah, well, things are a bit *irregular* around here at the moment. Come on, Tommy. As a favour."

Tommy thought about it, then he shrugged. "Don't tell anybody or I'll get in trouble."

You want trouble? I'll show you trouble. She pointed at one of the constables. "You, stay here and watch. You," she said to the other, "come with me."

Back in her office, she emptied the rest of her files out of the cabinets, and together she and the constable moved them up to the fifth floor. It took them two trips. Then they took the drawers out of her desk and took them and their contents upstairs and stacked them with the files in a corner of her new office.

"All right," she told the constable. "You can go back to whatever you were doing. I'll take the drawers back down myself." Once upon a time, she would have said 'thank you' as well, but today she didn't know who she was thanking.

When the constable was gone, she looked around the office. Desk, two chairs, filing cabinets. The view from the window looked weird this high up in the building, and she wondered if she would get the chance to get used to it.

She emptied the desk drawers onto the top of the desk and took them back downstairs. Her old office already looked unfamiliar to her. She stood looking at the map of *Wayland* occurrences on the wall and wondered what to do with it. If you looked out of the window, everything outside seemed perfectly normal, but it really wasn't. Maybe it never had been.

Fleet went by the open door, saw her, and looked into the office. "You okay, boss?"

"I'm not your boss anymore, Peter," Mellow said.

"I put in for a transfer to your squad," he told her.

She smiled. "You've literally been with Organised Crime for five minutes."

He lowered his voice. "This new bloke's going to be a disaster," he said. "He's talking about having a go at the Old Families."

There had been an official envelope waiting for her when she got back from Effie Fox's. The 'action plan' Kelly had talked about this morning. She hadn't been able to bring herself to read it yet.

She said, "A lot of stuff's going to be changing soon."

Fleet looked at her. "Are you sure you're okay?"

"It's been a long day." She walked to the door and turned out the light. "Maybe tomorrow will be better, eh?"

MELLOW'S SCHOOLDAYS HADN'T been a roaring success, so much so that she sometimes wondered how much influence her father's time in the force had had when it came to her own application. But she'd turned out to be a good copper, even if she'd been as surprised as everyone else when she was promoted out of uniform.

There had been one school report that was so catastrophically bad that she'd actually been afraid to go home and show it to her parents. She'd dallied after school, and then when there was no longer an alternative she'd gone home and walked past her house a dozen times, trying to work out what to do. Could she pretend she'd lost the report? That her teacher hadn't given it to her? That some bigger kids had beaten her up and stolen it? She'd been smart enough to know, as the daughter of a police officer, not to try that last one.

And now here she was, twenty-five years later, doing the same thing, cycling slowly up her street past the house, up to the main road, and back round again, going over and over the alternatives. She could just not tell her father that she knew about his involvement in hiding Courtenay Fox's body – she certainly had no intention of telling anyone else. She could confront him about it – what was he going to do, storm out of the house? Or she could just not go home at all. And those were the only available options, pretty much.

Well, she wasn't going to be driven out of her own home because her father had been stupid enough to go and help his ex-girlfriend fifteen years ago. She'd had a shitty, absurd day, and at the very least she deserved a cup of tea and an armchair by the fire.

She stopped at the garden gate, dismounted, and wheeled her bicycle up the path towards the front door. As she reached the house, she heard the slightest sound of boots scuffing on the paving stones, and she turned and saw someone standing on the path behind her. In the light from the living room window, she made out a figure dressed all in black, with a balaclava hiding its face. Mellow froze, still holding her bike, and the figure took a step towards her and raised its hand and pointed a pistol with a ridiculously long barrel. Then there was a quiet grunt of exertion and a swishing sound, and all of a sudden there was a sickening crunch and the masked figure's head seemed to crumple sideways and it dropped to the ground.

There was someone else standing on the path, this one tall and thin and wearing a long black coat. Inside the coat's hood, Mellow could see in the light from the doorway a clean-shaven, young-looking face.

"Thank you, Archie," she managed to say.

"You're welcome, Leonie," Archie Fox said. He was holding an old wooden baseball bat in one hand. "Are you hurt?"

She swallowed and shook her head.

"Ma sends her regards," Archie said. "She told me to keep an eye on you."

"Yes, I've seen you about." Mellow felt a sudden wave of dizziness, and if she hadn't taken a step back, she would have fallen over.

"Are you okay?" Archie asked.

She nodded, unwilling to speak. She went over to the fallen figure and knelt down beside it. She hesitated for a moment, wanting to know but not wanting to know, then she reached out and pulled off its balaclava. Underneath was a distorted but unfamiliar face, and she almost passed out with relief that it was a stranger. She thought she would have gone out of her mind if it had been someone she knew, someone she worked with. She went through his pockets, then reached out and picked up the gun and held it up to the light, looked at the silencer screwed onto the barrel.

"Leonie," Archie said gently, "I don't think you should stay here."

Mellow closed her eyes for a few moments, then opened them again and stood up. "Yes," she said. "Yes, you're right." She pointed at the body. "Put him round the side of the house out of sight," she said. "I'll be back in a minute." And she disappeared inside.

"HELLO, EFFIE," JACK said when Effie opened her front door. "You're looking well."

She looked at Mellow and Jack and Rocco and Archie, all standing there on her doorstep. "Well," she said. "I suppose you'd better come in, then."

Rocco wheeled Jack down the hall towards the kitchen. Mellow said, "Could I have a quick word?"

Effie gave her a long, level look. "Okay," she said. "Come into the office."

Mellow walked down the hallway. As she passed the living room door she glanced inside and saw half a dozen people with guns. "You're all under arrest," she called out.

"Fuck off," someone called back, not without some amusement.

In the study, Effie closed the door. "Your dad got old," she said.

"Someone just tried to shoot me," Mellow told her, taking out the silenced pistol. "If it wasn't for Archie, me and Dad would be dead. So, thank you."

Effie took the gun and looked at it. "Who was it?"

Mellow took an Oxford ID card and a little leather wallet from her pocket. "He was carrying these," she said. "The ID says he was Henry Russell." She let the wallet flap open so Effie could see the police badge.

"Sloppy of him to carry those," Effie said.

"He probably didn't think he was going to have any trouble."

"Still sloppy." Effie took the card and opened it. "What do you think? Transport Unit?"

Mellow shook her head. "I don't know. I didn't recognise him." Effie only lived a couple of streets away, but the walk here had felt as if it lasted a hundred years, and the whole way Mellow had been trying to work out why her disappearance had finally been ordered. Was it something to do with Adam not coming back from Compton Vale? Or had someone just had enough of her?

They looked at each other. "Well," Effie said. She handed the gun and the card back.

"You're right," Mellow said. "They're coming after you. Arrests, raids, the whole thing. There was a meeting this morning."

Effie nodded calmly. "How long have we got?"

"I don't know. Not long. Can you look after Dad and Rocco? I have to go and do something."

"Go where?"

"Compton Vale."

"What are you going to do there, *arrest* everybody?"

"I don't know, but I think that's where this all started. Someone else went over there yesterday, and they haven't come back." Effie didn't say anything, just looked at her. "I don't know what good I can do, but I'm not going to sit at home waiting for some other twat to come up the garden path with a gun."

Effie nodded and walked into the middle of the room. "You'll take Archie with you," she said.

"Look, I'm grateful to you for looking after me, but I'll attract less attention on my own."

"You'll take Archie with you," Effie said again. She pulled back the rug in the middle of the floor, and Mellow saw a little brass ring set in the floorboards. Effie lifted it, put her finger through it, and pulled, and a section of floor hinged up, exposing a short set of steps. "You'll need some supplies, too."

Mellow followed Effie down the steps and found herself in a basement lined with shelves and racks supporting enough weapons to start a war. Crossbows, shotguns, pistols, knives, automatic rifles, hunting rifles, and box after box of ammunition.

"I don't suppose there's any point telling you this is all illegal," she said. She pointed at a box of hand grenades. "Particularly those."

"Everyone else forgot what happened last time," Effie said. "We didn't." She took an automatic rifle down from its rack. "What happens if *you* don't come back?"

"Get Dad and Rocco out of the city and take them to Goring. Ask for someone called Coghlan; they'll take care of them. And you might want to think about going with them."

Effie smiled. "There's been Foxes in Headington for centuries, Leonie," she said. "I'm not going anywhere."

TWENTY-FIVE

THEIR TOUR OF the estate took most of the day, and after the first couple of hours Adam tuned out a little because it was all the same, a succession of small farms and holdings passing by in the rain. The estate was so big that they might have been out in the open countryside, except that the open countryside was wild and overgrown and everything on the estate was neat and tidy and efficient. All the people and animals he saw were healthy and well-fed and apparently content, and everywhere they went they were greeted by a cheering little crowd waiting to shake the hand of Father John. Hob was right; these people seemed to love him. And for his part, he loved the attention. He made little speeches, looked at baskets of potatoes, nodded enthusiastically as farmers introduced him to their horses and pigs and cows. And he actually meant it. It was quite extraordinary to watch; there was no knowing smirk, no sense that he was just indulging these people. Adam watched him and thought that, yes, it would have been entirely possible for him to convince people in Guz to mutiny.

Still, it didn't all seem entirely spontaneous. There was the little school where twenty or so children with freshly scrubbed faces recited a poem for them, and one farm they stopped at where lunch was waiting. Not a sandwich and some beer, but roast chicken and roast potatoes and green vegetables. John tucked in like a starving eight-year-old and got gravy on his shirt.

The light was beginning to fail as they turned back towards the house. It was visible even from the far side of the estate, many of its windows already lit up, and Adam wondered if that had been staged as well, a quite literal demonstration of power. There must be dozens of wind generators on the roof, but he'd seen few out among the farms.

"Tell you what, Adam," John said as they clambered down from the carts in front of the house, "why don't you join me for dinner this evening?" He asked the question as if it had only just occurred to him, and maybe it had, but Adam wasn't sure. The whole day was starting to feel like a huge play put on just for him.

Adam looked up and along the huge front of the house, and he could see the window of his room because it was the only one with bars over it. "All right," he said.

"Excellent!" John came over and shook his hand enthusiastically, as if they hadn't just spent all day sitting in a cart together. "Someone will come and collect you." And he marched off into the house.

The guards escorted Adam back to his room, where he found that the clothes he'd been wearing the previous day had been washed and dried and left neatly folded on the bed, alongside a suit and a white shirt. On the floor was a pair of black shoes. He tried one of them on and it pinched a little but not too badly. Someone had made a good guess at the size of his feet, and that was an attention to detail that he noted.

He showered and tried on the suit and shirt, and they also fitted quite well. He'd never worn a suit before, and it felt weirdly insubstantial and awkward. There was a tie as well, and he spent half an hour or so in a spirited attempt at working out how to tie it, but in the end he had to admit defeat and do without.

Not long after that, the guards turned up and led him along the corridors again to a big ornate room with an oval dining table big enough to seat twenty people. But there were just two places set, facing each other across the middle of the table, and John was rising from one of them and coming towards him, hand outstretched.

"Adam!" he exclaimed happily, even though it wasn't all that long since they'd last seen each other. "Good to see you." He nodded at the open collar of Adam's shirt. "Had trouble with the tie, did we?"

"I might have stood a chance if there was a mirror," Adam told him, allowing his hand to be shaken.

"Please, sit down," John told him, indicating the other place setting. "It's a dying art, you know, wearing a tie. Still, a miracle it survived at all, when you think about it."

"I imagine people have other things to think about," Adam said, sitting down.

"It's a sign of civilisation, a tie," John told him. He had changed his shirt, but he appeared to be wearing the same suit as earlier; Adam could see grease spots on his lapels. "Do people wear ties in Plymouth?"

"Can't you remember?"

John looked thoughtful. "Now you mention it, I can't, really. Long time ago. Are you a wine drinker?"

More people were entering the room now; a young woman wearing a black skirt and white shirt, pushing a trolley with a silver tureen on it, the older man who had served Adam's breakfast this morning, a boy with a small cloth draped over his forearm and a bottle in his hand. "I've never had a lot of opportunity," Adam said.

"Oh, you're in for a treat, then." The boy showed him the bottle, then poured a splash of wine into his glass. John took a sip and nodded, and the boy filled up his glass and came round the table to attend to Adam's. "The cellars here are *extraordinary*. A lot of the bottles haven't survived, of course, but there's wine down there that's nearly two hundred years old, and it's still drinkable. Give it a try."

Adam tasted the wine, but he couldn't tell what was supposed to be extraordinary about it. Meanwhile, the young woman was ladling soup into plates and passing them to the older man to place in front of the diners.

"You should make the most of it," John told him. "It could be decades before anyone makes wine again, if that's even possible anymore."

The waiters placed baskets of fresh rolls on the table, then they left, and John eagerly took up a spoon. "Tuck in, Adam," he urged. "Don't stand on ceremony."

The soup was a clear chicken broth with thin slivers of vegetables floating on the surface, and it tasted very good. John attacked his as if he was bailing out a boat.

"So," he said between slurps, "What do you think of the house?"

Adam looked about him. "It's very... big," he said.

"Extraordinary, isn't it? Dates back to 1705, you can feel how close to history you are. Churchill was born here." He saw the blank look on Adam's face. "You've heard of Churchill, surely. Winston Churchill?"

Adam shook his head.

"Well," John said in a disappointed tone of voice, "I don't know what they're teaching you down there in Plymouth. Churchill was one of the greatest of all Englishmen, a towering statesman. We could use someone of his stature in charge today."

"What happened to the people who used to live here?" Adam asked.

"Originally?" John thought about it. "No idea."

"No, when you arrived."

John smiled. "Oh, they're still here. Christians. Christians are great, salt of the Earth. They'll work all day and smile while they're doing it so God can see them."

This didn't sound like any Christians Adam had ever met, but he didn't say anything. He broke open a bread roll and buttered it.

"They'd already been farming on the estate for years," John went on, waving his spoon to punctuate his words. "But between you and me they were making a bit of a pig's ear of it, barely scraping by. They needed someone to get them organised."

"And that was you."

"Well, one doesn't like to boast, but organisation is *the* most important thing, don't you agree? Without it everyone's just running around in all directions and nothing ever gets done. We have that much in common, surely."

It was true that Guz was enthusiastic about organisation. Adam himself, not so much. The waiting staff came back, cleared away the soup course, and served plates of thickly sliced rare roast beef, boiled potatoes, more green vegetables. John doused his food with gravy and tucked in.

"Tell me," he said between mouthfuls, "do you think someone should be running the country?"

Adam thought about it. "The real question is whether it's a country at all, isn't it?" he said.

John smiled broadly and pointed his knife at Adam, conceding the point. "Yes!" he said enthusiastically. "Yes, that's the point, isn't it? I knew you'd understand. Where is England? Is it in the landscape? Is it in the hearts of the people? Is it possible that an entire country could simply cease to exist, just like that?" He snapped his fingers.

Adam didn't think John expected an answer. He ate some roast beef.

"What we have at the moment," John went on, "actually resembles the old Anglo-Saxon kingdoms. You have your own little kingdom down in the west, we have ours here. There's another out in Kent, I believe."

It was hard to think of Thanet as a *kingdom*, but he had a point, of sorts. Adam said, "So what?"

"So I ask you again, Adam, do you think someone should be running the country? Should someone unify these little kingdoms and make us a nation again?" John looked at him. "Oh, come on, Adam. Surely you have an *opinion*?"

"I'm usually too busy to have opinions."

"Well, if you'll forgive me for saying so, that's a luxury a lot of us can't afford. Take Richard and myself, we're experiencing something of a difference of opinion over what to do about Oxford. He believes we have to control the city at any cost, whereas I favour a more subtle approach."

"Who's winning that argument at the moment?" Adam asked.

"Oh, he is." John took a swig of wine. "He's currently whipping up unrest in the hope that he can scare the Colleges into cooperating with us."

"The way you did fifteen years ago?"

John smiled slyly. "Yes, well, guilty as charged. And it didn't *really* work back then; what cooperation we do have is grudging, at best. Chancellery doesn't work nearly as well as people think." He shrugged. "But that's what I meant about Richard only seeing the smaller picture. He wants to bully Oxford into submission, but he hasn't thought about what happens afterward."

Adam thought Hob had actually given a lot of consideration to what would happen if he got his hands on the Colleges' technological resources, and so had John, but he didn't say anything.

"Anyway," John said, "where were we?"

"Who runs the country," Adam said.

"Yes. Yes. Have you ever read Thomas Hobbes?"

Adam shook his head.

"Hobbes was a Malmesbury boy, just like me, and he studied at Oxford, just around the corner from where Chancellery is now. He reasoned that people are basically animals who'll fight each other to get what they want and kill to keep it, and really you only have to look at the state of the country today to see that he was right. There's no law, no organisation, the strong prey on the weak. Hobbes believed that the solution to this situation was for the people to come to an agreement with a strong leader, in which they would give up all their rights in return for his protection."

"Someone like you?"

John made a show of thinking about it. "Well, I was thinking about Churchill, but now you mention it..." He took another drink. "There can only be one leader, Adam. England *will* be a country again, the people have a deep connection, they still feel it in their bones. All they need is someone to organise them."

"Is that what this is all about, then? Who gets to be king?"

"It's about what kind of England we want," John said seriously. "Do we want it to be a place where people are free to live the way they want, or a military dictatorship where they're afraid to even open their mouths?"

"You just said that people had to give up their rights."

John didn't answer. Instead, he said, "Richard was nothing but a little farmer's brat when I first came here, couldn't read, could barely add two numbers together. I made him what he is, I gave him responsibility for Oxford. Now he's got above himself. He thinks he knows better." He waved his fork and gravy spattered the tablecloth. "He's been talking to your people for weeks now. He thinks I don't know, but I've listened to his radio transmissions. He's been begging them to come here."

"Why?"

John snorted. "Why do you think? He wants Oxford for himself, and he wants your people to help him get it. He's the one who issued the order to let you through the barricade, you know, but he made it *look* fake so no one would suspect him." He glanced at Adam. "You didn't know that?"

Adam thought about it, and he scowled.

John guffawed. "Your people have been *using* you, Adam. They sent you here to meet with Richard and receive his terms, and from the look on your face they didn't bother to tell you. You were supposed to arrive without any fuss and at some point Richard would have met you quietly, but the estimable but misguided Chief Superintendent Maxwell decided to have you arrested and then all of a sudden everybody was curious about you and Richard didn't dare approach you. I don't think he was expecting Inspector Mellow to take you home, either. And he *certainly* wasn't expecting Wayland."

"I keep telling everyone, that's got nothing to do with me."

"Our working hypothesis is that your people sent someone into the city after you, someone to whip up unrest among the great unwashed. Would they tell you about something like that?"

"Maybe not," he admitted.

John spread his hands. "Well, there you are, then. Wayland sneaks into the city and causes trouble, and that puts Richard on the back foot when he's negotiating with you."

It was mad enough to be something that the Bureau might come up with. If it was true, it had got entirely out of hand.

"Anyway," said John. "It's all academic now, isn't it, if you'll excuse the pun. What you've *actually* done is put Richard so far on the back foot that he's getting ready to put the city under martial law, and that's quite funny."

"Yes," Adam said. "I can almost hear Oxford laughing from here."

"One doesn't like to boast, of course, but something great

is happening here," John told him. "When we finally arrived in Cirencester, thirty-odd years ago, there were just three of us left – the others had died of cold or starvation. The Cotswolds was just a lot of frightened people scratching a life out of what was left after The Sisters, and we organised them. We taught them how to be better, how to be stronger. We started to build a nation out of the ruins – something the people in Plymouth really aren't interested in, by the way. There are almost a hundred thousand people living in the Cotswolds now, over ten thousand of them under arms. The garrison here on the estate is a thousand strong – I could ride into Oxford right now and take over the place."

"Except for the Colleges."

John smiled at him. "Well, it's a problem. I think it's a problem we can solve, if we're patient. Richard disagrees, of course." He laid his knife and fork down on his plate. "Adam," he said seriously. "You've seen what we've built here. We're not a threat to you, we just want to be left alone to live our lives in peace and solve our own problems."

"That doesn't solve the problem of who runs the country," Adam pointed out.

"Well, one day perhaps we can all meet and discuss that as friends," John told him. "But not now. Perhaps not even in our lifetimes."

"I'm not sure Guz would be willing to meet as friends, considering what happened the last time you met."

"Adam," John exclaimed, "that was *thirty years ago* and it was a *complete* misunderstanding." He sat back in his chair and spread his hands. "And *I* was the one thrown out into the wilderness. Surely if *I* can forgive and forget, your superiors can?" He held up a finger. "But if you try to meddle in our affairs again, we *will* fight back. I promise you."

Adam looked at the remains of his meal and put down his cutlery.

"So," John said, "will you take that message to your masters? Leave us alone and everything will be lovely. Bother us, and there will be trouble."

"You're just going to let me go?"

John shrugged. "Why not? You've done me no harm, really, caused me no real offence. It's actually been rather fun to meet you. You can leave tomorrow; we'll sort a horse out for you. We can even let you have some provisions."

"I'd rather walk," Adam told him.

"So *walk*, Adam. Walk back to your friends in the Chilterns, or all the way home, I don't care. Just tell them to stay out of our business."

Adam thought about it. "What about Hob?"

"Richard's not your problem. I'll deal with him when I'm ready." He clasped his hands in front of him. "Come on, Adam!" he said. "I'm going to let you go anyway. Someone will take you down to the gate tomorrow morning and you can just walk away. You're lucky we're not sending your head home in a box."

"That would probably be counterproductive," Adam mused. He shrugged. "All right."

John beamed at him. "That's the way! You see? Things get done when reasonable people sit down and talk."

And also when reasonable people were threatened with having their heads sent home in a box. He finished his wine; he had no idea if it was good or not, and he strongly suspected that John didn't either. Everything he knew about wine came from some book or other. He'd probably never even tasted it until he'd come here. But that was John. Everything about him was a front, a cover for a man ruthless enough to start a near-civil war in a city just to distract people from what he was really doing.

John got up and dropped his napkin on his plate. "Come on," he said. "Let's retire to the drawing room for a celebratory drink, shall we? We have some *excellent* brandy."

As if in response to some hidden signal, the waiting staff were coming back into the room to clear the table. Adam got up and followed John out of the door, where his two guards were waiting, and John led the way happily down the corridor.

"Who killed Professor Halloran?" Adam asked as they walked.

John glanced back at him. "Halloran? Sorry, old son, don't recognise the name."

"Doesn't matter." Up ahead, Adam could see Hob and another soldier standing in the middle of the corridor.

"Dick!" John said cheerfully as they reached them, "Adam's going to be leaving us tomorrow. Be a good chap and sort out someone to escort him down to the gate in the morning, would you? Make sure he's got some supplies to take with him."

Adam watched Hob thinking about this. His expression didn't change, not even when he said, "Kill them both," to the guard at his side.

For a fraction of a second, Hob and Adam were the only people on the landing who weren't surprised, and that gave Adam the chance to half-turn, punch the nearest guard in the face, and take his gun. He turned back and shot the second guard in the chest. The first guard was lying on the floor with a hand clutched to his face, and Adam shot him, too, and by then Hob and John were nowhere to be seen.

He searched the bodies quickly and found a couple of spare magazines for the rifle. Stuffing them in his pockets, he went back along the corridor to where the waiter and waitress were standing in the dining room doorway with horrified expressions on their faces. As he approached, they fled, and he ducked inside and locked the door behind him.

Going over to the window, he pulled the curtains aside. The window opened easily, and he poked his head out into the pouring rain. Every window in the house must have been lit up; he could clearly see the gravel forecourt three floors below, too far to jump. There was, though, a drainpipe to one side of the window. Without thinking about it, he slung the rifle over his back, got up on the windowsill, leaned over, and got a hand on the pipe.

He heard shouting in the corridor, and people running. The doorknob rattled as someone tried it. He gave the pipe a tug, and it felt firm. He got both hands around it and stepped over onto one of the brackets that held it to the wall. He paused a moment to make sure of his balance and his grip on the rain-wet metal of the pipe, then he started to climb down as quickly as he could.

He almost made it. He was just passing the first floor when his hands slipped and he fell backward off the pipe. There was a moment's freefall, just time to think, *fucking hell...* and then an impact that drove all the breath out of his body.

HE DIDN'T BLACK out, quite, but there was a brief period when everything was disjointed and confused, and when things made sense again he was being half-walked and half-dragged across the gravel between two soldiers and Hob was talking.

"I've had enough of this bullshit," he was saying. "I'll *make* them take me seriously."

"If you harm me, Guz will come here and completely fuck you up." It wasn't much, as threats went, but it was all he could muster. His right arm was in agony; he thought maybe he might have broken his elbow in the fall.

Hob snorted. "With *what*? The couple of hundred Marines you've got on the other side of the Vale of the White Horse? I've got a fucking *army*."

"It's not how many men you've got, it's what you do with them."

"I offered you *peace*!" Hob yelled into the night and the rain and the hail. "I offered you an *alliance*! And you came here and *completely* fucked things up. There's a fucking *insurrection* going on in Oxford right now, the Colleges have withdrawn from Chancellery, we don't get any more medical or technical support. It's going to take me *years* to repair the damage you've done."

"Let me go and I'll fix it," Adam tried.

"*Let you go?*" Hob shrieked. "Oh no. No, no, no."

Adam suddenly saw where they were going, and he dug his heels in and tried to twist himself free, but his arm hurt too much and he felt woozy and the soldiers had too good a grip, and they dragged him to the cross which stood at the edge of the gravel forecourt, all lit up by the light from the windows of the house.

"Bad idea," Adam said hurriedly. "This is a very bad idea." He tried to struggle but the soldiers stood him up against the cross and roped his arms to the crossbeam. Then one of them went away briefly and came back with a box and a hammer and a couple of long broad-headed nails. He put the box down beside Adam and stepped up on it. With one of the nails between his teeth, he positioned the other over Adam's wrist.

"Last chance," Adam said desperately. "You can still change your mind."

"No," said Hob, and the soldier drove the nail through Adam's wrist and into the wood behind it.

The world greyed out, came back as the soldier was hammering the second nail through his other wrist, greyed out again, came back.

"There," Hob said. "*Now* you know I'm serious."

"I know how you did it," Adam said quietly.

"What?" said Hob.

"I said I know how you did it," Adam said, lowering his voice until it was barely audible over the sound of the rain. He was fighting to hang on to consciousness for a little longer.

Hob stepped forward. "Know how I did what?"

"I know how you did it," and his voice was a whisper.

Hob stepped forward again until they were practically toe-to-toe. "How I did what?" he demanded, and Adam lunged forward as far as he could and fastened his teeth on Hob's nose.

Everything happened too quickly for the guards to react. Hob screeched and tried to pull away, but Adam concentrated and bit down hard and felt something crunch between his teeth. He jerked his head back and spat the end of Hob's nose onto the gravel in front of him.

Hob staggered back, shrieking, one hand clamped over the middle of his face and blood pouring between his fingers. "You *cunt*!" he screamed. He stepped forward and punched Adam awkwardly in the face, but there wasn't a lot of force behind the blow. He snatched the hammer from the soldier who had nailed Adam to the cross, then he seemed momentarily lost for what to do with it.

"*Cunt*!" he yelled again, and he raised the hammer and swung it round and down, and with a single blow he shattered Adam's right kneecap. Then he threw the hammer down and staggered back towards the house.

WELL, HE IMAGINED Chrissie saying to him, *there's no situation so bad that you can't think of a way to make it worse, is there?*

I thought it was worth it, considering, he imagined himself replying.

And did it make you feel any better?

Well, quite. He supposed he was going to die here, but it was a bit of a surprise to find that it didn't bother him all that much. A lot of that had to do with the pain, of course. His arms were starting to go numb, but it felt as if a bomb had gone off in his knee and he couldn't put any weight on it at all. Mostly, though, he realised that he had never expected to survive into old age. He did dangerous work – it was dangerous just moving around the country – and in the back of his mind he'd always accepted that the chances were that he'd succumb to something, even if it was as mundane as blood poisoning. You could be as careful as possible, and you would never think of everything. Crucifixion had never occurred to him, though. It turned out that life had one last surprise waiting for him, after all.

He looked out into the darkness down the hill and thought he could see lights far away between squalls of rain and sleet. Was that the barracks he'd seen earlier? The thousand soldiers John had told him about? And why had John told him that, anyway? Manpower strength was a secret you protected at all costs. Was it simple boasting? Naïveté? A flat-out lie?

Idiot. What does it matter? You're going to die.

He wondered if he was going to die here, if they'd just leave him until exposure and blood loss and starvation did the job, or if they'd cut him down and take him back to Oxford and spike him to the floor of that warehouse like Halloran and Courtenay Fox, as a piece of psychological warfare. Because that was all it was, a cheap, cruel trick to scare somebody. *Look. We have a monster on our side. You'd better give up.* The question was, who was it supposed to scare?

Idiot.

The two soldiers, possibly in an attempt to avoid having to explain to Hob why they had done nothing while Adam was biting his nose off, had taken up position on either side of the cross. He couldn't see their faces properly – the light from the house was behind them – but if he turned his head, he could see them standing there stoically in the pouring rain.

They stood there for a long time, the three of them. Adam's mind drifted, and there were moments when he wasn't there at all, although they were brief because the pain kept bringing him back. The strain of taking his weight on one leg became enormous.

A little group of people came out of the house carrying a lot of equipment. Without saying a word, some of them arranged lights on tripods in front of him, while another set up a camera. He watched all this in horrified fascination. Someone started to turn a hand-cranked dynamo, and the lights came on, weakly at first then brighter and brighter until Adam had to squint.

"We'll send your people a photograph," he heard Hob's voice say from somewhere on the other side of the wall of light. "That'll show them how serious I am."

Adam didn't hear the camera go off. The lights just suddenly went out, then the people in front of him were dismantling their equipment and taking it away, and then there was only Hob, this time standing a respectful distance away from the cross. There was a big wad of bloody dressing in the middle of his face, held on by bandage wrapped around his head. He didn't say anything, just stood there, vibrating with rage, and Adam thought he was winding himself up to come over and smash his other leg. But in the end, he just turned and walked back towards the house, and then it was just Adam and the guards again.

He lost track of time. The rain was occasionally relieved by a fall of hail.

"You could just let me go, you know," he told the guards. His voice was croaky and thin, and he might not have spoken at all for all the response he got. "Just pull the nails out and I'll take it from there."

Nothing.

"You do realise I'm Wayland, don't you?" he tried. "Have you any idea how many people I've killed? Most of them probably didn't deserve it, but I killed them anyway, just to make a point. Imagine what I'll do to people who *really* deserve it."

There was a sudden meaty thump and the guard on his left crumpled sideways holding his chest. In the light from the house, Adam saw a pointed metal rod protruding from his back. The second guard said something Adam didn't catch and started to move, and then there was a crunching noise and he dropped his rifle and fell to the gravel.

There was a moment's perfect silence, then a grunt of effort and another crunching thud. And another. And another. He turned head painfully slowly and saw a tall, skeletal figure dressed all in black hitting the fallen soldier over and over again with what looked like a baseball bat, and a whole series of images assembled themselves in his mind; a ragged scarecrow of a man offering him a bag full of human scalps, a half-glimpsed someone with the same body language standing outside the butcher's shop where they'd found the first *Wayland*, a hooded figure walking at the side of the road carrying a sack and a tin of paint.

Oh, he thought.

Then Mellow was standing in front of him, wearing a rain poncho and holding a crossbow and staring at the nails in his wrists. The tall figure kept hitting the guard, whose head no longer even vaguely resembled a head.

"Stop it, Archie," Mellow said. "He's dead."

"When I told you to get out of the city, this wasn't what I had in mind," Adam told her.

"This is Archie," she said as the figure with the baseball bat moved into his field of vision. He saw a tall young man with a kind, open face. "Archie, this is Adam."

"Okay," said Archie.

"We need to get him off this thing somehow."

"There's a hammer on the ground somewhere," Adam said.

Archie looked around and found the hammer where Hob had thrown it. He looked at its claw end, then came back to the cross. "This is going to hurt," he said.

"It *already* hurts," Adam told him.

It took Archie a long time to lever the nails out. Or maybe it just felt that way. When the second one came out, he pitched forward into Mellow's arms, head spinning with the pain.

"Can you walk?" she asked.

"Yes," he said, but when he tried to use his right leg, it felt as if it was made of fabric, not able to bear even the slightest weight. "No."

Mellow sighed. "We'll have to find another way out," she said. "He'll never get over the wall like this."

"We need to get him away from the house, whatever we do," Archie told her. "Otherwise, none of us are going anywhere."

They managed to get Adam slung between them, arms over their shoulders, and though he tried to bear as much weight on his undamaged leg as he could they wound up more or less carrying him down the hill and into the darkness beyond the light coming from the house. The rain pounded down, and wings of sleet kept sweeping across the estate.

"How did you find me?" Adam mumbled at one point, barely conscious.

"Someone painted *Wayland* on a big piece of wood and propped it up against the wall on the main road, so we decided to take a look and we saw you up there, all lit up," Mellow said. "And speaking of Wayland, what were you saying about him just now?"

But Adam had passed out and he never heard her.

TWENTY-SIX

HE HAD A terrible dream that he was back in his room at Blandings, and Commodore Templeman was, improbably, sitting by his bed. She was a stout woman with short grey hair, and she was wearing a black combat suit.

"So," she said. "Have we forgotten how to salute, Mr Hardy?"

"With respect, ma'am," he said, "you're not in uniform."

He knew it was a dream, because she smiled. "Insubordinate cunt," she said. "How do you feel?"

"I feel terrific," he told her.

"That's because you're full of painkillers and Christ only knows what else."

"I'd like to have those all the time, please."

She shook her head. "Not going to happen. I'll be expecting your report at the earliest possible opportunity. Or will we have to dress up for that?"

"I'm sorry, ma'am," he said. "I seem to be having an awful dream," and then the world went away.

*   *   *

IN ANOTHER DREAM, it was Betty Coghlan sitting beside the bed. "I was really hoping I wouldn't see you again," she was saying. "After what you did in the Parish."

"It was the monkey," he told her.

"What monkey?"

"It wouldn't stay in the box," he explained.

"You *butchered* people," she said.

"You've always known what's going on in Oxford," he said. "It just occurred to me, that's where you got the antibiotics you asked me to take to the Parish. You've got a contact in one of the Colleges, or in the hospital, and they've been smuggling stuff out to you."

She stared at him. "At least I haven't killed people."

"Can I have some more painkillers?" he asked.

IN ANOTHER DREAM, he said, "Trinity killed Halloran. They found out he was moving antibiotics out of the city, so they killed him."

"Why go to all that trouble, though?" asked Mellow. "Why not just quietly disappear him?"

"They wanted to send a message. They assumed he was giving the antibiotics to Hob, for this measles outbreak in Cheltenham, and they copied Courtenay Fox's murder to make a point. *Don't mess with us.*"

"But how did they know how Courtenay died?"

"Hob *told* them. He was too young to have been involved with Leviathan, but he'll have known what they did, and he boasted to the Colleges about it. *This is what we're capable of if you don't cooperate.*"

Mellow thought about it. "And you worked all that out for yourself? Just lying there?"

"I've had a lot of time to think."

She shrugged. "Well, it's not the maddest thing I've heard in the past few weeks. The chances of an arrest are slim, though."

"How did we get here?"

"Long story. We had to come the long way round, though. It took a while."

"Thank you."

She smiled. "You're welcome."

"How are things in Oxford?"

She sighed. "Judging by the radio messages it's pretty crazy there now. I'll be going back soon."

"Why?"

"Because I'm still a police officer," she said. She frowned. "Are you feeling okay?"

"Do you think you could ask them to give me some more painkillers, please?"

"WELL, WE MANAGED to save your leg, sort of," Chrissie was saying. "You might still lose your hands, though. They were pretty badly infected."

It seemed that he had been awake for some time without noticing. He looked down along his body, saw that his right leg was almost entirely encased in a framework of wood and metal pins and wires. His hands were huge soft white blobs, useless mittens wrapped in layers of bandage, and one of his arms was in a sling.

"Where's Mellow?" he asked.

"She went back to Oxford."

He sagged back against the pillows, suddenly remembering his dream. "For fuck's sake," he said.

"She said she had to make sure her father was all right," she told him. "We gave her some gear, a radio and stuff. She said she'd be in touch when she thinks it's safe."

"It's never going to be safe," he said. "Hob's monitoring radio traffic."

"She said she'd find a way. I was sorry to see her go, actually;

we could use her in the Bureau." She sniffed. "Not so sorry to see the boy go. He's *very* spooky."

Adam had to search for the name. "Archie," he said. He'd thought he'd hallucinated him.

"Archie," Chrissie agreed. "We could find a use for him, too, but I'm not sure I'd be happy letting him into Guz."

He thought of the boy hitting the guard over and over again, long after it was obvious he was dead. "I don't even know who he is," he said. "How long's she been gone?"

"They left yesterday. It's been a little over a week since she brought you here, a fortnight since you got hurt." She looked at him. "You're going to need debriefing, you know," she said.

"Not now," he said.

"No, not now. But soon."

"You already know everything about Oxford," he told her. "You knew even before you sent me there."

"Well," she said, "we knew a lot of things, but we didn't know how true they were."

"You knew from Hob."

"Mr Hob was very selective with the details," she told him. "There was a lot of stuff about how brilliant he was and how joining forces with him would be a great thing for us, but he never said a single word about Father John."

He sighed. "How long have you been talking to him?"

"A few months now. In fact, we still are. Well, we're *listening* to him, anyway. He's been all over the radio, shouting and ranting about us deserting him. Did you really bite his face off?"

"His nose," Adam said, although he wasn't sure if that had been an hallucination, too. "Not even all his nose."

"Well, he's *very* angry with you, and by extension with us, so thank you for that."

"You could have told me about it before you sent me off."

"We wanted you to go in there with no preconceptions and come back and report," she said. "That's your job."

"You wanted me to go in there and cause trouble."

"You managed to do that all right," she told him. "Whether we wanted you to or not."

Adam closed his eyes. "I'm tired," he said.

"We need to talk about it, Adam," she said.

"Yes," he said. "But not right now. I need some more painkillers."

He heard Chrissie getting up to go. "We need to talk about that, too."

"So," Chrissie said, "it was all about the Colleges?"

"Some of it," Adam said. "It's very complicated."

"So try and make it simple for me."

He thought about it and shifted uncomfortably. In recent days he'd been allowed out of bed, although he needed help to move. He was sitting in a chair by the window, his leg propped up on a pair of footstools. "The thing about Oxford is, it looks like a working city," he told her. "But it's not. It's a bunch of groups, all of them cooperating because they have no choice. The city and the Colleges depend on each other, and neither of them likes it. They all sit in Chancellery and twice a year they put on robes and they make a big show of unity, but really they're just manoeuvring for advantage all the time."

"And then there's the criminals."

"The Old Families," he said. "They're not all criminals, just people whose families have lived in Oxford since before The Sisters. Some of them represent the city in Chancellery. But they all resent the authorities. It's a mess, and the mad thing is that it actually worked reasonably well until John started to meddle with it twenty-odd years ago."

Chrissie sat back in her chair and looked at him. In all the hours of his debriefing she had not taken a single note, but she had an unnaturally good memory. "It's hard to believe he survived at all," she said, "let alone wound up in a position to take over a community the size of Oxford. Are you sure it's the same Father John?"

He stared at her. "I can go back and ask him, if you'd like."

She shook her head. "No. He and his friends literally left Guz with nothing; if they'd stopped for five minutes to collect a change of clothes, they'd have wound up being put against a wall and shot. How did he wind up running the Cotswolds ten years or so later?"

Adam shrugged and winced as a bolt of pain went through his injured elbow. "How did he talk so many people in Guz into rebelling? He tells people what they want to hear, promises them greatness, and it sounds convincing if you don't think too hard about it and he manages to keep you fed."

Chrissie looked towards the window. Outside, the extensive – and extensively boobytrapped – grounds of Blandings were being lashed by hail and sleet, but in here everything was warm and dry and cosy. It was easy to forget that beyond the walls of the estate – beyond the boundaries of Guz or the Bypass ringing Oxford – the majority of the country still had no electricity and little or no medical care, was still just one bit of bad luck away from starvation.

She said, "It's hard to believe this fantasy about England."

"An England with money."

Chrissie made a rude noise. "Money." There was a warehouse in Guz half-full of bales of money, century-old plastic notes brittle as old leaves. Nobody knew what to do with the stuff; the warehouse wasn't even guarded. "That was one of his bright ideas, thirty years ago. He called us Communists."

"He's moved on since then; he's calling us a military dictatorship now."

She shook her head.

"He also says there wasn't a coup," he told her. "He says we threw him out."

She narrowed her eyes at him. "And what do you think of that?"

"I don't know, to be honest."

"Well, when we get back, I'll introduce you to some people who were around back then. Not Bureau, not Committee, ordinary people who lost friends and family. They'll tell you what happened."

"I'll hold you to that." He shifted again, trying to get comfortable.

"Are you all right?"

"Yes."

"You look tired," she said. "We can pick this up tomorrow, or the day after."

He shook his head. There was another operation on his leg scheduled for the end of the week, and he'd be unable to function properly for days afterward. "I'd rather get it over with."

She watched him for a moment. "I'm still not clear about this Leviathan business."

Leviathan. Chrissie was perfectly clear about it; she'd shared some of the information from Mellow's debriefing with him. What she wanted was his perspective. "John made a mistake in Guz," he said. "He moved too soon and he barely got out alive, but he's learned patience. He's had to, because he needs the things the Colleges have. He's not short of technicians and engineers – he's got a whole valley full of little factories making weapons and God only knows what else – and they can copy designs for wind generators and whatever, but there's other stuff he can't copy."

"Medicines," Chrissie said. "Antibiotics. Vaccines."

Adam nodded. "He just doesn't have the expertise for that. The problem is, the Colleges are basically little independent states, and they keep strangers out, so he couldn't infiltrate them. The next best thing was to infiltrate the city's administration and use that to try and manoeuvre the Colleges into giving him what he wanted."

"So what went wrong?"

"Nothing went wrong. He brought people in over a period of years, in ones and twos, without anyone noticing, and they found themselves jobs in Chancellery. And the more people he got into Chancellery, the easier it became to put more people into position. But all those people were in admin; they still didn't have anyone at a policy level, so they couldn't stop the police when they decided to crack down on the families and trouble broke out. What they *could* do was move a squad of killers in one night, take over a police station, and use it as a base for putting the fear of God into the gangs. And when that was over, they had thirty-odd new police officers, all waiting to be gradually promoted into senior positions." He sniffed. "It all worked out rather well really, from John's point of view. They spent the next fifteen years quietly getting their feet under the table; now they more or less run the city."

"Everything but the Colleges."

"It's quite funny, if you think about it. All that work, and they still can't get what they want."

"It's not *really* funny, though, is it?" she said.

"You've got to get your laughs where you can," he told her.

Chrissie thought about it. "Inspector Mellow told me what you said about this Halloran bloke. Do you know that as a fact, or was it just the painkillers talking?"

So it hadn't been a dream after all. "Now *that's* funny." They were trying to cut down his painkillers gradually, but it was leaving him sweaty and shivery and in a lot of pain, and he was assailed by terrible nightmares. "Did you ask Betty about it?"

She nodded. "She's being a bit cagey, but she admits she was getting antibiotics and some other stuff from the hospital, which would have been nice to know."

"It's a sod, isn't it? Not being told everything?"

"Stop being snarky. I don't suppose we can blame her for wanting to keep it quiet; she's got a lot to protect here." She looked thoughtful. "Still, it's only a guess, isn't it? You don't have any evidence that the Colleges killed Halloran."

"I didn't go there to solve a murder," he grumbled and closed his eyes. "This leg's starting to hurt a lot again."

"No painkillers till this evening." She looked at him lying on the bed and wondered whether she should mention the package that had been delivered the previous day, left on the ground outside the front gate of Blandings and weighted down with a stone, containing a photograph of him nailed to the cross outside Father John's palace. She'd never trusted Hob's appeals for help, but now it seemed he was quite unhinged. She said, "This thing about the measles in Cheltenham is interesting. Be a shame if John's little kingdom had a measles epidemic."

He opened his eyes and looked at her. "Tell me I didn't just hear you say that."

She shook her head. "Just thinking out loud."

They were quiet for a while. Hail rattled on the window. Adam said, "Have you heard anything from Mellow?"

"No," she said. "That doesn't mean anything, though. If she has any sense – and I think she does – she'll be keeping her head down."

"We should send somebody into Oxford and try to make contact with her."

"And we probably will," she told him. "But not you. You're not going anywhere. If nothing else, we'd quite like to extract this boy Rocco. This radio source in Yorkshire sounds interesting; we haven't been able to pick it up here."

"So, what happens next?"

"I think that depends a lot on who winds up on top over there. What do you think?"

He thought about it. "John says he isn't interested in a fight with us; Hob isn't interested in us at all."

"Do you believe them?"

"Of course not. They're not going to march an army into Devon and try to take Guz; John at least knows that would be impossible. But they're getting ready to butt heads with us sometime in the future, somewhere else. They're establishing a presence in the Vale of the White Horse, and I'd be surprised if they don't have people in Abingdon as well. I think John still wants to take the Chilterns, but I don't think he's in a great hurry."

"And you didn't see what happened to him."

Adam shook his head, suddenly feeling a great weariness settling over him.

"Well," Chrissie said, "it'll be monsoon in a couple of weeks, and then it'll be winter, and then it'll be monsoon again, so nobody's going to be doing anything until next summer. We'll move some more people along the coast and stage them up here through Southampton while the weather holds, but if John's really got a thousand-strong garrison handy we can't fight them."

"I don't think he's got that many people," he said. "He just wants us to think he has."

"Anyway, a little civil war between John and Hob wouldn't be the worst outcome," she said. "It'd keep them busy for a while, if nothing else. Maybe we'll wait a bit and then see if we can't repair things with him." She paused. "Might have been better if you hadn't bitten off his face, though."

"His nose," he said. "Not even all of his nose."

There was a silence, then he heard her standing up. "The weirdest thing is this Wayland business," she said. "Are you *sure* that wasn't you?"

"I'm sure," he said wearily.

"And who killed Harry Kay? Did Trinity think he was in it with Halloran?"

"I don't know." He blinked blearily at her. "Someone broke

into his house looking for something; they might have thought he had some of Halloran's stuff. I think the murder was a coincidence, although I'm willing to bet Hob's behind the graffiti and the attacks on College staff."

"Well, it sounds as if that's blowing up in his face, if what Inspector Mellow says is right." She went over to the door and put a hand on the handle. "But we still don't know who killed him and wrote Wayland's name on his bedroom wall in the first place."

Adam closed his eyes again and thought about the scarecrow figure he'd met in the Parish, offering him a present of human scalps, and considered the insane possibility that everything that was happening in Oxford right now was the result of an accident, a collision of coincidences.

He opened his eyes and said, "I stashed Gussie in a house south of Oxford."

Chrissie sighed. "You and that fucking gun."

That fucking gun had almost cost him his life, more than once. "It's a good gun," he said. "I stashed a lot of my field gear there, too. I've got the map reference."

She looked at him for quite a long time. "I'll send someone to retrieve it."

"Thank you." Something else occurred to him. "I had this weird dream," he told her. "Something about the commodore being here."

She smiled brightly and opened the door. "Oh, that wasn't a dream," she said.

TWENTY-SEVEN

MORTY WAS LOST again.

He'd thought, when he spotted Wayland leaving the city and followed him, that they were finally coming close to the purpose of their mission, but Wayland was on a bicycle and Morty was on foot, and very quickly Wayland had vanished into the distance, leaving him with no option but to plod along and try to catch up.

Eventually, he'd fallen in behind a group of workers making their way along the side of the road, and he'd spotted Wayland in the back of a cart being taken through a gate in a high wall. Could this be their final destination? The place where Wayland would tell him what to do?

By now, Morty was desperate for an answer, and he didn't know what to do other than putting Wayland's name on a sign and leaving it near the road. When that didn't bring any results, he set out to walk along the wall surrounding the estate. It was a long way, and it took him a couple of days because he had to keep hiding from patrols of armed people.

In a far corner of the estate, he found a spot where a tree

had come down in a storm and was leaning exhaustedly against the wall. He used it to climb over and spent another day or so wandering around. There were a lot of people about, but it was a big place and there was plenty of cover, and he was even able to paint Wayland's name on a couple of sheltered buildings, but again there was no response, and eventually he climbed back out into the countryside beyond the wall.

He didn't know what to do. And as if that wasn't bad enough, Albie Dodd's head, decayed and covered in mould, had stopped talking and a day or so later the other head, the fresher one, had fallen silent, too. Nothing he did could make them talk to him, and in a fit of rage he'd thrown them into a flooded ditch and now he had nobody to talk to.

At one point, he came across one of the armed people patrolling alone, and he killed them and took their weapons. The automatic rifle in particular was very fine, and it went some way towards making him feel better.

It didn't solve his problem, though. He'd lost Wayland, he didn't know what to do, and he didn't know where he was. There was a big village nearby, but unlike Oxford it wasn't big enough for him to lose himself in a crowd, and when he walked along its main street he felt out of place and obvious, as if everyone was looking at him. One night, he used the last of his paint to write Wayland's name on a big official-looking building, and the next day he saw a work-gang scrubbing it off the stone, and in a distant sort of way he thought that pretty much summed up his situation.

He retreated some distance into the countryside, where he found a ruined house in which he could shelter, and he spent hours stripping and reassembling the rifle and pistol he'd taken from the guard while he tried to work out what to do. There was plenty of food, on farms and in household henhouses, and he had somewhere to hide, but what came after that? He couldn't just stay here like this for ever; he'd thought that he had, in a dim and confused way, a sense of purpose, something which had been entirely absent from his life, and now it seemed to have disappeared into thin air.

He hid in the house for days, staring out at the steadily worsening weather. It had never been a huge factor in his life when he was a farmer – the farm was a couple of dozen acres of rubbish whatever the weather – but he'd done it for long enough to be able to recognise the coming autumn monsoon and know that winter wouldn't be very far behind. There would be howling blizzards, ice storms, snowdrifts as tall as he was. It would kill him, unless he found himself somewhere to wait it out.

Very gradually, he began to think about returning to Oxford. It began with the memory of the last house he'd occupied, which had a stove and a fireplace and an intact roof and was actually in better shape, structurally, than his farmhouse in the Parish. And once that memory popped up, it wouldn't go away. Morty was used to living rough, but he had, by his own low standards, been happy in that house.

And the thing about Oxford was, there were lots of houses like that there. Big parts of the city were almost deserted but still not ruined, there was plenty of food to be had if you were careful about stealing it, and he had already discovered that nobody noticed him when he was out on the streets.

The more he thought about it, the more attractive it seemed. It occurred to him that Wayland would also be aware of the coming winter; it wouldn't be unreasonable for him to have found a place around here where he could lay up during the worst of the weather. Perhaps that explained things. Wayland hadn't vanished; like any wise predator he'd found himself a lair. That made a lot of sense to Morty. He could spend the winter in Oxford and come back here when the weather improved.

In the world as Morty experienced it, this was a perfect solution. He could picture himself in an isolated house in

Oxford, warm and cosy while he looked out into a howling snowfall. He could picture himself setting out in the dying days of the spring monsoon, returning here – wherever *here* was – in the dying days of the spring monsoon, and finally coming face to face with Wayland and asking the question. *What do you want me to do?*

For the first time in days, Morty felt his mood lifting. He'd existed for so long without a plan, without a purpose, that it was rather a heady feeling to look beyond the day after tomorrow and think, *that's what I'll do.*

It was in this spirit that he set out the next morning in the pouring rain and made his way to the Oxford road. The rain didn't bother him. Nothing bothered him; he had weapons and he had a plan, and he felt that old sense of invincibility beginning to stir in him again. Everything was going to be all right.

He'd been walking for an hour or so when he saw a horse and cart standing at the side of the road. When he got closer, he saw that the driver's seat of the cart was empty and the reins had been looped over an overhanging branch. The horse was cropping unconcernedly at the roadside vegetation.

Morty walked up to the cart, briefly got up on tiptoes to look into the back, but it was empty. He went and stood by the horse, which paid him no attention, and looked about him. A few moments later, a rustle in the bushes beside the road announced the return of the driver, a stringy-looking man with a red face and a shapeless leather hat. Morty carefully arranged the Morty Face, but he didn't move.

"What do you want?" the driver said, coming out of the bushes adjusting the fastenings of his trousers.

"Are you going back into the city?" Morty asked.

The driver narrowed his eyes. "What if I am?"

"I'm going that way," said Morty. "Maybe you could give me a lift."

The driver snorted. "Maybe you could fuck off. The walk'll do you good."

Morty looked around again. He couldn't see anyone else, there were no buildings nearby, nobody on the road in either direction. As the driver went by him to climb up onto the driver's seat, Morty stabbed him once under the armpit and once in the throat and pitched him into the bushes to bleed to death out of sight.

He took the reins down from the branch, got up onto the cart, and clicked his tongue a couple of times. The horse lifted its head, and when Morty flapped the reins, it took up the strain and started to pull the cart along the road towards Oxford. By the time they'd gone half a mile, Morty had forgotten the driver had ever existed.

The sudden appearance of the cart was proof that he was doing the right thing. He hadn't necessarily needed transport back to Oxford – and he was going to have to abandon it in order to sneak back into the city – but it made his journey easier. He could be back through the barricades before dark, find somewhere to hide for the night, and start to look for a new hideaway tomorrow. After despairing about being lost, everything was suddenly going his way.

He was so pleased about the turn of events that he didn't immediately register the fact that someone was calling to him. When he did notice the sound, he turned his head and saw a figure wading chest-deep through an overgrown field towards the road. He didn't stop, just let the horse plod slowly along, but he took the pistol out of his pocket and laid it on the seat beside him.

He didn't think he had anything to worry about, though. As he watched, the figure tripped and fell headlong, and when it reappeared a moment later it was covered in mud. He watched it burst out of the undergrowth and onto the road, and he put a little tension on the reins and the horse came to a stop.

The figure was a man in a long raincoat that was a little too small to do up, and it flapped forlornly around him. Underneath, he was wearing a suit and shirt, torn and soaking wet and muddy. Morty had never in his life seen a man in a suit, but it seemed a poor choice in all-weather clothing.

"I say," the stranger said breathlessly, trotting up to the cart. "I say, you there. Do a chap a favour?"

Morty sat where he was and looked down the road.

The stranger came level with him and reached up to grasp the side of the cart, as if he thought that would stop it moving away again. Morty's hand moved close to the pistol.

"Go on," the man said. "Do a chap a favour. I just want a bit of a lift." He put his hand in a pocket and Morty's fingers brushed the butt of the gun, but when the man brought his hand out, he lifted it so that Morty could see a palm full of coins. "I don't want to go far. I can pay, look."

Out of sight, Morty's fingers drummed slowly on the butt of the pistol.

"Oh, go on," the stranger said. "Give a hand to your fellow man." He lifted the palmful of money higher. "I've got *loads* more of this where I'm going, you can have it all." He kept looking up the road, as if expecting to see someone chasing him. "Will you help me?"

Morty thought about it, then he composed the Morty Face and looked down and smiled and watched the stranger try not to wince.

"Yes," he said.

ABOUT THE AUTHOR

DAVE HUTCHINSON WAS born in Sheffield in 1960 and read American Studies at the University of Nottingham before moving into journalism. He is best known as the author of the critically accalimed *Fractured Europe* series of novels, as well as being the author of six collections of short stories and the editor of three more. His novella, *The Push*, was shortlisted for the BSFA Award in 2010 and *Europe in Winter*, book three in the *Fractured Europe* series, won the BSFA Award in 2016. He has also been shortlisted for the Arthur C. Clarke Award, the John W. Campbell Memorial Award and The Kitschies.

Dave lives in London with his wife and a varying number of cats.

DAVE HUTCHINSON

"One of the UK's foremost writers" – *Guardian*

SHELTER

BOOK ONE OF THE AFTERMATH

⊙ SOLARISBOOKS.COM

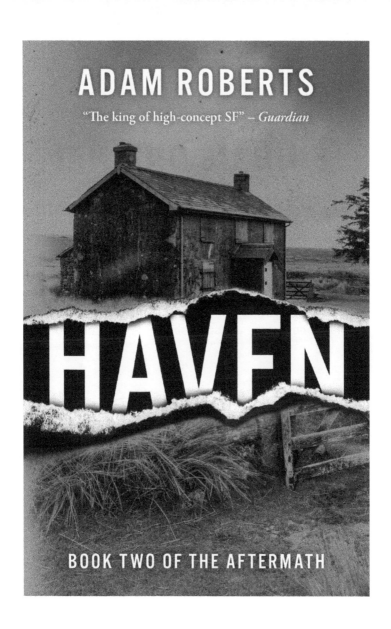

ADAM ROBERTS

"The king of high-concept SF" – *Guardian*

HAVEN

BOOK TWO OF THE AFTERMATH

⊙ SOLARISBOOKS.COM

FIND US ONLINE!

www.rebellionpublishing.com

/solarisbooks /solarisbks /solarisbooks

SIGN UP TO OUR NEWSLETTER!

rebellionpublishing.com/newsletter

YOUR REVIEWS MATTER!

Enjoy this book? Got something to say?

Leave a review on Amazon, GoodReads or with your
favourite bookseller and let the world know!

Milton Keynes UK
Ingram Content Group UK Ltd.
UKHW011041231123
433129UK00004B/257